EXTRAORDINARY PRAISE FOR

"UNIQUE . . . A [illegible] thoughts, actions [illegible] bers of the Soviet [illegible] of both technical [illegible], Peters has provided us with a provocative and illuminating book."

—*Milwaukee Journal*

"FRIGHTENINGLY REALISTIC . . . Must reading for anyone involved in military matters."

—Harold Coyle, author of *Team Yankee* and *Sword Point*

"BRILLIANTLY EXECUTED . . . Fusing knowledge of Soviet fighting techniques and Russian history, Ralph Peters presents credible military situations and characters who are archetypes rather than stereotypes."

—*Publishers Weekly*

"AWESOME IN ITS CONCEPT . . . POWERFUL AND TROUBLING . . . Peters has breathed life into the kinds of soldiers and officers that all of us have known. . . . The author has captured the essence of Men at War: he has produced a fiction treatise on leadership that will challenge the best historical treatment of real battlefields in retrospect. . . ."

—James C. McBride, Colonel, Armor, (Ret.), *Officer Review*

"PETERS' BATTLE SCENES ARE MASTERPIECES OF PERSPECTIVE. . . . IT IS HARD TO IMAGINE A BETTER PORTRAYAL OF MODERN WAR."

—*Newsweek*

"Soldiers at last may have found an author who can imagine World War III from their perspective: the mud soldier's muse. . . . VIVID."

—*Army Times*

"A FAST-PACED, TOTALLY BELIEVABLE TALE . . . what makes Peters' scenario so effective is that, unlike most military authors, he does not neglect the psychological dimensions of combat. . . ."

—*Topeka Capital Journal*

"THE BEST LOOK YET INTO THE MINDS AND HEARTS OF THE RUSSIAN SOLDIER . . . Peters is unsurpassed . . . in the depth and richness of his characters."

—*Flint* (MI) *Journal*

"The Soviets are portrayed with all of their personal dreams, hopes, fears and ambitions while they fight a desperate and bloody war to reach the Rhine. . . . Suspense and sheer storytelling power move the tale to a surprising ending."

—*Library Journal*

"Detailed and intelligent . . . a first-rate military novel that can be read and appreciated by a general audience . . . Outstanding battle scenes, and above all, a superb understanding of war."

—*Kirkus Reviews*

"A BOMBSHELL FINISH . . ."

—*San Diego Union*

"With thunderous prose and relentless drive, author Ralph Peters *out-Clancys* Tom Clancy with this gripping and impressive novel of World War III. . . . Wonderfully sympathetic and very human protagonists . . . ONE OF THE FINEST THRILLERS EVER WRITTEN."

—*Rave Reviews*

"There is no high-tech gimmickry here. . . . Indeed, what comes out of this very readable novel is a feeling that while the wars change, the soldiers remain the same."

—*New York Times Book Review*

"Riveting stuff all through, told with both compassion and precision."

—*Insight Magazine*

"Vivid detail . . . Sure to raise some hackles about the effectiveness of the whole NATO defense concept . . . Ralph Peters performs with great literary skill in reducing the philosophical to the day-to-day feelings of human beings who happen to be soldiers."

—*Richmond News Leader & Times Dispatch*

"MOST SURPRISING OF ALL THE TWISTS IS THE ENDING. GIVEN HIS KNOWLEDGE OF THE MILITARY BALANCE IN EUROPE, HOW MR. PETERS CHOOSES TO CLOSE *RED ARMY* IS CHILLING. . . ."

—*Raleigh News and Observer*

"HARROWINGLY REAL AND PERSUASIVE."

—*Newsday*

RALPH PETERS

POCKET BOOKS

New York London Toronto Sydney Tokyo Singapore

This book is a work of fiction. Names, characters, places and incidents are either the product of the author's imagination or are used fictitiously. Any resemblance to actual events or locales or persons, living or dead, is entirely coincidental.

The views expressed in this book are those of the author and do not reflect the official policy or position of the Department of the Army, Department of Defense, or the U.S. government.

Maps designed by Tony Fradkin

An *Original* Publication of POCKET BOOKS

POCKET BOOKS, a division of Simon & Schuster Inc.
1230 Avenue of the Americas, New York, NY 10020

ISBN: 0-671-67669-5

First Pocket Books paperback printing March 1990

10 9 8 7 6 5 4 3 2 1

Printed in the U.S.A.

FOR MARION . . .
comrade in all of life's campaigns

"Here, across death's other river
The Tartar horsemen shake their spears."

—T.S. Eliot
"The Wind Sprang Up
At Four O'Clock"

RED ARMY

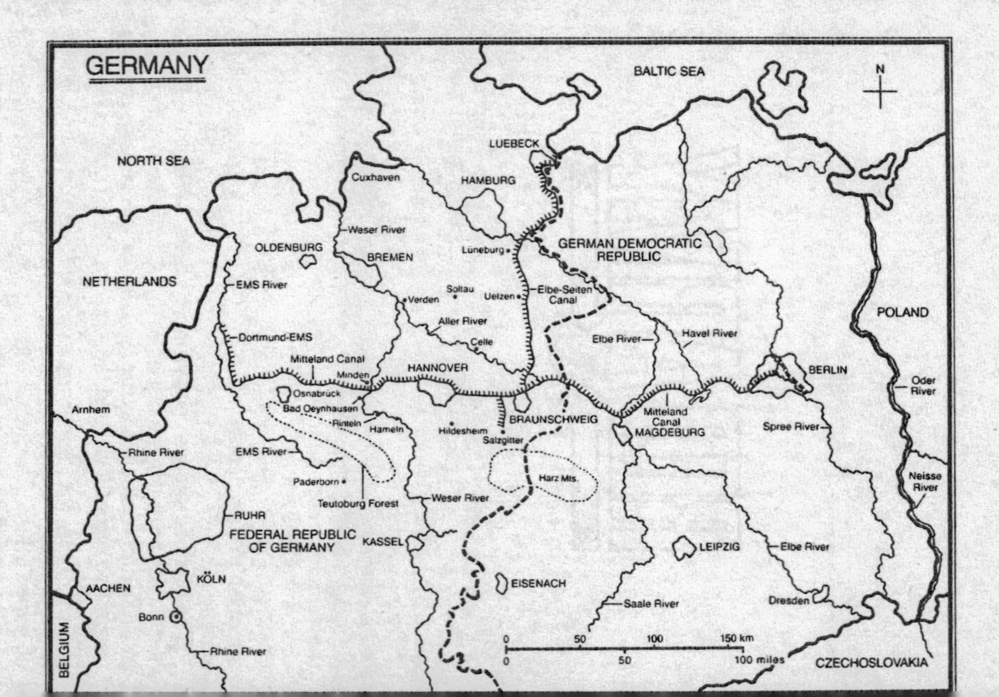
GERMANY
N
NORTH SEA
BALTIC SEA
NETHERLANDS
BELGIUM
POLAND
CZECHOSLOVAKIA
GERMAN DEMOCRATIC REPUBLIC
FEDERAL REPUBLIC OF GERMANY
LUEBECK
HAMBURG
Cuxhaven
Weser River
OLDENBURG
BREMEN
EMS River
Dortmund-EMS
Mitteland Canal
Minden
Osnabrück
Bad Oeynhausen
Rinteln
Hameln
Verden
Soltau
Lüneburg
Uelzen
Elbe-Seiten Canal
Aller River
Celle
HANNOVER
Hildesheim
Salzgitter
BRAUNSCHWEIG
Elbe River
Havel River
BERLIN
Oder River
Mitteland Canal
MAGDEBURG
Spree River
Harz Mts.
Arnhem
Rhine River
EMS River
Paderborn
Teutoburg Forest
Weser River
RUHR
KASSEL
EISENACH
LEIPZIG
Elbe River
Neisse River
Saale River
Dresden
AACHEN
KÖLN
Bonn
Rhine River
0 50 100 150 km
0 50 100 miles

Prologue

Night came to Germany. In among the pines, the low, sharp-prowed hulls of the infantry fighting vehicles turned black, and the soldiers gathered closer into their squad groups, huddling against the weak rain. Whenever possible, the vehicle commanders had tried to back off the trails in such a way that the nearby trees formed a protective barrier, allowing a safe sleeping space. Those who failed to pay attention to such details risked being crushed during a night alert.

The bivouac site was not virgin territory. When the unit had pulled in under the last afternoon grayness, which was more an ambience than a true light, it was evident that other troops had recently vacated the area. Huge ruts and waves of churned mud, the signatures of tracked vehicles, had ruptured the trails and broken the forest floor. Tins and scraps of paper littered the remaining islands of moss and pine needles, and the smell of human waste was almost as strong as the odor of vehicle exhaust. It was all instantly familiar to Leonid, who had just over a year's experience of training areas in East Germany, and he recognized his unit's good fortune in occupying the site while there was still a bit of visibility. The vehicles were much too cramped to sleep in, even had it been permitted, and when you arrived at a new location at night you had no idea where you might decently lie down.

For the first few days after the unit hurried out of garrison, they had moved about only during the hours of darkness. But now the roads were constantly filled, and this last move had been conducted entirely during daylight, covered only by the overcast sky. Everyone craved news. It was evident that this was not a routine exercise, but little information reached the soldiers. Leonid had already heard enough rumors to cause him to worry. All of his life, his teachers and youth activities leaders had drummed into him that the United States and the other Western powers were anxious to unleash a nuclear war against the Soviet Union, and the descriptions of the horrors of such a conflict had been sufficiently graphic to stay with him. Now he wondered what in the world was happening.

Seryosha, the big man and unofficial leader of the squad's privates, sat under the awning of the vehicle's camouflage net, assuming its limited bit of protection against the elements as his due. He had opened an issue of combat rations. He picked at the food, telling more stories about his experiences with women. Seryosha was muscular and handsome, and he was from Leningrad. He loved to parade his sophistication.

Seryosha's audience, to which Leonid belonged, sat in a rough circle. All lights were forbidden, but the officers had disappeared to wherever officers went, and several of the squad members smoked now. Along with the last feeble twilight, the welling glow of drawn cigarettes lent an eeriness to faces and objects that did nothing to improve Leonid's mood. Off behind the trees, metal clanged against metal, and a voice fired a loud volley of what could only be curses in some Asian language. Then the local silence returned, coddled in the distant humming of the roads.

Sergeant Kassabian, their squad leader, came back from a

trip into the woods. Leonid knew he was upset to find that Seryosha had broken open the reserve rations, but Kassabian paused before saying anything.

Seryosha ignored the sergeant's return. "And city girls," he went on, "know their way around. No nonsense, lads. They like it, too, and they know you know it." He noisily fed himself another bite of dried biscuit.

"We're not supposed to be eating those rations," Sergeant Kassabian said suddenly, finding his courage.

Leonid could feel Seryosha grinning. Seryosha had a wide, ready grin that seemed to overcome all troubles. Leonid pictured that grin loaded with the chewed mush of the biscuit now. He resented Seryosha's power but could do nothing about it.

Seryosha moved over to make room under the camouflage for another body. "Come and sit down," he told Kassabian. "You can't eat promises. If we wait for the battalion kitchens to feed us, it'll be the same story as last night. Come on, sit down. If there's a problem, I'll handle it."

Kassabian obediently took a seat beside Seryosha, as if the bigger boy's natural authority might expand to include him. The rumble of another unit moving nearby seemed to bring a tangible weight to the darkness. The shadowy form of the sergeant seemed very small, almost childlike, beside the broad-shouldered outline of Seryosha. Kassabian was really just a conscript like the rest of them, except that he had been chosen for a few months of extra training, after which he had received the rank of junior sergeant. Perhaps in another squad, he might have gained more authority, but here Seryosha was impossibly powerful. When the officers were around, Kassabian passed on military orders and seemed to rule. But in the barracks, Seryosha was incontestably in charge.

"Seryosha," Leonid asked tentatively, desperately wanting to be included in the intimate circle of the group, "you think it's the real thing?"

The question was unexpected, and the seriousness in Leonid's voice spoiled the atmosphere of imagined women and the freedom to touch them. Leonid realized that he had used poor judgment, but it was too late. When Seryosha answered him, irritation undercut the practiced nonchalance of his voice.

"Think they'd trust us to lug around live rounds if it wasn't?" Seryosha laughed spitefully. "You think maybe we're going to the range and we've just been lost for the last several days? You think you're just out for a target shoot and snooze, boy?" Yet it was evident that Seryosha himself did not want to believe that they might truly go to battle.

Leonid tried to back out of his dilemma. "Lieutenant Korchuk didn't actually say there was going to be a war."

"Korchuk?" Seryosha said. "That sissy boy never says anything worth listening to. The Party loves you. The Party says, don't play with yourself in your bunk at night. The Party says, don't take a crap without a signed certificate giving you permission."

It was always odd to hear Seryosha ridiculing Korchuk, the unit's political officer, since Seryosha nevertheless went out of his way to cultivate Korchuk's favor, and the political officer was so impressed by Seryosha that he frequently designated him to lead group discussions and badgered him to sign up for the whole Party program. Korchuk seemed to be struggling to win over Seryosha's soul. But behind his back, Seryosha's commentary on the downy-faced lieutenant was merciless.

Everyone laughed at Seryosha's attack on Korchuk—except for Leonid. When the lieutenant had come by earlier to cheer them up, he had only managed to frighten Leonid badly. Leonid had counted himself lucky to be assigned to the Group of Soviet Forces in Germany. He had hoped that in the German Democratic Republic, so close to the West, he might be able to collect a few unusual rock music records or tapes from special groups whose recordings were unavailable or very expensive back home. Instead, he had spent his first year restricted to barracks like a prisoner or on sodden training ranges, except for one escorted tour to a war memorial and a museum in Magdeburg. Then the routine had suddenly collapsed. The unit responded to an alert, hastening to its local deployment area. That much had been normal enough. But the accustomed return to garrison at the end of the test had been delayed. Instead, the unit had remained out all day, and at night they had marched their vehicles to a forest in the East German countryside. After that, the unit had shuttled about in a seemingly random manner for days. And then Lieutenant Korchuk had come by to ask them if they had any problems, and to encourage them to keep their spirits up. But the political officer had clearly been nervous about something, and he had talked a little too much and too earnestly about sacrifices for the Motherland and Internationalist Duty for Leonid's peace of mind.

Leonid just wanted his two years of conscripted service—easily the most miserable period of his life—to end so that he could go home to the state farm outside of Chelyabinsk, to his mother and his guitar.

"And this girl, Yelena, she's got a sister who wants to know what's going on, see?" Seryosha went on with his tales. "Her father's this big wheel in the Party, though, and everybody else is afraid to lay a finger on her. So I'm up in this fancy apartment, waiting for Yelena to come home . . ."

Everything seemed to come so easily to Seryosha. Leonid tried to master the prescribed military skills, but his uniform was never quite neat enough, and he bungled the physical execution even of tasks he clearly understood in his mind. But Seryosha seemed to be able to do everything perfectly the first time. And he made fun of Leonid, who was included in the squad group, but only as a member of the outer circle. Now, however, Leonid felt compelled to reach out to the others, to get through to Seryosha that matters were serious, indeed, and that something had to be done, although he had no idea what that something might be.

Seryosha finished his startlingly vulgar story, in which he was, as usual, a hero of dramatic capabilities. As the admiring laughter subsided Leonid tried again to reach the others, despite the risk.

"I think," Leonid began, searching nervously for the right words, "I think that things are . . . things must be bad."

He could feel Seryosha turning in the darkness. "Things are," Seryosha said imperiously, "the way they always are. In the shit. If you're not in one kind of shit, you're in another." Seryosha laughed bitterly, then began again, speaking in exaggerated English, "Leonid, *baby.* Mister Rock and Roll." Then he collapsed into Russian. "You've been in pig shit all your life out on your collective farm, haven't you?"

"State farm," Leonid corrected.

"Out there in Chelyabinsk," Seryosha continued. "No, I mean from *beyond* Chelyabinsk. You must know what it's like to be in the shit."

Leonid desperately wanted to express something. But he did not know exactly what it was. He thought of Lieutenant Korchuk's pale cheeks and scrawny mustache, and of a mental collage of troubling images. But none of it would fit into words.

"I wish we had some music," Leonid said, drawing back again. It seemed to him now that he had never been happier than when he had been at home, with his small, precious collection of rock and blues music, his Hungarian jeans, and his guitar. He had dreamed of going to Leningrad, where a real music scene existed. Or at least to Moscow, where you could hear good blues. Now that he knew Seryosha, he had ruled out Leningrad. That garbage? Seryosha had said, when Leonid tried to talk to him about music. That's old hat. *Nobody* listens to the blues. They'd all laugh at you in Leningrad. Everybody listens to metal music now, everybody who knows what's going on is a metallist. You'd be lost in Leningrad, you little pig farmer.

The intensity of the drizzle picked up slightly, and the soldiers herded closer, each maneuvering for a greater share of the leaking protection of the camouflage net and stray bits of canvas.

"You know what?" Seryosha said. "If there is a war, I'm going to take care of one of those German bitches with her nose in the air. And I don't care if she's West German or East German, unless you can prove there's a difference between a capitalist piece and a socialist one. It just drives me crazy when we're driving by them and they act like they don't even see you, like they're looking right through you." He paused as they all remembered deployments that took them through tidy German towns where the handsome women showed no regard for them at all. "I'm going to take care of one of them," Seryosha resumed. "And when I'm done, I'm going to turn Genghiz loose on her for good measure."

The group laughed. Even Leonid laughed at this image. Genghiz was their nickname for Ali, their Central Asian antitank grenadier. Ali did not understand enough Russian to get the jokes, but he always laughed along. Once, during the squad's first field exercise, Ali had tried to sneak more than his share of the rations. Seryosha had begun the beating, and they had all joined in. The squad had almost gotten in trouble over the incident, but in the end, Ali had not needed to stay in the sick bay overnight, and Seryosha had concocted a tale to bring in Lieutenant Korchuk on the side of the squad. Ali never repeated his mistake, and he carefully did exactly what Seryosha told him to do as long as the task was clearly explained.

"No music," Seryosha said wistfully. "No women. And nothing to drink. My father used to say, 'War solves all your problems.' My old man was in the big one, and he had a girl or two. Hell, he was on his third wife when I popped out."

"You father," Ali said happily, surprising them all. "You no know you father, Russian bastard."

The group laughed so hard they swayed and banged their shoulders against one another in the little circle. Even Seryosha laughed. It was a great moment, as if a dog or cat had spoken.

The squad grew boisterous. Everyone was supposed to be quiet, on precombat silence. But there were still no officers around, and you could clearly hear the other squads nearby.

Leonid wondered where the officers had gone, and why it was taking them so long. He wondered what in the world was going on.

Suddenly, a vehicle engine powered up a few hundred meters away. Then another vehicle came to life, closer this time.

"Here we go again," Seryosha said disgustedly.

They rode crouched in their armored vehicle, with the troop hatches closed. Only the driver and the vehicle commander were allowed to look outside. The interior was cramped and extremely uncomfortable, even though the squad was understrength with only six soldiers. The smells of unwashed bodies and of other men's stale breath mingled with the pungency of the poorly vented exhaust. The jittering of the vehicle's tracks seemed to scramble the brain. Leonid knew from experience that he would soon have a severe headache.

"Where do you think we're going this time?" a voice asked from the darkness.

"Paris," Seryosha said. "New York."

"Seriously."

"Who the hell knows?"

"I think we're going to war," Leonid said with helpless conviction.

All of the voices went heavily silent. The whine of the engine, the clatter of the tracks on the hard-surface road, and the wrenched-bone noise of shifting gears surrounded the quiet of the soldiers.

"You don't know," Seryosha said angrily, doubtfully. "You're just a little pig farmer from the middle of nowhere."

Leonid did not know why he had said it. He recognized that, in fact, he did not know where they were going. But somehow, inside, he was convinced that he was correct. They were going to war. Perhaps it had already begun. NATO had attacked, and men were dying.

The vehicle stopped with a jerk, knocking the soldiers against one another or into the metal furnishings of the vehicle's interior. Road marches were always the same. You went as fast as you could, then came to a sudden, unexplained stop and waited.

"Leonid?" a voice asked seriously, just loud enough to be heard over the idling engine. "Has somebody told you something? Do you really know something? What makes you think we're going to war?"

Leonid shrugged. "It's just my luck."

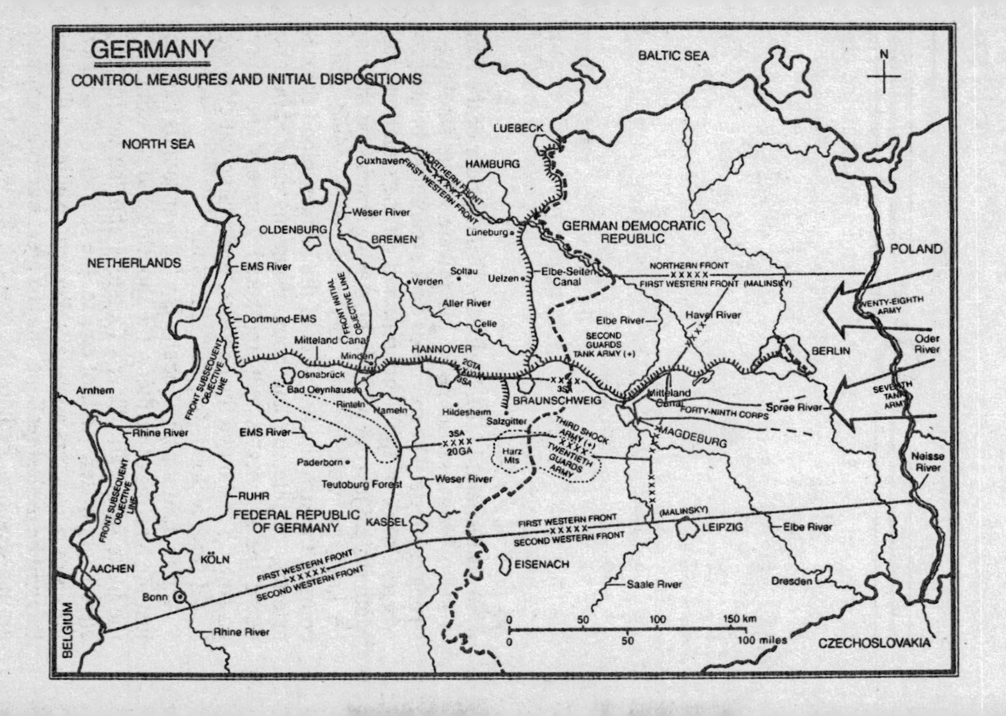
GERMANY
CONTROL MEASURES AND INITIAL DISPOSITIONS
NORTH SEA
BALTIC SEA
N
NETHERLANDS
BELGIUM
POLAND
CZECHOSLOVAKIA
GERMAN DEMOCRATIC REPUBLIC
FEDERAL REPUBLIC OF GERMANY
LUEBECK
HAMBURG
Cuxhaven
NORTHERN FRONT
XXXXX
FIRST WESTERN FRONT
Weser River
OLDENBURG
BREMEN
Lüneburg
EMS River
Verden
Soltau
Uelzen
Elbe-Seiten Canal
NORTHERN FRONT
XXXXX
FIRST WESTERN FRONT (MALINSKY)
Aller River
Celle
Dortmund-EMS
FRONT INITIAL OBJECTIVE LINE
Mitteland Canal
Minden
HANNOVER
2GTA
3SA
Elbe River
Havel River
SECOND GUARDS TANK ARMY (+)
BERLIN
Oder River
Osnabrück
Bad Oeynhausen
Rinteln
Hameln
Hildesheim
Salzgitter
BRAUNSCHWEIG
Mitteland Canal
FORTY-NINTH CORPS
Spree River
Arnhem
FRONT SUBSEQUENT OBJECTIVE LINE
Rhine River
EMS River
3SA
XXXX
20GA
Harz Mts
THIRD SHOCK ARMY (+)
XXXX
TWENTIETH GUARDS ARMY
MAGDEBURG
Neisse River
Paderborn
Teutoburg Forest
Weser River
RUHR
KASSEL
(MALINSKY)
FIRST WESTERN FRONT
XXXXX
SECOND WESTERN FRONT
LEIPZIG
Elbe River
AACHEN
KÖLN
EISENACH
Dresden
Saale River
Bonn
Rhine River
0 50 100 150 km
0 50 100 miles

One

Army General M. M. Malinsky, Commander of the First Western Front, sat alone in his private office, smoking a strong cigarette. The room was dark except for a bright pool where a bank of spotlights reflected off the situation map. Malinsky sat just out of the light, staring absently at the map he knew so well. Beyond the office walls, vivid action coursed through the hallways of the bunker, blood through arteries, despite the late hour. From his chair, Malinsky heard the activity as half-smothered footsteps and voices passing up and down the corridor, resembling valley noises heard from a cloud-wrapped mountain.

And that, Malinsky thought, is what war sounds like. Not just the blasting of artillery, the shooting and shouting. But the haste of a staff officer's footsteps and the ticking of a clerk's typewriter. And, of course, the special, half-magical noises of computers nowadays. Perhaps, Malinsky thought, this will be the last real one, the last great war fought by men aiming weapons. Perhaps the next big one would be fought entirely by means of cybernetics. Things were changing so troublingly fast.

But there would always be a next time. Malinsky was certain of that. Even if they were foolish enough to toss great nuclear bombs across oceans, Malinsky was convinced that enough of mankind would survive to organize new armies to fight over whatever remained. Mankind would remain mankind, and there would always be wars. And there would always be soldiers. And, in his heart, Malinsky was convinced there would always be a Russia.

A discreet hand knocked at the door.

"Enter," Malinsky called, leaning back deeper into the shadows.

A fan of light swept the room, then disappeared as the door shut again. A staff major padded up to the map without a word and realigned unit symbols.

Malinsky watched in silence. Germany, east and west. Virtually his entire adult life—more, even his straight-backed adolescence as a Suvorov cadet—had been directed to this end. Elbe, Weser, Rhine and Maas. Mosel and Saar. With the low countries and the fields of France beyond, where Colonel of the Guards Count Malinsky had raised his curved saber against the cavalry of Napoleon.

Malinsky believed he knew exactly how to do it. How to apply his own forces against the enemy on the right bit of earth along the correct operational directions, in the most efficient order, and at a tempo that would be physically and psychologically irresistible. He knew where the turning movements had to come, and where and when it would be necessary to drive on without a backward glance. He even believed he knew his enemies well enough to turn their own efforts against them.

His enemies would come, at least initially, from the Northern Army Group—NORTHAG—which was, in turn, subordinate to the Allied Forces Central Europe, or AFCENT. NORTHAG was, potentially, an operational grouping of tremendous strength. But intelligence assessments led Malinsky to believe that NORTHAG, with its defense straddling the terrain compartments of northern West Germany, had three great weaknesses, none of which the Westerners seemed to recognize. Certainly, NORTHAG was far more vulnerable than its sister army group—CENTAG—to the south. Despite possessing splendid equipment and well-trained cadres, the enemy leadership did not understand the criticality of unified troop control—there was reportedly so much political nonsense allowed that NORTHAG resembled a Warsaw Pact in which the Poles, Czechs and East Germans were permitted veto power over even the smallest details of military planning and operations. Compounding the first problem, the enemy clearly undervalued speed. When you watched them on their exercises, they did everything too slowly, too carefully, stubborn pedestrians in a supersonic age. Finally, Malinsky believed that his enemies underestimated their opponents, that they had hardly a glimmer of how the Soviet military could and would fight. Malinsky expected the defense by his enemies to be stubborn, bloody, and in vain. He was fond of repeating three words to his subordinate commanders, as a sort of personal motto: "Speed, shock, activeness."

"What's that?" Malinsky leaned forward, cigarette thrusting toward the map like a dagger. "What's that supposed to tell me?"

The major quickly backed away from the map, as though he had received an electric shock. "Comrade Front Commander, elements of the Seventh Tank Army have begun closing on their appointed staging areas, but, as you see, there is a conflict with the trail elements of the Forty-ninth Unified Army Corps. The Forty-ninth is behind schedule in its move to its assembly areas west of the Elbe River."

Controlling his voice, Malinsky dismissed the staff officer, a clever, crisp-talking Frunze graduate. When the door had shut behind the major's retreat, as if the fan of light had swept him away, Malinsky reached for the intercom phone.

"Is the chief of staff there? Give General Chibisov the phone."

For a moment, Malinsky listened to the faint pandemonium of the briefing room on the other end. Then Chibisov's familiar voice, ever perfectly controlled, came on the line.

"I'm listening, Comrade Front Commander."

"Is Anseev here yet?"

"He just came in."

"Tell him to come down and see me." Malinsky considered for a moment. "How are we doing otherwise?"

"A few are still missing. But they'll be here in time."

"The Germans?"

"Yes. Nervous as puppies."

"Good. I like them best that way."

"The Polish liaison officers are here from the Northern Front. You can imagine how happy they are."

Malinsky could well imagine. He was always impressed by the talent of ranking Polish officers, but he could never bring himself to trust them. He saw them as always attempting to barter their way out from under their responsibilities, and he dealt with them more harshly than was his habit with others.

"Just send Anseev down to me," Malinsky said. "And let me know when we have them all assembled."

Malinsky hung up the phone. A waft of smoke hovered between him and the brilliantly colored map, as though the battle had already begun amid the clutter of arrows and lines. Malinsky lit another cigarette.

He thought of his son. Anton. Anton Mikhailovitch Malinsky. His son was the newly appointed commander of a maneuver brigade in the Forty-ninth Corps, a youngish, handsome Guards colonel. Anton was the type of officer over whom the ladies at the Imperial Court had once swooned. Malinsky was terribly proud of his son, and although Anton was in his middle thirties, Malinsky always thought of him as "the boy," or "my boy." Anton was his only child. Malinsky had gone to extremes to insure that there was no favoritism, that Anton earned his own way. He could never be certain, of course, and no doubt the name had its effect—doubly so now that the old military families were back in style again. But Malinsky was determined not to behave like the patriarchs of so many military families, bashing down doors for their children. Anton was a Malinsky, and the traditions of the Malinsky family demanded that he be a fine officer of his own making.

They had been counts, if only of the second order, with estates not far from Smolensk. Before the Revolution, of course. Russian service gentry, with traces of Polish and Lithuanian nobility in their veins. At the hard birth of the eighteenth century, a Malinsky fought under Peter the Great at Poltava and on the Pruth. It was during Peter's wars along the Baltic littoral that a Malinsky first heard the German language spoken. Then Vassili Malinsky lost an arm at Kunersdorf in the hour of victory over the soldiers of Frederick the Great in 1759. Vassili went on to serve under Potemkin in the Turkish wars, and Catherine, the German-born czarina, rewarded Vassili's services with the title of "count." One Malinsky, the shame of the family, served with Suvorov in Italy and the Alps, only to be condemned for cowardice after the debacle at Austerlitz. But his brother rode through the streets of Paris in 1814 at the head of a regiment of lancers. Malinskys fought in the Caucasus and in Central Asia, and one claimed to have beaten Lermontov at cards. During the long afternoon of the nineteenth century, a Malinsky died of plague in camp before Bukhara, and another died of cholera in a ditch at Sevastopol. At Plevna in 1877, Captain Count Mikhail Malinsky won the George, Second Class, and as a general, he fought the Japanese in 1905. Major Count Anton Mikhailovitch Malinsky fell before Austrian machine guns in the Carpathians in the Great War, and his brother Pyotr Mikhailovitch joined the Revolution as an engineer captain. The Malinskys had been there, always, to serve Russia, whether as diseased young Guards officers in St. Petersburg or as reformers in the officer corps and on their estates. Malinskys had drunk themselves to death and struggled to rationalize agriculture on a modern scientific basis. While some did their best to gamble away the family fortunes, others had counted Herzen and Tolstoy among their friends. It was a family full of all the contradictions of Russia, unified by a single name and the habit of wearing army uniforms.

After the Revolution, it had almost come to an end. Malinsky's grandfather, Pyotr Mikhailovitch, had been eager to join the Revolution, dreaming sincerely of a new and better Russia. But the Revolution had not been so enthusiastic about the Malinskys. The nobility, progressive or regressive, were all oppressors of the workers and peasants. Making the situation worse, Malinskys appeared on both sides in the Civil War, with two cousins serving under the counterrevolutionary Denikin, while Pyotr fought against the Whites as a military specialist and adviser to an illiterate commander of more bravery than skill. Then Pyotr had been allowed his own command in the Polish War, although his young wife, son, and mother remained hostages of the careful Bolsheviks. Pyotr fought like a savage, not so much for the Bolsheviks as for Russia. The Civil War and the fighting against the foreign enemies of the Revolution grew more and more merciless, but Russia towered over it all, absorbing the blood in her earth, relentlessly driving her sons.

In the end, it was a very near thing. Only his high level of technical expertise as an engineer and staff officer saved Pyotr. He received an assignment to the newly organized military academy, which would later become the Frunze. He taught mathematics and cartography to eager officers who had virtually learned to read and write on horseback during the Civil War.

The estates were gone, of course. No Malinsky dared go near them. But an officer's life remained a good one compared to the sufferings and dislocations Pyotr witnessed around him. At times, he considered an attempt to leave Russia with his family. But, he told himself, the Bolsheviks would pass, too, while the army would always remain. He looked for the good in the Revolution and in the strange new leaders it brought forth, still eager to believe in the good in men after swimming through seas of blood.

Pyotr's son, Mikhail, entered a military academy in 1926. The tradition had almost been broken, since the Workers' and Peasants' Red Army did not want the sons of former noblemen. But even then, there had been enough survivors among the military specialists recruited from the Czarist ranks to quietly find the boy a place.

In 1938, Colonel Pyotr Mikhailovitch Malinsky was arrested, tried, and shot by the secret police. His son, a captain, was arrested and sent to the camps near Kolyma. Captain Malinsky's wife and son remained behind with no knowledge of whether he was alive or dead until, finally, after a year, a particularly brave comrade of the captain's revealed that Malinsky was alive in a camp in the east, and his family could write to him, so long as great care was taken in what was said.

In his well-furnished office in a bunker deep in eastern Germany, the son of the captive sat now, remembering how he had scribbled notes to a distant, half-remembered father. His mother always insisted that he add something, either a note of his own or, when there wasn't enough paper, a few scratched words on his mother's neat pages.

His father survived. When the Hitlerite Germans invaded on the twenty-second of June, 1941, even Stalin was soon forced to realize the extent of his folly. Imprisoned officers who were still healthy enough and whose records were not too black were returned to service. Malinsky's father fought from Tula to Berlin. Not for Stalin. And not for the Communist Party, although he was reinstated as a member. But for Russia.

Malinsky's father had looked sixty when he was in his late forties. The camps had ruined his health, and perhaps only his strength of will kept him going through the war and beyond. He had entered Berlin as a rifle division commander, with fewer than two thousand able soldiers on the divisional rolls. He died in a military sanatorium in the Caucasus in 1959. His son had come in his dress uniform to visit him, towing his own six-year-old boy, and in the quiet of a general's sickroom, the old man had looked his son in the eyes and said, "I outlived that bastard. And Russia will outlive them all. Remember that. Your uniform is the uniform of Russia."

In the year after the invasion of Czechoslovakia, Malinsky had found himself on an inspectorate tour that took him through Smolensk. Hard drinking was still fashionable in the officer corps then, and the officers with whom he was traveling were a particularly hard-drinking bunch. One morning while they snored into their hangovers, he had taken the staff car out to the state farm where once his family estates had counted thousands of souls.

The great house was long gone, destroyed by the Germans during the Great Patriotic War. The Sovkhoz buildings were nondescript barns, shacks and sheds of tin and cinder block. Malinsky parked the car and walked beyond the litter of the state into the newly harvested fields. From a low rise he could see the chronicle of his blood stretching brown and yellow and green over tens of gently rolling kilometers. And he wept, taking off his hat. Not for the loss of land. Nor because he wasn't called a count, even though in intimate moments he thought of his wife affectionately as his countess. Rather, he wept for Russia, without understanding himself. With blurred vision, he stared off into the distance where the fields met the vast, empty sky, caught up in its timelessness, suspecting that good men had always wept for Russia, that there was no choice, ever.

The gagging of a stalled tractor roused him, and he walked back through the characterless plot of farm buildings. Upon his approach, an old woman, an eternal peasant of a woman, called out:

"No special bargains for officers here, Comrade. You can go stand in line like all the rest."

Major General Anseev came in cautiously. As he approached the island of light in front of the situation map Malinsky motioned for him to take a seat. A visitor's chair had been carefully positioned so that the guest could turn slightly to his left and address the map or twist to the right and face Malinsky, but with no possibility of comfort in either position. The chair was positioned exactly so that, whenever the guest had to turn toward Malinsky, one of the small spotlights that lit the map dazzled the subordinate's eyes. Malinsky was not a cruel man, but he firmly believed in establishing and maintaining control under all circumstances, and he believed in precision and in the importance of the smallest detail to the greatest military operations.

Malinsky knew Anseev well enough. During Malinsky's tour of duty in Afghanistan—easily the most frustrating assignment of his life—Anseev had commanded a combined arms unit. Anseev had been bold, a great improviser, where others were routinely overcautious. Once, denied the use of mountain roads by the dushman, he had personally led his armored vehicles up a dry riverbed to relieve a besieged garrison. But he did not pay enough attention to little things, and his casualties were always high. Each of his commanders had his own peculiar weaknesses, Malinsky reflected. Anseev just needed to feel the bit now and then.

Anseev had been given the command of a corps structured to perform optimally as an operational maneuver group, with the mission of thrusting deeply and rapidly into the enemy's operational rear, unhinging the enemy's ability to reorganize his defenses, seizing key terrain or striking decisive targets, and convincing the opponent that he had been defeated before the military issue was actually settled. Anseev had been selected for the command because of his boldness and the speed with which he moved. Yet here was a situation in which one of his subunits could not even clear its staging area on time. Malinsky suspected he knew the reason, but he wanted to hear Anseev's tale.

Holding out his cigarette case, Malinsky leaned forward into the light. Anseev was normally highly self-confident, even brash, and he was a chain-smoker like Malinsky. But now he waved away the proffered smoke with almost unintelligible thanks.

"Come, Igor Fedorovitch, you like a smoke."

Anseev obediently took one of the short paper tubes that bled dark tobacco from both ends.

From Anseev's behavior, Malinsky could tell that the man knew what the problem was, and that he had hoped it would slip by the front commander.

Malinsky leaned back into the shadows.

"Igor Fedorovitch," he said in a friendly, almost paternal voice, "are you aware that your trail brigade is still in its staging area, holding up another unit?"

"Yes, Comrade Front Commander."

"What's the problem there?"

"The roads are just too crowded," Anseev said anxiously. Anseev was a mongrel, with a great deal of Tartar blood and the guarded eyes of an Asian. "The supply columns from the front and army matériel support brigades are undisciplined. They act as though they are under no control whatsoever. I have tanks colliding with fuelers, and nobody can decide who has priority unless a senior officer is present. The commandant's service has not deployed adequate traffic controllers. You should see how it is along my routes, Comrade Front Commander. The river-crossing sites are an absolute nightmare."

"Igor Fedorovitch, do you imagine it will be easier to move in combat? Do you expect the British or the Germans to control traffic for you?" Malinsky paused for effect, carefully holding his voice down to a studied near-whisper that could be chilling and fatherly at the same time. "We're not in Afghanistan now. This is a real war, with mechanized opponents, with enormous mechanized armies the like of which the world has never seen in battle. Moving to war on the finest road networks in the world. And you, my cavalryman, are perhaps the most important formation commander in this front. Yet you can't move a lone brigade on time? Igor Fedorovitch, we've had reasonable weather, a little rain, but nothing to stop a good cavalryman. If the supply columns have no control, why didn't you take control? If you can't maneuver around a pack of field kitchens, how do you expect to get to the Rhine? How can I trust you even to get into combat on time?"

"Comrade Front Commander, this will *not* happen again. It's just—"

"No 'just,'" Malinsky said, his voice lowering in pitch and suddenly as cold as winter in the far north. "Fix the problem. And never let it happen again."

"Yes, Comrade Front Commander. By the way, I have to tell you that your son's brigade is the best in my command. Well-disciplined, and he moves his tanks like lightning."

It was the wrong approach to try with Malinsky, who instantly realized how shaken Anseev must have been to try anything so tactless and naive. Anseev would need watching as the pressure mounted.

"Guards Colonel Malinsky is no special concern of mine," Malinsky said emphatically. "He's one commander out of many. Anseev, did you personally review your march tables and routes in detail?"

"Comrade Commander, I flew the routes myself."

"Did you personally review the march tables? Was your movement plan fully cleared with my chief of the rear and my movement control officers? Or did you bend the schedule you were allowed by the front? Did you even know all that had been done or left undone in your name?"

"Comrade Front Commander, the automated support mechanism—"

"Yes or no?"

"No, Comrade Front Commander."

Malinsky drew on his cigarette, letting its glow briefly light his face. Anseev was clearly distraught. As he deserved to be. But Malinsky did not want him to return to his unit that way. And there was the final review to get through with all of the other commanders, the front staff, and the special representatives.

Anseev turned his face to the map, as though seeking a way to reach out and correct his error in front of Malinsky's eyes.

"Igor Fedorovitch," Malinsky began, weighting the paternal tone in his voice, "you are . . . perhaps the finest fighting commander I have. I frankly admired you in Afghanistan. You know that. It was a bad war for all of us, not really a war—a trial we were never permitted to win. But you did so well with what you had, under the worst possible conditions . . . we always counted on you in the desperate moments. And I am counting on you now. We're all counting on you. Of all the formations in the First Western Front, it is most critical that your corps and its brigades be responsive and exactly on time. You must always be there first." Malinsky sucked on his cigarette, blowing the smoke back out with a faint sigh. "We all have flaws, Igor Fedorovitch. And I'll be frank. Your flaw is that you see everything in bold, broad terms. This may also be your virtue. But a commander must take the time for the details. If the artillery arrives but the ammunition doesn't show up, the artillery is useless. Precision saves lives, Igor Fedorovitch. It is perhaps the most important aspect of discipline for an officer. The soldier of the Soviet Motherland will give you everything he has. I will not see his life wasted because a commander was too busy to attend to administrative details."

"I understand, Comrade Front Commander. I won't forget."

Malinsky allowed a short silence to drain the tension.

"I'll see you in a few minutes then, Igor Fedorovitch. At the final review."

Anseev understood this form of dismissal. He rose sharply and presented his respects.

Malinsky nodded.

With Anseev gone, Malinsky lit a final cigarette, attempting to gather his thoughts. He wanted to keep the review short so that his commanders could get back to their formations, but he also wanted to insure that every last-minute question had been answered. There would be no time once the great machine had been set in motion. He tried to enumerate his last-minute concerns, but his mind strayed determinedly to his son, as if Anseev had cursed him. He suddenly felt as though, if he were a religious man, he would pray for the boy.

But pray to whom? To Russia? It was, Malinsky considered, the closest thing he could imagine to a god. Something so much greater than its children. Its stubborn, passionate, dreaming children, who always seemed to seek the most difficult solutions to life's problems. The idea of Russia remained hopelessly mystical, verging on melodrama. Intellectually, he could pick it apart, yet it was emotionally irresistible to him.

Spare my boy. And I will do everything for you.

And Paulina. How they had wanted more children. But those children had never come, and Paulina had endured the dreadful lieutenant's quarters on the edge of the world, with communal kitchens and the filthy shared latrines. And the separations, the lack of fine things that only those much closer to the Party, or those whose sense of duty was to themselves, would ever have. Paulina, his soldier's wife. His countess. Paulina, he thought, if I could choose, if I had to choose, I would send you back your son.

Malinsky felt ashamed of himself. He knew he hadn't a moment to squander on nostalgia and personal matters. He needed to concern himself with the movement of tens of thousands of war machines, of hundreds of thousands of men. There was no time for emotionalism.

The intercom phone rang. It was the chief of staff and first deputy commander, the newly promoted Lieutenant General Pavel Pavlovitch Chibisov. The chief was a self-contained, coldly brilliant man with an analytical bent and almost obsessive self-discipline whom Malinsky had rescued from another ineradicable aspect of the Russian character—anti-Semitism. Chibisov was an ethnic Jew whose family had long ago renounced their religion, but he still felt compelled to struggle relentlessly against every last vestige of his Jewishness. And Chibisov was correct—his Jewishness never would be fully laid to rest in the eyes of many of his fellow officers. Malinsky felt a close personal bond to Chibisov, a deep, if quiet, affection. They were both outsiders, in their very different ways. In any case, Chibisov was the perfect chief of staff, a born mathematician and organizer, leaving his commander free to concentrate more of his own energies on the military art. Chibisov was the first of his fellow officers whom Malinsky had ever trusted to the extent that he allowed himself to depend fully on another, and he smiled to think of Chibisov the man, a lifelong bachelor who could express everything except emotion with utter clarity.

"Comrade Front Commander, they're all here except the chief of the political directorate—he's still occupied at the KGB site," the familiar clipped voice reported.

"All right. Have they had their tea?"

"They're settled in. We're ready. At your convenience."

"Good. I'm on my way."

Malinsky laid the phone to rest, then crushed out his stub of a cigarette.

But he did not move at once. He stared hard at the map one last time. The deep red arrows of his plan cut through the carefully detailed hopes of his enemies. He had waited for this all his life. But he had never quite believed the day would come.

Major General Dudorov, Malinsky's chief of intelligence, described the enemy dispositions in remarkable detail. Dudorov was clever and a good student of the enemy, but best of all, to Malinsky, he had worked the enemy problem so long that he had acquired not only many Western tastes but even something of a Western outlook. To Malinsky, it was the next best thing to having an intelligence chief right from the enemy's ranks. Malinsky had a great hunger to know his opponents, to fully digest their strengths and weaknesses. He recognized that, in order to apply the precepts of Soviet military science and art to fullest effect, detailed and accurate intelligence was indispensable.

The briefing room stank with the swampy smell of wet uniforms, and the audience shifted restlessly. For many of the officers present, Dudorov's portion of the briefing had gone on far too long. Dudorov was short and overweight, and he spoke like a condescending professor—exactly the sort of figure combat commanders tended to despise. And Malinsky knew that his subordinate commanders were anxious to return to their formations in order to put last-minute corrections into effect. But he took no action to shorten Dudorov's remarks. He placed great confidence in Dudorov's professionalism, and, as with Chibisov, he had carried Dudorov along with him as he rose to positions of ever-greater authority.

Malinsky wanted his subordinates to know their enemies, whether they felt interested or not. It was a common thing for tank and motorized rifle commanders—especially those who had not served in Afghanistan—to swagger about, assuming that the enemy was merely something to be used for target practice. But Malinsky believed their level of interest would rise sharply after a taste of the battlefield.

"And so," Dudorov began his summary, "we face a partially prepared defense. Engineer preparations have been most extensive opposite the Third Shock Army in the British sector, where a unilateral decision apparently was made to execute their obstacle plan early on. The Germans, on the other hand, appear to have been reluctant to dig up their countryside, but all-out preparations are now underway. The Dutch and Belgian efforts at engineer preparations only began within the past twenty-four hours. Overall, we face a much more favorable situation than the one facing our comrades in the Second Western and Southwestern fronts opposite NATO's Central Army Group. Of course, the limited aims of the Northern Front make it a secondary consideration. All of the matériel aspects of force reduction have clearly favored us. Even in the British sector, our most recent calculations do not indicate that the known preparations will significantly degrade our highly favorable operational correlation of forces and means."

"Any sign of Americans supporting NORTHAG?" Malinsky asked.

Dudorov pointed at the map. From his seat, Malinsky really couldn't see the details, but he had the map memorized. "The single U.S. brigade garrisoned in the north," Dudorov stated, "has apparently been withdrawn into a deep reserve role. Their exact location is presently unknown. There are no indications at present of additional U.S. ground forces opposite the First Western Front."

Timing is everything, Malinsky thought. He was not overly fond of the General Staff, but he had to admit that their calculations on how quickly NATO would detect and, more importantly, muster the decisiveness to respond to a Warsaw Pact mobilization had been almost exactly correct. Discounting the period of discreet measures, it had taken seven days of overt activities to adequately prepare the key Soviet, East German, Czech, and Polish units and formations and to position them forward in a manner that decisively shifted the correlation of forces and means. Of the seven days of all-out measures executed by the Warsaw Pact, the first four had been almost completely free. NATO's intelligence evidently detected, evaluated, and reported the situation within twenty-four hours, but individual member governments of NATO had vacillated for several days. At his meeting with the commander-in-chief of the Western Theater of Strategic Military Action earlier in the day, Malinsky had been astonished by Marshal Kribov's stories of frantic diplomatic efforts that seemed absurd beyond belief. Kribov was not known for his sense of humor, but he had smiled as he remarked to Malinsky that, while he believed they could beat NATO's armies, he was absolutely convinced they could beat NATO's governments.

"Other questions?" Dudorov asked the assembly.

Lieutenant General Starukhin, the commander of the Third Shock Army, stood up. Malinsky smiled to himself.

Starukhin always stood up, always had something to say. Starukhin was a bully, a heavy drinker despite the change in fashion, and a brutally tough and aggressive commander. Exactly the sort of man to command in the breakthrough sector. Malinsky had known Starukhin for years, and he well knew the man's long list of bad habits. But he also knew he could trust him to fight.

"Dudorov," Starukhin began, posing for his circle of paladins, "you stand there and tell me that the British engineer preparations don't make a significant difference. Maybe you'd like to ride in my lead tank."

Malinsky watched to see who laughed along with Starukhin. The army commander's subordinates, of course, and the commander of the Twentieth Guards Army and his companions. The East German officers laughed tentatively, while the Poles appeared disinterested. Trimenko, the commander of the Second Guards Tank Army, remained stone-faced, as did his clique. Trimenko and Starukhin were long-standing rivals, as different as summer and winter. It was a rivalry that Malinsky carefully exploited to draw the best efforts from each man.

None of the members of the front staff laughed at Dudorov. Malinsky and Chibisov took great pains to build a tight, loyal staff where backbiting was not tolerated.

Malinsky waited for the laughter and secondary comments to die down. Starukhin still stood posing, with a stupid grin on his face.

"If you're so worried, Vladimir Ivanovitch," Malinsky said coolly, "perhaps you'd like my chief of intelligence to command your army for you."

Now Trimenko's boys and the front staff smiled as a collective. But in the end, Malinsky did not want to further any contentiousness between his staff and his commanders. He only wanted to insure that everyone knew who was in control.

"My chief of engineers assures me that he will get you across the initial canal line and through the British obstacles," Malinsky told Starukhin. "I certainly don't underestimate the difficulty of the Third Shock Army's mission. No one does, Vladimir Ivanovitch. But I am certain you will accomplish it." Malinsky turned to the chief of staff. "General Chibisov, review the army missions."

The chief of staff exchanged places with Dudorov at the map. The bunker's ventilation system performed sluggishly in wet weather, and tobacco smoke filled the room with dirty wisps at the level of a standing man's shoulders. Chibisov was asthmatic, and Malinsky knew he survived such briefings on sheer strength of will. The chief of staff was the only officer in whose presence Malinsky limited his smoking. But in such a forum, such niceties were impossible, a mark of weakness, and Chibisov was on his own.

"The First Western Front attacks at 0600 Moscow time to seize an initial objective line here"—Chibisov traced a line on the map that ran just west of the Weser River, allowing for operational bridgeheads—"and a subsequent objective line that includes bridgeheads on the Rhine north and south of the Ruhr metropolitan complex. Follow-on missions or additional objectives will be designated by the High Command of Forces, Western Theater of Strategic Military Action, as the situation develops."

Malinsky watched Chibisov survey the crowded room, making high-speed calculations and judgments. The issue remained open as to whether the offensive would continue into the low countries and France. Although the plans already existed, even Malinsky did not know if the final political decision had been made to implement them. The chief of staff continued in a clear, controlled voice, dominating in its self-assurance.

"The Front conducts its attack with three reinforced armies in the first operational echelon.

"In the north, the Second Guards Tank Army, reinforced to a strength of five divisions, attacks in the Uelzen—Verden—Arnhem operational direction, with the immediate missions of crossing the Elbe-Seiten Canal in multidivisional strength on the first day of operations, locating and exploiting the boundary between the Netherlands Corps and the German Corps, and rapidly penetrating the Netherlands operational grouping in depth." As Chibisov reviewed the Second Guards Tank Army's mission, the formation's commander, Colonel General

Trimenko, wore a mask of hard determination, but his fingernails fought anxiously with the shell of one of the pistachios that were his only public vice. "The line of Autobahn E4/A7 is to be reached by multiple forward detachments not later than local midnight on the first day of operations," Chibisov continued. "Not later than midnight on the second day of operations, initial bridgeheads will be established on the Weser line. The Second Guards Tank Army has two secondary missions. Its initial exploitation of the corps boundary is to be followed by a southerly turning movement into the tactical, then into the operational rear of the German Corps. The army also conducts a supporting attack, from the initiation of hostilities, against the frontage of the German Corps, with the objective of fixing the Germans as far forward as possible, facilitating their subsequent envelopment and encirclement. Upon the commitment of the army's second echelon, those first-echelon units not occupied in guaranteeing the flank of the breakthrough against German counterattacks and not involved in the closing of the ring behind the Germans will contain residual Dutch elements northwest of a line drawn here, from the north of Bremen to Buxtehude."

Chibisov paused for breath, disguising the break as an opportunity for the audience to ask questions. But all of this had been covered before, in much greater detail, and Trimenko and those supporting him knew the plan thoroughly.

"In the south," Chibisov continued, saving the central breakthrough operation for last, "the Twentieth Guards Army attacks in the Duderstadt—Paderborn—Dortmund operational direction, with the mission of developing a rapid penetration in the Belgian sector, thereby creating an early crisis in the vicinity of the enemy's army group boundary. In this instance, as in the example of the Second Guards Tank Army in the north, it is our expectation that early penetrations on its flanks will force the enemy's Northern Army Group—NORTHAG—to commit its available reserves early and in a piecemeal fashion as it attempts to stabilize both of its flanks. Finally, upon receipt of the appropriate order, the Twentieth Guards Army is prepared to execute a turning movement to unhinge the British defense just to the north, should that prove necessary."

Chibisov breathed deeply, poisoning his lungs. "In the center, ultimately making the front's main attack, the Third Shock Army, reinforced with one East German division to a strength of five divisions, attacks in the Hannover—Osnabrueck—Venlo operational direction. Initially, the Third Shock Army's offensive is phased slightly behind those of the flanking armies, allowing NORTHAG to identify the threat to its flanks and commit its reserves, thus robbing the center of any depth. The initial structure of radio electronic combat operations will allow the enemy to maintain the necessary communications to identify the threat to his flanks and to initiate movement of his reserves. To that end, we will initially attack the enemy's air–ground and fire-support communications, but as soon as we have confirmation of the movement of the enemy's reserves to commitment, we will redirect the full weight of our radio electronic combat effort against NORTHAG's command and control and intelligence links."

As Chibisov spoke Malinsky watched Starukhin, the Third Shock Army's commander. Starukhin was always restless, looking for a fight or for a superior's attention. Now he sat fitfully, obviously swollen with energy and nerves, rubbing at his stubbly chin and blotched nose. Malinsky knew it was only a matter of time until Starukhin opened his mouth again. Malinsky could not help feeling a personal distaste toward Starukhin, even as he valued the man's unrivaled ability to smash his way through problems.

Starukhin managed to rein himself in a bit longer, and Chibisov continued smoothly, a perfect staff officer, choosing each word exactly without losing the rhythm of his speech. "In support of the front's plan, the Third Shock Army initially structures its attack to give the appearance that all four of its organic divisions have been committed, while actually holding the bulk of the Seventh and Tenth Tank divisions and all of the attached East German division as a ready second echelon. The commitment of this second echelon is not contingent upon the commitment to battle of the enemy's reserves, only upon the confirmed movement of those reserves to the north and/or south, or upon the personal authorization of the front commander.

"Third Shock Army has the primary mission of seizing multiple bridgeheads on the Weser River not later than 0600 on the third day of the war, and of thus facilitating the immediate commitment of the Forty-ninth Unified Army Corps to breakout and exploitation operations from the Weser line. The corps functions as the front's initial operational maneuver group.

"Third Shock Army has the secondary mission of supporting the Second Guards Tank Army's encirclement and destruction of the enemy grouping in the German Corps pocket.

"In the second operational echelon, Seventh Tank Army follows Third Shock but is prepared to release one division to Third Shock Army upon order of the front commander. Seventh Tank Army also prepares for options calling for it to repel an operational counterattack launched by CENTAG to relieve the pressure on NORTHAG, or to follow Twentieth Guards Army, should the initial success prove greater in that sector.

"In the north, Twenty-eighth Army follows Second Guards Tank Army. The primary mission of the Twenty-eighth is to break out from the Weser line and conduct exploitation operations that culminate in the establishment of operational bridgeheads on the Rhine. Twenty-eighth Army also prepares to release one division to Second Guards Tank Army upon order of the front commander if reinforcement of the Second Guards proves necessary to contain and reduce the German pocket.

"Other reserves or follow-on forces will be allocated to the First Western Front from the High Command of Forces based upon the developing military and political situations."

Malinsky believed it was as good a plan as could be devised with the available forces and technical support. An apparent pincer movement on a grand scale to draw off the enemy reserves, then a smashing blow to splinter a fatally weakened center. And the real beauty of it, as only Malinsky knew, was its function as a trap within a trap. Marshal Kribov expected Malinsky's breakthrough to draw off NATO's last operational reserves from the south, possibly even units stripped from CENTAG's front line. At that point, a powerful, sudden thrust would be directed against the weakened German–American defenses in the south in the Frankfurt and Stuttgart directions, employing follow-on forces that had, up until then, been portrayed as following Malinsky's armies. It was a series of blows of ever-increasing intensity, always directed at the unexpected but decisive point, on an ever-grander scale.

"Questions?" Chibisov asked.

Starukhin, the Third Shock Army commander, rose. Usually, when Starukhin got up a second time, it was to voice a legitimate concern. Malinsky watched Trimenko, the Second Guards Army commander, as Trimenko watched Starukhin. Trimenko was the type who never whined or complained, who just coldly went about the business at hand with the available tools.

"While I'm content with the allocation of indirect fire assets," Starukhin declared, "I remain troubled by the initial unavailability of fixed-wing air support. The Air Army needs to be reminded that it is ultimately under frontal control—*army* control. In my case—in all of our cases—it's imperative to deliver a crushing blow that reaches the enemy's tactical–operational depths simultaneously with the main assaults against his front. My attack helicopters can barely support water-obstacle crossing operations and the accompaniment of air assault missions—which are heavily scheduled. I say nothing about their use as a highly mobile antitank reserve." Starukhin paused, gauging the other commanders in the room. "The present allocation of fixed-wing aircraft allows the armies very little control over the battle in depth."

There was no question about it. Starukhin had a point. But there were never sufficient assets to please everyone. Malinsky had made his decision based upon his evaluation of the situation within the constraints imposed by the High Command of Forces. In any case, he was a habitual centralizer, having experienced too much subordinate incompetence over the years, and he felt the army commanders already had more assets than they could effectively manage.

Malinsky stood up and approached the map. Both Chibisov and Starukhin took their seats, leaving the front commander as the only focal point in the room.

"Vladimir Ivanovitch has a strong case," Malinsky said, surveying them all. As his eyes passed over the East Germans he almost laughed. He doubted they were the men their fathers and grandfathers had been. They looked as though they expected to be fed to the serpents. Starukhin would insure that they were employed to the best possible effect.

"However," Malinsky continued, maintaining his straight-backed, straight-faced gravity, "I am convinced that the key to the ground war is the air battle. I fully support Marshal Kribov's decision to employ the bulk of the air and deep-fire weapons of all the fronts to support the initial air offensive. If we failed to reach a single ground objective on the first day of the war, if your units did not accomplish a single mission of the day, but we managed to destroy the enemy's air power on the ground or while it was in a posture of reaction, I'm certain we could recover lost time in the ground battle. Since the withdrawal of his intermediate-range missiles and ground-launched cruise missiles, the enemy has only his air power to rely upon to reach deep and attempt to rupture our plans. His air power is the cornerstone of his defense. Remove it, and you can knock his military structure apart with relative ease." This time it was Malinsky's turn to pause for effect, making eye contact with his leading commanders and finally settling his gaze on Starukhin. "I am committed to the initial requirement to destroy the enemy's air defense belts and his fixed-wing combat capability. Even if it meant diverting maneuver forces, I would do it. A parochial attitude begs for defeat.

"Now," Malinsky continued, stalking through the mist of cigarette smoke, "I also understand that some of you are worried about the enemy's possible employment of weapons of mass destruction. That will always remain a concern. But, as Comrade General Dudorov told us, we have no indications that we are presently in a nuclear-scared situation. If you accomplish the tasks assigned to each of you within the plan, I believe we can defeat the nuclear bogeyman. *Speed . . . shock . . . activeness . . .*" Malinsky surveyed the group of officers, each one a very powerful figure in his own right. "Once we are deep in their rear, intermingled with their combat and support formations, how will they effectively bring nuclear weapons to bear? The object is to close swiftly with the enemy, to achieve and exploit shock effect, to penetrate him at multiple points, and to keep moving, except to destroy that which you absolutely cannot outmaneuver." Malinsky turned to face his chief of missile troops and artillery. "I also understand that some of you are troubled by my targeting priorities. Let it be on my shoulders. But I do not believe it is possible to destroy every nuclear-capable system in the NATO arsenal. Anyway, why cut off the fingers and toes when you can more easily lop off the head? Once our trap has been sprung, the targets for the front and army reconnaissance strike complexes must be the enemy's command and control infrastructure and his intelligence-collection capability. If he cannot find us, he cannot hope to place nuclear fires on us. And without effective command and control systems, the requirements of both nuclear targeting and conventional troop control are insoluble. Yet even such targeting must be selective. For example, we know what we want the enemy to see and how we want him to respond initially. That, too, must be factored into our decisions regarding what targets to attack and when to attack them. Modern warfare is not merely a brawl. It is both a broad science and an uncompromising art. If you have not asked yourself every possible question, the unasked question will destroy you."

Malinsky considered the men before him one last time. The anxious and the stubborn, men of finesse and born savages. He never ceased marveling at the varieties of character and talent the military required or could at least manage to exploit. Ambitions as different as their secret fears, Malinsky thought.

"I know you are all anxious to return to your formations and workplaces. There's always too much to do and too little time in which to do it, I know. And every man among us has his own devils, his own worries. *My* concern in these last hours is that the enemy might strike first. But I know, in my mind and in my heart"—Malinsky touched his fist to his chest—"that once we have begun, no power on earth will be able to stop us. Each of you wears the trappings of tremendous power, commanders and staff officers alike. Consider what your badges of rank represent. Each of you has come to personify the greatness, the destiny of the Motherland. And your actions will ultimately decide that destiny."

Malinsky thought of his son, a flashing instant of worry, affection, and pride intermingled. "I hope at least a few of you get a bit of sleep, too. I just want to leave you with one final caution. Most of you have heard it from me many times. If there is one area in which I profoundly disagree with the theoreticians, it is in regard to casualties. I believe that none of us, on either side, is prepared for the intensity of destruction we will encounter. Not everywhere. But at the points of decision, and in priority sectors, I expect some units—on both sides—to suffer unprecedented losses. Certainly, the number of soldiers who fall on a given field will not rival the casualty counts of antiquity. But we have not yet found the algorithm to relate modern systems losses to preindustrial manpower losses. The manpower losses will be severe enough, but the losses in what might appropriately be termed the 'capital' of war will appear catastrophic to the commander who is weak or has not prepared himself sufficiently. I hope . . . that each of you is just sufficiently better prepared than your opponent . . . to remain steadfast when he wavers, to impose your will on him when he takes that fatal pause to count his losses. You must be hard. Each of us will experience things that will haunt him for the rest of his days. That goes with the rank and position."

Malinsky thought for a moment, searching for the right closing words. "This is not my permission to take needless casualties. One life lost unnecessarily is too much. But . . ." He reached for words. Without sounding weak, he wanted to tell them to value the lives of their men, and without callousness, he wanted to communicate to them what needed to be done, to prepare them. "Simply do your duty."

Malinsky strode abruptly toward the door. The officers jumped to attention. Malinsky could feel the collection of emotions grown so intense in the men that it almost demanded a physical outlet. The door opened before him, and a voice barked down the hallway. Malinsky marched back toward his private office in a press of concerns that obscured the braced figures he passed in the long corridor. He wondered if any of them really understood what was about to happen. He wondered if it was humanly possible to understand.

Two

The meeting broke up behind Malinsky. Officers hurriedly folded maps and pulled on their wet-weather garments. A few lower-ranking officers gleaned the remnants of the refreshments that had been set out earlier, while others discussed problems in low, urgent voices. The images were the same as those at the end of a thousand other briefings, but the air had an unmistakably different feel to it, an intensity that would have been rare even in Afghanistan.

Chibisov had another meeting to attend, and a host of actions to consolidate or check on, but he hoped to sneak a few minutes outside of the bunker, breathing fresh air. The East German medicine he took for his asthma now was better than that available in the Soviet Union, but the smoke-filled briefing room nonetheless made his lungs feel as though they had shrunk to the size of a baby's and would not accept enough oxygen to keep him going. The fresh night air, thick and damp though it might be, would feel like a cool drink going down. But Chibisov could not leave until all of the other key officers had cleared off. Patiently, ready with answers to any of their possible questions, he watched the others leave, judging their fitness for the tasks at hand.

Starukhin, the oversized Third Shock Army commander, suddenly veered in Chibisov's direction, followed by his usual entourage, augmented now by a lost-looking East German divisional commander and his operations officer. Starukhin was the sort of commander who was never alone, who always needed the presence of fawning admirers and drinking companions. He was a tall, beefy, red-faced man who looked as though he belonged in a steel mill, not in a general's uniform. His heavy muscles were softening into fat, but he still cultivated a persona of ready violence. Starukhin was definitely old school, and he only survived the restructuring period—bitterly nicknamed "the purges" by its victims—because Malinsky had protected him, much to Chibisov's surprise.

Chibisov and Starukhin had known each other on and off for years, and they casually disliked one another. At the army commander's approach, Chibisov drew himself up to his full height, but he still only came up to Starukhin's shoulders. The army commander smoked long cigars, a habit he had acquired as an adviser in Cuba. Now he stepped very close to Chibisov, releasing a cloud of reeking smoke that carried a faint overtone of alcohol. And he smiled.

"Chibisov, you know that's nothing but crap about the aircraft." Starukhin gave his admirers time to appreciate his style. They gathered around the two men, smirking like children. "The Air Force always wants an absurd margin of safety. There are plenty of aircraft. I know, I've examined the figures personally. And Dudorov, that fat little swine, needs to get his head out of the clouds and do some real work. You know the British won't give up all of their tank reserves. I'll be stuck in unnecessary meeting engagements when I should be pissing in the Weser."

"Comrade Army Commander," Chibisov said, "the front commander has taken his decision on the matter of aircraft allocation." He chose his usual armor of formality, even though he and Starukhin wore the same rank now and Starukhin was technically subordinate by virtue of their respective duty positions. In an odd way, though, he sympathized with Starukhin. Beyond the dramatics, Starukhin, too, was a tough professional. Now he was trying to build his own margin of safety, a type of behavior the shadow system taught every perceptive officer as a lieutenant. But there was nothing to be done.

"Oh, don't tell me that, Chibisov. Everybody knows he does whatever you want him to do. Comrade Lieutenant General Chibisov, the grand vizier of the Group of Forces. Just get me a few extra aircraft, say one hundred additional sorties. And tell Dudorov his number-one job is to find the British reserves so I can send the aircraft after them. Oh, and Nicki Borisov tells me I need more one-five-two ammunition."

"Two more units of fire per gun would be good," Borisov put in from Starukhin's side. Borisov was a talented enough officer, a recent Voroshilov graduate who was betting on Starukhin to pull him along.

"Comrade Army Commander," Chibisov said, "at present, you have received a greater proportion of the front's allocation of virtually every type of ammunition than your comrades. You have more march routes with fewer water obstacles. You have more hauling capacity than any other army. You have more rotary-wing aircraft of every type. You have *two* deception battalions in support of you, as well as an extra signal battalion that came right out of the front's hide. You have the lion's share of the front's artillery division, you—"

"I have the best maneuver terrain"—Starukhin cut him off—"and I have forty-six percent of the tactical bridging assets to cross under thirty-four percent of the projected water obstacles. Don't play numbers with me, Chibisov. I also have the main attack, and the toughest opponents. In addition to which I expect half of the German Corps to come down on my northern flank when Trimenko gets stuck in the mud."

"That's nonsense. The Germans will hold on too far forward and too long. It's a given. And if they hit anybody, it'll be Trimenko."

"A few damned aircraft, Chibisov."

Chibisov could tell now that Starukhin was sorry that he had initiated the exchange and that he was looking for a token prize so that he would not be embarrassed in front of his officers.

"Comrade Army Commander, as the aircraft become available, I promise you will have priority."

"But I need to *plan.*" Suddenly, Starukhin lost his temper. "Listen, I don't have to beg you, you little . . ."

Say it, Chibisov thought, looking Starukhin dead in the eyes. Go ahead, say it, you cossack bastard, say the word. Chibisov knew Starukhin better than the army commander realized. Dudorov had a finger in everything—he was a superb chief of intelligence—as a result of which Chibisov knew that Starukhin strongly encouraged his officers to affiliate with Pamyat, a right-wing nationalist hate group that wanted to revive the days of the Black Hundreds and to rid the sacred Motherland of Asians and other subhuman creatures, such as Chibisov himself. Oh, he knew the bully with the big cigar. His grandfathers had come for a drunken frolic in the ghetto, coming by the hundreds, to cut a few beards and perhaps a few throats, to rape the women . . . and to steal. The Slav was a born thief. And Chibisov's ancestors, but a few generations removed, would not have resisted. They would have bowed and prayed.

Those days were over. And the Starukhins of the world would never bring them back. Even for officers who were not Party members, such affiliations were illegal. Pamyat had even reprinted *The Protocols of the Elders of Zion,* the infamous Jew-baiting book of the Czarist Okhrana so beloved of the Hitlerite Germans. Chibisov needed all of his self-control now not to spit in the army commander's face. He consoled himself with the thought that he could destroy Starukhin, if it proved absolutely necessary.

"You were about to say something, Comrade Army Commander?"

"Pavel Pavlovitch," Starukhin began again, switching suddenly to the ingratiating tone that Russian alcoholics always kept at the ready, "our concerns should be identical. The Third Shock Army has a terribly difficult mission to accomplish under unprecedented time constraints. I only want to insure that we have covered every requirement."

He would really have to watch Starukhin now, Chibisov realized. Now and forever. In a moment's embarrassment, they had become eternal enemies.

No, Chibisov corrected himself, the enmity between them had merely been uncovered. The Starukhins and the Chibisovs of the world had always been enemies.

"Comrade Army Commander, I am convinced that our concerns are truly identical. As soon as ground-attack aircraft become available, you'll have your fair share of sorties."

Staruhkin looked at him. Chibisov had great faith in Starukhin's ability to bully his way through the enemy. But just in case there were problems, he wanted to be certain that they fell on Starukhin's shoulders, and that there were as few excuses as possible available to the man.

"About the ammunition," Chibisov went on, "I believe I can help you with that. Front can provide an additional point-five units of fire for your heavy guns, and perhaps even for your multiple-rocket launchers, if we can align the transport. There's a projected movement window opening up behind your divisions in midafternoon. Have your chief of the rear call Zdanyuk and tell him where you want it delivered. We'll bring it right to the divisional guns. And the best of luck tomorrow, Comrade Army Commander."

Starukhin went off without thanks, without even an acknowledgment, like a man turning away from an empty shop window. When the army commander's entourage had left the room, Chibisov turned to one of his staff assistants.

"Tell Colonel Shtein that I'm a bit behind. Then see that Comrade Army Commander Trimenko has some refreshments and ask if he needs access to any communications means. Have Shtein begin the tapes as soon as General Trimenko has settled in. I'll be down in a few minutes. Oh, and make sure Samurukov knows he's to sit in."

The staff officer turned smartly to execute his mission. The handful of technical and service officers remaining in the room had no immediate call on Chibisov's time, and he went out into the hallway, fighting back his cough.

Even the stale air in the corridor felt refreshing after the smog of the briefing room. Chibisov strolled down the hall to the main tunnel corridor, not allowing himself to hurry. The officers and men of the front staff were careful to allow plenty of room as Chibisov passed. But the chief of staff was not prowling for defects tonight. He just wanted to breathe.

As soon as he reached the backup stairwell and found it deserted, he nearly collapsed with pent-up coughing. He felt as though his face must be changing color with the intensity of the struggle for breath. He went up the stairs slowly, lungs clotted shut. With no one to see him, he spit as though ridding himself of wreckage. He hurriedly took one of his steroid pills, which were only to be used in emergencies, washing it down with his own saliva. In the cemented stairwell, his coughing sounded especially destructive.

What did that bastard Starukhin see when he looked at him? An asthmatic little Jew? Chibisov had come up through the airborne forces, and he had been a martial-arts specialist as a young officer. He had done everything possible to toughen himself, to reject every weak, infuriating image clinging to him from a thousand years of pathetic East European Jewish history. He resolutely turned his back on all aspects of Jewishness. He worked to be a better Soviet patriot than any of them, a better *Russian* patriot, as had his father and his grandfather, the first enlightened members of a fiercely traditional family. He even downplayed his intellectual abilities when it came to studying the theoretical aspects of socialism and communism, since he felt it was too Jewish to overly master political philosophy. Instead, he had turned to military engineering and mathematics, to cybernetics and troop control theory. Then they tried to turn him into an instructor, the star young theorist on the staff of the Ryazan Higher Airborne Command School. But he maneuvered his way back into a fighter's job, even volunteering, although already in his middle thirties, for training as a special operations officer.

Accepted despite his age, he survived the agonizing training only to be defeated by an unreasonable and unexpected enemy: asthma. It was as though a millennium of weak-lunged Jewishness, of reeking ghettos, had taken their revenge on him, as though some bitter and malicious Jehovah were having his little joke. He completed his training only to collapse and end up in a military sanatorium in Baku. His jumping days were over.

But he refused to give in. He fought to remain an officer, obsessive in his determination to wear the uniform. He knew they did not understand him. He had never in his life attended a Jewish service. He had no understanding of the Jews who wanted to leave the Soviet Union, to leave Russia, their home. To Chibisov, the émigrés were incomprehensible, weak, and selfish. For him, Israel was a distant land of superstition and fascist enthusiasms. And yet he knew that his fellow officers always saw him as the little Jew, a born staff man, perhaps meant to be a senior bookkeeper in some great Jewish banking house, or a student of arcane texts, shut in a musty study. Chibisov, the little Jew who wanted to be a Soviet paratroop officer.

Chibisov left the stairwell, sweating, near exhaustion. He labored up the ramp to the massive blast-proof entry doors. The interior guards saluted with their weapons, and, behind a glass panel, the duty officer jumped to his feet. Everyone knew the little Jew chief of staff, Chibisov thought bitterly.

He stood in limbo for a moment as the inner door shut behind him. Then the outer door began to slide back, and the cool air raced in, carrying flecks of rain and a multilayered drone of constant noise from the trails and roads and highways. The forecast called for a wet first day of the war, and Chibisov felt lucky to emerge from the bunker at a moment when the rain had softened to little more than a mist. As the outer door closed Chibisov stood still, breathing as deeply as his lungs would permit, almost gasping. The nearest sounds came from the departing helicopters that carried away the more important briefing attendees. The blades hacked at the darkness to gain lift. Underlying the throb of the rotors, countless vehicles groaned toward carefully planned destinations. Chibisov's mind filled with timetables. It had been a key consideration that the Soviet forces could not close on their jump-off positions too early. It was unthinkable to put everything neatly into place, then wait in a silence that telegraphed to the enemy that you were ready to attack, with your final deployments even telling him where the main effort would come. The plan kept forces on the move, shifting, realigning toward a fluid perfection that would appear no different than the preceding days of road marches and hasty bivouacs, but that would allow the swift convergence of overwhelming forces at the points of decision, achieving tactical surprise, and even a measure of operational surprise. Chibisov looked at his watch. If the march tables were on schedule, the noise in the distance would be from one of the divisions of the Seventh Tank Army, leapfrogging closer to the Elbe. As the lead echelons moved into the attack the follow-on forces would already be closing on their vacated positions, leaving as few exploitable gaps as possible. Chibisov had confidence in the mathematical model and in its tolerances. Yet he recognized that, to the drivers and the junior commanders out on the roads, it probably seemed like chaos. It was important to cultivate Malinsky's talent for standing back, Chibisov thought. Not to get caught up in the frustrating details, even though you remained aware of them. From the grand perspective, the minor scenes of confusion on the roads or in assembly areas simply disappeared, consumed by the macro-efficiencies of the model.

It only seemed remarkable to Chibisov that the enemy had not reached out to strike a preemptive blow. He and Dudorov had discussed the situation at length with Malinsky. In the twenty-four hours prior to the attack, the posture of virtually all of the Warsaw Pact forces, and especially their supply and rear services deployments, was terribly vulnerable. But so far, NATO had done nothing. Dudorov was convinced that there was absolutely no danger of NATO striking first. But neither Chibisov nor Malinsky could quite believe that the enemy would passively wait to receive the obviously impending blow.

Chibisov tasted the night air. The passages of his lungs had reopened slightly, and he felt like a man reprieved. He thought that the plan for a high-powered, relentless offensive would be like depriving a man of oxygen. NATO would have its wind taken away by the initial impact, and it would never be allowed to regain its breath. The damp night air felt vivid with power; the vehicle noise sounded as if the earth itself were moving. In just a few hours, the first wave of aircraft would be on their way. And still the enemy did nothing.

A lone helicopter growled by overhead. Probably Starukhin, Chibisov thought. But the army commander had already receded in his mind.

The last faint rain stopped. Chibisov could feel that it would return, stronger than before. But for the moment, he stood peacefully in the spongy air and thought of Malinsky, who had saved him. Recovering from his collapse in the sanatorium, Chibisov found that paperwork had been initiated without his knowledge to remove him from active service. The old anti–Semitism. He struggled through the bureaucracy until he managed an interview with the deputy commander of the Transcaucasus Military District. That was the first time he met Malinsky. Comrade Deputy Commander, the army is my life. I'm as good as any officer in this uniform. Malinsky listened, watching him in silence, unlike the blustering, self-important general officers with whom Chibisov was familiar. The Starukhins of the world.

Malinsky put a stop to the separation proceedings and gave Chibisov a trial job in his operations department. They were designing contingency plans for the invasion of Iran at the time, and they needed someone with a solid background in airborne matters. Chibisov quickly discovered something new in himself. Perhaps because of his technical training, he had an eye for the telling detail, and he almost intuitively understood how to make a plan intelligible to its executors. He loved the work.

He especially enjoyed working under Malinsky. Brilliant operational concepts and dazzling variations seemed to come effortlessly to Malinsky. Chibisov had never seen anyone who could grasp the overall context and true military essentials of a situation as thoroughly and as quickly as Malinsky. The two men seemed fated to work together, Malinsky rich with ideas and Chibisov perfectly suited to turn those ideas into the words and tables, the graphics and the monumental paperwork that moved armies and brought them efficiently to bear. In the end, Afghanistan had put all of the Iran plans on hold, possibly forever. But Chibisov had gone with Malinsky to the general's first military district command, his trial run, in the Volga Military District. Chibisov had been the most junior military district chief of staff in the Soviet Army, and he did not underestimate the jealousies, or the pressure Malinsky received over the matter. The two men had worked together almost constantly since then, and it was Chibisov's sole regret that he was not the sort of man who could ever tell Malinsky how deeply grateful he was to him.

Breathing regularly now, Chibisov turned back toward the bunker. There was no more time to waste. Trimenko, the Second Guards Tank Army Commander, would be almost through watching the videotapes now, and Chibisov did not want to waste any of the man's time. He had no doubt that Trimenko, whose horizons did not extend beyond the strictly military, would be angry, impatient, and skeptical by now.

The tape was still running as Chibisov entered the darkened room. He stood until his eyes adjusted to the darkness, watching the colorful footage of destruction and disaster, some filmed on rainy days, other segments reflecting good weather in order to be prepared for either circumstance. Then he made his way to the chair that had remained empty for him between Colonel General Trimenko and Major General Dudorov. Samurukov, the front's deputy commander for airborne and special operations forces, sat on the other side of Trimenko. Colonel Shtein, the master of ceremonies, stood beside the television screen.

Chibisov had seen the footage before, but it still seemed remarkable to him. The filmed destruction of a West German town that had not yet been taken in a war that had yet to begin. Shtein had been sent to the First Western Front directly from the special propaganda subdepartment of the general staff in Moscow. As Chibisov watched he was convinced by the sights and sounds that this was, indeed, what modern war must look like. The filming was magnificently done, never too artful, never too clear. The viewer always had the feeling that the cameraman was well aware of his own mortality. Chibisov could not understand the

German voice-over, but it had all been explained to him the day before, when he and Malinsky saw the film for the first time. Only then had certain directives suddenly made sense to them. Malinsky had been furious that he had not been trusted longer in advance, and he was sincerely uneasy about the whole business. There was something old-fashioned, almost gallant about Malinsky, and this particular special operation was not well-suited to his temperament. The staff called Malinsky "the Count" behind his back, half-jokingly, half in affection. Such a thing would not even have passed as a joke when Chibisov was a junior officer, and he forbade the use of the nickname. But he secretly understood how it had developed. It was not just a matter of the well-known lineage, which Malinsky vainly imagined might be ignored. There was something aristocratic about the man himself.

Malinsky had readily agreed with Chibisov's suggestion that he handle the matter with Shtein, freeing the commander for battlefield concerns. Chibisov had recognized the arrangement immediately as the only practical solution. Personally, he remained undecided on the potential effectiveness of the planned film and radio broadcasts. The approach was to attempt to convince populations under attack that it was only their resistance that made the destruction of their homes inevitable, and, further, to convince the West Germans that their allies took a cavalier attitude toward the destruction of their country. The goals were to create panic and a loss of the will to fight, while dividing the NATO allies. Chibisov doubted that such an approach would be effective against Russians, but Western Europeans remained something of an enigma to him.

Colonel Shtein commented on a few salient points as the film reached its climax. Then the screen suddenly fuzzed, and Shtein moved to turn up the lights.

Trimenko turned to Chibisov. It was clear from the bewildered look on the army commander's face that he had not grasped the total context. Chibisov felt a certain kinship with Trimenko, although they were both men who kept their distance. Both of them were committed to the development and utilization of automated troop control systems as well as sharing the no-nonsense temperaments of accomplished technicians. In staff matters, they were both perfectionists, although Trimenko was quicker to ruin a subordinate's career over a single error.

"At least," Trimenko said coldly, "I now understand all the fuss about rapidly seizing Lueneburg. It never made military sense to me before—and I'm not certain it really makes military sense now." Trimenko glanced at Shtein, hardly concealing his disgust. "Our friend from the General Staff has explained his rationale to me. But I frankly view the scheme as frivolous, a diversion of critical resources. And"—Trimenko looked down at the floor, then back into Chibisov's eyes—"we're not barbarians."

Trimenko's concern mirrored Chibisov's own. But the chief of staff knew he had no choice but to support the General Staff's position. Overall, he was relieved that there had been so little interference with the front's plan. Marshal Kribov's approval had been good enough. This matter with Shtein was a special case, and it was important not to make too much of it. But Trimenko had to support it, one way or another.

"Comrade Army Commander, let me try to put it in a better perspective," Chibisov said, unsure that he could manage to do what he was promising. "As you know, we are living in an age in which there has been something of a revolution in military affairs. Personally, I would say a series of revolutions—first the nuclear revolution, which may have been a false side road in history, then the automation revolution, with which you are intimately familiar. In the West, they speak of the 'information age,' and perhaps they're correct in doing so. The Soviet system has always realized the value of information—for instance, the power of correct propaganda. Today, the powerful new means of arranging and disseminating information have opened new possibilities. In light of the successes of our propaganda efforts in the past, we must at least be open to the new and expanded opportunities offered by technology. Certainly, we both realize the value of battlefield deception, of blinding the enemy to your true activities and intentions, of confusing him, or even of steering him toward the decision you desire him to make. But how do we define the battlefield today? If warfare has expanded to include conflict between entire systems, then perhaps we must also be prepared to redefine the battlefield, or to accept that there are, in fact, a variety of battlefields. This little film is an information weapon, a deception weapon, aimed above the heads of the militarists. It targets the governments and populations of the West."

"If the film is as accurate as Colonel Shtein tells us it is," Trimenko said, "what's the point of diverting a portion of my forces to actually destroy this town?"

"Lueneburg has been carefully selected by the General Staff," Chibisov said, parroting Shtein's own arguments now. "It is easily within the grasp of our initial operations, it is defended by one of the weak sisters, and it has great sentimental value to the West Germans because of its medieval structures. Yet the town has no real economic value. Colonel Shtein's department went to great expense to construct the model of the town square and other well-known features so that they could be destroyed for this film. The wonders of the Soviet film industry, you might say. But when this film is broadcast twenty-four hours from now, it must be augmented with additional dating footage, and, most importantly, it must stand up to any hasty enemy attempts at verification. The historic district must be flattened. We must destroy the real town now that we have filmed the destruction of the model."

Trimenko was not yet ready to give in. Chibisov knew him as a hard and stubborn man, and he recognized the locked expression on the army commander's face. "But what good does it do? Really? One of my divisions squanders its momentum, you tie up air-assault elements needed elsewhere, aircraft are diverted, and perhaps irreplaceable helicopters are lost. For what, Chibisov? So we can show the West Germans a movie? So we can broadcast to the world that we *are* barbarians after all?"

Chibisov sympathized but could not relent. Malinsky had commented that this was the sort of thing the Mongols would have done, had they possessed the technology.

"But you see," Chibisov said, "the broadcasts will portray

future incidents of this nature as avoidable. Tomorrow we will have film crews all over the battlefield. I expect Goettingen will be a positive example of what happens when there is little or no resistance. We'll see. But what the West German people and their government get is a threat that, if resistance continues, there will be more Lueneburgs —because of their resistance, not because of any will to destruction on our part. They'll also see undestroyed cities and towns where we were not forced to fight. Anyway, we can easily convince a substantial portion of the West German population that the Dutch are more responsible for the town's destruction than are we, simply because they chose to fight to defend it. *We* would not have harmed the town, had *they* not forced us into a fight."

"What if the Dutch don't fight for Lueneburg?"

"Immaterial. You saw the film. Even if the Dutch fade away tomorrow, they will still have caused the destruction of that town on the film. And film doesn't lie, Comrade Army Commander. Technically, the Dutch may have proof to the contrary. But frightened men have no patience with involved explanations. What could the Dutch, or NATO, bring as an effective counterargument? A bluster of outrage? Denials are always weaker than accusations. It's elementary physics, you might say."

Colonel Shtein interrupted the conversation. As a representative of the General Staff on a special mission, he was not about to let slight differences in rank get in his way.

"Comrades," he told them, lecturing, "it is the assessment of the general staff that the West Germans have grown so materialistic, so comfortable, that they will not be able to endure the thought of seeing their country destroyed again. They have lost their will. The Bundeswehr will fight, initially. But the officer corps is not representative of the people. This operation will complement your encirclement of the German corps and its threatened destruction. And consider its veiled threat should NATO look to nuclear weapons for their salvation. It sets up numerous options for conflict termination."

The army commander looked at the staff colonel. "And if

it doesn't work? If they simply ignore it? Or if they fight all the harder because of it?"

"They won't," Shtein said. "But no matter if they did respond that way initially. We have similar film for Hameln. And we may actually be required to strike one mid-sized city very hard, say Bremen or Hannover. But in the end, the General Staff is convinced that this approach will help bring the war to a rapid conclusion, and on very favorable terms."

Trimenko turned to Chibisov. "I don't like it. It's unsoldierly. We mustn't divert any assets from the true points of decision."

Chibisov noted a change in Trimenko's voice. The army commander was no longer as adamant in tone, despite his choice of words. He would accept his responsibility, as Chibisov had accepted his own. Now it just required another push, for form's sake.

Chibisov turned to Dudorov, the chief of intelligence. "Yuri, what do you think of all this? You understand the West Germans better than any of us." Dudorov always preferred to be called by his first name without the patronymic, another of his Western tastes.

Dudorov looked at Chibisov and the army commander with all of the solemnity his chubby face could manage. And he was unusually slow in speaking.

"Comrade Generals . . . I think this is absolutely brilliant."

Chibisov wandered down to the operations center after seeing Trimenko off. The local air controller did not want to clear Trimenko's helicopter for takeoff, due to expected traffic. The air controller did not know that the traffic would be the beginning of the air offensive, only that he had been ordered to keep the skies cleared beginning one hour before military dawn for priority air movements. The clearance had required Chibisov's personal involvement, and the delay further contributed to Trimenko's bad mood. He needed to be at his army command post now. Shortly, the skies would be very crowded indeed, as aircraft shot to the west, their flights cross-timed with the launch of short-range missiles and artillery blasting corridors through the enemy's air defenses. Then the entire front would erupt.

The operations center was calmer, quieter than Chibisov expected. The calm before the storm, he thought to himself. Malinsky was still napping, and Chibisov let him sleep. Tomorrow, Malinsky would move forward to be with the army commanders during critical periods and to direct operations from the front's forward command post closer to the West German border. He needed all the rest he could get. Chibisov required less sleep than the front commander, and they had an unspoken arrangement between them on that, too.

An officer-clerk moved to the big map now and then, while other officers took information over telephones. The bank of control radios remained quiet, except for routine administrative traffic that the enemy would be expecting. Out in the darkness, formations and units were sending just enough routine transmissions, usually from bogus locations, to lull the enemy into a sense of normalcy. But the critical war nets still slumbered.

Seven minutes, and the first plane would take off from an airfield in Poland. Then the other aircraft between Poland and the great dividing line would come up in sequence, a metal blanket lifting into the sky. Chibisov agreed with Malinsky. The air offensive was critical.

Chibisov walked around a bank of data processors to the second row of desks back from the master situation map. He stopped at the position of the front's radio electronic combat duty officer. He put his hand on the shoulder of the lieutenant colonel, signaling him to remain at his screen.

"Everything all right?"

"Yes, Comrade General."

"No surprises?"

"Not yet. We won't know for at least half an hour, maybe longer if it gets really bad. Nothing on this scale has ever been attempted before."

Chibisov was aware of the potential problems. When you attempted to employ these weapons of the new age, attacking the enemy's communications complexes and radars, there was always the worry that you would strike your own critical networks—that, somehow, key aspects had been overlooked or inadequately tested. There was so much that was about to happen for the first time. Chibisov pictured the electromagnetic spectrum as crowded with an almost visible flood of power. The manipulation of nature itself, Chibisov thought, of natural laws and properties, more of the deadly wonders of technology. Yet he knew that there were men out there, waiting to blast and fill and tear at the border barriers, waiting at the literal edge of war, who were as frightened as their earliest ancestors had been when they came out of their caves to do battle.

Chibisov moved on to check the latest returns on fuel consumption.

THREE

Nobody wanted to touch the body. The soldiers stood around the corpse in the drizzling rain, staring. The rain tapped at the open, upturned eyes and rinsed the slack mouth under the glare of the lantern. Bibulov, the warrant officer who had been left in charge of the vehicle transloading, tried to remember the soldier's name. He recalled that the boy was a Tadzhik. But the elusive Asian consonance of his name escaped him, teasing just beyond his mental grasp. The boy had come to the unit unable to speak any Russian beyond the primitive sounds necessary for survival. And all of the prissy, well-intentioned efforts of the language skills collective had not brought him to proper speech. The boy had done as ordered, imitating when he did not understand, and had waited as mutely as a resting animal between jobs. It seemed to Bibulov as though the boy had set his mind to endure the two years in uniform required of him with the minimum of personal engagement. To do as he was made to do, uncomplainingly, until it came time to return to his distant home. Now he was dead, and the war had not even begun.

Bibulov believed that there would, indeed, be a war, and that it would come soon. But now there was only the frantic shifting of cargoes in the middle of a rainy night. The guns had not yet begun to squander their accounts of ammunition. Yet the boy was absurdly dead, as though fate could not wait a few more hours or another day. Bibulov shook his head, attempting to select the correct response, the course of action that would result in the least trouble.

Somehow, it was in the natural order of things. If not this, then something else. The premature death accorded with Bibulov's view of the world and of his own place in it. What more could reasonably be expected?

And what did they expect, when exhausted soldiers were detailed to trans-load the unwieldy crates of artillery charges and rounds in the rain with their bare hands, without even the most rudimentary tools? It seemed to Bibulov as though nothing of significance had changed in a hundred, perhaps a thousand years. Oh, there were the trucks, of course. The big trucks from the army matériel support brigade brought the cargo from the army's forward supply base to the transshipment point at division. Then brute strength—wet, splinter-riddled hands—shifted and hoisted and lugged the stone-heavy boxes through the mud to the smaller trucks of the artillery regiment or to the shuttling division carryalls. The trucks were fine. But between the full and empty trucks lay a pool of timelessness, where animal labor continued to dominate.

Bibulov had watched helplessly in the muted glow of the safety lights as the unbalanced crate began to slip. It started with a fatal shift on the shoulders of weary boys. Then it proceeded relentlessly, a dance of silhouettes, as the crate slowly edged forward, quickening, then dropping very fast as the struggling boys abandoned it one after the other in a swift chain reaction. At the climax of the brief drama, the Tadzhik was a last tiny shape, twisting in a moment's terror and sprawling backward under the weight, padding its fall with his chest. By the time they heaved the crate off to the side, the boy was dead.

Bibulov tried to get the thing in perspective. The rain licked at the back of his neck. How big an event was the boy's death now? In a training exercise, everything in the unit would have come to a halt. But events had moved fatally beyond training exercises. The inevitability of war had come home to him the evening before, when the responsible officers had suddenly stopped demanding signatures of receipt on their delivery inventories. Bibulov had never known such a thing to happen, and it jarred him profoundly. At the same time, the grinding pace of the past few days had increased to an inhuman tempo.

Bibulov decided that, although the boy's death was undoubtedly a very significant event to somebody, somewhere, there was nothing to be done about it here and now. And the cargo had to be transferred.

He stared down, tidying up his conscience with quick last respects. The corpse appeared ridiculous and small, an ill-dressed doll. The flat Asian face shone in the cast of the lantern as though the rain had polished it with wax.

"Pick him up," Bibulov ordered. "We're wasting time."

When the soldiers responded merely by shifting their positions, milling a little closer as each one waited for another to begin, Bibulov hardened his voice.

"Pick him up, you bastards. Let's go."

It was always like this, Bibulov consoled himself. The big men decide. And there's nothing to be done but obey, hoping you're not the one who gets crushed in the mud.

Shilko woke abruptly in response to the careful hand on his shoulder. "Has it started?" he asked, with the urgency of disorientation.

Before Captain Romilinsky could respond, Shilko had gained sufficient mastery of himself to realize that everything was still as it should be, and that his big guns had not yet begun their work. The only sounds were the dotting of rain on the roof of his range car and the background noise of vehicles in movement that had not ceased for days. The local area had its own little well of rain quiet. The battalion was ready. Waiting.

"Sleep well, Comrade Commander?" Romilinsky asked.

Shilko liked his battalion chief of staff. Romilinsky was wonderfully earnest, an officer of excellent staff culture. It had been no plum for him to be assigned to a battalion whose commander obviously was not soaring through the ranks like a rocket. Lieutenant Colonel Shilko was easily the oldest battalion commander in the high-powered artillery brigade, perhaps in the entire Second Guards Tank Army. He was, in fact, older than the new-breed brigade commander. But if Romilinsky felt any disappointment at his assignment, he never let it show. The captain was a good officer and a fine young man. Shilko wished that his daughters had chosen husbands more like Romilinsky.

"Sleep, Vassili Rodionovitch?" Shilko said, moving his tired body in the seat and drawing up his reserves of good humor. "I slept like a peasant when the master isn't looking. What time is it?"

"Two o'clock."

Shilko nodded. "Always punctual, Vassili Rodionovitch. But I'm keeping you out in the rain. Go back inside. I'll join you in a moment."

Romilinsky saluted and trotted off toward the fire-control post. Shilko shifted in the seat, wishing he were younger or at least wore a younger man's body. His kidneys ached. He had slept only a few hours, but it had been the plunging, hard sort of sleep that wants to go on for a long time. The preparations for war had exhausted most of the officers and men. What effect would war itself have on them?

Despite his seniority, Shilko had never been to war. Instead, his son had gone to Afghanistan as a junior lieutenant, fresh from the academy, and he had come back after only four months, with neither his legs nor a career. Shilko continued to be haunted by guilt, as though he had sneaked out from under his responsibilities intentionally, sending his son in his stead, although that certainly had not been the case. Meeting his returned son for the first time in the military hospital, with the medal "For Combat Services" and the Order of the Red Star pinned to his pajamas, and the bottom half of the bed as flat as the snow-covered steppes, had been the most painful experience in Shilko's life.

Overall, he counted himself a lucky man. He had a good wife, and they had had healthy children together. He had work he didn't mind, and he enjoyed the personal relationships that developed in the small unit families where he had spent most of his career. He had never expected to be a marshal of the Soviet Union, recognizing even as a young man that he was not cut out for special honors. So he simply tried to do that which was required of him as honestly as possible, content to be at peace with himself. His daughters had always seemed like the real fighters in the family, and it seemed to him as though they only married so they would have new opponents against whom to try their tempers. He could not understand it. His wife, Agafya, was a fine big happy woman, well suited to him. But the girls were an untamed, greedy pair. Perhaps, Shilko thought, trying to be fair, Romilinsky was much better off just as he was.

Pasha had been different from the girls. He had excelled at sports but had not been overly proud, with nothing of the bully about him. All things considered, he had been a kind boy, and decent to the girls. He had never given Shilko any serious trouble, and he had done well enough at the military academy.

Shilko had been proud to see the boy off to Afghanistan, although ashamed that he himself was staying behind. Then Pasha had come back missing parts. The boy had stubbornly tried to make it on his own, but the reception for the *Afgantsy* was not a good one. Shilko could not understand what was happening to the country. Instead of being respected, veterans were ignored, or even mocked and slighted. Pasha had been denied ground-floor living quarters, despite his handicap and although such an allocation had been easily within the powers of the local housing committee. And, as Pasha himself bitterly told it, when he complained about the low quality of his prostheses to the local specialist, the doctor had replied, "What do you expect *me* to do? *I* didn't send you to Afghanistan." The prostheses had not changed much since the Great Patriotic War over forty years earlier. But something in the spirit of the people had changed.

No, Shilko told himself, that was probably incorrect.

Even the Great Patriotic War had undoubtedly had its little human indignities and examples of ugliness. That was human nature. Yet . . . somehow . . . there was something wrong.

Shilko fitted his cap to his head. He avoided wearing a helmet. He valued small comforts. And he was conscious of how foolish he looked with his big peasant face and potato nose under the little tin pot. He had no illusions concerning his appearance. He had grown fatter than he would have liked, and he would never appear as the hero in anyone's fantasies. But that was all right, as long as he didn't look like a complete fool.

He swung his legs out into the slow drizzle, then grunted and huffed his body out of the vehicle. He stood off to the side for a moment, relieving the pain in his kidneys. Then he moved toward the shelter of the fire-control post at a pace that compromised between his desire to get in out of the rain and his body's lethargy.

Inside, behind the flaps of tentage, the little control post was bright, crowded, and perfumed with tobacco smoke. Shilko felt instantly alert, comfortable with the reassuring sensory impressions of a lifetime's professional experience. The feel of the place was right, from the pine branches spread over the floor to keep the mud at bay to the intense, tired faces and the iron smell of the command and control vehicles that formed office compartments at the edge of the tentage.

The crew snapped to attention. Shilko loved the small tribute, even as it always embarrassed him just a little.

"Sit down, Comrades, sit down."

A sergeant bent to draw tea from the battered samovar, and Shilko knew the cup was for him. They were all good boys, a good team.

"Your tea, Comrade Battalion Commander."

Shilko took the hot cup lovingly in both of his big hands. It was another of life's small wonderful pleasures. Hot tea on a rainy night during maneuvers. The army couldn't run without its tea.

He caught himself. It wasn't a matter of maneuvers this time. He stepped into the fire direction center vehicle and bent over the gunnery officer's work station, where a captain with a long wave of hair down in his eyes poked at the new automated fire-control system.

"And how are we progressing, Vladimir Semyonovitch?"

The captain looked up. His face had a friendly, trusting look. It was the sort of look that Shilko wanted every one of his officers to have when their commander approached. "Oh, it will all sort out, Comrade Commander. We're just working out a few bugs in the line. The vehicles keep cutting our wires. But the battery centers are each functional individually."

Shilko put his hand on the man's shoulder. "I'm counting on you. You can't expect an old bear like me to figure out all of this new equipment." Although he said it in a bantering tone, Shilko was serious. He understood the concepts involved and what these new technical means theoretically offered. And he was willing to accept any help they could give, just as he was ready to lay them aside if they failed. But he was personally frightened by the thought of sitting down behind one of the forbidding little panels and attempting to call it to life. He suspected that he would only embarrass himself. So he gladly let the young men pursue the future, and when they performed well, he was grateful, and he encouraged them to go on attacking the problem.

He approached his battalion chief of staff. Romilinsky and a lieutenant sat bent over a field desk covered in manuals, charts, and loose papers. The lieutenant worked on a small East German-made pocket calculator that always seemed to be the most valuable piece of equipment in the battalion.

Romilinsky looked up. Shilko knew the man's expressions well enough to know that, beneath the staff discipline, Romilinsky was frustrated.

"Comrade Battalion Commander," Romilinsky said, "no matter how we do it, the numbers will not come out right. Look here. If we fired every mission assigned under the fire plan, as well as the projected number of response missions for the first day, we would not only have fired more units of fire than we have received under our three-day allocation, but we would not even have time to physically do it. The division's expectations are unrealistic. They're not used to working with our type of guns, and they think we can deliver the sun and the moon."

"Well, Vassili Rodionovitch, we'll do our best."

"If we were to conform fully to the tables, if we used the normative number of rounds per hectare to attain the designated level of suppression or destruction for each mission they've assigned us, it just wouldn't come out. The numbers refuse to compromise."

"Everyone wants the big guns," Shilko said. Then, in a more serious tone, he asked, "But we can meet each phase of the initial fire plan?"

Romilinsky nodded. "We're all right through the scheduled fires."

"And the rest," Shilko said, "is merely a projection."

"We're looking at minimum projection figures."

"Don't worry. We'll manage. If they keep dropping off ammunition the way they've been dumping it since yesterday, we may end up with too many rounds and not enough vehicles to move it when we displace."

"But the matter of the physical inability to fire the missions within the time constraints?"

Shilko appreciated Romilinsky's nervous enthusiasm. He liked to have a worrier as chief of staff. "I have confidence in you," Shilko said. "You'll make it work, Vassili Rodionovitch. Now tell me, has Davidov gotten his battery out of the mud yet?"

Romilinsky smiled. There was a slight rivalry between Romilinsky and Davidov, and Shilko knew that the chief of staff had been amused at Davidov's embarrassment. He had delighted in helping the battery commander recover his bogged guns as publicly as possible.

"He's out and in position. But he was in a heat. We teased him a little. You know, 'Getting one gun stuck may be an accident, but getting an entire battery mired begins to look like a plan.' He still hasn't calmed down completely."

Shilko stopped smiling for a moment. He truly did not like their fire positions. The terrain over which they had been deployed seemed like a German version of the Belorussian marshes. You had to go carefully, and there were areas where you absolutely could not get off the roads. The precious little islands and stretches of reasonably firm ground were absurdly overcrowded. His own guns were too close to one another, batteries well under a thousand meters apart. And still their position was not completely their own. A chemical defense unit, which, to Shilko's relief, appeared utterly unconcerned about the war, and an engineer heavy bridging battalion had both been directed to the same low ground. There was so much steel out there in the darkness that it seemed to Shilko as though the woods and meadows should sink under the weight. He worried that they would all become hopelessly intermingled when it came time to move, and, more seriously still, that his ability to displace, due both to trafficability problems and the unavailability of alternate sites, would be dangerously restricted. The evening before, he and Romilinsky had conducted a reconnaissance, looking for alternate fire positions, but they had not found a single suitable piece of ground that was unoccupied. Now he was waiting for the division to whose divisional artillery group his battalion had been attached to designate alternate sites for his guns. In the meantime, he comforted himself with the thought that he was positioned in depth, thanks to the long range of his pieces, and that the worst initial counterfires would be directed against batteries much closer to the direct-fire battle than his own. But he still had difficulty maintaining an even temper when he imagined his battalion attempting to displace and sticking in the bogs and sodden byways of East Germany, unable even to make it across the border. He was certain of one thing—space on the roads was going to be at a premium.

On the other hand, the initial fire plan in support of the opening of the offensive was just fine with him. Romilinsky's concerns notwithstanding, Shilko had been pleased when he reviewed the schedule of targets, his "gift list" to be sent to the enemy. The staff officers who had compiled it under the direction of the division commander and his chief of missile troops and artillery were clearly professionals. Shilko prided himself on the traditional professionalism of the Soviet and the earlier Russian artillery. This fire plan did it right, emphasizing concentrations of tremendous lethality at the anticipated points of decision, as well as on known and suspected enemy reserve and artillery concentrations and in support of what Shilko suspected were deception efforts. The concept for maneuvering fires in support of the attack had a good feel to it. Now it was a matter of executing a good plan.

"Anything else, then, before we all go to war?" Shilko asked. He tried his usual easy tone, but the word "war" did not come off with the intended lightness. The moment that would forever after punctuate their lives had drawn too close.

"Well, we received another delivery of the special smoke rounds," Romilinsky said. "I still don't see why we have to post so many guards on them. It's a waste of manpower, and we're short enough as it is."

Romilinsky was speaking of the new obscurant rounds that had been compounded to attenuate the capabilities of enemy observation and target designation equipment. The existence and purpose of the rounds were well known, but the security personnel still insisted that they be handled as though they were vital state secrets.

"Be patient," Shilko said. "We'll fire them up tomorrow, and then we won't have to guard them." He had learned long ago not to argue security issues. "Have all of the troops been fed?"

Romilinsky nodded. He had an exaggerated manner of nodding, like a trained horse determined to please his master. "I'm not certain it was the finest meal we ever served, but it was hot."

Shilko was glad. He tried to feed his battalion as though they were all his own children, although it was very hard. Now he didn't want them going to war on empty stomachs. The food in the Soviet military was of legendarily poor quality, but his battalion's garrison farm was one of the finest in the command. Shilko himself came from peasant stock, and he was proud of it. In the past year, his battalion had been able to raise so many chickens that they not only exceeded the official meat allocation per soldier but were able to sell chickens to other units for almost five thousand rubles. His soldiers were better fed than those in any other battalion of which Shilko was aware, yet he used only six soldiers full-time in the agricultural collective . . . although each boy had been carefully selected because of his background and expertise. The brigade had gotten quite a bit of mileage out of the accomplishments of Shilko's "gardeners," and their achievements had even been featured in a military newspaper as an example to be emulated by all. It had been Shilko's finest hour with the high military authorities and the Communist Party of the Soviet Union.

Shilko slipped into one of his old peasant attitudes. The Party. He was in the habit of occasionally going down and working a bit with the soldiers in the garrison garden and poultry sheds. He had realized too late how much he loved the land and animals and the sense of growing things, and he suspected that he really had been born to be a farmer, like his forefathers. But, as a young man, he had viewed life on the collective farm as hopelessly drab and unsatisfying. Now, when he dug, the political officer got nervous. Publicly, Shilko received praise for his spirit of proletarian unity and his vigorous conformity to the essential principles of the Party. In fact, however, he knew very well that it made the full-time Party boys very nervous when lieutenant colonels took up shovels and hoes. Afraid they might have to do a little proletarian duty themselves. Shilko had half expected to be denounced as a Maoist, and, while he had in fact been a full member of the Party for twenty years, he had never taken that membership too seriously. It was something you did because you had to do it, like wearing the correct uniform for the occasion. But all of the theory had been a bit too much for him. He liked things he could do with his hands.

His son was another matter. Pasha had a better mind than his father; he was clever and quick. Although he had been an enthusiastic Young Pioneer and a good Komsomolist, Pasha had never immersed himself in the theoretical aspects of Marxism-Leninism to any unusual extent. He had simply accepted the Party as a fact of life, as did most young men of reasonable ambition. Then he had come back, legless, from Afghanistan, to find himself last on the list for everything. No salutes for the boy without legs. And Shilko had watched his son turn from a loving, open youth into an extraordinarily dedicated member of the Party. The Party accepted Pasha the invalid, seeking to exploit him even as they genuinely sought to help him. But Pasha had turned the full weight of his talents and his anger to exploiting the Party. Shilko knew from experience that that was the kind of ambition on which the Party thrived. At first, upon his son's return, Shilko had worried about the practical aspects of his well-being. Then he had watched the legless boy develop himself into a man with long arms.

Pasha was doing very well within the Party apparatus. He seemed to have developed a taste for manipulation, and Shilko had no doubt that his son would become a powerful man, that he would long ride the ribbons he had been given to compensate for his missing legs. Shilko no longer needed to worry about the mundane aspects of his son's welfare. Pasha would have a fine ground-floor apartment, or an apartment in a building where the elevator worked. But the simple, loving father in Shilko worried now about other aspects of his son's future.

And in a matter of minutes, there would be a war. It still seemed unreal to Shilko, as though this could not possibly be a rational decision. But there was no mistaking the level of preparation, the intensity, the inevitability of it all. Shilko wondered if the decision to begin this war had been made by the kind of men his son was coming to resemble. The men who knew best, for each and every living creature.

Well, Shilko thought, it didn't matter. He and his boys would fight and fight well, no matter who made the decisions. The event was infinitely greater than the men caught up in it.

The mood in the fire control post had begun to change. The frantic action tapered off. Officers began to sit down. Men looked up at the master clock above the communications bank.

It would not be long now. Shilko looked at his watch, even though he had just glanced at the clock. He went to the samovar and tipped himself another cup of tea. Then he took his chair near the situation map, proofing the schedule of fires one last time.

The radios were silent. Romilinsky sat down beside Shilko and nervously patted the handle of the field telephone, the wires of which led directly to the gun batteries. Soon it would be time to pick it up and say the single word that would unleash the storm.

Shilko was almost as proud of the big guns with which he had been entrusted as he was of his men. When he had entered the service, his first unit had been equipped with field pieces designed before the Great Patriotic War, towed by Studebaker trucks from the war years. Now the enormous self-propelled pieces in his battalion made those little towed weapons seem like toys. Shilko felt that he had seen enormous progress in his lifetime.

"Comrade Battalion Commander," Romilinsky said, "you seem admirably relaxed."

"The sleep did me good," Shilko said, content to wait and think through these last minutes.

But the chief of staff wanted to talk. "I believe we are as ready as possible."

Shilko accepted that the needs of other men were different from his own. If his chief of staff needed to talk away the final minutes of peace, Shilko was willing to oblige him.

"I'm confident that we're ready, Vassili Rodionovitch. This is a good battalion. I have great faith."

"I can't help thinking, though, of things we should have done, of training that should have received more stress . . ."

Shilko waved the comment away. "No one is ever as prepared as they should be. You know the dialectic. A constant state of flux."

"Five minutes," a voice announced.

Shilko looked up at the clock. Then he sat back. "You know," he began in his most personable voice, "when I was a junior lieutenant, I was horrified by the conditions I found upon arrival at my first unit. Nothing seemed to be as we had been promised at the academy. Nothing was as precise, or as rigorous, or even as clean. I was very disturbed by what I viewed as a betrayal of the high standards of the Soviet military. Oh, I wasn't especially ambitious. I never expected to change the world. But this unit didn't seem as though it could go to war against a pack of dance-hall girls. Half of the equipment didn't work. The situation seemed intolerable to a brand-new lieutenant who had been coached to go up against the capitalist aggressors at a moment's notice. Anyway, my commander was a wise man—a veteran, of course, in those days. He watched my struggles with some amusement, I think. Then, one day, he called me into his office. I was worried. It wasn't so common for a battalion commander to speak to a lieutenant in those days. And it usually didn't happen because the lieutenant had done something to be proud of. So I went to his office in quite a state. I couldn't think of anything I'd done incorrectly. But you never knew. Anyway, he asked me how I enjoyed being in the army, and how I liked the unit. He was teasing me, although I didn't realize it then. I talked around my real feelings. Finally, he just smiled, and he called me closer. Very close to his desk. And he said he was going to reveal to me the one military truth, and that if only I remembered it, I would do very well in my military career."

Shilko looked around. Everyone was listening to him, despite the unmistakable tension.

The clock showed two minutes to go.

Shilko grinned. "You know what he said to me? He leaned over that desk, so close I could see the old scars on his cheek, and he half whispered, 'Shilko, wars are not won by the most competent army—they are won by the least incompetent army.' "

His audience responded with pleasant laughter. But the undercurrent of anticipation had grown so intense now that no man could fully master it. The tension seemed almost like a physical wave, rising to sweep them all away.

Romilinsky gripped the field telephone, ready.

Less than one minute to go.

In the distance, a number of guns sounded, startling in the perfect stillness. Someone had fired early, either because of a bad clock or through nervousness.

Shilko looked at the clock one final time. Other batteries and full battalions took up the challenge of the first lone battery, rising to a vast orchestra of calibers. Shilko turned to Romilinsky, utterly serious now.

"Give the order to open fire."

FOUR

Junior Lieutenant Plinnikov wiped at his nose with his fingers and ordered his driver forward. The view through the vehicle commander's optics allowed no meaningful orientation. Rapid flashes dazzled in the periscope's lens, leaving a deep gray veil of smoke in their wake. The view was further disrupted by raindrops that found their way under the external cowl of the lens block. Plinnikov felt as though he were guiding his reconnaissance track through hell at the bottom of the sea.

The shudder of the powerful artillery bursts reached through the metal walls of the vehicle. Suddenly, the armor seemed hopelessly thin, the tracks too weak to hold, and the automatic cannon little more than a toy. Occasionally, a tinny sprinkling of debris struck the vehicle, faintly audible through Plinnikov's headset and over the engine whine. He could feel the engine pulling, straining to move the tracks through the mud of the farm trail.

"Comrade Lieutenant, we're very close to the barrage," his driver told him.

Plinnikov understood that the driver meant *too* close. But

the lieutenant was determined to outperform every other reconnaissance platoon leader in the battalion, if not in the entire Second Guards Tank Army.

"Keep moving," Plinnikov commanded, "just keep moving. Head straight through the smoke."

The driver obeyed, but Plinnikov could feel his unwillingness through the metal frame that separated them. For a moment, Plinnikov took his eyes away from the periscope and looked to the side, checking on his gunner. But Belonov was all right, eyes locked to his own periscope. Three men in a rolling steel box. There was no margin of safety in personnel now; everyone had to do his job without fail. Plinnikov had never received the additional soldiers required to fill out his reconnaissance platoon for war, and he had no extra meat, no dismount strength in his own vehicle. As it was, he could barely man the essential positions in each of his three vehicles.

It was impossible to judge the exact location of his vehicle now. If everything was still on track, his second vehicle would be tucked in behind him, with Senior Sergeant Malyarchuk to the rear in an overwatch position. Plinnikov laughed to himself. Overwatch. You couldn't see ten meters. He glanced at his map, anxious to orient himself.

He could feel the trail dropping toward a valley or ravine. Artillery rounds struck immediately to the front.

"Keep going," Plinnikov said. "Get down into the low ground. Stay on the trail as long as the smoke holds. *Fast* now, *move.*"

Plinnikov sensed that they were very close to the enemy. Clots of earth and stone flew into the air, hurtling across his narrowed horizon. Plinnikov guessed that, if he moved off the trail, there might be mines, but that the trail itself would only be covered by direct fires—which would be ineffective in the confusion of the Soviet artillery preparation.

"Lieutenant, we're catching up with the barrage. We're too close."

"Keep going. We're already in it. Go right through."

"Comrade Lieutenant . . ." It was Junior Sergeant Belonov, his gunner and assistant. The boy's face was milky.

"It's all right," Plinnikov told him through the intercom. "Just spot for targets. If we wait and try to sneak through, they'll get us for sure."

An unidentified object thumped against the vehicle so hard that the vehicle jolted, as though wincing in pain.

"Go *faster,*" Plinnikov shouted to the driver. "Just stay on the road and go as fast as you can."

"I can't see the road. I lose it."

"Just *go.*" Plinnikov brushed his fingers at his nose. He felt fear rising in his belly and chest, unleashed by the impact of whatever had hit the vehicle.

Suddenly, the artillery blasts seemed to swamp them, shaking the vehicle like a boat on rough water. Plinnikov realized that if they threw a track now, they were dead.

"Go, damn you."

In the thick smoke, the lights of the blasts seemed demonic, alive with deadly intentions.

"More to the left . . . *to the left.*"

The tracks seemed to buckle on the edge of a ditch or gully, threatening to peel away from the road wheels.

"Target," Plinnikov screamed.

But the sudden black shape off to their right side was lifeless, its metal deformed by a direct hit. The driver swerved away, and the tracks came level, back on the trail again.

Plinnikov broke out in a sweat. He had not seen the shattered vehicle until they almost collided with it. He wondered, for the first time, if he had not done something irrevocably foolish.

Slop from a nearby impact smacked the external lens of Plinnikov's periscope, cracking it diagonally, just as the vehicle reached a pocket where the wind had thinned the smoke to a transparent gauze. Several dark shapes moved out of the smoke on a converging axis.

"Targets. Gunner, right. Driver, pull left *now.*"

But the enemy vehicles moved quickly away, either uninterested in or unaware of Plinnikov's presence. The huge armored vehicles disappeared back into the smoke, black metal monsters roaming over the floor of hell. None of the turrets turned to fight.

"Hold fire."

The enemy were evidently pulling off of a forward position. The fire was too much for them. Plinnikov tried his radio, hoping the antenna had not been cut away.

"Javelin, this is Penknife. Do you hear me?"

Nothing.

The heaviest fire struck behind them now. But the smoke, mingled with the fog and rain, still forced them to drive without points of orientation. Plinnikov worried because he had once turned in a complete circle in a smokescreen on a training exercise, in the most embarrassing experience of his brief career. He could still hear the laughter and the timeworn jokes about lieutenants.

"Javelin, this is Penknife. I have a priority message."

"Penknife, this is Javelin." The control station barely came through the sea of static.

"Enemy forces in at least platoon strength withdrawing from forward positions under fire strike. I can't give you an exact location."

"Where are you? What's your location?"

"I'm in my assigned sector. Visibility's almost zero. We just drove under the artillery barrage. We're in among the enemy."

"You're hard to read. I'm getting a garbled transmission. Did you say you're *behind* the artillery barrage?"

"On the enemy side of it. Continuing to move."

There was a long silence on the other end. Plinnikov sensed that he had surprised them all. He felt a bloom of pride. Then the faint voice returned.

"Penknife, your mission now is to push as far as you can. Ignore assigned boundaries. Just go as deep as you can and call targets. Do you understand?"

"Clear. Moving now."

Plinnikov switched to the intercom. The smoke thinned slightly. His first instinct was to move for high ground so he could fix his location. But he quickly realized that any high ground would not only reveal his presence but was likely to be occupied by the enemy.

"Driver, follow the terrain, stay in the low ground. Just watch out for ditches and water."

He switched again, this time to his platoon net, trying to raise his other two vehicles.

"Quiver, this is Penknife."

He waited. No answer. He tried again and still received no response. He swung the turret around to get a better view, straining to see through his cracked and dirty optics.

There was nothing. Misty gray emptiness.

"Penknife, this is Stiletto." Plinnikov heard Senior Sergeant Malyarchuk's voice. "I can't hear any response from Quiver. My situation as follows: moving slowly with the barrage. Can't see a damned thing. I lost you twenty minutes ago."

"This is Penknife. Clear transmission. Continue to move on primary route. Watch for Quiver, he may be stuck out there. End transmission."

His other vehicle might be broken down or mired. But, he realized, it was more likely that they were dead. He was surprised to find that he felt little emotion, and ashamed to experience how swiftly his thoughts turned to the implications the loss of the vehicle and crew had for him.

"Driver, get on that trail to the right. That one."

The vehicle moved sharply now, with the worst effects of the barrage well behind it. Plinnikov's optics had deteriorated severely. The crack in the outer lens allowed water to seep in.

"Slow. See the trail into the trees? *Slow.* Take the trail."

The vehicle eased onto a smooth forest trail that appeared very well-maintained. Plinnikov hoped to find a spot to tuck into for a few minutes so they could clean off all of their vision blocks and lenses and tighten the antenna. One barrage had already passed over the forest, and patches of trees had been splintered and blackened. The driver worked the tracks over a small fallen trunk. He drove the vehicle cautiously, with no desire to throw a track in such close proximity to the enemy.

"Comrade Lieutenant, I can barely see," the driver said. "Can I pop open my hatch?"

"No," Plinnikov said. "Stop right here. I'll get out and clean the blocks."

The vehicle rocked to a standstill. Plinnikov unlatched

the safety bolt and pushed up his hatch. The sudden increase in the noise level was striking. The weight of the artillery preparation was incredible, and the fires sounded much closer now. It was difficult to imagine anything surviving such an effort.

In the wet green woods, fresh forest smells mingled with the stink of blown ordnance. Raindrops worked through the overhanging branches and struck Plinnikov's nose and cheeks, touching cool at his lips. The hatch ring felt slimy with moisture and dirt.

Just ahead, another trail crossed the one along which they had moved. The other trail was deeply rutted and black with mud, evidence that several tracked vehicles had passed along it.

Plinnikov drew himself back down into the turret. "Belonov," he told the gunner, "make sure the autocannon's ready to go. I don't think we're alone."

"Comrade Lieutenant, let me check the exterior."

"No. You stay on the gun. Just be ready." Plinnikov stripped off his headset and snaked out of the turret. The deck seemed to slide away under his boots, and he grasped the long, thin barrel of the automatic cannon to steady himself, crouching.

The armament appeared to be all right, with no metal deformities. But there were numerous spots on the vehicle exterior where the paint had been stripped away and where the bolt-on armor had been gashed or even sheared away. One fender twisted toward the sky. An external stow-box was gone, and the spare track pads were missing. The shovel was gone. The main antenna for the high-powered radio set was nicked, but functionally intact.

Unidentifiable objects ripped through the foliage, their noises an occasional whisper. Big raindrops burst like shells on his skin. More rain coming. Plinnikov hurriedly cleaned all of the optics with a rag, trying not to smear them too badly.

He got back into the turret as soon as he reasonably could. "The trail looks clear enough up ahead, but you can't see very far. The enemy has either passed through these woods or he's still somewhere in here with us."

"Perhaps we should wait here for a while, Comrade Lieutenant. See what the enemy does, you know?" Belonov was clearly frightened. Plinnikov hoped the gunner would be able to work his weapon when the time came.

Plinnikov twitched his nose, then rubbed at it with his dirty knuckles. "No. We have to get a fix on our location. And if we just sit, the artillery will roll back over us. We're moving."

The truth was, Plinnikov realized, that he was afraid to remain motionless, afraid he couldn't handle the stress of inactivity.

"Driver, can you see all right now?"

"Better, Comrade Lieutenant."

"Let's go. Nice and easy." Plinnikov wanted to make sure he spotted the enemy before they spotted his lone vehicle. He knew it would be impossible to detect moving vehicles until they were fatally close, due to the noise of the artillery preparation.

The vehicle dug itself into the peat of the trail, then gripped and lurched forward. Plinnikov unlashed his assault rifle. He expected to fight with the automatic cannon and the on-board machine gun, but he wanted to be prepared for anything. He stood up behind the shield of his opened turret, weapon at the ready, headset flaps left open so he could hear a bit of the world around him.

The vehicle pivoted into the rutted trail. The rain picked up, slapping Plinnikov, making him squint. Nervously, he ejected a cartridge from his weapon, insuring it was loaded and ready.

"Belonov?"

"Comrade Lieutenant?"

"How well can you see?"

"I can see the trail."

"If I duck down and start turning the turret, be ready."

"I'm ready."

Plinnikov heard the nerves in both of their voices. He was furious about the lack of soldiers to fill out his crew. He wanted all of the fighting power he could get. He wished his lost vehicle was still with him.

The tracks slid and plumed mud high into the air behind

the vehicle. The immense roar of the artillery seemed part of another reality now, clearly divorced from anything that would happen in these woods.

Black vehicle shapes. Thirty meters through the trees.

Plinnikov dropped into the turret, not bothering to close the hatch behind himself. He took control of the turret, forehead pressed against his optics.

"See them? Fire, damn you. *Fire."*

The automatic cannon began to recoil.

"There. To the right."

"I have him."

"Driver, don't stop. Go."

The vehicle pulled level with a small clearing in the forest where two enemy command tracks stood positioned with their drop ramps facing each other. Two light command cars were parked to one side.

A third track that had been hidden from view began to move for the trail.

"Hit the mover, *hit the mover."*

The automatic cannon spit several bursts at the track, which stopped in a shower of sparks.

"Driver, front to the enemy."

Plinnikov swung the turret again.

The enemy fired back with small arms, although one man stood still, helmetless, in amazement, as though he had never in his life expected such a thing to happen.

The automatic cannon and the machine gun raked the sides of the enemy tracks. All good, clean flank shots, punching through the armor. The track that had made a run for the trail burned now. The driver's hatch popped up, and Plinnikov cut the man across the shoulders with the on-board machine gun.

The man who had stood so long in such amazement slowly raised his hands. Plinnikov turned the machine gun on him.

Plinnikov was afraid he would miss one of the dismounted soldiers, and he left the on-board weaponry to Belonov, standing behind the shield of his hatch with his assault rifle.

Just in time, he saw an enemy soldier kneeling with a

small tube on his shoulder. He emptied his entire magazine into the man, just as Belonov brought the machine gun around to catch him as well.

Plinnikov pulled a grenade from his harness, then another. As quickly as his shaking fingers allowed, he primed one and tossed it toward the enemy vehicles, then followed it with the second grenade. He dropped back inside of his vehicle.

The explosions sounded flat, almost inconsequential, after the artillery barrage. Plinnikov realized that his hearing was probably going.

"Sweep the vehicles one more time with the machine gun. *Driver.* To the rear, ten meters."

"I can't see."

"Just back up, damn it. *Now.*"

The gears crunched, and the vehicle's tracks threw mud toward the dead and the dying.

"Driver, halt. Belonov, I'm going out. You cover me."

He felt as though he would have given anything imaginable to have his authorized dismount scouts now. If there was a price to pay for the system's failure, he'd have to pay it. The idea did not appeal to him. He felt as though he were going very, very fast, as though he had the energy to vault over trees, but his hand shook as he grasped the automatic rifle. He didn't bother to unfold the stock. It was challenging enough to snap in a fresh magazine.

It felt as though it took an unusually long time to work his way out of the turret. He was conscious every second of how fully he was exposed. As soon as he could, he swung his legs high and to the side, sliding down over the side of the low turret, catching his rump sharply on the edge of the vehicle's deck.

He hit the mud and crouched beside the vehicle. Great clots of earth hung from the track and road wheels.

He checked to his rear.

Nothing. Forest. The empty trail.

To his front, the little command cars blazed, one with a driver still behind the wheel, a shadow in the flames. Between his vehicle and the devastated enemy tracks, Plinnikov could see three enemy soldiers on the ground.

One of them moved in little jerks and twists. None of them made any sounds. Another body lay sprawled face down on the ramp of one of the command tracks, while yet another—the antitank grenadier—had been kicked back against a tree by the machine gun. The grenadier hardly resembled a human being now.

The vehicle that had tried to escape burned with a searing glow on its metal. The type and markings made it Dutch. Plinnikov kept well away from it as he worked his way forward.

One of the command vehicles had its engine running. Both of the command tracks bore West German markings, and most of the uniforms were West German. Plinnikov skirted the front of the running vehicle, taking cover in the brush. As methodically as his nerves would permit, he maneuvered his way around to the enemy's rear.

He halted along the wet metal sidewall of the running vehicle, feeling its vibrations. Above the idling engine, he could hear the razzle of a radio call in a strange language. He wondered if it was a call for the station that had just perished.

Someone moaned, almost as if he was snoring. Then it was quiet again.

Plinnikov breathed in deeply. He felt terribly afraid. He could not understand why he was doing this. It seemed as though he was meant to be anyplace but here. He looked at the grenadier's contorted remains. Somehow, it had all seemed a game, a daring game of driving through the artillery. And if he had been caught, he would have been removed from the game. But the man slopped against the tree was out of the game forever. For a length of time he could not measure, Plinnikov simply stared at the tiny black, red, and gold flag on the rear fender of the far vehicle, as if it could provide answers.

He took a last deep breath, fighting his stomach. He pulled his weapon in tight against his side and threw himself around the corner of the vehicle onto the drop ramp.

He had forgotten the dead man on the ramp. He tripped over the corpse, flopping over the body and smashing his elbow. He landed with his mouth close to the dead man's ear, and, in an instant of paralysis, he felt the lifelike warmth of the body through the battle dress and sogging rain. The dead man had fine white hairs mixed in with the close-cropped black on the rear of his skull, and Plinnikov saw the red pores on the back of the man's neck with superhuman clarity.

As soon as he could, Plinnikov pushed off of the corpse and twisted so that he could fire his weapon into the interior of the vehicle. But he knew that if anyone still had been capable of shooting, he would be dead already.

The running vehicle bore a stew of bodies in its belly. The accidents of dying had thrown several men together as though they had been dancing and had fallen drunkenly. The inside of the cluttered compartment was streaked and splashed with wetness, and uniforms had torn open to spill filth and splinters of bone. Plinnikov realized that some of the rounds that had penetrated the near side of the vehicle had not had the force to punch out the other side and had expended themselves in rattling back and forth inside the vehicle, chopping the occupants.

In the track parked opposite, a lone radio operator sat sprawled over his notepads, microphone hanging limply from a coil cord. On the radio, a foreign voice called the dead.

Plinnikov was sick. He tried to make it to the trees, out of some elementary human instinct, but he stumbled over the dead man on the ramp for a second time and vomited on the corpse's back. As he looked down at his mess Plinnikov panicked to see blood smeared over his own chest before realizing that it had come from his embrace of the middle-aged corpse.

Plinnikov felt empty, his belly burning with acid and his heart vacantly sick. He stared at the slow progress of his vomit down the angled ramp. He wanted to be home, safe, and never to see war or anything military ever again.

He wiped the strands from his lips, wondering if his crew had watched his little performance. The taste in his mouth made him feel sick again. He realized, belatedly, that the amazed man with his hands up had been trying to surrender, and that it had been wrong to gun him down. But during the fighting, it had never occurred to him to do anything but shoot at everything in front of him.

The voice on the radio called again. Plinnikov imagined that he could detect a pleading tone.

Suddenly, he braced himself. He stared at the silver ornaments on the epaulets of the corpse on the ramp. This was a command post. There would be documents. Maps. Radio communications data.

Stomach twisting, Plinnikov turned to his task.

Senior Lieutenant Filov failed to grasp what was happening until it was too late. He brought his company of tanks on line behind the smokescreen, moving at combat speed toward the enemy, maintaining reasonable order despite his spiky nervousness. Then the tanks began to sink in what had appeared to be a normal field.

Reconnaissance had not reported any difficulties. Now his command tank stood mired to the deck, and none of his vehicles succeeded in backing out. Their efforts only worked them deeper into the marshy soil. His entire company had ground to a halt in a tattered cartoon of their battle formation.

Filov attempted to call back through the battalion for more smoke and for recovery vehicles. But the smokescreen began to dissipate noticeably before he could establish radio contact. The nets were cluttered with strange voices.

"Prepare to engage, prepare to engage," he shouted into his microphone. When his platoon commanders failed to respond, he realized with a feeling of near-panic that he had been speaking only through the intercom. He switched channels, fingers clumsy on the control mechanism, and repeated his orders.

"Misha, I'm stuck," one of his platoon commanders responded.

"We're *all* stuck. Use your call sign. And mine. And use your head."

Filov tried to raise battalion again. Without more smoke, they'd be dead. Filov was sure the enemy had trapped them, that this was a clever ambush, and that enemy antitank gunners were waiting to destroy them.

The smoke continued to thin.

Nothing on the battalion net. It was as though battalion had vanished from the earth. Filov's gunner, a Muslim from Uzbekistan, was praying. Filov slapped him hard on the side of his headset.

"God won't help, you bastard. Get on your gunsight."

Flares popped hot bright through the last meager smoke. From the angle of their arc, Filov could tell that none of his people had fired them. In any case, the use of flares was inappropriate. Even with the rain and smoke, there was still plenty of light. Probably a distress signal, Filov thought. But he had no idea who could have fired.

He tried the battalion net again, begging the electronics to respond. The gun tube of his tank was so low to the ground that it barely cleared the wild grasses.

Filov wondered if they could dig themselves out. He knew how to recover tanks in a classroom, when the problem allowed nearby trees. But now they were stuck dead center in a meadow. He was about to order all of his vehicles to begin erecting their camouflage nets and to send one of his lieutenants back on foot to locate the rest of the battalion when the last smoke blew off.

The battlefield showed its secrets with painful clarity, the light rain and mist offering no real protection. Less than five hundred meters from his line of tanks, set at an angle, Filov saw five enemy tanks. The enemy vehicles were also bogged down almost to the turrets.

"*Fire,*" Filov screamed, paying no attention to which channel he was riding, forgetting all fire discipline and procedures. His gunner dutifully sent off a round in the general direction of the enemy. Filov tried to remember the proper sequence of fire commands. He began to turn the turret without making a decision on which enemy vehicle to engage.

The enemy fired back. Filov's entire line fired, in booming disorder. Nobody seemed to hit anything.

Filov settled on a target. "Loading sabot. Range, four-fifty."

The automatic loader slammed the round into the breech.

"Correct to four hundred."

"Ready."

"Fire."

The round went wide, despite the ridiculously short distance to the target. But another one of the enemy vehicles disappeared in a bloom of sparks, flame, and smoke under the massed fires of Filov's right flank platoon. Filov's headset shrieked with broken transmissions.

"I've lost one. I've lost one."

"Range, five hundred."

"Wrong net, you sonofabitch."

The enemy tanks fired as swiftly as they could, their rounds skimming through the marshy grasses. Filov could not understand why he could not hit his targets. He had always fired top scores on the range, perfect fives. He tried to slow down and behave as though he were back on a local gunnery range.

Filov's gunner sent another round toward the enemy tank. This time it struck home.

The enemy tank failed to explode. After a bright flash, the big angular turret was still there, settling back down as though its sleep had been disturbed. But the vehicle's crew began to clamber out through the hatches, clumsy in their haste.

Out of the corner of his field of vision, Filov saw the turret of one of his own tanks fly high into the air, as though it were no heavier than a soccer ball. Then another enemy tank flared up in a fuel-tank fire.

It was too much. Filov opened his hatch and scrambled out. This was insane. Murder. All of his visions collapsed inward. His headset jerked at his neck, and he tore it off. He stumbled down over the slippery deck of his tank, then abandoned his last caution and jumped for the grass. He saw other men running across the field in the distance.

It was senseless to stay. For what? They'd all die. Just shoot until they all killed each other. What would it accomplish?

The *whisk* and thunder of the tank battle continued behind him, punctuated occasionally by the metallic ring and blast of a round meeting its target. The sopping marshland clutched at Filov's boots. In his panic, he began smashing at his legs, as if he could slap them into cooperation, as if he could beat the earth from underfoot. He ran without looking back.

Plinnikov stood up in his hatch, fumbling to ready the smoke grenade. He heard the helicopter before he saw it. The weather had an odd effect on the sound, diffusing it against the background of the artillery barrage, so that it was difficult to identify the exact azimuth of the aircraft's approach. All at once, just offset from Plinnikov's line of sight, the small helicopter emerged from the mist, a quick blur that swiftly grew larger and began to define itself. Plinnikov tossed the smoke canister so that the wind would lead the colored fog away from his vehicle. He could tell immediately that the pilot was one of the Afgantsy, a real veteran, by the way he came in fast and very low, despite the rain and reduced visibility.

The pilot never really powered down. His copilot leapt from the settling aircraft and raced through the drizzle, bareheaded. Plinnikov jumped from his track, clutching the rolled maps and documents. The maps and some of the papers were stained with blood and the spillage of ripped bodies, and Plinnikov was anxious to be rid of them. He held them out to the aviator like a bouquet.

"Anything else?" the copilot shouted. The wash off the rotors half submerged his voice.

Plinnikov shook his head.

The smoke spread out in a shredded carpet across the green field. The enemy would see it, too, and there was no time to waste.

The copilot raced back to his helicopter. He hurriedly tossed the captured materials behind his seat, and the pilot began to lift off even before his partner was properly seated. The aircraft rose just enough to clear the trees, then shot off in a dogleg from its approach direction.

Plinnikov vaulted onto the deck of his vehicle, almost losing his balance on the slippery metal. He dropped into the turret.

"Let's move. Back into the woods."

The vehicle whined into life, rocking out across the

furrows of the field until it could turn and nose back into the trail between the trees. Plinnikov studied his map again, searching for a good route deeper into the enemy's rear. No obvious routes suggested themselves, and his calculations began to seem hopelessly complicated to him. In irritation, he ordered the driver to double back onto the trail that had proven so lucrative earlier, hoping a course would be easier to develop while working through the actual landscape than it was on the map.

At a trail crossing, he turned to the map for reference. It was a very high-quality map, with extensive military detail. But it almost seemed as though the trails in the German woods created themselves out of nothing, as though the forest were haunted.

He chose the trail that seemed to head west. At first, it was a fair dirt track. Then the forest began to close in. Plinnikov found himself pushing wet branches away from the vehicle. His uniform was already soaking and uncomfortable, and his spirits dropped suddenly, as though someone had pulled a cork.

"Depress the gun tube. It's catching the branches. Driver, go slowly."

Then Plinnikov's fortunes seemed to change. The trees thinned again, and the terrain began to show slight undulations. A hollow off to his right discharged a small stream that then flowed parallel to the track. He checked his map again, hoping the feature and the trail, side by side, would allow him to orient himself. But he could not identify his location; the only possibilities on the map didn't really seem to make sense in terms of the distance he estimated they had traveled. He needed a clear landmark, or an open view.

Through all of his trials, Plinnikov tried not to think of the dead enemy, to hold their creeping, insistent reality at a distance. He sought harmless thoughts, gleaning his memories of the military academy and the seemingly endless dilemmas of the lieutenancy that followed graduation. But all of the forced images faded into the vivid sights, sounds, and smells of the recent combat. He could not help refighting the action over and over again, scrutinizing his failures. The dead men died again and again, their reality already changing slightly, as though warping and mutating in his overheated memory.

Unexpectedly, the forest ended. The vehicle lay fully exposed where Plinnikov ordered it to halt. He shook off the last of his daydreams. A church spire rose above a copse of trees, dark against the low gray sky. He wiped the back of his fingers across his nose and reached down for his map.

He neither saw nor heard the round that killed him. It tore into the hull of the vehicle below the turret, ripping off his lower legs and mincing his hands as it exploded. The quick secondary blast shot his torso up through the commander's hatch, breaking his neck against the hatch rim and shattering his back as the pressure compressed his body through the circular opening and blew it into the sky like a bundle of rags.

FIVE

Captain Kryshinin had never faced such a frustrating problem. As commander of the forward security element, it was his job to move fast, to locate the enemy and overrun him, if possible, or, otherwise, to fix the enemy until the advance guard came up, meanwhile searching for a bypass around the enemy position. Textbook stuff. Yet here the enemy had already pulled back. And his element was blocked by nothing more than a mined road crater and an unknown number of mines in the surrounding meadows.

He had no idea where the combat reconnaissance patrol had gone, or how they had gotten through. They should have warned him of this situation. Now Kryshinin was stuck. His engineers had become separated from his element in the confusion of initial contact and penetration of the enemy's covering troops. He had no mine-clearing capability without them.

He judged that the advance guard was no more than twenty minutes behind, unless they had gotten bogged down in more fighting. Leading the Second Guards Tank Army attack, the division's lead regiments had struck the thin enemy deployments so hard that it had been surprisingly easy to force a gap. Kryshinin had not lost a single vehicle in combat. He was only missing the wandering engineers. Until the lead infantry fighting vehicle attempted to work around the road crater. A mine had torn out its belly and butchered the crew.

Now Kryshinin's element was static. Thirteen infantry fighting vehicles, three tanks, a battery of 122mm self-propelled guns, and over a dozen specialized vehicles with ground-to-air radios, artillery communications, antitank missiles, and light surface-to-air missiles were backed up along a single country road. It was a tough little combat package, well-suited to the mission and the terrain. But now, without engineers, it was helpless.

Kryshinin dismounted and began walking swiftly forward along the bunched column. But before he reached its head, he saw one of his lieutenants flush all of the soldiers out of their fighting vehicle. The lieutenant got into the driver's compartment and, after a jerking start, edged slowly toward the blasted vehicle.

The lieutenant guided his vehicle behind the hulk and began pushing it. Kryshinin stood still for a moment in surprise. Then he began to shout at the motorized rifle troops who were standing around watching as casually as if this was a training demonstration. He came back to life now, as if awakening, stirred by his lieutenant's example. He ordered the vehicles into a more tactical posture. He was suddenly ashamed of himself. He had allowed them all to back up on the road like perfect targets while he had waited for inspiration.

The lieutenant had not been able to push the destroyed vehicle in a straight line. Finally, he just edged it out of the way, crunching and grinding metal. The mine-struck vehicle had peeled off a track, and the hulk curled off to the left as its naked road wheels bit into the turf and sank.

The lieutenant drove slowly forward, seeking a safe path to the roadway on the far side of the crater. He was a new officer, and Kryshinin had had little sense of him. Another lieutenant. Now the boy had taken the lead when his superior had failed.

Kryshinin stood in the disheartening German rain, painfully conscious of his inadequacy. He regretted all of the opportunities he had let slip to better train himself and his officers, to get to know his lieutenants a little better.

The infantry fighting vehicle's engine had a girlish sort of whine, even grinding forward in the lowest gear. Kryshinin watched, fists clenched, as the vehicle neared its destination.

The left side of the vehicle suddenly lifted into the air, lofted on a pillow of fire.

Kryshinin instinctively ducked against the nearest vehicle. When he looked up, the lieutenant's vehicle stood in flames.

Without looking around, Kryshinin could feel the crushing disappointment in all of the soldiers. They had been united in their hopes for the lieutenant. Now expectation collapsed into a desolate emptiness.

As Kryshinin stood helplessly again a young sergeant ordered all of his soldiers out of their vehicle. And the sergeant drove slowly in the lieutenant's traces until the prow of his track crunched against the flaming rear doors of the newly stricken vehicle. Then he applied power.

Before the sergeant finished working the burning vehicle out of the way, a tank pulled out of the column and carefully worked its way up along the shoulder of the road, ready to take its turn in case another probe vehicle was needed.

Kryshinin knew it was all right then. They would get through. He began to shout encouragement. Following his lead, his soldiers began to shout as well.

The flaming wreck veered out of the way, and the sergeant aimed at the roadway beyond the crater.

Kryshinin felt as though he could win the war with just a handful of men such as these. He was suddenly eager to get back on the move, to find the enemy.

"Could it be a deception?" Trimenko said, asking the question more of himself than of his audience. He reached into the leather tobacco pouch in which he carried his pistachios. Eating them was a habit he had picked up during his years in the Transcaucasus Military District. In Germany, his staff went to great lengths to keep him supplied. Often, he hardly tasted the nuts, but he found that peeling away the shells had a soothing influence on him, draining away nervousness the way worry beads worked for a Muslim.

"The documents appear to be genuine," the army's deputy chief of staff for operations said. "They were reportedly taken from a command post that was completely destroyed."

"Have you seen the documents? Has anyone here seen them?"

"They're on their way up from the division. We only know what the chief of reconnaissance reported from his initial exploitation. But it makes sense," the operations chief said, pointing at the map. "It puts their corps boundary here, not far from where we had assessed it."

"Far enough, though," Trimenko said. "It makes a difference. We need to execute the option shifting Malyshev's division onto the central tactical direction with Khrenov. The combat power has to converge." He slipped the bared pistachio between his lips.

"Comrade Army Commander, that may slow the seizure of Lueneburg."

At the mention of Lueneburg, Trimenko's temper quickened. But his facial expression gave no indication of any change. He still chafed at the thought of the Lueneburg operation. He had not been allowed to explain its purpose to anyone else; as far as his staff knew, it was a serious undertaking with a military purpose. But it irritated Trimenko that none of them seemed to question it. To him, it was obviously a stupid diversion of combat power. Yet his officers accepted it without a murmur. He looked at his operations chief. The man's mind was too slow; he was always too ready to state the self-evident. Trimenko felt disgustedly that he could think at least twice as fast and several times more clearly than any of his subordinates. He reached for another pistachio.

"If we rupture their corps boundary," Trimenko said in a voice that was clearly unwilling to accept further discussion, "we'll turn Lueneburg from the south at our convenience." He felt as though he were lecturing cadets at one of the second-rate academies. "I'm going to split them like a melon under a cleaver." He turned to his chief of staff. "Babryshkin, order Malyshev and Khrenov to execute the center option. Adjust the boundary accordingly." Suddenly, he stood up, unwilling to trust the staff to work incisively and swiftly enough to meet the demands of the situation. "Put the boundary here. Just offset from Route 71. Get Malyshev moving. If he hasn't made his preparations properly, I'll relieve him. Has Khrenov reported on the status of his crossing?"

"Comrade Army Commander, the divisional crossing operation is underway at this time."

Trimenko sensed that his operations officer didn't know any further details. He almost lashed out at the officer but managed to control himself. His fingernails worked at the pistachio shell. "All right. Everyone get started. Babryshkin, get me the front commander on the line. If he's not available, I'll talk to General Chibisov. And get my helicopter ready. I'm going forward. Make sure my pilot has a good fix on Khrenov's forward command post. If Khrenov isn't there, I'll take over his division myself."

Trimenko felt a familiar fury. He could not make them move at the pace he believed appropriate to the occasion. But he realized that if he drove them any harder now, they would only grow sloppy in their haste. He kept his hand on the throttle of the staff, striving for the maximum effective control of his officers, for the highest possible levels of performance and efficiency. And when he paused to reflect, he realized that his was a good staff, as staffs went. But the human animal was simply too slow, too inconsistent for him. You had to drive it with a lash, applying pain skillfully so that it spurred the animal onward but did not cause permanent injury. Occasionally an animal was too weak, and it failed and had to be destroyed. Other animals learned to respond to the very sound. But the requirement for the lash never disappeared, although the form taken by the instrument might change.

Trimenko was determined to fulfill the front plan so well that Malinsky would be forced to change it, cutting back Starukhin's role. He believed he would have an ally in Chibisov, Malinsky's clever little Jew, whom he took pains to cultivate. Trimenko regarded Starukhin as grossly overrated, a holdover from another, more slovenly era. Trimenko didn't believe modern war was for cossacks. Not at the operational level. Now it was for computers. And until they had better computers—computers that could replace the weaker type of men—war belonged to the men who were as much like computers as possible: exact, devoid of sentiment, and very, very fast.

Captain Kryshinin finally heard from the missing combat reconnaissance patrol. They had run into enemy opposition and had slipped off further to the south of Bad Bevensen. On Kryshinin's map, the patrol had moved outside of the unit's assigned boundary. But the good news was that they had seized a crossing site on the Elbe-Seiten Canal.

Kryshinin had gotten his forward security element on the move again, and the minefield and the lieutenant's sacrifice lay several kilometers to the rear. Kryshinin felt as though he would need to perform very well now to make up for his earlier lapse. He wondered what his other officers thought of him now.

He tried to reach division on the radio, and, when that failed, he attempted to reach the advance guard that was somewhere on his trail. He needed someone in a position of authority to make a decision on further violation of the unit boundary. But his element's route led through low ground now, and all he could hear was static and faint strains of music. He was not sure whether his radio was being jammed or if the nets had simply gotten out of control. Earlier, foreign-language voices had come up on his internal net, having a conversation.

Kryshinin desperately wanted to report the seizure of the crossing site. He suspected that, under the circumstances, division would order him to hurry to the support of the tiny patrol, despite the boundary problem. The lieutenant who led the patrol reported that they had come up on an east–west underpass, wide enough for tanks, where the elevated canal passed over a farm road. The tunnel had been guarded only by a few Dutch soldiers with small arms, and the patrol surprised them. Now the lieutenant was crying out for support.

Kryshinin tried both stations again.

Nothing.

He halted his column, then called for his senior artillery officer and the air force forward air controller who had been detailed to accompany the forward element to meet him by the air force officer's easily recognizable vehicle, a modified personnel carrier. The forward air controller was positioned closely behind Kryshinin, but the artilleryman was to the rear, leading the guns but prepared to come up to join the commander as soon as they were deployed. Kryshinin stood in the slow rain, waving for the artillery captain to hurry.

"Can either of you talk with your higher?"

The artillery captain shrugged. "I'm monitoring all right. I haven't tried to talk."

"I have a link back to division main and army central," Captain Bylov, the air force officer, stated, as though it was the most obvious thing in the world.

"Listen," Kryshinin said, "I want both of you to raise any stations you can. Then give my call sign and tell them my direct links aren't working. Listen carefully." Kryshinin unfolded his map, trying to protect it as much as possible against the fine drizzle that refused to come to an end. "We're changing our route of advance. We're going further south. To right there. The combat reconnaissance patrol has a crossing, but they won't be able to hold it for five minutes once they get hit."

The artillery captain, Likidze, looked at Kryshinin as though the element commander was crazy. "That's out of our sector. I won't be able to call up any fire support."

"That's what your battery's for. Look, our mission is to find a passage to the west. We've gotten this far, and it seems as if the enemy's covering plan has come apart. But the hardest part is getting across that damned canal. And now we have a crossing. I'm not going to pass it up just because it's a few kilometers out of sector. But you have to call back and tell higher what we're doing."

"What *you're* doing," the artilleryman said. "You have no authorization to cross a sector boundary. That site may even be one of the targets scheduled in our neighbor's fire plan."

Kryshinin wanted to shake the artilleryman, who had articulated Kryshinin's own doubts and fears. He realized that no one would share this responsibility with him. But he thought again of his earlier failure to act when confronted with the minefield, and of the lieutenant who had been so much braver and clearer-thinking than his commander. Now there was another lieutenant waiting for help who had managed to find a way across the canal. Kryshinin looked at the artilleryman in disgust, seeing himself and a hundred other officers he knew.

"Correct," Kryshinin said. "It's on my shoulders. Now let's get moving."

Time pressed harder on Kryshinin's mind than it ever had before. The patrol commander reported incoming artillery on his position. Kryshinin realized that he might well get away with his decision as long as he proved successful in holding onto the crossing site. After all, that conformed to the essential mission. But if he had taken the wrong decision, and if the crossing site was lost and he had no results, he would pay.

He lost radio contact with the patrol.

Kryshinin spurred his element on as fast as it could go. He felt oddly lucky now that he had lost his engineers, since the big tank-launched bridge would never have been able to keep up with the increased speed of the march column. When one of his vehicles broke down, he left it for the advance guard to collect. The tanks set the pace, gripping the wet road with their whirring tracks.

At a crossroads, they raced by a bewildered enemy military policeman. The soldier emptied his machine pistol in the direction of the flying column, then ran for the trees. A bit further along, a medical clearing station had been set up in the courtyard of a farm, obviously intended to support the enemy's covering troops. Kryshinin's element left the site undisturbed in their muddy wake. Kryshinin sensed that the enemy had lost control of his forward battle now, and that his own location was not known to them. He wondered if, perhaps, his element had already penetrated the enemy's main defenses. It was impossible to tell. Unlike the exercises to which Kryshinin was accustomed, where you knew generally how it was all laid out and usually received tip-off information so the unit would look good, real war seemed ridiculously confusing. Kryshinin had expected battle to have more formality to it, for combat to be more structured and to make better sense.

When an enemy field artillery battery appeared under drooping camouflage nets at the edge of an orchard, Kryshinin ordered his column to shoot it up from the march without deploying. He did not want to get bogged down. It was critical to maintain a single focus, and to act with speed.

The column crested a low hill, and Kryshinin saw the monumental line of the canal running north and south. He could not understand why the low ground had not been inundated. In a marvelous piece of engineering, the canal passed smoothly over a local farm trail, built up like a medieval fortress wall with a great open gate. Under the stout concrete tunnel, a single Soviet infantry fighting vehicle covered the near bank.

Kryshinin could not understand why the enemy had not blown the overpass immediately. He hastily got on his radio and ordered the artillery to deploy in the open hollow off to the left on the near bank. One platoon of motorized rifle troops would secure the near side of the crossing and protect the guns. Everyone else was to follow Kryshinin to the far side of the canal.

As he finished his transmissions the enemy artillery came again. The rounds exploded along the ridge on the far bank that paralleled the canal. The patrol's vehicles had been well-concealed, and it appeared as though the enemy was simply delivering area fires, attempting to flush the Soviet scouts into the open. A stout, walled farm complex, just to the right of the road as it wove up onto the crest of the ridge, provided an obvious focus for the efforts of both sides.

Kryshinin pulled his vehicle out of the line and personally took the lead. He raced down into the low ground, skidding to a stop beside the guardian vehicle at the mouth of the tunnel. In the watery field beside the road, the bodies of four enemy soldiers had been laid in a row. A senior sergeant greeted Kryshinin, wincing at the still-distant artillery blasts.

"Comrade Captain," he shouted, "the lieutenant's up in those farm buildings."

Kryshinin contracted back into his vehicle. "Move out," he ordered the driver. "Up the road. To the farmyard."

On the far side of the tunnel, a blasted enemy fighting vehicle lay like an animal carcass where it had been taken by surprise. Kryshinin spit into his mike. "Tank platoon to the treeline straddling the crest. Second rifle platoon, north of the road. Third platoon, cover the south side. Establish a hasty defense. Antitank platoon, disperse to cover the entire perimeter. All other vehicles shelter behind the farm buildings. Quickly. End."

Through the random eruptions of incoming enemy artillery, Kryshinin could now see two fighting vehicles drawn up on a small plateau beside the farmyard walls. One had tucked in behind a fertilizer mound, and the other had found a sunken position between two apple trees.

Kryshinin told his driver to halt fifty meters to the rear of the vehicles, in a low section of the road. As he dismounted a soldier waved him into the cluster of buildings. Kryshinin ran, carrying his soggy map and his assault rifle. He could feel the wash of the artillery rounds as the enemy gunners reached toward the canal itself.

Inside the neat little courtyard, a rifleman lowered his weapon at Kryshinin, then suddenly pulled it away.

"In here, Comrade Captain. Up the stairs."

Kryshinin vaulted through the doorway. The hallway of the house was littered with glass and smashed potted plants, the aftermath of the nearby artillery strikes. He jumped the stairs two at a time.

A lieutenant knelt low behind a broken-out window on a landing just below the second floor. He gazed through a pair of binoculars, man-packed radio at his side with the antenna angled out through the window frame. He looked around suddenly.

"Comrade Captain, you're here!"

The boy's voice sounded as though he had just experienced the relief of Leningrad. Loaded with complex emotions and thoughts, Kryshinin sensed that his arrival, in the lieutenant's mind, had meant salvation, an end to all troubles. Yet Kryshinin could only feel how little combat power he had brought to the scene. Now they would need to hold out until the advance guard of the division arrived. If they were coming.

"Look," the lieutenant said. "You can see them across the valley, by those woods. Orient on the lone house. They're getting ready to come at us." He held the binoculars out to Kryshinin.

One quick look. Tanks. Big, modern, Western tanks. Approximately thirty-five hundred meters off.

The artillery came back, shaking the farmhouse.

"They spotted us maybe twenty minutes ago," the lieutenant shouted. "They came marching up the road like they were on parade. We had to open up to keep them away from the tunnel. A few minutes after that, the artillery started."

Kryshinin looked at the baby-faced lieutenant. Somebody's sweetheart. He touched the boy on the shoulder. "Good work. Good work, Lieutenant. Now let me see what I can do about those tanks."

The concussion of a nearby artillery blast almost knocked him off his feet. Someone screamed.

"In the barn," the lieutenant said. "The Germans. The family. They were still here, hiding. I didn't know what to do."

It had never really come home to Kryshinin before that warfare could have such complex dimensions. He thought for a long moment. The screaming clearly came from a female throat.

"They can take care of themselves," Kryshinin said, turning away to organize his battle.

Kryshinin called the artillery battery commander, ordering him to either come up and act as a forward observer the way he was supposed to, or send someone else. He was prepared for another argument, but the artillery officer's attitude had undergone a distinct change. He was excited now, too. He had contacted division, reporting that Kryshinin's element had reached the crossing site. The chief of missile troops and artillery had personally informed the division commander. He had approved Kryshinin's decision, and the advance guard from Kryshinin's regiment was on the way.

"How far back?" Kryshinin asked.

"Didn't say."

"Find out. We have enemy tanks coming for a visit. They want us out of here." He passed the grid where the enemy tanks were forming up. Then he hastened to the air force officer's control vehicle. The hatches were sealed, and Kryshinin had to bang on the metal with the stock of his assault rifle.

Bylov, the forward air controller, opened the hatch one-handed, holding an open rations tin in the other.

"Taking a break," he told Kryshinin.

Kryshinin almost gave up. At the same time he realized, jealously, that he had eaten nothing since the previous night. But there would be time, he consoled himself. Later. If they were still alive.

"Have you informed your control post of our situation?" Kryshinin demanded.

The air force officer nodded, forking up a hunk of potted meat so strong-smelling that its aroma penetrated the garlic-and-onions stink of the artillery blasts.

"Listen," Kryshinin said, "we're going to need air support. If you want to be alive at suppertime, you'd better get some ground-attack boys or some gunships in here. The valley just beyond the ridge is filled with enemy tanks."

Bylov finished chewing and swallowed. "I'll see what I can do. But if they can't give me something that's going up now, it won't help."

"*Try*. And get out where you can see what's going on. Up there by the apple trees. Anywhere."

Kryshinin jumped back down off the vehicle, splashing in the mud. His camouflage uniform had been soaking wet since before dawn, and his trousers had been chafing his crotch. But the discomfort had disappeared in his current excitement. He raced for the tank platoon, instinctively running low, even though the enemy artillery had lifted for the moment.

The tank platoon had a problem. The platoon commander could not find any suitable firing positions along the ridgeline. In order to sufficiently decline their gun tubes to engage an approaching enemy, they would need to expose themselves to observation and fires.

"All right," Kryshinin said. "I have a better idea. Pull back onto that low hill over there, just north of the road we took to come up here. There. See it? Hide where you can watch the approaches to the tunnel. Counterattack any enemy armor that gets through. Don't wait for orders. Just hit them. We'll try to hold around the farm buildings. Do your best."

The lieutenant of tank troops saluted and immediately began talking into his microphone. The tanks belched into readiness.

Kryshinin hurried back toward his own vehicle. But before he was halfway, the sounds of combat came back, changed.

His infantry fighting vehicles and wheeled antitank vehicles were engaging. The enemy was on the way.

Kryshinin looked back across the canal. Still no sign of movement. Kryshinin cursed the artillery officer, wondering what was keeping him. He needed someone to call fires. Otherwise, they would be overrun before the guns did any good.

His tank platoon rolled powerfully down across a saddle and veered toward their new position. Kryshinin felt confident that they would do their job. The lieutenant had had a crisp professionalism about him.

One of the antitank vehicles had profiled too high on the ridgeline. Now it caught a round in the bow and lifted over on its back, throwing scraps of metal upward and outward in a fountain. Kryshinin felt a sting on his shoulder, as though he had been bitten by an oversized insect. He almost tripped but managed to keep running.

The nearest platoon of motorized riflemen had dismounted, but their officer had not properly positioned them. They were simply lying in a close line with their machine guns, assault rifles, and antitank grenade launchers, protected only by the small irregularities of the ground.

Kryshinin shouted at the officer in charge. "Are you *crazy?* Get these men into the buildings. It's too late to do anything else now. *Hurry.*"

The lieutenant stared at him as though he understood nothing at all. Suddenly, Kryshinin went cold inside at the thought of what the situation was probably like in the platoon that had lost its lieutenant in the minefield. He felt overwhelmed by the need to do everything himself. He ignored the lieutenant now, grabbing the first soldier he could reach, a machine gunner.

"*You.* Get inside the buildings. Take your pals. Fight from there."

Kryshinin ran along the line. Where the lieutenant had positioned the men, they would have been not only hopelessly vulnerable, but useless. They had no fields of fire. Kryshinin could not believe he had failed so thoroughly to train his officers and soldiers. He had complied with every regulation, and his training sessions usually had gone well, with the company receiving mostly fours and fives. Now it all seemed meaningless, as though they had all merely been going through the motions, without really learning. And now it was too late. They would have to fight in the state in which war had found them.

"All of you. *Get up,*" he shouted, rasping to be heard above the chaotic battle noise. One of the machine gunners had opened fire, and firing began to spread along the line, although some soldiers simply lay still on the ground. "Stop it. *Stop.* They're still out of range." Even on his feet, Kryshinin could not see the enemy from the position of the firing soldiers. "Get into the buildings and get ready to fight. This isn't a country outing. *Stop your firing.*"

Then he saw the helicopters. Approaching from the wrong side.

"*Come on,*" he shouted, voice already cracking. He ran for the cover of the buildings, with the motorized riflemen all around him. Behind them, an infantry fighting vehicle positioned in the orchard sent off an antitank guided missile.

"Where's the air defense team?" Kryshinin wondered out loud.

The helicopters throbbed over the trees, ugly, bulbous creatures with dark weaponry on their mounts and German crosses on the fuselages. The markings confused Kryshinin, who was sure he was still in the Dutch sector. He stopped to fire his assault rifle at the aircraft, and a few others fired as well.

The helicopters, four of them, churned overhead without firing. Kryshinin felt relief at their passing. But a moment later, he heard the hiss of missiles coming off launch rails.

The artillery, Kryshinin remembered. The battery was sitting out in the open. Kryshinin watched helplessly as the enemy attack helicopters banked playfully above the landscape, teasing the desperate gunners on the ground, destroying the self-propelled pieces one after the other.

Why didn't the air defense troops fire? Kryshinin wondered.

In less than a minute, the helicopters peeled off to the south, leaving the wrecked battery in a veil of smoke pierced now and then by the flash of secondary explosions.

Kryshinin made a hurried stop at his own vehicle. It had moved nearer to the crest, and its main gun fired into the distance. He leaned into the turret, grabbing the gunner by the sleeve, shouting to be heard.

"Back into the courtyard. Get her behind the walls. I need the radios."

The gunner stared up at him. "Comrade Captain. You're bleeding." Kryshinin followed the gunner's eyes down to his shoulder, then over his chest and sleeve. Much of the uniform was shockingly dark, much darker than the rain alone could have made it. At the sight, Kryshinin felt a momentary faintness.

"Hurry up," he said, almost gagging. "Get into the courtyard." But he suddenly felt weaker, as if his realizing that he had been wounded had unleashed the wound's effect. He remembered the little sting. It seemed impossible that it could have done this. He was not even aware of any pain.

He trotted beside his vehicle, guiding it through the gates as the direct-fire battle increased in intensity. But the forward air-control vehicle had blocked the courtyard, taking up more than its share of the space. Kryshinin ran to make the air force officer move out of the way just as the artillery came thumping back.

The barn roof collapsed. The concussion of the blast knocked several of the men in the courtyard to the ground. One soldier had blood draining from his ears, and Kryshinin felt deafened. But he still had enough hearing to recognize the sound of a tank gun closer than expected. In the misery of the courtyard, soldiers screamed for aid and choked on the dust of the smashed barn. Then the rain abruptly increased in intensity, as if the enemy controlled that, too.

"Everybody into the buildings," Kryshinin shouted. "Don't just stand around." But the soldiers were hesitant. After watching the roof of the barn cave in, Kryshinin could hardly blame them. Nonetheless, the remaining buildings provided better protection than the open courtyard. And it was impossible for all of the men to fight effectively from the courtyard. "*Move,* damn you."

But they were already scrambling to obey him. It was only that they had been stunned into a slowed reaction by the confusion that seemed to worsen with every minute. Now those who didn't understand Kryshinin's Russian simply followed their peers.

The sounds of moving tanks crowded in with the noises of missile back-blasts and automatic weapons. Kryshinin bounded back into the house and up the stairs, crunching glass underfoot. The lieutenant remained at his post. But he didn't need his binoculars anymore.

"Those tanks," he told Kryshinin, "at least a company. Working up along the treelines. We got two of them."

A round smashed into the wall of the house, shaking it to its foundation. But the building was old and strong, built of masonry.

The lieutenant noticed Kryshinin's bloody tunic.

Kryshinin held up his hand. "No real damage done," he

said, hoping he was correct. He couldn't understand where the pain was hiding. The arm still worked, if stiffly.

"One of the officers went up on the roof with a radio," the lieutenant said. "He looked like an air force guy."

"*Where* is he?"

"On the roof. There's an attic stairway back there. The roof has dormer windows."

The enemy tanks had closed to within a thousand meters. Kryshinin watched them for a moment, catching a glimpse of dark metal now and then through the local smokescreens the enemy vehicles laid down with their smoke grenades. Their movement struck him as very clever, very disciplined, but slow. They seemed to move in cautious bounds. Kryshinin watched one of his own antitank missiles stream toward the enemy tanks, then spring out of control, soaring briefly into the empty sky, then plunging into a meadow. He turned away in disgust.

He followed the directions toward the attic. He felt unusually light, almost as though he were floating, yet it was a hard climb going up the narrow stairs. He began to feel as though his torso could fly but his feet were weighted down with irons. When he reached the attic, he found it cluttered with forgotten property, stinking with mildew. The trash of generations troubled his course, barring his feet with old framed pictures and antique household machinery, all strewn with ragged fabric.

The roof windows had been shattered. Kryshinin leaned out through the nearest, which opened toward the canal.

Bylov lay sprawled on his belly on the roof tiles, talking into a radio set, with a satchel of gear open beside him.

Kryshinin could not understand a single word the air force officer said. The level of noise was incredible, maddening. It seemed to give the air a tangible thickness, as though you could stir it with your hand.

Kryshinin tugged at Bylov's leg.

The air force officer held up a finger. Wait. He rolled onto his back, scanning the gray sky.

Kryshinin followed Bylov's line of sight but could see nothing. Nonetheless, Bylov reached into his satchel, retrieving a flare pistol and two explosive canisters of colored smoke. He spoke once into his microphone, then rose to his knees on the slick tile, just high enough to peer over the roofbeam.

With a sure motion, Bylov threw a smoke canister to the right, then quickly hurled another to the left, marking the line of friendly troops. He fumbled briefly at the flare pistol, then fired two green flares in succession in the direction of the enemy.

Bylov threw his satchel at Kryshinin, knocking him back into the attic. The air force officer followed the bag, quick as a cat, dragging his radio after him. Without a look at Kryshinin, Bylov flattened onto the floor, hands over his ears.

Kryshinin swiftly imitated him.

A powerful rush of jet engines seemed to pass right through the room, shaking the floor even more powerfully than had the artillery blasts. The passage was closely followed by small blasts, then by enormous booms that seemed to tear several seconds out of their lives. The air itself drew tighter.

"Fuel air explosives," Bylov shouted. "Great stuff."

"Good work," Kryshinin shouted back.

"Count on the air force," Bylov told him. "We serve the Motherland and all that."

"How did you get the sorties?"

Bylov looked at him in honest surprise. "We've got top priority. I've got more on the way."

Bylov methodically began to gather his spilled tools, checking his radio, a technician of the sky. In his own little world of airplanes, Bylov had not noticed—or, at any rate, had said nothing about—Kryshinin's wound. But Kryshinin felt changes coming over his body now. He was losing strength fast. He needed to have a look at the wound, yet he was afraid that the sight of his damaged flesh, of his own blood on his own skin, might paralyze him. And he was determined to hang on, no matter what happened.

Kryshinin slowly raised himself and worked his way back down the stairs to the lieutenant's observation post. The lieutenant's torso lay, smashed against a wall, head and limbs twisted out of any skeletal sense, eyes bulging. From behind another wall, a machine gun fired.

Kryshinin peered out of the battered window frame. The valley had filled with black smoke.

Then he saw the first enemy tank in close. The airplanes had missed at least a platoon. Four enemy tanks came over the crest, one after another. One tank trailed fire off its deck, resembling a mythical dragon. They drove beside the farm complex, leaving Kryshinin's field of vision.

He hurried back down the stairs to the accompaniment of blasts and rapid fires. Men shouted in a contest of complaints and commands.

From the doorway, the farmyard appeared chaotic. Kryshinin watched as his own vehicle attempted to pull off, only to explode in the entrance gateway. The heat of the blast reached into the foyer of the house, rinsing Kryshinin with a wave of unnatural warmth.

Above the billows of smoke, he saw two more helicopters appear. But these were from his side, "bumblebees," loaded with weaponry. They flew an orientation pass. Kryshinin wanted to get into the fight, to insure that his tank platoon had moved to intercept the enemy tanks that had broken through. But flames blocked the gateway.

He searched hurriedly through the ground floor of the house, hunting for a side door. Nothing in the building seemed to be left whole. In the kitchen, he found two soldiers casually sitting against a cupboard, as though they were on an authorized rest period.

"Come with me," Kryshinin shouted, heading for the open space where a door had been ripped from its hinges.

Outside, the black smoke covered the landscape between the farm buildings and the original positions of the enemy tanks. The amount of firing that continued seemed incredible, first because it seemed as though all of the ammunition should have been used up already, and, second, because it was hard to believe so many survivors remained. But Kryshinin felt reassured that so many of his men continued to engage the enemy.

He heard the beat of the Soviet gunships returning. And

the battle noises clearly revealed a tank fight going on down toward the canal.

The two riflemen followed Kryshinin obediently, simply waiting for his instructions. Kryshinin hustled around a corner. One of his infantry fighting vehicles sat in perfect condition, scanning for targets, even as the battle had passed it by. Kryshinin let it stand as a sentinel. Growing weaker and dizzy almost to nausea, he worked along the wall of the ruined barn, weapon ready, seeking a view back toward the canal. He came up behind a rain barrel, and, taking a chance, he raised his head.

The finest, most welcome sight of his life awaited him. The twin ridgeline on the eastern side of the canal streamed with Soviet vehicles. Air-defense elements raced across the high fields to find correctly spaced positions, and self-propelled guns bristled their tubes at the sky. In the valley bottom, the enemy tanks that had penetrated Kryshinin's thin line burned away like lamps to light the rainy day. Soviet tanks roared through the tunnel, blooming out into a long, beautiful line and heading straight for Kryshinin's position.

Kryshinin collapsed against the wall of the barn, letting go at last.

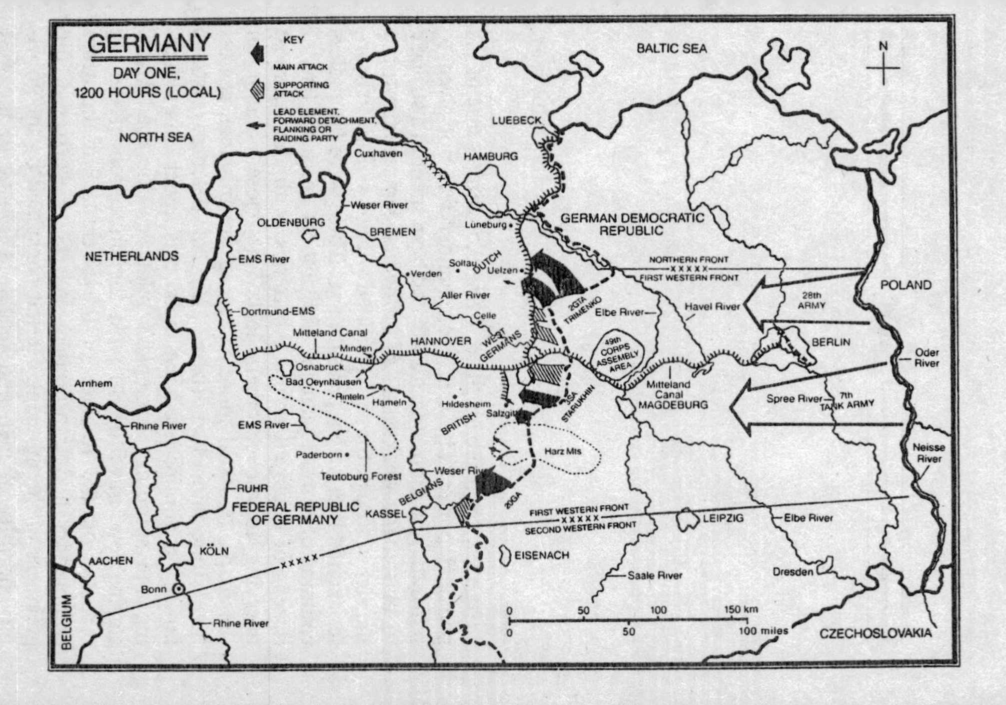

GERMANY
DAY ONE,
1200 HOURS (LOCAL)
KEY
MAIN ATTACK
SUPPORTING ATTACK
LEAD ELEMENT, FORWARD DETACHMENT, FLANKING OR RAIDING PARTY
NORTH SEA
BALTIC SEA
N
LUEBECK
HAMBURG
Cuxhaven
Weser River
OLDENBURG
BREMEN
Lüneburg
GERMAN DEMOCRATIC REPUBLIC
NETHERLANDS
EMS River
Soltau
DUTCH
Uelzen
Verden
NORTHERN FRONT
XXXXX
FIRST WESTERN FRONT
POLAND
28th ARMY
Aller River
Havel River
2GTA TRIMENKO
Elbe River
Dortmund-EMS
Celle
Mitteland Canal
Minden
HANNOVER
WEST GERMANS
49th CORPS ASSEMBLY AREA
BERLIN
Oder River
Osnabruck
Bad Oeynhausen
Mitteland Canal
MAGDEBURG
Arnhem
Rinteln
Hameln
Hildesheim
Salzgit
3SA STARUKHIN
Spree River
7th TANK ARMY
BRITISH
Rhine River
EMS River
Harz Mts
Neisse River
Paderborn
Teutoburg Forest
Weser Riv
RUHR
BELGIANS
20GA
FEDERAL REPUBLIC OF GERMANY
KASSEL
FIRST WESTERN FRONT
XXXXX
SECOND WESTERN FRONT
LEIPZIG
Elbe River
KÖLN
AACHEN
XXXXX
EISENACH
Bonn
Saale River
Dresden
0 50 100 150 km
0 50 100 miles
Rhine River
BELGIUM
CZECHOSLOVAKIA

Six

The view from the air filled Trimenko with a sense of his personal power. The army commander was not given to self-indulgent emotions; his life had been spent in a struggle to master the weaknesses of individual temperament, but the sight through the rain-speckled windows of the helicopter excited him with a pleasant awe. These were *his* endless columns of combat vehicles and support units, *his* tens of dozens of deployed artillery batteries, with the rearmost hurrying to move, others locked in close column on the roads, and still more executing fire missions against the stone-colored horizon. *His* air-defense systems lurked on hilltops like great metal cats, radar ears twitching and spinning. Trimenko's pilot flew the road trace, staying low, unwilling to trust the protection of the big red star on the fuselage of the aircraft. But the army commander had transcended such petty worries in the greatness of the moment. He felt consumed by the growling enormity of men and machines flowing to the west like a steel torrent, absorbed into a being greater than the self.

In detail, it was a far-from-perfect vision. Some columns were at a standstill. Here and there, crossroads teemed with such confusion that Trimenko could almost hear the curses and arguments. Soviet hulks had been shoved off the roadways where the enemy's air power or long-range artillery fires had caught them. Incredible panoramas opened up, then closed again beneath the speeding helicopter.

Trimenko realized that, to those on the ground, waiting nervously for a column to move or for an order to come, the war probably seemed like a colossal mess on the edge of disaster. But from the sky, from the god's-eye view, the columns moved well enough. For every march serial that had bogged down, two or three others rushed along parallel routes. And the flow carried them all in the right general direction. Trimenko knew that one division already had pushed its lead elements across the canal a bit to the north, even as a major assault crossing operation was being conducted in another divisional sector. Some units had penetrated to a depth in excess of thirty kilometers from their start lines, and one reconnaissance patrol had reported in from a location fifty-two kilometers west of the border. Meanwhile, the enemy's power to strike out to halt the flow of Soviet forces had proven surprisingly weak. Trimenko had already heard the fearful casualty reports from the morning's engagements. Kept in perspective, the numbers were acceptable—and he had no doubt that they were somewhat exaggerated in the heat of combat and in the process of hastily relaying data up the echelons. The prospect of inaccurate data for his forecasting calculations troubled Trimenko more than did the thought of the casualties themselves.

Jet aircraft, invisible in the haze, passed nearby, and the sound slammed into the helicopter. Trimenko thought that Malinsky had been absolutely correct to support the air offensive so heavily. With the low number and limited range of the surface-to-surface missiles available to the enemy now, air power had been the great enemy threat. In his private, less-assured moments, Trimenko had worried that NATO would catch them right at the border-crossing sites, where the engineers had opened gaps in the frontier barriers. But the threat had not materialized. NATO's ground attacks with aircraft were deadly, but haphazard, and Trimenko suspected that many of NATO's aircraft had, indeed, been caught on the ground. Starukhin had been an ass to press the issue of initial close air support with Malinsky, and the present obviousness of it pleased Trimenko. Starukhin, he mused, was the sort of Russian officer he himself most despised, and a type still far too common—the man who raged and stamped and shouted to announce his own power and grandeur, to convince a skeptical world of how much he mattered. Trimenko, no less concerned with his own importance, found tantrums inefficient and primitive. He believed that the times called for a more sophisticated approach to the exploitation of resources, whether material or human.

Trimenko stared out over his army as it marched deeper into West Germany. The spectacle offered nothing but confusion to the man with a narrow, low-level perspective, he realized, but it revealed its hidden power, incredible power in an irresistible flood, to the man who could look down.

"Afterburners now."

"Fifty-eight, I'm still in the capture zone. I'm hot."

"Open it up, Fifty-nine. Flares away. Get out of the kitchen."

"He's on me. *He's on me."*

"Turning now. *Go."*

The junior pilot in the wing aircraft fired his flares and banked, engines flushing a burst of power.

"More angle, little brother. *Pull it around."*

Pilot First Class Captain Sobelev watched as an enemy air-defense missile miraculously passed beside his wingman's aircraft and carried about five hundred feet before exploding. Sobelev felt his own aircraft buck like a wild horse at the blast.

"Steady now. Keep her steady, Fifty-nine."

The planes had come out two and two, but the trailing pair had been shot down before they even reached the Weser

River. Now, deep in the enemy's rear, the air defenses had thinned. But it was still nightmarish flying. It was not at all like Afghanistan. Flying in and out of Kabul and good old Bagram had been bad enough. With the eternal haze over Kabul, filthy dust on the hot wind, and later the horribly accurate American Stinger missiles. But all of that had been child's play compared to this.

"Fifty-eight, my artificial horizon's out."

Shit, Sobelev thought. "Just stay with me," he answered. "We're going to do just fine."

Sobelev sympathized with the lieutenant's nervousness. It was their second combat mission of the day, and today was the lieutenant's first taste of war. If Afghanistan had been this bad, Sobelev thought, I might have quit flying.

"Stay with me, little brother. Talk to me."

"I'm with you, Fifty-eight."

"Good boy. Target heading, thirty degrees."

"Roger."

"Keep those wings level now . . . final reference point in sight . . . go to attack altitude . . . *talk* to me, Fifty-nine."

"I have the reference point."

"Executing version one."

"Correcting to follow your approach."

"On the combat course . . . *now* . . . hold on, it's going to be hot."

"Roger."

"Target . . . ten kilometers . . . steady . . . I have visual."

Sobelev saw the airfield coming up at them like a table spread for dinner. Enemy aircraft continued to land and take off.

"Hit the apron. I've got the main runway."

"Roger."

Air-defense artillery suddenly came to life in their path, drilling the sky with points of light.

"Let's do this clean . . . hold it . . . *hold straight . . . straighten your wings."*

In Afghanistan, you flew high and tossed outdated ordnance at the *kishlaks* with their mud buildings that had not changed for a thousand years. The bombs changed them in an instant.

Sobelev was determined to bring his wingman out. Wingboy, he thought, children at war, already forgetting how young he had been on his first tour of duty in Afghanistan.

Sobelev led them right into the general flight paths of the NATO aircraft taking off, making it impossible for the air-defense guns to follow them.

"Now."

The lieutenant shouted into the radio in childish elation. The two planes lifted away from the enemy airfield, and, as they banked, Sobelev caught a glimpse of the heavy damage that already had been dealt to the base by previous sorties. Black burned patches and craters on the hardstand. Smoking ruins in the support area. Emergency vehicles raced through corridors of fire. Sobelev heard his flight's payload detonate, adding to the destruction.

"Let's go home, little brother . . . heading . . . one . . . six . . . five."

An enemy plane suddenly shot straight up in front of Sobelev. He recognized a NATO F-16. As the plane twisted into the sky, disappearing from view in the grayness, Sobelev's mouth opened behind his face mask. He had never seen a plane . . . a pilot . . . maneuver like that. It shocked him.

After a long, long few seconds, he spoke. "Hostiles, Fifty-nine . . . do what I do . . . do *exactly* what I do . . . do you understand?"

"Roger." But the exuberance was gone from the lieutenant's voice. He, too, had seen the enemy fighter's acrobatic climb. Now they both wondered where the enemy aircraft had gone. Sobelev looked at his radar screen. It was a mess. Busy sky.

"Follow me *now,* Fifty-nine," Sobelev commanded. And hope I know what I'm doing.

Major Astanbegyan leaned over the operator's shoulder, watching the scanning line circle the radar display.

"Does *anyone* respond to query?" the major asked.

"Comrade Major," the specialist sergeant said, with weary exasperation in his voice, "I register responses. But it's all so cluttered that they intermingle before I can sort targets. Then the jamming starts again."

Astanbegyan told the boy to keep on trying. He was beginning to feel like a unit political officer in his struggle to maintain a positive collective outlook in the control staff. He had begun the morning by shouting when things went wrong, but he had soon shouted himself out. There were so many unanticipated problems that he quickly realized he was only making the work harder. Now he simply did what he could to keep the entire air-defense sector from collapsing into anarchy.

He turned away from the boy at the console. He knew the sergeant was trying, that he sincerely wanted to do what was right. The officers manning scopes and target allocation systems were doing no better. The NATO aircraft were using the same penetration corridor in sector as those of the Warsaw Pact, and it was a hopeless muddle. Out on the ground, the batteries were operating primarily on visual identification.

The battle management computers were a disappointment as well. So far, they were handling systems location and logistics data fairly well—or seemed to be, since there was no way of knowing how accurate all of the inputs and outputs were at this point. But the sorting and assigning of targets was going badly. Astanbegyan had no doubt that aircraft were being knocked out of the sky. He had over a dozen reported kills. But he was less certain about who was being shot down.

"Comrade Major," a communications specialist called to him. "The commander of Number Five Battery wishes to report."

"Take his report, then."

"He wishes to report to you personally, Comrade Major."

Astanbegyan stepped over to the communications area and took the receiver from the specialist.

"Six-Four-Zero. Go ahead."

"This is Six-Four-Five. I have two systems down. Enemy air-to-surface missiles, antiradiation, I think. We got the bastard, though."

"All right," Astanbegyan said, although he was far from

happy with the news. What could you do, order your subordinates to go back and start from the beginning and not lose the systems next time? "How are you receiving your encoded instructions?"

There was a momentary silence on the other end.

"This is Six-Four-Five," the voice returned. "I haven't received any for the last hour."

Astanbegyan felt his self-control drain away. "Damn it, man, this isn't an exercise. We've been sending constantly. Check your battery console."

"Checking it now."

"And next time don't wait until you have to call me and tell me you've lost the rest of your battery."

"Understood." But the voice shook. "Listen, Comrade Major . . . we're running low on missiles."

"You can't possibly have fired everything on your transporters."

"Comrade Maj—I mean, Six-Four-Zero, I haven't seen the trucks all day. The technical services officer became separated from the unit. You wouldn't believe what the roads are like out here."

"You find those damned trucks. If you have to walk to Poland. Better yet—*you* walk *forward.* Send somebody else to the rear. What the hell good are you without missiles? You ought to be court-martialed."

"You don't know what it's like out here."

"Comrade Major," a radar-tracking specialist shouted, interrupting. "Multiple hostiles, subsector seven, moving to four."

Immediately, the shriek of jets flying low penetrated the walls of the van complex, shaking the maps and charts on the walls, and drawing loud curses from electronics operators whose equipment flickered or failed.

"Where did they come from?" Astanbegyan screamed, giving up his last attempt at composure.

"They were ours, Comrade Major."

Astanbegyan ran his hand back over his scalp, soothing himself. A good thing, too, he thought.

Seven

Colonel Tkachenko, the Second Guards Tank Army's chief of engineers, watched the assault crossing operation from the lead regiment's combat observation post. Intermittently, he could see as far as the canal line through the periscope. He had studied this canal for a long time, and he knew it well. There were sectors where it was elevated above the landscape, with tunnels passing beneath it, and other sectors, like this one, where the waterway was only a flat, dull trace along the valley floor. This sector had been carefully chosen, partly because of its suitability for an assault crossing, but largely because it was a point at which the enemy would not expect a major crossing effort, since the connectivity to the high-speed roads was marginal. Surprise was the most important single factor in such an operation, and the local trails and farm roads would be good enough to allow them to punch out and roll up the enemy. Then there would be better sites, with better connectivity, at a much lower cost. Tkachenko refocused the optics, looking at the sole bridge where it lay broken-backed in the water. A few hundred meters beyond, the smokescreen blotted out the horizon. Under its cover, the air assault troops had gone in by helicopter to secure the far bank, and now the assault engineers on the near bank appeared as tiny toys rushing forward with their rafts and demolitions. Beyond the smoke-cordoned arena, the fires of dozens of batteries of artillery blocked the far approaches to any enemy reserves.

A flight of helicopters shuttled additional security troops, with portable antitank weapons, to the far bank. Yet the action appeared very different now than it looked in the demonstration exercises in the training area crossing sites. The only order seemed to be in the overall direction of the activity, and the noise level, even from a distance, cut painfully into the ears. There was no well-rehearsed feel to this crossing, only the desperation of men hurrying to accomplish dangerous tasks, with random death teasing them. The banks of the canal were steep and reinforced with steel. There were no easy points of entry for amphibious vehicles. Everything had to be prepared. Ingress, egress. With the enemy's searching fires crashing down.

The enemy artillery shot blindly at the banks of the canal. The Soviet smokescreen had been fired in along a ten-kilometer-long stretch of the waterway, and the enemy gunners were forced to guess the exact location of the crossing activities. Despite the difficulties, occasional shells found their mark, shredding tiny figures, hurling them about on waves of mud, and setting unlucky vehicles ablaze.

A flight of two Soviet gunships passed overhead, flying echelon right. Another pair followed the first, then a third couple came by. They flew heavily across a sky the color of dishwater, then disappeared into the smoke.

Gutsy pilots, Tkachenko thought. Not a good day to be an aviator.

Along the canal line, a ragged series of demolitions began. The explosions on the near bank were soon followed by blasts from the western bank. Tkachenko tried to keep count. At least eight points of entry.

More low blasts punctuated the horizon.

Tkachenko felt pride in the courage of the engineers down on the water. At New Year's, 1814, bridging trains from the Imperial Russian Army had supported the Prussian crossing of the Rhine. Only the Russian engineers had had the equipment and the skill to force the great river. Now Tkachenko intended to repeat the earlier event, and he wondered how many days it would take to fight all the way to the Rhine. The engineers would have plenty of practice on the way, given the dense drainage pattern of northern Germany.

Tkachenko turned to the motorized rifle regiment commander, a major.

"You can get a company of infantry fighting vehicles across now. No promises on the quality of the egress cuts, but we'll winch them out if we have to. As soon as you get your first wave across, we'll put in the assault bridges."

The enemy artillery barrage intensified again, as if they sensed the progress along the canal. The blasts and smoke made it difficult to see. But Tkachenko soon made out a column of infantry fighting vehicles, prepared for swimming. They emerged from a hide position several hundred meters back from the bank, then began to deploy on line, searching for their markers and guides.

Tkachenko left the periscope. Time to go forward. He waved his hand at the commander of the engineer assault bridging battalion.

"It's time. Let's get them in the water."

Together, the two engineers slogged through the mud, past the local security troops with their machine guns and shoulder-fired antiaircraft missiles. Tkachenko began to climb laboriously into the younger commander's control vehicle.

"Comrade Colonel?"

Tkachenko looked around at the handsome young Estonian. Fit. The new breed. Tkachenko knew he was getting too old for all of this. It was time for a good teaching position, where you slept in a soft, warm bed every night and there were no real risks to be taken.

"I'm going with you," Tkachenko told the younger man. "You don't begrudge a grandfather a little fun, do you?"

The younger officer looked confused. Tkachenko continued to work his bulky way into the cramped armored vehicle. Of course, the battalion commander would not particularly want the chief of engineers looking over his shoulder. But that was just too bad, Tkachenko told himself. He didn't want to miss the actual crossing. All of his military career, he had been waiting to use his skills for a serious purpose. Now it was his duty to be down there with them all, putting in the bridges and running the ferries.

The Estonian battalion commander yanked the hatch shut behind them and tugged on his headset. Tkachenko relaxed as best he could in the cramped interior, hunkering against a shelf of radios. It was up to the younger man to deliver them to the crossing site. Tkachenko figured there was nothing he could do to protect them from bad luck or to deflect an enemy round. Content, he sat and waited.

Once before, he had thought that he was to have an opportunity to put his skills to practical use. He had been selected for a posting as an adviser to the Angolans. The assignment had brought him the greatest disillusionment of his life. He had hated the Angolans. They were greedy and subhuman to him. Filthy. Inhuman to each other. And the Cubans, in their clever, degenerate way, had been worse. None of them had even once shown the appropriate level of respect for the Soviet Union or for Soviet officers. It was all lip service, meaningless agreement, and lies. He had spent most of his tour drinking Western liquor and building barracks and bridges to house and carry the future of the developing world. He had even gone into combat once, when the situation in the south had deteriorated to the point that the Soviets themselves had been required to stabilize the front. Yet how could you call those worthless grasslands or the deadly junglelike forests a front? It was a place where men scarcely dignified by ragtag uniforms murdered each other in horrible ways, torturing prisoners gleefully, like children tormenting small animals just to hear them scream. It wasn't even really a matter of interrogation. They flayed men alive. Or cut them up a piece at a time. And there were no particular efforts to spare the women. They were all counterrevolutionaries, of course. Africa, Tkachenko thought, with the same sort of disgust another man might feel at the word syphilis. It was a pit of disease, bad water, and poisonous creatures, all wrong for a Russian.

Tkachenko chuckled at a turn in his memories. Wrapped in his headset, eyes fixed to his optics, the younger officer had no sense of the old colonel behind him. Tkachenko remembered that he had had visions of tropical cities in the moonlight, of native women who were somehow clean and cheaply willing, and of serving a worthy cause as well. His illusions had not lasted one week in-country. They had hardly lasted a day.

In an odd way, the cumulative effect of the system of bribery had been even worse than the violence, against which Tkachenko had normally been shielded. It had been a never-ending frustration, and not a matter of little gifts to get your name moved up on the waiting list for a television set like back home. The Angolan officials looked for big bribes before they would allow you to do things for their people. Tkachenko often suspected the Cubans and Angolans of collusion to milk every last drop from the Soviet cow. A Soviet officer could not touch certain Soviet matériel that had been off-loaded at Luanda. A gift from the Soviet people, the matériel had become Angolan property. The Soviets in the military assistance group then had to barter to obtain key supplies in order to accomplish their assigned tasks in support of the Angolans, who controlled the matériel. And the whoring Cubans had been in the middle of it all. Tkachenko had watched the Cubans go to pieces in Angola. Perhaps there had been a few good ones, a few believers. But most of them had exploited the situation to their own advantage in every possible respect. Tkachenko himself had returned from Angola with a bad liver, a persistent skin disease, and a hatred for everything that was not Soviet from west of the Urals, everything that was not Greater Russian. In Luanda, Western businessmen had commanded more respect and courtesy than a Soviet officer. That wasn't socialism. Africa was a swamp of insatiable greed and corruption. The corruption of the spirit and of the flesh. Tkachenko had come home convinced that the Soviet Union had nothing to gain in Africa.

Nearby blasts rocked the vehicle, snapping Tkachenko back to the present. The vehicle turned off the road and bumped across broken ground. Tkachenko gripped at a metal brace, holding on. He told himself again that he was getting too old for this.

The Estonian ripped off his headset and grabbed his helmet.

"We're here."

The bridgehead appeared hopelessly confused at first. A column of tanks had come up too soon, and the big truck-launched bridge sections had to be worked around them. Vehicles backed antitank guns toward temporary positions, and a ditcher bit at the muck, beginning to prepare bridgehead fortifications. Engineers and commandant service troops, whose mission it was to control traffic, waved arms and flags, and another wave of amphibious infantry fighting vehicles skidded down through blasted mud into the water of the canal. The vehicles began swimming awkwardly, struggling to gain control, like limbless ducks. As Tkachenko watched, one vehicle took a chance direct hit, exploding into the water, resurfacing in shreds, then sinking finally beneath the surface, carrying its occupants down with it. Another vehicle hit trouble at the far bank, unable to find enough purchase to haul itself out of the water.

A huge blast clubbed Tkachenko's ears, and he threw himself on the ground. Only the presence of one of the misdirected tanks saved him from the flying debris. Men screamed in agony, or in the fear of agony, and other voices called for medical orderlies.

The Estonian battalion commander shouted orders and waved his arms, reminding Tkachenko of an old joke which insisted that whenever engineers were at a loss, they started waving their arms as though signaling something important.

Tkachenko reset his helmet and scraped the worst of the mud off the front of his uniform with his hands. He headed for the canal on foot, puffing resolutely along. At the edge, he took over the supervision of the first bridging column, irritated by the slowness now and secretly glad to be able to take charge. He even guided individual trucks as they angled back to release their cargoes of pontoons into the water.

Tkachenko didn't mind the splashing. He was already soaked. When the first half dozen bridging sections were floating in the canal, he leapt out onto a bridge deck where engineer troops strained at stabilizing the sections and linking them to one another.

"Down."

Tkachenko fell flat on the bobbing deck as a flight of jets tore overhead. Antiaircraft guns opened fire, and missiles hissed skyward. Then came the blast of the aircraft-delivered ordnance.

"Work," Tkachenko shouted, "unless you want to die right here, you bastards." He seized a tool from one of the clumsier soldiers.

Down along the canal, more entry points underwent preparation, and more and more bridging sections slithered into the water from the backs of their trucks. The battalion commander had already gotten two tactical ferries into operation, and the first tanks crossed the water obstacle on their decks. Tkachenko, studying the engineering plans on the canal, had insisted adamantly that no tanks should attempt snorkeling. The banks were much too steep, and he doubted the tankers could find their points of egress once submerged. He suspected the tankers had been relieved by the recommendation.

Power boats half circled out into the canal. The engineers on the pontoons shoved the long bridge off from the bank with staves, allowing the boats to work in along the side. Shrapnel plunked in the dirty water like especially large raindrops. Tkachenko stood upright on the deck, wiping the broth of sweat and rain from his forehead.

The bridge slowly turned perpendicular to the near bank, buoying out into the waterway, reaching across the canal under the guidance of the power boats. Tkachenko watched more ferry sections maneuvering in the water, readying themselves for heavy cargo. The first ferries headed back to load more tanks.

Half an hour, Tkachenko thought. If they don't counterattack hard with ground forces, with tanks, in half an hour, it'll be too late. They'll never close the bridgehead on us. He listened carefully to the dueling artillery. It sounded as though the Soviet guns dominated the exchange. Attacking the enemy batteries, and throwing a protective curtain of steel down between the bridgehead and the enemy.

The end of the pontoon bridge found the far bank, sending a shock along the deck and through Tkachenko's knees. The ramp slapped into the mud. They were going to need matting, Tkachenko thought. And the guides had to go up. He began shouting again, happy as a child.

Leonid worried about drowning. It seemed absurd to him to be in the middle of a battle, trapped inside a bobbing steel box. The infantry fighting vehicle's propulsion system seemed to have no thrust at all. Leonid felt as though they were trying to cross an ocean. His head ached from the exhaust fumes, and the view out of the troop periscopes along the side of the vehicle only confirmed that the water level was perilously close to the vehicle's deck. More than anything, Leonid just wanted to push open the roof hatch and see the sky.

But he was afraid. Afraid of being punished. Afraid of swamping the vehicle. Afraid of the artillery fire. Driblets and thin trickles of water snaked through the vehicle's seals. And when the gunner fired at some distant, unseen target, the vehicle rocked as though it was bound to capsize.

Leonid prayed. He did not know if he believed in a god or in much of anything. But his mother had never given up her little peasant shrine and her timid, warbling prayers. Leonid clutched his rifle tightly against himself and closed his eyes. He prayed as best he could, trying to imagine what kind of approach you would need to take to convince a neglected god you were really sincere at the moment. It seemed a little like coaxing a solemn, avoided teacher to believe that you had honestly intended to do your homework.

The vehicle thunked against something solid, knocking the crammed soldiers against one another. The engine whined and strained. The spinning of the tracks buzzed through the metal walls.

Suddenly, miraculously, the vehicle found enough traction to surge up onto the bank. The solid, jouncing throb of tracks on gravel seemed like a blessed event without precedent in Leonid's life.

The vehicle leveled out and changed gears, rushing forward. Leonid could hear thundering noises around them now, and the main gun pumped out rounds, filling the poorly vented troop compartment with gases. The broken terrain tossed the soldiers about, smacking them against one another or drawing them toward the sharpest bits of metal in the vehicle's structure. The soldiers complained and cursed one another, but it felt as though their souls were not present in the voices, as though every man had retreated into a private world of anticipation.

The order came to lay down suppressive fire through the firing ports. Leonid twisted around and did as he had been told, glad to have something to do, to occupy his hands. He couldn't see any targets through the clouded periscope, but he quickly emptied magazine after magazine, adding to the acidic stink inside the troop compartment.

The vehicle jerked, almost stopped, then cruised forward slowly.

"Dismount," the squad leader, Junior Sergeant Kassabian, yelled.

The vehicle's rear doors swung open. The soldiers tumbled out in a clumsy imitation of their endlessly repeated drill. Leonid's legs cramped, but he forced them to go. He banged his shoulder in his haste to exit the vehicle, and he stumbled, almost falling over Seryosha, catching a strong vinegar smell on the machine gunner. Seryosha didn't appear to feel the impact, or to be aware of anything at all. He moved like a very fast sleepwalker.

"This way, *this* way."

The air clotted gray and thick, twinkling with quick points of color, like red and yellow holiday lights. The noise engulfed Leonid's body, a physical presence. He ran laterally through the rain, trying to find his position in the dismounted line.

Ali ran by him, screaming unintelligibly, wielding his antitank grenade launcher over his shoulder like a spear.

There were no targets in sight, only a close line—much closer than in the rehearsed battle drills—of Soviet combat vehicles, peppering away into the smoke.

Leonid trotted forward, vaguely conscious of Seryosha off to his left. Seryosha's muscular presence, trotting forward with the machine gun, seemed protective. Leonid shouted as loud as he could, letting the sounds come randomly. He squeezed the trigger on his assault rifle, firing into the vacant grayness ahead of him, frantic to effect something, to gain some sort of control over his fate. He quickly ran out of rounds in the first magazine and slowed to change it.

He dropped the full magazine. As he bent to retrieve it from the mud an infantry fighting vehicle almost ran over him. It seemed to be out of line with the others. But glancing around, Leonid realized he was no longer certain exactly how the line faced. Hot lights teased out of the smoke, then disappeared. All around him, the small-arms fire continued without a discernible focus.

Another vehicle snorted past him. Leonid followed in its wake, mud sucking at his boots. He had no idea where his squad mates had gone so quickly.

He saw his first casualty. A strange Russian boy, pawing at the sky as though reaching for the bottom rungs of a ladder hanging just beyond his reach. The boy strained his arms, calling for his mother through a bloody hole of a mouth, a bloody face under bloody blond hair. The boy gargled the single word, "Mother," over and over again, clawing at the sky and slapping the back of his head in the mud.

Leonid rushed by in horror. He fired his weapon in the general direction of his progress, clearing his own way, hopelessly disoriented.

An infantry fighting vehicle exploded off to the side, shooting brilliant colorations through the murk. Leonid found himself sitting down, baffled by how he had left his feet.

Where was the enemy? He couldn't see anything except running shadows and huge black vehicles that grumbled unexpectedly out of the smoke only to disappear again. If he was going to die . . . if he was going to die . . . he realized he did not even know what country he was in. They had driven so long. Was this still the German Democratic Republic? Or had they counterattacked to the west? Who was winning? How could you ever tell?

A ripple of artillery shells nearly deafened him, their force tearing at his uniform like a brazen girl. He kept his footing and trotted vacantly forward, out of tune with the danger of the exploding rounds. He passed a vividly burning vehicle around which blackened bodies lay. A voice barked in an Asiatic language, and a collection of small arms rattled in the mist.

Leonid discovered a machine gunner lying behind a low mound. For a moment, he lit with hope: Seryosha!

No. It was a stranger. Leonid flopped down beside him anyway, glad for any companionship. He began to fire his weapon in the same direction as the machine gunner.

An officer appeared, shrieking at them for their stupidity. The wild, red-faced captain waved his pistol and ordered them to go forward. Leonid and his companion lifted themselves off the wet grass and moved cautiously in the direction the officer had indicated.

Dead men. Dead men. Uniforms peeled back. Blood and bone and the strewn offal of slaughtered pigs. Vehicle bonfires. And still no sight of the enemy.

Vehicle engines screamed at the side of a hill. Leonid tried to follow the sound. Then he heard tank guns, quite near, easily recognizable to anyone who had ever camped on a training range.

Trees. Leonid headed for the dark trunks, still keeping pace with his anonymous companion, neither of them consciously leading the way. Leonid wanted to get out of the paths of the careening vehicles.

Small-arms fire erupted close by. Leonid stood, out of breath, remaining upright for several seconds before he realized that the muzzle flashes were aimed in his direction. His companion had already dropped behind a log, sweeping the wet woods with his squad machine gun, drawing magazines mechanically from a pouch.

"Over there," he shouted to Leonid. *"In the brush."*

Leonid tried to fire, but he had let his magazine go empty again. He hurried to change it, fingers refusing to behave with any discipline. He could not understand how anyone could tell friend from enemy. Perhaps everyone was simply shooting at everyone else. Leonid fired into the maze of trees.

Light. Heat. Painful noise. Leonid saw the machine gunner's body coming up from the side of his field of vision. The boy rose off the ground as though jolted by electricity, then his body seemed to hover for an instant before coming apart. He was a lifeless ruin as he flopped onto Leonid, covering him with waste.

Leonid screamed. He pushed and slapped at the body, trying to drive it away. He did not want to touch it. Yet he frantically wanted to scour the mess off of himself.

Dark figures bounded through the mist. Leonid pawed at his weapon, hands greased with another man's death. But the figures vanished like phantoms.

Leonid crawled in close behind a pile of weathered stones and matted leaves. Time had gotten out of control; the rhythm was all skewed. From beyond the edge of the trees, he heard a rising shout from many voices, a middle pitch between the high notes of rounds in flight and the bass of armor at war. He struggled to his feet, relieved to find his own body intact. As fast as he could run, he went toward the sounds of battle. He did not think even briefly of rejoining the fight. He simply wanted to be close to other living men.

EIGHT

Lieutenant Colonel Shilko stepped outside of his battalion control post and had a smoke under the tarpaulin. Each time a nearby battery let go a volley, the tarpaulin shivered water onto the ground. The rain had picked up again. It was miserable weather for a war.

Shilko wished he knew what was happening up front, in the direct-fire war. So far, he had received no updates on the situation, only an overload of fire missions. The targets moved deeper and deeper into the enemy's territory, which was a positive sign. On the other hand, his battalion deputy for technical affairs, in the process of trying to locate spare parts, had heard a rumor that the regimental- and divisional-level artillery units positioned closer to the forces in contact were taking severe punishment from enemy counterfire. His uncertainty left Shilko in limbo. Personally, he found the war thus far not much different from a training exercise, except that far more ordnance had been expended and operations had an especially frantic air about them. But no enemy rounds had landed anywhere near his batteries, and the occasional planes overhead merely screamed by on their way to other rendezvous.

The battalion's greatest problems at the moment were a hopeless backlog of missions and a rate of ammunition expenditure already running over twice as high as had been projected. Plenty of ammunition had been dumped on the ground by the guns for the initial fires in support of the plan, but Shilko faced the problem of dealing with a supply system in the division he supported that was totally unused to handling rounds in the appropriate caliber. He did not trust that system to dependably feed his guns once the battlefield really began to move. The system was supposed to push the correct ammunition forward to him from higher-echelon ammunition depots, but Shilko worried that his orphaned battalion might too easily be forgotten.

In order to remind the division rear services and the artillery technical support staff of his existence, Shilko had ordered half of his resupply trucks to dump their cargoes by the guns. Then he had sent the trucks off to draw more ammunition under the guidance of his deputy commander for political affairs. One thing Shilko trusted about the battalion's political officer was the man's ability to play the system within the system to acquire whatever the battalion really needed. If the rear services officer made no progress, the political officer could work through his own counterpart to move the system. If the rounds were anywhere to be had, Shilko knew his requisition would be satisfied—as long as the trucks could make their way on the jammed-up roads.

The difficulty with the lagging missions required a different sort of improvisation. The division's targeteers continued to send Shilko's guns more missions than they could possibly fire, whether the ammunition held out or not. First Romilinsky, the battalion's chief of staff, then Shilko himself had tried to explain the situation to division. But the missions continued to queue. Everyone wanted support from the big long-range guns. Finally, Shilko gave up on formal processes. He had been an artilleryman long enough to recognize what kind of missions were not worth firing after too long a delay, and he quietly took it upon himself to periodically purge the target schedule without notifying anyone outside of the battalion. Shilko always considered himself a conscientious officer. But he also recognized the need to be a practical one.

Shilko tossed the butt of his cigarette into the mud. One thing that he could say now that he was technically a veteran was that war was a noisy business, even by an artilleryman's standards. The earth lay under a constant low thunder. He remembered what he had been doing when he received the alert order. He had been at his desk, working with Romilinsky on the endless paperwork necessary to requisition materials to build a unit smokehouse. The unit's gardening and animal-raising efforts had been going extraordinarily well, and they were endeavors in which Shilko took great pride. In the weeks just before the order to prepare for war, the smokehouse question had seemed like one of the most important matters in the world to him. Now the project appeared trivial to the point of hilarity. Yet there was a part of Shilko that could not quite get used to the idea of being at war even now.

Captain Romilinsky stepped out of the busy vehicle complex and ducked under the tarpaulin with Shilko.

"Comrade Battalion Commander, Davidov's complaining about his ammunition situation again."

Shilko smiled, as much at the company of his chief of staff as at the thought of Davidov's endless entreaties. Shilko did not like to be alone, and he especially liked to be surrounded by his officers. But in the midst of the urgent efforts of his officers and men, he had suddenly experienced a sense of his own futility, a budding suspicion that he had only gone through the motions of his professional life for years, and he had felt the unaccustomed impulse to step outside and stand alone for a bit. Now Romilinsky offered relief from the unwelcome prospect of further solitude.

"Davidov always complains," Shilko said. "He complains until he tires me out and I give him what he wants." Shilko offered Romilinsky a cigarette, then drew another for himself. "But today he'll have to wait like the others." Romilinsky offered a light, and Shilko bent over the younger man's unspoiled staff officer's hands. In comparison, Shilko's hands looked like big knuckles of smoked pork.

"Besides, Davidov's a clever one. He always has more than he admits to having. He knows how to play the system. He'd make a good factory manager, our David Sergeyevitch. Or better yet, a farmer." Shilko chuckled at the thought of his battery commander swearing convincingly to the authorities that they had assigned his state farm totally unreasonable production quotas. "Well," Shilko concluded, "he'll come through. It's just his way."

Romilinsky nodded. He looked tired. They had been waiting or moving or setting up since the afternoon before, and they had all begun the war as tired men. Now, since the fighting had begun, it felt as though every hour counted for three or four in exhausting a man.

"Davidov's right, in a sense," Romilinsky said, temporarily putting aside his rivalry with the other officer. "Matching the number of missions assigned against the allocation of rounds prescribed by the effects norms, you can see that someone isn't thinking very far ahead."

Shilko suspected that Romilinsky was right, that the officers responsible for targeting were so overcome by the excitement of the moment that they were acting more on impulse than rigorous calculation. But he did not want to discourage the younger man, and he settled on a milder response.

"When you think about it," Shilko said, "it appears that the norms to achieve desired effects were developed by artillerymen like us, who wanted to make damned sure that the mission's objective was achieved, while our allocation of units of fire was designed by rear services officers out to make equally certain that we damned artillerymen don't get too carried away with ourselves. It's the way the system has of coming up with a compromise."

"Until now," Romilinsky said, "I always thought the units of fire were rather generous."

Shilko shrugged. "In some ways . . . it's a very generous system. The art lies in knowing when to be satisfied."

To Shilko, his chief of staff, standing unshaven and with dark circles ringing the moving targets of his eyes, looked exactly as an artillery officer should look. Shilko realized that he himself was far from the dashing type. But

Romilinsky looked quietly heroic to him. Shilko was proud of the younger man, and he liked him. He liked all of his officers, although it was easier to feel affection for some than for others. They were good boys, his gunners. Russian gunners had outshot the cannoneers of Frederick the Great. Why not the Bundeswehr as well?

Another volley tore into the sky, and thin smoke rose over the treeline a few hundred meters away.

"How would you like to be on the other end of that?" Shilko asked. The power of the guns continued to amaze him, even after twenty-odd years and long-ruined eardrums.

Romilinsky had positioned himself poorly, and the cascade of water from the tarpaulin caught him between the collar and his neck. He jumped as though touched by fire.

"Direct hit," Shilko said, grinning.

A lieutenant thrust his face out of the control post. "Comrade Battalion Commander. Orders. Our forces are across the Elbe-Seiten canal, and we're to prepare to displace."

"Now?" Shilko said, thinking of the rounds piled on the ground and of his trucks that had not yet returned.

"We're to be prepared for movement within two hours."

Shilko relaxed. Two hours was a long time. "Have they assigned us new fire positions?"

The lieutenant shook his head. "Division says things are moving very fast. Fire positions will be designated when we receive the order to execute movement."

"All right," Shilko said. According to the manuals, his batteries already should have displaced several times to avoid discovery by the enemy. But there was no place to go on the overcrowded terrain. "Good. Vassili Rodionovitch, call down to the batteries and tell them we're going to fire everything we can't lift." He looked back at the lieutenant. "Son, get me the current gift list, and we'll see what presents we can send the enemy."

The lieutenant pulled his head back into the tentage like a turtle returning to its shell.

"Standard movement drill?" Romilinsky asked.

"No," Shilko said, suddenly adamant, thinking of the possibility of losing control of his battalion on the hectic roads. It was as bitter as the thought of abandoning his children. "The rules are off, Vassili Rodionovitch. We'll all move together. Or we won't see our batteries again until the war's over."

"But if we receive interim missions? And no one's in position to fire?"

"We can always say we ran out of ammunition," Shilko said, determined to maintain control of his unit, and delighted at the prospect of engrossing activities that would, at least temporarily, drown his self-doubts.

Another huge ripple of fire punched the sky. This time, the spillage off the tarpaulin caught Shilko. The water was cold and unwelcome. But Shilko shrugged it off.

"Direct hit," he said.

Major General Khrenov's divisional forward command post had been hastily composed around a liberated country inn. In the parking lot, communications vans hid half-heartedly under sagging camouflage nets, and command vehicles lurked under dripping trees. Windows had been smashed out of the building to admit cables, and handyman soldiers spliced and taped and carried boxes of staff clutter up the steps to the building's main entrance. Bad-tempered warrant officers supervised the physical activities, monitored, in turn, by staff officers who occasionally ventured out into the damp air to find out why everything was taking so long.

The scene was instantly familiar to Trimenko, and he didn't like it. This was a souring conclusion to the elation of seeing his army on the march from the vantage point of the helicopter. He wanted Khrenov on the move, not setting himself up to hold court. But the army commander decided to hear what the division commander had to say before letting the hammer fall.

"Comrade Army Commander," Khrenov greeted him, smiling, clearly quite pleased with himself, "I hope you had a good flight."

Trimenko made a noise at the back of his throat, noncommittal. He strode beside Khrenov from the meadow that served as a helipad to the building. The rain-rinsed air felt unseasonably cold.

"Comrade Army Commander," Khrenov tried again, "you no doubt have been informed that we have secured our bridgehead, and that we are expanding it at this time. It's a solid bridgehead. We already have forward detachments out."

Trimenko had not known. The information must have missed him in flight. What in the world was Tkachenko, his chief of engineers, doing? He was supposed to keep his army commander informed on the crossing situation. Trimenko wondered what else had happened of which he was unaware, what other events had occurred in the army's sector of which his staff had failed to properly inform him. He had only known that a forward element had seized a good crossing site in the vicinity of Bad Bevensen almost by accident and that Khrenov's crossing operation was underway. But this was rapid success, if Khrenov was accurately reporting his situation.

"I need the details, not generalities, Khrenov," Trimenko said, as though none of the division commander's revelations had surprised him.

Their boots slapped up the cement steps. Inside, staff maps and remote communications gear had been set up in a public dining room. The appointments were far too comfortable for Trimenko's image of a division's forward command post in wartime.

"You're carrying a lot of your staff forward with you, Khrenov," he said.

Khrenov looked at him in mild surprise. "The bastards hit my main command post with a fire strike. Around noon. I thought you knew. Over fifty percent destruction. I'm running everything but rear services and traffic control from here until we get the alternate running hot."

Trimenko was furious now, although he carefully held his temper inside the mental box he had fashioned for it over the years. He realized that so much was happening so swiftly that it was impossible to know it all. But his staff had the mission of sorting out those details that were truly vital and keeping the army commander informed. These gaps in his knowledge only convinced him more fully of the inability of average men to cope under the conditions of modern war. The machine was superior to the man.

"I'm sorry, Khrenov. I didn't know that." For a moment, Trimenko framed the problem in terms of the officers lost, undoubtedly some very good men. But he quickly rejected any sentimentality. "The important thing is not to lose control now. We must keep close control of the troops. Confusion is the enemy now. Confusion and time."

Khrenov nodded. "Comrade Army Commander, if you'll have a seat at the map, I'll brief you myself."

Really pleased with himself, Trimenko thought. Otherwise, he'd have one of his staff officers brief me. Trimenko took a seat beside a table, fronting on a map that had been unfolded and tacked to the wall. A staff officer slipped a packet of looted cigarettes, matches, and a cup of tea onto the table, then nimbly disappeared. Trimenko ignored the little gifts, reaching into his tunic pocket for his tobacco pouch of pistachio nuts. He scattered a few on the tabletop and told Khrenov to go ahead.

"The overall situation in the sector of the Twenty-first Motorized Rifle Division is quite favorable at this time. We have firmly established a divisional bridgehead . . . here . . . following a successful assault crossing against the canal line. At this time, forward elements have penetrated the line of Highway 4, and the division's right flank regiment, following a tactical turning maneuver north from the bridgehead, is fighting on the southern outskirts of Uelzen."

"Don't get bogged down in a city fight," Trimenko interrupted. "Just get the roads. Let the follow-on forces deal with any pockets. Don't divert any more forces to deal with them than absolutely necessary to provide security."

"Comrade Army Commander, our only interest is in securing the Highway 71 axis. Our forces are only engaged in the Uelzen area to firmly establish control of the local road network. A forward detachment detailed from that regiment has already passed into the enemy's rear, and its last reported location puts it in light contact eighteen kilometers west of Uelzen along the supporting network corollary to Highway 71 in the Soltau-Verden direction. The division's mission of the day should be accomplished within one to two hours."

The reported locations were almost stunning to Trimenko. But he adamantly refused to show it in his facial expression. He slowly peeled another nut, slipped it between his lips, and stared at the map. Khrenov had reason to be pleased with himself. This was splendid. The enemy had lost control in the sector. Now it was time to hit them even harder.

"Are you in contact with the Two Hundred and Seventh Division on your southern flank?"

Khrenov's face fell. "Yes, Comrade Army Commander. Dalyev reports that both of his initial crossing attempts have failed. The Germans . . . appear to be giving him a bad time."

Trimenko nodded. "Dalyev's got a lot of frontage. Too much to expect real results. He's paying the price for you to succeed in your own little area, Khrenov."

Khrenov bent forward, as though Trimenko had dropped a physical weight onto his shoulders. It was evident that the division commander was anxious to turn the briefing back to his own successes.

"I don't mind so much," Trimenko said. "Somebody always has to pay the price. I just want Dalyev to keep the Germans so busy up front that they miss what's happening on their flanks. I *want* the Germans to perceive success. But I want to keep enough pressure on them so that they worry, too. So that they stay put. Dalyev's taken severe losses, Khrenov. While your forward detachment's heading for Soltau, perhaps even the Weser itself, waving at the girls and singing the 'Internationale,' no doubt. But let me pose a problem for you. Suppose Dalyev can't keep the Germans occupied long enough. We've already had reports of German antitank helicopters working the Dutch sector, trying to brace up the front. Really, it's only a matter of time until they hit you with a brigade, maybe more. How are you going to hold the southern shoulder of the penetration?"

"Comrade Army Commander, defensive positions are being prepared at the bridgehead itself. Otherwise, in a fluid, breakthrough situation, I must be prepared to accept open flanks . . . to a degree . . ."

"Oh, don't recite your academy notes to me, Khrenov. Neither do I want you to slow down. If anything, I think you're lagging a bit just now," Trimenko lied. "But you do need to get your antitank battalion and some mobile obstacle detachments up. And detail an armored reserve. Start your antitank defenses somewhere around that wishbone on Highway 4. Right about there, oriented to the south. And keep laying them in as fast as you can while you move west. Be generous with the antitank mines."

"Comrade Army Commander, I don't have the routes. Not yet. You must have seen what the roads are like. I've loaded my assault forces forward, the bridgehead's packed, and everybody's screaming for more ammunition. In any case, one antitank battalion can't cover even the flank we've got now, and I need them on the bridgehead. I can't even get my casualties out," Khrenov said, in his bitterest tone of the day, "and they're heavy."

Trimenko dropped a flame-shaped pistachio back onto the table and waved his hand. "And you'll have worse difficulties yet. The war has hardly begun. I'm giving you a full antitank regiment. And an additional battalion of engineers to tuck them in and lay minefields along your flank. But getting them here is your problem."

Khrenov caught the signal. He was doing well. He was being reinforced. The army commander counted his efforts a solid success.

"Now tell me," Trimenko continued, "about support issues. What are the real problems?"

Khrenov sighed. It was almost a womanish gesture. In the background, plates rattled. Soldiers fooling around in the kitchen, eating when they needed to be working. Trimenko let it pass for the moment.

"Comrade Army Commander," Khrenov began. It was almost a litany, the way he said it, and it annoyed Trimenko. "I have too many reports of excessive tank main gun and artillery ammunition consumption to ignore. If it were one unit, or two, I'd assume they were overreacting, or just getting greedy, trying to stock up. But I have several reports of tanks shooting up their entire on-board units of fire in their first engagements. And the artillery is loaded down with calls for fire. It was all right as long as we were on the phased fire plan, but now, even with the battle-management computers, we can't really tell exactly who is in firing position or who's still on the road, who's low on ammunition or who's just sitting around with his elbow up his ass. My chief of missile troops and artillery is out on the ground trying to sort it out personally."

Trimenko thought for a moment.

"But no fuel problems?" he asked.

Khrenov shook his head. "Not a whisper."

"Of course not," Trimenko said. "But get me better details on the ammunition problems. Not just generalities. Numbers. And burn this into your brain, Khrenov. I don't want any unit stopping just because it runs out of ammunition. They can just go on a sightseeing ride to the Rhine. We're on the edge of cracking those bastards now. You can feel it, Khrenov. The battlefield's gotten away from them. And a tank with nothing but a few belts of machine-gun ammunition is still a tremendous weapon if it's deep in the enemy's rear." Trimenko sat back and smiled one of his thin, rare smiles. "Think of it. If you were a fat rear-area soldier and you woke up to find enemy tanks all over your comfortable little domain, would you stop to ask yourself whether or not they had ammunition on board?" Trimenko tossed a shell toward the map. Then he locked his facial muscles once again.

"Make sure you maintain good communications with Malyshev as he comes up. Cooperate, and no nonsense. I want his division's tanks across the autobahn tonight. I expect you to ensure personally that all control measures for his forward passage have been worked out and fully agreed upon. There must be no pauses, no letting up. Hit them, Khrenov. Get them down on their backs, and drive your tanks and fighting vehicles right over them." Trimenko paused at the power of his mental vision. "Let me know when the first vehicle crosses the autobahn line. That triggers the deep air assaults on the Weser crossing sites." Trimenko stared at Khrenov, measuring this man who had already accomplished so much this day. "You have the opportunity to do great things, my little major general. Great things. But first you need to stop building yourself a headquarters palace here. I find this sort of indulgence totally inappropriate. Commanders should be farther forward. I can hardly hear the guns from here," Trimenko exaggerated. "You need to get moving, Khrenov."

"What's your hurry, you little bastard? You're going the wrong way, anyway. You think this is a retreat?"

In response, Captain of Transport Troops Belinsky looked up fiercely at the tall major of motorized rifle troops. Around them, their vehicles—Belinsky's cargo trucks and the major's battalion of combat vehicles—had intermingled with smashed headlamps, shouts, curses, and confusion. No traffic controllers had been posted at the intersection. Now the combat troops were in a self-righteous rage, furious that a lowly transport unit had muddled their progress.

"First of all, Comrade Major," Belinsky said calmly, "you're on a support route. This is not a combat artery."

"You're the one who's on the wrong road, you snot. Now you can get those trucks off out of my way, or I'll drive right over them."

"Major, this is my road, and I'm carrying important cargo."

"To the *rear?*" The tall major laughed. He pawed his foot at the ground like a prancing stallion, head thrown back in mocking hilarity.

Belinsky glowered up into the other man's eyes. Bully's eyes, beneath a dripping helmet rim. Belinsky was already unhappy with his unexpected mission, but he was determined to carry it out.

"Come with me, Comrade Major. Just for a moment. You need to have a look at my cargo." And he turned his back on the man, drawing the motorized rifle officer along behind him by the magnetism of his insolence.

The major followed Belinsky down the crumbling, rain-slicked road, cursing as though the outcome of the war depended on his vulgarity. Belinsky casually slipped off his glasses and dropped them into the pocket of his tunic. He felt no need to inspect his cargo in detail yet again.

The tall major did not even have to stretch to see into the bed of the first cargo truck. As Belinsky drew back the tarpaulin, admitting the smoky daylight, the sounds of raw human misery greeted the two officers. Belinsky watched the major's face change expression. And it kept changing, unable to settle on an appropriate mask.

Abruptly, the major slapped down the canvas and stalked off. Belinsky hurried along beside him. "This motorized rifle battalion," Belinsky said coldly, "is *returning* from the front, Comrade Major. The complement of ambulances was a bit short, as were the stretchers."

But the major wasn't listening. He simply shouted orders in multiple directions, telling his men to edge to the side of the road and let the damned trucks pass.

NINE

Guards Colonel Anton Mikhailovitch Malinsky sat in his command car, eyes lowered to his map, thinking about Chopin. His fingers tapped and touched delicately at the milky plastic map bag, forming chords and absentminded arpeggios across the routes and rivers, cities and towns of central Germany. Remembering a favorite passage, a quick flourish into melody, he closed his eyes, the better to hear the vibrating strings and wires of memory. He loved Chopin. Perhaps, he thought to himself, it was the Polish blood that had poured heatedly into the Malinsky lines back in the days of hussars with ornamental wings rising from their armored backs.

Anton regretted the war, although his formation had not even been introduced into combat as yet. He regretted his spectacular rise to the command of a premier maneuver brigade at a jealousy-inspiring age. He regretted all of the things his father had never been able to see clearly. The old man made such a fuss about accepting no patronage for Malinskys. Yet, Anton thought, were it not for his position, it's unlikely I would be more than a middling major. Were it not for the name, the name and its iron burden of traditions, I would hardly be a soldier. Colonel of the Guards. Guards colonel. It sounded marvelously romantic, the stuff of operettas and oversized epaulets. Strauss might have had a grand time with such a character. Or Lehar. Better yet, a more common touch. Romberg. Well, you could not dismiss light music so easily. There was a need for more lightness in the world.

Anton peered out at the grim German sky beyond the camouflage net. He was alone now, his officers attending to their endless chores. He had sent his driver splashing off through the mud in search of something warm to drink. His driver was a good boy, not really cut out to be a soldier either. Quite frightened of the great, brooding colonel, son of one of the most powerful officers in the Soviet military establishment. Anton remembered how the sickly colored mud had grabbed the boy's ill-fitting boots. A lean Russian boy in a dismal training area in the Germanies, waiting for orders. Waiting for orders like all of them.

Anton had heard that the war was going very fast up front, even faster than the plan had called for in some sectors. The combination of modern killing technologies and the barely controllable mobility of contemporary armored vehicles and aircraft had torn the orderliness of situation maps apart with a rapidity alarming even to the side enjoying success. Anton remembered the baffled faces at the corps briefing he had attended earlier in the afternoon. Everyone had expected a tougher initial fight. But the fairy-tale endings of countless dreary exercises had suddenly come true. Even the careful Tartar eyes of Anseev, the corps commander, had revealed an odd disorientation, unsettled by the velocity of events.

In his heart, Anton felt that the war could not go too slowly for him. He recalled the detritus of enemy bombings on the approaches to the Elbe River crossing site north of Magdeburg. The long lines of burned-out trucks and the hapless rows of burned bodies had not even made it into the war in the traditional sense. Hours away from the border and the stew of combat, death had come without warning. If war had ever had any glamour, Anton thought, it was surely gone now. *If* war had ever had any glamour. Now complex, inhuman systems flew overhead, or perhaps just somewhere in the middle distance, beyond the reach of the human eye, and computers told the machines what to do and when to do it, and the earth erupted with hellfire. Anton had counted thirty-seven wrecks in one area, over fifty in another. The crossing sites themselves were little more than vehicle graveyards, the riverbanks blackened. His brigade had lost several vehicles during the Elbe River crossing, including precious air-defense systems. Now the survivors sat hidden in an assembly area in the Letzlinger Heide, topped off with fuel, organized into combat march serials, ready to move on the last, most difficult leg of their journey into battle. The corps commander projected a resumption of the march within twelve to eighteen hours, and a rapid movement to commitment, with no scheduled rest stops or halts at provision points. When the vehicles moved again, their destination would be combat.

As soon as the Guards colonel told them to move. As soon as the corps commander told the Guards colonel. As soon as the front commander gave the word to the corps commander.

Anton thought helplessly of his father. He truly loved the old man. And admired him. Of course, it was easy to admire Army General Malinsky, Commander of the First Western Front. But Anton wondered how many other men truly loved him. His father had always seemed enormous and heroic to him. And blind, as heroes had to be in the social architecture of the Soviet system. Anton was convinced that his father was scrupulously, almost absurdly honest. The old man meant it when he said he wanted no special treatment for his son. But the system was not equipped to handle such requests. Anton knew well that he would have had to commit a string of outrageous public follies even to slow his career. Malinsky's son. Promote him. And get him out of here.

Even if he had it all to do over again, Anton doubted he

would follow his own desires. The old man was too big, too grand to be resisted. And disarmingly demanding, in his aristocratic way. He had never threatened or bullied Anton into becoming an officer. He had just assumed it would be so with such unshakable conviction that Anton had found himself powerless to resist.

Zena wanted him to quit. She wanted him to find his own life. It was far too late now, of course, to think seriously about becoming a concert pianist. Too many years had gone by. His fingers had stiffened around too much military hardware. But, she pointed out, he could perhaps become a professor of music, and a critic. He had a good name, and the good names were back in fashion at last, a new novelty for the privileged elite. And then they could be together always.

Zena.

She was a fine, loving, exuberant chaos of a woman, absolutely inappropriate for the role of an officer's wife. She could never remember the ranks of the other wives' husbands; she was only half-aware that Anton wore a rank himself. If Zena liked her, a lieutenant's child bride was as good as a marshal's dowager. And naturally, since she was married to a Malinsky, the wives from the upper echelons assumed that Zena purposely snubbed them. Zena was an open, honest, naïve, hated woman who danced jauntily through it all, never fully aware of the nastiness behind the smiles, singing her little Beatles' songs learned from Western tapes. He played Scriabin, and she listened, curled up like a cat on an old peasant stove. But left to her own devices, she buoyed in and out of rooms, delighted and frenetic with life, singing in her phonetically memorized English, "Honey Pie, you are making me cra-a-zy . . ."

Tears came to his eyes as he pictured her, straight red hair draping a white throat made for jewels. Jeans and jewels. Zena. He touched his eyes, dreading discovery, and a queasiness that had been nipping at his stomach for the last few hours twisted in him again. He hoped he was not getting sick, even as the beginning of illness soured his mood still further.

He felt now that his entire life had been a masquerade. The brooding, serious officer. It had been all right as long as there wasn't a real war. He had not even had to go to Afghanistan. Instead, he had been shipped off to Cuba, under the protection of General Starukhin, the senior Soviet military representative in Havana. Starukhin was an abusive drunkard, clever and talented enough to survive, and indebted to Anton's father. He had treated Anton carefully. And Cuba had been a good assignment. Anton had run the motorized rifle troops and several special training programs. But life had been slower in the tropics, and there had always been a little time to live, and he had even been able to take Zena with him. The Cubans had had no interest in socializing with Russians beyond the requirements of official functions. But he and Zena had lived in a world all their own, going down to the beach together when a bit of free time could be scavenged, or spending a rare weekend in Havana, in the splendid, run-down aftermath of decadence. "What fine little capitalists we might have made, darling," Zena had teased him. "Wicked rum and the stars on the water, a casino perhaps, and my Anton in that dreaded capitalist uniform, a dinner jacket."

Now he was here, in Germany, in the mud, and everything was painfully real. The war was real. And he did not know if he could accomplish his assigned tasks, if he could really be his father's son. He knew all of the phrases and the drills, all of the wisdom of the classroom and the training range. But would he be able to lead men into battle? Would he be able to manage the complexity? Would he be able to do it right when it really mattered? In his heart, he doubted his adequacy.

Perhaps the hard men of the Revolution had been correct. Perhaps the old families were no more than parasites. Useless. Perhaps the Bolsheviks should not have stopped until they had purged every last man, woman, and child.

Anton thought of his father again, and the theory fell apart. His father would pay the Soviets in full for what little they had given him; he would overpay them. But he was not a Soviet man, no matter what he said and no matter what they said. His wonderful Russian father, as great as the low hills and the endless steppes. As great as summer and winter. Anton smiled. Surely, the old man was in his glory now, as strong as his son was weak. Perhaps this time the plaudits would outstrip those gained at the gates of Plevna. Or the entry into Paris.

Yes. Paris. And Zena. One of their many fantastic dreams. But he had pictured it all a bit differently than this.

His driver came around the trees, plopping through the mud, struggling to balance two steaming cups. Tea. And Chopin. And Zena.

Anton shook his head in wordless sorrow.

"Flight Leader, I have you on my screen. You are cleared for auxiliary runway number two. Don't screw around. We have more hostiles on the way."

"This is Zero-Five-Eight. Roger. Auxiliary number two. Coming straight in."

"Watch for the smoke, Flight Leader. We have burning fuel."

"With me, Fifty-nine?" Sobelev called to his wingman.

"Roger, Fifty-eight."

"You're in first. Number two's longer than it looks, but it comes up suddenly behind the trees. Don't flare early. You'll be just fine."

But Sobelev himself was unprepared for the sight of the airfield. Fuel fires raged, and black smoke rose thickly against the gray sky. Vehicles with warning lights ran along the apron, and planes lifted through what appeared to be great hoops of fire. From several kilometers out, the litter NATO raids had left behind challenged the pilot's confidence.

"Flight Leader, this is Control. I have you visual."

"I'm rolling out. My wingman's coming in first."

"Roger. Do you need assistance on the ground?"

"Negative. Not unless we bugger it up."

"Your runway."

The lieutenant, Sobelev's wingman, took his aircraft in cleanly. Sobelev remained surprised that they had made it this far, that they were still alive. For at least one more mission. He came around and followed his wingman in, bouncing on the runway.

"Talk to me, Control. Where am I going?"

"Proceed onto taxiway four. Move out. Hard hangars, crescent B."

"Numbers?"

"Just take the first open bay. This is war, my distinguished Comrade Aviator."

Sobelev guided his plane through the trailing smoke and the wreckage of planes that had been caught on the ground. It struck him that all of this was an incredible waste, but now that he was on the ground, he realized that the focus of his life was to get to a latrine.

Sobelev's legs quivered as he stood on the concrete of the hangar floor, and his thighs felt spongy as he walked to the tunnel and collected his wingman. After a latrine stop, they reported to the mission room, deep underground. Muffled blasts sounded through the layers of earth, steel, and concrete. The enemy aircraft had returned.

As Sobelev and his wingman entered the mission room, the occupants went silent, and each face turned to see who had made it back. Several men offered greetings, but their voices were hollow with the knowledge that their survival might only be a temporary affair. Sobelev drew himself a cup of dark, steaming tea from the samovar. Conversations resumed, but the mood was serious, almost somber, unlike the swaggering tone of peacetime exercises. Now there was no question about who had passed and who had failed. Sobelev took a chair, listening to the patchwork dialogues of the other men and trying to calm his insides. His lieutenant took a seat close by, as though they were still in the air and he still required shepherding. There was one basic subject to which all of the talk returned.

"Sasha's down over Guetersloh. I couldn't see a chute."

"It's hard to see anything in this weather."

"Has anybody seen Profirov?"

"Profirov went deep."

"Vasaryan got clean, though. Good canopy opening."

"He'll come out all right. Luck of the Armenians."

"Couldn't even see what was shooting at us. The visibility was some of the worst I've ever flown in."

"And this forward air controller was absolutely worthless. Couldn't locate the enemy, couldn't get a fix on me . . ."

Sobelev began to grow conscious of less dramatic physical sensations now. His flight suit felt greasy and cold on his skin, stinking with the sweat of fear. The strong tea burned his empty stomach.

"How many more sorties do you think we'll run today?"

"They're not going to try to do this at night, are they? With these planes? In this weather?"

"Is there anything to eat around here? Any biscuits?"

The entrance of a staff officer interrupted the pilots' conversations. The outsider strode to the blackboard, positioned himself for authority, and began to call names. Several times, the selected names met no response, and Sobelev realized that the staff did not have a firm grasp on which pilots were available at this point.

At the end of the grim roll call, Sobelev, his wingman, and six other pilots were ordered to report to a special top-security briefing room. The major could not tell them anything about their mission, only that their aircraft were being prepared with the correct ordnance packages.

Sobelev led the way down the grimy corridor. He was seriously worried about his ability to keep going without making deadly mistakes. He could accept the fact that the enemy might get him even if he performed perfectly. But he did not want to die because of an error.

He looked at his wingman. The boy looked as though he had been sick for a week. "Feeling all right?"

The lieutenant nodded. "Was it ever this bad in Afghanistan?"

"Not even remotely. No comparison."

They rang a bell for admittance at the oversized steel door. The special facility was identified only with a number. A lieutenant colonel from the intelligence services opened the door slightly, looked them over, then allowed them inside. Maps and aerial photographs, some of which were impressive blowups, covered the walls of the briefing chamber.

"Sit down, Comrades. I must ask you to remain in this room and only this room. If any of you need to visit the latrine, you'll have to go back outside. This complex is restricted to intelligence personnel only. Now, can I offer you some tea?"

The pilots declined as a group.

"Well," the briefer began, "you're all in luck." He glanced from face to face, an eager lieutenant colonel, conditioned to the paper reality of staff work. "This ought to be the easiest mission anyone's had all day." He turned to the map with his pointer. "This is the city of Lueneburg. Actually, more of a large town. The photos on the walls show the air approaches to the heart of the old town and various key features, such as the town square, the town hall, and so forth. Your mission consists of the destruction by aerial means of certain physical structures within the town. Each of the photographs on the far wall shows a specific target. They're very clearly identified, as you can see. There are three targets, or target groups. Two planes to a target. The last pair of aircraft—let's see, that would be . . . Bronchuk and Ignatov—will take pictures."

"Just a moment," one pilot said. "What's the military value of the target?"

The lieutenant colonel appeared surprised at the question. "The target," he said, "is just the town itself. Don't worry, we assess a minimal air defense threat in sector. You'll be safe. Our own troops are already in the vicinity."

"But what's the military purpose? The enemy's bombing the hell out of our air bases, and we're attacking little towns nobody's ever heard of?"

The staff officer's last hesitant smile disappeared. The exchange was underscored by a series of blasts thudding dully up on the surface.

"You will do as you're told," the briefer said. "There is no time—or allowance—for argument. You will all do exactly as you're told."

Kryshinin lay on the canvas litter, waiting for the ambulance to begin moving again. He felt inexplicably weak now, tired beyond reason. He kept his eyes closed because it was so much easier. He could not understand why his wound did not hurt any worse. There was only a dull discomfort, an unwillingness on the part of his torso to move. He felt lightheaded, and he was no longer sure that he was conscious without interruption. Over and over again, the scenes of battle played back in his head, and he was vaguely aware of calling instructions, trying to warn his men. Bylov, the air controller, sat on the roof, and the world was in flames, and Bylov was eating his lunch as though unaware of the violence and waste around him.

"Vera," Kryshinin said. "Vera, I have to explain." He could not understand where Vera had gone. Only a moment ago, his wife had been beside him. Now he could not remember where she had gone.

His immediate surroundings returned. The grimy interior of a battlefield ambulance, waiting, sickening with exhaust fumes and the smells of ruined bodies. Two medical orderlies chatted with each other between the packed litters.

"This one's gone."

"Can't be helped. Nothing to do. If they want to hold us up for everybody in the army to get past, we'll lose them all. None of our doing."

"Have a look. See if it's still tanks going by."

"You have a look if you want. I can tell by the sound that it's tanks."

"You're closer to the door."

They were stuck in a minefield, Kryshinin realized. They needed someone to lead them. He wanted to explain to them how it could be done, but they wouldn't wait for him. He struggled to speak, muttering, but unable to get the words out in order.

"This one looks bad. He needs a transfusion quick," an orderly said. "He's white as snow."

"Unless piss works, he's out of luck."

Kryshinin suddenly realized that they were talking about him. And he wanted to reply. But he did not know what to say, or how to say it now. And it seemed as though it would take an absurd, unreasonable amount of energy to speak.

"Well, to hell with them, anyway. At least they're officers and they get to die in an ambulance."

Vera. He knew he had seen her. She had been there a moment before, wearing her green dress that was growing a bit too tight. No. *No. Grip reality.* Vera is far away. Hold on to the actual. Don't let go . . . . But it was all so difficult.

He had not thought of Vera once during the battle. Perhaps that was a sign of how far apart they had grown. Nothing had worked out as planned. Nothing ever quite worked between them. They fought over trivial things, and he knew he drank too much at the officers' canteen, but he did it anyway. And Vera carried her resentment in silence until it suddenly exploded into vicious, public anger, for all of the families in the officers' quarters to hear.

But it could all be mended. Kryshinin felt the warmth of conviction. If only he could see her now, it could all be put right. It was all foolishness. And they must have children. When he found out that Vera had had two abortions without telling him, he had beaten her so badly that she could not go outside for almost two weeks. *Two* abortions. As if she wanted to kill every part of him that could have gotten inside of her.

"Get away from the window," Kryshinin shouted. "Get back."

But the lieutenant failed to obey the command. He reached to catch an object hurtling through the air, and he burst apart as though his body were the climax of a fireworks display.

"I need support, can you hear me? *I need support.* We can't hold. They're all over us. *Please.*"

Vera surrounded by clouds of black smoke.

"Sounds as if this one had an interesting day," one of the orderlies said in amusement.

"It just gets on your nerves after a while," the other replied.

Halfway between the improvised helipad and the concealed forward command post of the Third Shock Army, the range car carrying Lieutenant General Starukhin down the muddy trail backfired once, shook, and sank to a stop. The sudden absence of mechanical noise startled the general. The world seemed to stop inside the big perceived silence, despite the vigor of the rain and the dull, distant sound of the war like a hangover in the ears. Each rustle of uniforms and wet leather straps seemed amplified, and the sour smell of tired men in damp uniforms grew unaccountably sharper.

Overcoming his initial bewilderment and horror, the junior sergeant behind the steering wheel clumsily tried to restart the vehicle, but the engine would not come to life. Instead of waiting for the dispatch of his own vehicle from the headquarters, Starukhin had hurriedly commandeered the immediately available range car, unwilling to lose the extra ten or fifteen minutes. Now he sat heavily in the little vehicle, with no means of communication, still several kilometers from his command post, mocked by the barrage of rain on the canvas roof.

The young driver carefully avoided looking around, fixing his eyes on the dashboard as though his stare might bully the machine back to life. The two aides accompanying Starukhin remained carefully silent. Starukhin listened to the boy's fumbling for as long as he could bear it, then shouted:

"You can't *coax* it to start, you drizzle ass. Get out and look at the engine."

The boy shot out of the vehicle, banging against the door frame with bruising haste. Beyond the rain-smeared windshield, Starukhin could see him fumbling with the engine cover. In the blurred background, the rain seemed to have scoured all of the color out of the sky and landscape.

"And *you* two," Starukhin bellowed, turning on his aides. "Get out there and help him. What's the matter with you jackasses?"

The aides moved with the panic of men caught in a terrible crime. One of them, a lieutenant colonel, jostled wildly against Starukhin in his anxiety, and the army commander gave him a hard shove toward the door. Soon the two aides stood glum-faced beside the driver in the steady rain.

They were hopeless. All of them. Starukhin sat back, squaring his shoulders, convinced that he had to carry the entire army on his back. All of his life, he thought, he had had to drive his will head-on into the ponderous complacency characteristic of the system into which he had been born. Every day was a struggle. When something broke, those responsible would sheepishly sit down and wait to be told to fix it. Then they would take their own good time about the task. Unless you drove them. And Starukhin had learned how to drive men. But now, during the great test of his lifetime, he feared his inability to move the men under his command.

More than anything, he feared failure. He feared it because he believed it would reveal some secret incompetence hidden within him. Deep within his soul, where no other human being had ever been allowed to penetrate, Starukhin doubted himself, and nothing seemed more important to him than the preservation of his pride.

The damned whoring British would not break. It seemed incredible to him that he could not simply will his way through them, hammering them to nothing with his personal determination and the tank-heavy army under his command. He drifted back and forth between his bobbing doubts and waves of immeasurable energy. Now, as he envisioned the defending British, he sensed that it would be impossible for them to resist.

Yet the British were resisting, fighting bitterly for every road and water obstacle, seemingly for every worthless little village and godforsaken hill. While to the north, that bastard Trimenko was breaking through. Starukhin knew that Trimenko's Second Guards Tank Army was already ahead of schedule, splitting the seam between the Germans and the Dutch. While he, Starukhin, had to butt head-on against the British.

That little Jewish shit Chibisov undoubtedly had a hand in it, Starukhin was convinced. He stared through the mud-speckled windshield at the soaking trio bent over the vehicle's engine, feeling a strange pleasure at the thought of Chibisov. The hatred he felt was so intense, so pure and unexamined, that it was soothing. After the war . . . the Chibisovs would be made to pay. The Motherland had to be purged yet again. It was time to settle accounts with the Jews and the Jew-loving writers, with the leeching minorities and false reformers. In the wordless clarity of the moment,

Chibisov embodied everything foul in the Soviet Union, all responsibility for the failures of Starukhin's own kind. And yet Starukhin recognized that he hated Chibisov not merely for his Jewishness, but for his easy, controlled brilliance as well. Everything came too easily to Chibisov. Malinsky's staff Jew could perform offhandedly tasks that confronted Starukhin with agony and consternation.

Surely, Starukhin decided, Chibisov was sabotaging him, poisoning Malinsky against him and cleverly throwing the front's support behind Trimenko. As he sat in the hard, low vehicle seat under canvas vibrant with rain Starukhin imputed to Chibisov every action that he would have taken in the other man's place.

And Malinsky. How could Malinsky fail to support him, even at the expense of Trimenko? Trimenko was nobody's friend. But Starukhin had served as a baby-sitter for Malinsky's son in Cuba. Just to keep the boy out of Afghanistan. Starukhin was certain that the posting had been no accident. No, Malinsky must have fixed it up for the boy. And Starukhin clearly understood who possessed power and how much. He had known what would be tacitly expected of him. Keep the son out of trouble.

Of course, the kid had not been so bad. He worked hard enough. As the officer responsible for training, he had done all that was required, even a bit more. Young Malinsky was clever at solving problems. Yet somehow, there was so little to the boy. It was as though he was never fully present, as though his heart really wasn't tucked inside the tunic of his uniform. There was no *fire.* Young Malinsky had gone through all of the paces, performing with ease. But he just did not seem like a real soldier.

Young Malinsky didn't even drink like a man. In Cuba, the boy had spent all of his spare time cuddled with his redheaded bitch of a wife, following her around like an excited dog. Starukhin doubted that the boy would have had the strength to raise his hand to his wife even if he had caught her in the act of being unfaithful to him. Not that Starukhin had any evidence that she had betrayed young Malinsky. No, the little cunt was probably too smart for that. She knew what she had to do to have it good. But she was still a whore. One look at her and you knew. You could smell it. And her independence of manner, her lack of respect . . . the boy seemed to have no control over her. You had to treat women the same way you treated the men beneath you. Break them down. Force your will on them. Get them by the ears and shove it down their throats.

Starukhin thought briefly, disgustedly, of his own wife. A sack of fat. The woman had no pride, no respect for her position. She had the soul of a peasant, not of a general's wife. Young Malinsky's wife, now—she at least looked the part. But she was a calculating little tramp.

Hearing a series of distant explosions, Starukhin pounded his big fist on the frame of the car. The war would not wait for him. *His* war. The opportunity of his lifetime. Even the daylight seemed to be floundering, failing, letting him down. Everything was running away from him, while he sat in a broken-down vehicle in the mud. He felt as if the universe had conspired to humiliate him. And Trimenko and Chibisov and all of the whoring Jewish bastards of the world were leaving him behind. Starukhin felt as though he would explode with the enormity of his anger.

He threw open the door of the car and clambered out into the mud just as the rain picked up again. He stared at the sergeant and the two aides. They were tinkering dutifully with the engine, but it was clear that not one of them knew what to do.

"You're *relieved,*" Starukhin told the two officers. "I don't want to see your goddamned faces anywhere around the headquarters. Your careers are finished."

Suddenly, two NATO aircraft roared in low overhead. The sound of their passage was so big it shocked the ears like an explosion. The aides and the sergeant threw themselves into the mud. But Starukhin only raised his wide face to meet the jets, automatically sensing that they were after something bigger than a stranded range car. In the instant of their passage, he clearly saw the black squared crosses and the hard colors of the West German air force. A moment later, the tactical helipad that served the army's command post threw a bouquet of fire high into the heavens, followed quickly by a second bloom, orange, yellow, and a ghostly red, tricking the eyes as it singed the air to black. The mud grasping at Starukhin's boots turned to jelly, and waves crossed the surface of the puddles. Then the sound of the blasts arrived with an intensity that seemed to penetrate the skin as well as the ears.

Without a word or backward look, Starukhin turned down the swamped trail toward his forward command post, raging at the rain that fell on him, cursing every man and woman who crossed his mind, marching, almost running in the slop, fervent and vicious with fear.

TEN

Lieutenant Colonel Gordunov braced in the helicopter doorway, drenched with rain. His headset perked with the worries and technical exchanges of the pilots. Their talkativeness grated on him. Like junk-sellers in a bazaar. But he kept his silence and watched the crowded trace of the highway in the wet, fading light. The formation of gunships and transport helicopters throbbed between the last green hills before the target area.

Gordunov knew helicopter pilots, and he knew their machines. He knew the fliers who never thought of themselves as anything but fliers, the amateur killers, and he knew the warriors who just happened to be aviators. Far too few of the latter. And he knew the warning sounds that came into a pilot's voice, requiring firm commands through the intercom. In Afghanistan, the troopships sagged through the air, swollen birds who had eaten too rich a diet of men. The mountains were too high, the air too thin, and the missiles came up at you like bright modern arrows. You learned early to command from a gunship that carried a light enough load to permit hasty maneuvers. You swallowed your pride and hid in the midst of the formation. If you were a good airborne officer, you learned a great deal about killing. If you had no aptitude for the work, or if you were not hard enough on yourself and your men, you learned about dying.

Gordunov forced his thoughts back to the present. The valley road beneath the bellies of the aircraft intersected the rail line. They were very close now. Gordunov knew the route along Highway 1 from the ground; he had traveled it just months before on mission training, disguised as a civilian assistant driver on an international transport route truck. The highways and roads leading to Hameln had impressed him with their quality and capacities, and by the swift orderliness of the traffic flow. Now those same roads were in chaos.

Intermittent NATO support columns heading east struggled against a creeping flood of refugee traffic. At key intersections, military policemen sought desperately to assert control, waving their arms in the dull rain. As the helicopters carrying the air assault battalion passed overhead soldier and citizen looked up in astonishment, shocked by this new dimension of trouble. Some of the more disciplined soldiers along the road opened fire at the waves of aircraft, but the small-arms fire had no effect beyond exciting the pilots. The aircraft returned the fire, nervous pilots devastating the mixed traffic with bursts from their Gatlings.

Gordunov let them go. As long as they didn't overdo it. Terror was a magnificent weapon. Gordunov had learned his lessons from Afghanistan. War was only about winning. Killing the other one before he killed you. They killed one of your kind, or perhaps just made the attempt, and you responded by killing a dozen, or a hundred, of them.

Olive-painted transport trucks and fine, brightly colored German automobiles exploded into wild gasoline fires. Drivers turned into fields or steered desperately over embankments. Others smashed into one another. Gordunov's rain-drenched face never changed expression.

He knew the garrison slang terms that sought to degrade,

to cut him and those like him down to size. "Afghanistan mentality. Blood drinker. Crazy *Afgantsy.*" Name-calling that in the end only betrayed the nervousness, the awe and even fear of those who had not gone.

The destruction on the roads had a purpose. Purposes. Create panic. Convince the enemy that he is defeated. Convince him that further resistance is pointless and too expensive to be tolerable. And tie up the roads. Immobilize the enemy. It cut both ways, of course. But with any luck, the British or the Germans would clear the roads just in time for the Soviet armored formations that would be on their way to cross Gordunov's bridges over the Weser.

Your men died. You could not let the fate of individuals weaken you. It was imperative to learn to regard them as resources, to be conserved whenever possible, but to be applied as necessary. In Afghanistan, and now in Germany, the missiles and the heavy machine-gun fire traced skyward, and the ships burst orange and yellow in a froth of black smoke. No passenger ever survived the fireball.

But it was all right now. Gordunov had been prepared for the loss of up to fifty percent of his battalion going in. But the air defenses had been depleted along the penetration corridor. He could not be entirely certain, but from what he had personally observed, and from the pilot chatter, he believed he would get on the ground with over seventy-five percent of his force. Now it all depended on the air defenses at Hameln and what happened on the landing sites.

The rail tracks below the helicopter paralleled the main road, Highway 1, down into the sudden clutter of the town. Crammed into the valley on both sides of the Weser River. Suddenly, they were over the first buildings.

"Falcon, what do you have up there?" Gordunov spoke into the headset mike, switching the control to broadcast. He wanted a report from his battalion chief of staff, who was tucked into the first wave, just behind the advance party.

Pilot confusion bothered the net, with one transmission spoiling another.

"Eagle, this is Hawk," the aircraft commander called him. "The rail yards are packed. You want us to hit the rolling stock?"

Gordunov could just make out the funnel-shaped expansion of the rail yards.

"This is Eagle," he said. "Only strike combat-related activities. If there's any vehicle off-loading, hit them."

"Zero observed. But I've got heavies. I'm taking heavy machine-gun fire."

Without waiting for his orders, the pilot and copilot-navigator of Gordunov's aircraft began to bank the big gunship away from the rail line.

"Damn it," Gordunov told them, "just go straight in. That's nothing. Don't break the formation."

The pilots corrected back onto course. But the formation had grown ragged.

The chief of staff, Major Dukhonin, finally came up on the net. "One heavy on the northern bridge, Eagle. Clearing him now. Scattered lights. It's manageable."

Good. All right. Just put them down on the far bank, Gordunov thought.

"Eagle, Falcon," Dukhonin called again. *"Tanks further north.* Poor visibility, but I count five . . . maybe six. Heading east. Crossing tactical bridges down in the water."

"Get the bumblebees working on them," Gordunov ordered, using the old Afghanistan slang for the dedicated gunships. "Hawk, did you monitor my transmission?"

"Working them now, we're working them."

"Falcon, can they range the landing zone?"

"Not mine. Not without maneuvering back. *Shit. Beautiful. We're hitting."*

"Get the troop ships down."

Even with the headset cups over his ears, Gordunov could hear ordnance cracking, and dull thumps.

"We're hitting. Got one tank dead in the middle of the river, burning like a campfire. Two on the banks. We're all right."

Immediately to the right of his aircraft, Gordunov watched a troop transport fly directly into the side of a high-rise building, as though the pilot had done it on purpose. Another story that will never be told, Gordunov thought. He was used to occurrences that seemed to make no outward sense during air-assault operations. Pilots misjudged, or briefly lost control, and aircraft smashed into mountainsides. The blast wave from this latest crash felt as though it stripped the rain from his face.

Fewer tools to do the job. Seize and hold the northern bridge at all costs. Seize and hold the southern bridge, if possible. Tactical crossing sites to be destroyed if they could not be controlled.

The command gunship pulled to the right, entering its assault approach. "Don't shoot up the traffic on the main bridges," Gordunov ordered. "I want them clean."

"This is Falcon. *We're on the west bank.* Lead elements en route to the northern bridge," Major Dukhonin reported. "I'm going in myself."

"Let's go," Gordunov told his pilot. Moments later, his own aircraft and two others split north, away from the element headed for the landing zone south of town and the southern bridge. The lead element had gone in on the far bank to secure the primary bridge in the north. The plan called for Gordunov, his headquarters element, and two squads from the special assault platoon to jump from a rolling hover onto the roof of a hospital building from which fields of fire commanded the west-bank approaches to the primary bridge, and from where Gordunov could control the initial actions of his battalion. The other special assault troops had been designated to block to the northeast, but they had been lost in flight. Now the main highway from the north on the near bank would be uncovered. And Dukhonin had tanks crossing up there.

The hospital came up fast, emerging from the gaps between other buildings. Gordunov spotted the river. He fixed the bridge. The burning hulk of an infantry fighting vehicle stood at its eastern approach. Last random traffic crowded in an urgent attempt to reach the western bank.

Gordunov felt the press of events now. He had time for one more brief transmission.

"Hawk, have the gunships clear to the north and west. Don't pull out of here until you've cleared those tactical crossing sites in the north, or I'll kill you myself."

Gordunov unhooked his safety strap, then glanced over

his shoulder. His command party was ready to go. Terrified. Faces all nervous energy and fear in a volatile mixture.

"Slow now. Damn it, *slow,*" he told the pilot.

He stripped off his headset and threw it forward. He pulled on his helmet and unhitched his assault rifle. The helicopter moved in a slow, hovering forward roll along the flat roof of the designated building, just high enough to clear the assortment of vents and fans.

Always a bad moment. No matter how many times you did it.

Miss the vent, watch the vent.

Gordunov jumped through the door, one foot skidding on the wet lip. As he leapt clear he could already feel the pressure of the next man behind him.

He hit the roof with one foot leading, and the pain toppled him over and jerked him into a curled-up roll. *Hell,* he thought, furious at his beginner's clumsiness. Right foot. Or the ankle. He couldn't isolate the pain yet.

Now. Now of all possible times.

Gordunov hugged his weapon as if he could squeeze the pain into it, while the slow rain teased his neck below the helmet rim. A blast hurt his ears. He climbed out of his preoccupation with his misfortune. An antitank missile slithered off the launch rails of a nearby helicopter, hunting a target off to the north. In a few seconds, Gordunov heard a clang and a roar.

Just don't be broken, Gordunov told his injury. You can't be broken, damn you. And he forced himself to roll over and cover his field of fire.

The roof was clear to the south. He heard friendly voices now. Shouted names. Yan. Georgi. Misha.

A hand touched Gordunov's back. "Are you all right, Comrade Battalion Commander?"

Gordunov grunted and pushed the hand away. Disorganized small-arms fire sounded from several directions.

"First squad reports that the upper floor is clear. No opposition. But the hospital is full."

It was Levin, the deputy commander for political affairs, a little puppy dog who had learned to quote Lenin and the current Party lords. Gordunov suspected that Levin even believed half of it or more. And he wanted to be a soldier. Well, Captain Levin was about to get his chance.

Gordunov pulled himself up on his knees behind the low wall rimming the roof. The pain was definitely in his ankle now, and it was excruciating. Perhaps it was just a sprain, he thought. Sprains could hurt worse than breaks. He made a deal with his body. He would accept any amount of pain, as long as the ankle was not broken.

"Communications. Bronch," Gordunov shouted. "Damn it, Comms. I need to talk."

The soldiers of the command section came scrambling along the roof. A rifleman swiftly leaned his weapon over the balustrade and fired a burst down into the street. He had not unfolded the stock of the assault rifle, and he had little control of it. But he crouched lower, almost a cartoon of a warrior, and fired a second burst. Then the boy hunkered behind the protective barrier.

Gordunov could tell that the boy had no idea what he was shooting at. In combat, it made some men feel good just to fire their weapons. And there were others you had to beat with your fists in order to get them to let off a single round.

Sergeant Bronchevitch held a microphone out to him.

"The battalion net is operational, Comrade Commander."

Gordunov grasped the mike. "Now get the long-range burster up," he told his communications specialist. A gunship passed overhead, then another, flying off in echelon.

Where were they going? Gordunov knew the helicopters had not finished their area-clearing mission.

"Bronch. Put me on the air frequency. *Hurry."*

Sergeant Bronchevitch messed through his papers. His pockets were crammed with cards and printed sheets. Meanwhile, the battalion net came to life. Major Dukhonin's voice. "Those sons of bitches are clearing off. The gunships are clearing off. Eagle, I've got more tanks down here."

"I *know,* damn it. I'm trying to get them now. I'll be off this net."

Heavy machine-gun fire. Not Soviet. Another pair of

gunships pulsed overhead. Gordunov tried to stand up, struggling to wave at them, to communicate somehow.

They were leaving. The bastards were leaving.

At the head of the parched valley, in the rocks, high above the treeline, the transports had set them down. The dushman had waited with superb discipline. Savages with superb discipline. They had waited until the helicopters hurried off. Then they fired into the company position from all directions. The mountains had come to life, monstrous, spitting things. And Gordunov had watched his men fall as though in a film. The helicopters always cleared off too soon. Afraid. And Gordunov had waited to die in a mountain desert pass in a worthless land. They waited all afternoon. All night. When relief forces finally arrived the next day, only eleven men remained from the entire company. Gordunov never understood why the dushman had not come in to finish them off. And when they took him back to the base, he left his ten subordinates without a word and went to the pilots' quarters. He smashed the first aviator he saw in the face, then he attacked the next one, and the one after that, calling them cowards and sons of whores. It took half a dozen men to get him under control. But in the end, he had only received a verbal rebuke. He was already considered one of the crazies then, and they gave him a medal and leave as a reward for losing his company, and the helicopters continued to desert the combat area as soon as possible. But Gordunov had not cared any more. He simply killed what there was to kill and waited to die. Yet foolishly, crazily, he had expected better here.

"Comrade Commander," Bronch spoke in a nervous, embarrassed voice, "I don't have the flight frequency. They didn't give it to me."

Gordunov almost hit the boy. But he caught himself. It would not do any good. Suddenly, he relaxed, as in the presence of an old friend. Even the pain in his ankle seemed to diminish.

So. That was that. They were on their own. The way it was in the mountains. Now there was only the fighting, and nothing else mattered in the world. Gordunov felt the familiar rush of exhilaration.

"Levin."

The political officer looked at him obediently. Levin was the most annoyingly conscientious officer Gordunov had ever known. He did everything the Party told him to do and more. He didn't drink. He studied tactics because the political officer was supposed to be able to take over from fallen comrades in battle. He spent more time out on the ranges than the company commanders. And he had an attractive wife who deceived him. Gordunov did not have much regard for political officers, in any case. But he despised any man who let a woman control him or bring him embarrassment. In formulating the plan of operations, Levin had protested against landing atop the hospital building, even though it was the only possibility if they were to control the crossing site from the outset. Gordunov doubted that the enemy would have any scruples about using the structure. But Levin had cited the laws of war and endless paragraphs of rubbish. Gordunov himself had no special desire to use the hospital, but it was a question of practicality. Now he was going to give his cuckold captain the opportunity to apply some of the military knowledge he'd been cramming into his narrow little mind.

"Levin, I want you to take the first squad and get down to the bridge. Clear out anybody who's still resisting. Leave one machine gunner on the roof where he can cover your movement. I'm staying here with the radios until I find out just what we managed to get on the ground. Just clear the approach to the bridge and hold on until Major Dukhonin comes up. And watch for tanks from the north. We'll try to cover the approach, but keep your eyes open. Understand?"

The political officer saluted.

Gordunov slapped the hand down. "No more of that shit. This isn't a November Parade in Red Square."

"Comrade Commander," Bronch, the communications specialist, said, "the burst radio is operational."

Captain Levin moved out along the roofscape, gathering the first squad. Gordunov still did not know what to make of him. He turned to the matter of informing higher headquarters of the unit's arrival at the objective. He felt in his breast pocket and pulled out a small booklet, then leafed through the pages. It was increasingly hard to see in the rain-darkened evening light.

Bronch waited to copy the message.

Gordunov gave him the code groups for safe arrival, approximate percentage of strength, main bridge intact, and combat action. Then he carefully buttoned the booklet back in his pocket.

The firing on the near side of the river had no logical pattern to it. Probably exchanges with bridge guards and perhaps a few military policemen or support soldiers. But the firing on the western side was much more intense. Dukhonin had a real fight on his hands.

"Falcon, this is Eagle. What's your status?"

Dukhonin's voice was clearly that of a man pressed by combat. "I've got tanks all around me. They took out the last aircraft on the ground. I've got at least a platoon over here, playing hide and seek with us. Older tanks, I think they're M48s. German. Maybe reservists. But plenty of trouble."

"Any of your men closing on the bridge?"

"Not yet. Karchenko's working most of his company down toward it. But we've got a mess over here."

"Listen, I don't think the bridge is prepped to blow. Just my instinct. But Karchenko needs to get down there, no matter what it takes, before somebody thinks clearly enough to start fixing charges. I've got a good view up here, but I can't cover the entire span. Kick Karchenko in the ass. And let the tanks into town. It's easier to work them among the buildings. Especially at night."

"Right. Moving now."

"Vulture, this is Eagle."

"This is Vulture," Captain Anureyev, the ranking officer of the southern landing party, answered. "You're coming in weak."

"Just tell me what you have on the ground down there."

"No combat action. A bit of sniping. I have about a combat company, and half of the mortars. I think they put the antitank platoon down across the river by mistake."

"Battalion support?"

"They just kicked out cases of ammunition. We're sorting it out now. Half of them broke open. I think the handlers went down."

"Leave a detail to sort that out. You get onto the southern bridge as quickly as you can. Be prepared to reinforce the northern bridgehead. And I want an accurate account of who made it in with you. Get everybody under control before it's too dark."

"We're missing at least a company's worth of troops. And the air defenders."

"Engineers?"

"I haven't seen them. They might be over with the antitank platoon."

"Sort it out. And move fast."

A tank fired in the distance. Across the river. Dukhonin was probably right. Reservists. There was nothing to fire a tank main gun at. It was the machine guns that did the work in close. Unless they cornered you in a building.

Bronch scrambled in close. "Transmission passed and acknowledged. Higher send their congratulations, Comrade Commander."

"They can save it. Round up your boys and find a good site on the top floor. We can't all stay up here. And I don't want to lose the radios."

Bronch moved out. Gordunov respected the communications specialist. The boy was a radio buff from his school days, when he had been active in DOSAAF, the organization for imparting military skills to the nation's youth. He could make an antenna out of anything but ground meat. Bronch's radios worked dependably—something that was not always the case in Gordunov's career-long experience.

Gordunov undid the clasps and wet laces of his right boot. Then he pulled the laces in so tight that the discomfort of the constriction vied with the pain of the injured ankle. It was time to move. Gordunov sensed things bogging down. And they were so close. It made him furious that his men were not on both bridges already.

* * *

Gordunov gave instructions to the sergeant in charge of the remaining assault squad. Cover the approach road and the bridge. Then he started down the steps of the service stairwell, bracing hard on the hand railing as soon as he was out of sight of the soldiers. The pain was an unanticipated, unwelcome enemy.

Inside the hospital, there was another, separate world. A nurse cried hysterically. And, despite the growing darkness, the corridors remained well-lit. The air was warm and dry. A few nurses and doctors stood defensively in the hallways beside litter patients. A glance revealed that the hospital was overflowing with military casualties.

The crying nurse erupted into a scream. Gordunov turned on the oldest of the doctors, assuming he would be in charge. "Shut your little whore up," he told the man in Russian. "And turn the damned lights out."

The doctor did not understand. He touched Gordunov's sleeve, jabbering in incomprehensible German. Gordunov pushed past him and, when the doctor persisted, Gordunov shoved the muzzle of his assault rifle into the man's face. Then he turned the weapon on the overhead lighting panels and let go a burst.

"Understand?" Gordunov asked him. He shot out another sequence of lights. The other doctors and nurses threw themselves down on the floor. Gordunov yelled at one of his soldiers who stood idly by. "You. Get all of these people out of the hallway. And see that they turn out the lights in the entire building."

A machine gunner and a rifleman covered the main entrance on the ground floor. Gordunov ordered the rifleman to follow him, as much because he did not know how much longer he could manage the pain in his ankle as to have a runner for communications.

Automatic weapons fire chased them between automobiles in the parking lot. The bridge was very close, but there was an open square just off of the main feeder road that had to be crossed to get to it. An enemy fire team positioned on the far side of the main route covered the direct approach. The street itself had cleared of traffic now, except for a few burning or abandoned automobiles and the smoldering wreck of the infantry fighting vehicle that had been destroyed by the gunships.

There was no sign of Levin or the squad he had taken with him. "I'll kill the bastard," Gordunov promised himself, wondering where the political officer had gone. Gordunov was sorry now that he had not put more men down on the roof of the hospital. It had seemed too great a risk, and he had not even told his superiors about that small detail of the plan. Too many officers assigned to airborne and air-assault units and formations still had not been to Afghanistan. Too many of them were soft, and weak-willed, like Levin, and they might have objected to even the most limited use of the hospital. Gordunov felt as though he had enemies to overcome in both camps.

"You go back," Gordunov told his rifleman companion. "Get up on the roof." Gordunov pointed to the southwest corner of the hospital building. "Up there. Tell Sergeant Dubrov I said to put suppressive fires on the far side of the street."

Before the rifleman could sprint off, a ripple of grenade blasts dazzled along the far side of the street, shattering the glass in the last intact storefront windows. Hard after the blasts, rushing forms took the enemy position from behind. In a matter of seconds, automatic rifle bursts cut in and out of the buildings, and enemy soldiers stumbled out of the shadows with their hands in the air, calling out in a foreign language.

The near end of the bridge was clear.

Captain Levin had taken the assault squad well around behind the enemy position. Gordunov understood at once, feeling simultaneous relief that an immediate problem was out of the way and a peculiar sort of embarrassment that the political officer had performed so well.

Gordunov caught the rifleman by the arm. "Forget what I told you before. Just go up to the top floor and tell Sergeant Bronchevitch to bring the battalion command radio down to me. Do you understand?"

The soldier nodded. There was fear in the boy's face. How

much of it was fear of battle and how much was fear of the commander, Gordunov could not tell.

As the rifleman scrambled back toward the hospital, Gordunov raised himself for a dash across the street, weaving behind the partial protection of wrecked cars in case any enemy troops remained on the scene. Each step on his bad ankle meant punishment.

Levin had already sent a team forward onto the bridge. The action continued on the far bank, but there was no more firing on Gordunov's side of the river. Levin was excited, elated. His delight in his accomplishment made him look like a teenager.

"Comrade Battalion Commander, we have prisoners."

"I see that."

"No. I mean *more.* We surprised them." He turned to the alleyway. "Sergeant . . . bring up the prisoners."

The night had grown full around them. But the hot light shed by the burning vehicles revealed a string of eight more men in strange uniforms, all of them thirtyish or older, and some of them clearly not in shape for combat.

"They were up the road," Levin said. "I think they were trying to decide what to do. We just came up on them. And we helped them decide."

"You know all the uniforms. These are Germans?"

"Yes, Comrade Battalion Commander. Enlisted soldiers. This one is equivalent to a senior sergeant."

The prisoners looked pathetic. In Afghanistan, when you managed to take the enemy alive, he showed one of two faces. Either the prisoner was sullenly defiant, or he blanked all expression from his face, as though already dead. Which he soon would be. But these men looked frightened, surprised, sheepish. They didn't look like soldiers at all, really.

"The others are British. The ones who were shooting. We have three of them."

In the background, two tank main guns fired in succession. Across the low arch of the bridge, streaks of automatic-weapons fire cut the fresh night. The rain had slowed almost to a stop, and the damp river air carried acrid battle smells.

"This town," Levin went on, his speech rapid with

nervous energy, "you have to see it to believe it, Comrade Battalion Commander. When we were enveloping the enemy we came from back there." Levin gestured toward the dark alleyway. "It's like a museum. So beautiful. The houses in the center of town must be four or five hundred years old. It's the most beautiful town I've ever seen."

"This isn't a sightseeing trip," Gordunov cut him off.

"Yes, Comrade Battalion Commander. I understand that. I only meant that we must take care to minimize unnecessary damage."

Gordunov looked at the political officer in wonder. He could not understand what sort of fantasy world Levin lived in.

"We must try to keep the fighting out of the old part of town," Levin continued.

Gordunov grabbed the political officer by his tunic and slammed him against the nearest wall. In Afghanistan, you stayed out of the villages when you were on your own. The villages were for the earthbound soldiers in their armored vehicles. When a village was guilty of harboring the dushman, it was surrounded with armor. Then the jets came over very high, dropping their ordnance. After the aircraft, the artillery and the tanks shelled the ruins for hours. Finally, the motorized riflemen went in. And there would still be snipers left alive, emerging from a maze of underground tunnels. Like rats. Gordunov hated fighting in the towns and villages. He liked the open country. But there had been times when the worthless Afghan People's Army officers had gotten their troops in a bind. And the Soviet airborne soldiers had had to go in to cut them free. It was always worst in the towns. Towns were death.

The political officer did not attempt to defend himself. He only stared at Gordunov in bewilderment. Clearly, the two men did not understand one another.

Gordunov released the younger man. "Be glad," he told Levin. "Just be glad . . . if you're still alive this time tomorrow."

Sergeant Bronchevitch hustled across the cluttered street, carrying the command radio strapped across his shoulders.

Despite the darkness, he found his way straight to Gordunov, as if by instinct.

"Comrade Commander. Falcon needs to talk to you right away."

Gordunov took the hand mike. "Falcon, this is Eagle."

At first, Gordunov did not recognize the voice on the other end. "This is Falcon. Dukhonin . . . the chief's dead. All shot up. We're in a mess."

It was Karchenko, a company commander. Gordunov had expected more self-control from the man.

"This is Eagle. Get a grip on yourself. What's the situation close in on your end of the bridge? Can I get over to you?"

"I don't know. We have the bridge. But we're all intermingled with British soldiers. And German tanks are working down the streets. Their actions aren't coordinated. But they're all over the place."

"Just hold on," Gordunov said. He released the pressure on the mike, then primed it once more. "Vulture, this is Eagle."

Nothing. Twilight static.

"Vulture, this is Eagle."

Only the noise of firing in the distance.

Gordunov turned to Levin. The political officer did not back away. There seemed to be no special fear in him after the rough handling, just a look of appraisal. "Two things," Gordunov said. "First, get the prisoners shut up somewhere so that one man can watch them. Don't waste time. Then get down to the southern bridge and find Captain Anureyev. Just take a rifleman or two, you'll be safer if you're quiet and quick. If Anureyev has control of his bridge, take one of his platoons and work up the far side of the river. Don't let yourself be drawn into a fight that has nothing to do with the bridges. I want this bridge reinforced. If Anureyev has the antitank platoon with him, bring two sections north. And tell that bastard to listen to his radio."

Gordunov turned to his radioman. "Come on," he told Bronchevitch. "Stay close behind me. We're going across the river."

Gordunov took off at a scuttling run, limping, crouched

like a hunchback. As he passed the walkway along the riverfront he fired a burst into the low darkness. There was no response, only the feeling of coolness off the flowing water.

No one fired at them as they continued over the dark bridge. It was a strongly built, two-lane structure that would easily carry heavy armored traffic. And they had it in their possession. Gordunov was determined to keep it.

The pain in his ankle seemed strangely appropriate now. Toughening. A reminder that nothing was ever easy.

At the far end of the bridge, a Russian speaker called a challenge. Sergeant Bronchevitch answered, and they were allowed back onto firm ground.

"Where's the commander?" Gordunov asked the guard.

"Up that way. Up the street somewhere."

Gordunov didn't wait for anything more. He didn't want to stop moving until he had found Karchenko. Until the situation was under some kind of control.

A few hundred meters up the road, a hot firefight raged between the buildings. Closer to the bridgehead, friendly positions had been established to cover the main road and the lateral approaches. Machine guns. Antitank weaponry.

"Do you know where your company commander is?" Gordunov asked a waiting machine gunner.

The dark form mumbled, raising its blackened face from its weapon.

"He doesn't understand Russian," a voice said from the shadows.

"Where's Captain Karchenko?"

"He was here a while ago. But he's gone." Then the tone of the voice changed significantly. "Excuse me, Comrade Battalion Commander. I didn't recognize you."

"Where's your lieutenant?"

"Putting in an observation post down by the water line."

Too much time wasted already. "Bronch. Give me the mike."

The sergeant fumbled for a moment, then produced the microphone.

"Falcon, this is Eagle."

"This is Falcon."

"I'm on your side of the river. Are you in that action up north?"

"Just below it. Along the main road."

"All right. I'm close. Watch for me coming up the street." Gordunov handed the mike back to the communications specialist and took off at a limping trot. "Come on."

A blast shook the last scraps of glass from nearby windows. Gordunov kept moving. At the far end of the street, several buildings had caught fire. Occasional forms dashed past the flames, but it was impossible to tell if they were Soviet or enemy.

"Over here."

Gordunov rushed across the road, rolling once and throwing himself into the doorway. His body already bore numerous scrapes and bruises, the inevitable wounds of urban combat, and, along with the ceaseless pain in his ankle, the collection of injuries made Gordunov feel like a wreck himself. But he knew the ordeal had hardly begun.

Sergeant Bronchevitch waited for Gordunov to clear the doorway, then he followed quickly, unable to roll with the radio on his back.

In the pale glow from the flames up the block, Karchenko appeared as though he expected the sky to fall on him at any moment.

"Do you have any damned control of this mess?" Gordunov demanded.

"Comrade Commander . . . we're *fight*ing."

"Who's in charge up the road?"

"Lieutenant Svirkin's directing the blocking action. Gurtayev's putting in the positions around the bridgehead."

Directing the blocking action, Gordunov thought. What he meant was that the lieutenant was hanging on for dear life. Gordunov calmed slightly. "And what are you doing?" he asked Karchenko.

"This is my company command post. Between the bridge and the blocking force."

"Where's Major Dukhonin?"

"He's dead."

"I know. But where is he? Where's the body?"

Karchenko didn't answer.

"I said, where's his body?"
"I don't know."
"You left him?"
"No. I mean, he was dead."
"And you left him?"
"He was in pieces. We had to move. There were tanks."
"You left him," Gordunov said in disgust, arctic winter in his voice. It wasn't a matter of emotionalism. Gordunov considered himself a hard man, and he was proud of it. He had been the toughest cadet in his class, and the best boxer in the academy. And he prided himself on his strong stomach. But the first time he had seen what the dushman did to the bodies of the Soviet dead, he had been unable to speak. The sight of the bodies had filled the bottom of his belly with ice. That was why airborne soldiers brought back their dead. And they never let themselves be taken prisoner. Because the bodies of dead soldiers were only for practice.

Now Gordunov made no mental distinction between dead comrades in Afghanistan and those killed by British troops or Germans. It was simply a matter of military discipline, of pride, as routine as wearing a clean, well-fitted uniform on parade. Airborne soldiers brought back their dead.

"The tanks would have killed us all," Karchenko said, pleading for understanding. "We had to organize the position."

Dukhonin had been all right. Another veteran. A professional. Dukhonin had been in the terrible fighting up in Herat in Afghanistan. And his chest was sewn up so that it looked as though there were a zipper across it. Now he was gone.

"Ammunition all right?" Gordunov asked, in a controlled voice.

"We got our full load in. I think Anureyev's flight was hit a lot worse than ours."

"More targets," Gordunov said. "Listen. I sent Levin down to fetch you another platoon. I want you to block one hundred and eighty degrees off the river. You can weight the defense to the north, but don't take anything for granted. Move your command post closer to the bridge. You could be overrun up here before you knew what was happening. And push out observation posts."

A series of explosions crashed along the street.

"I'm surprised they're shooting everything up," Karchenko said. "The houses are full of people, you know. You don't see them. But they're here. Six of them in this basement. They thought we were going to eat them."

"Keep the soldiers under control. How do you see the enemy over here? More Germans or more British?"

"Seems like a mix. The tanks are all German. I think we caught a German tank unit crossing the river up on the tactical bridges. But there was a British support unit tucked in near the landing zone."

"Well, the British won't care what they shoot up. It isn't their country."

"They're tough. Especially for rear services troops."

"We're tougher. Get this mess under control." Gordunov looked at his watch. "In ninety minutes, I want you to meet me in the lobby of the hospital across the river. Bring Levin, if he's still with you. I'll get Anureyev up. I want to make damned sure that, come first light, every man is where we need him. We got the bridge easily enough. Now it's just a matter of holding it."

"For how long? When do you think they'll get here?"

A spray of machine-gun fire ripped along the street, punching into the interior wall above their heads.

"Sometime tomorrow." And Gordunov got to his feet and launched himself back into the darkness, with Sergeant Bronchevitch trailing behind him.

Karchenko might not make it, Gordunov thought. But he did not know with whom he could replace him. Dukhonin had been his safety man, his watchdog on this side of the river. Now Dukhonin was gone. There was no one left he could trust.

He thought of Levin, the political officer. Levin didn't have any experience. But he would have to use him, if it came down to it. Perhaps Levin on the eastern bank, while he took personal command in Karchenko's area. Or wherever the action was the most intense. Gordunov hated the thought of relying on the political officer. But then he hated to rely on any man. He could only bear counting on Dukhonin because they had both come from the *Afgantsy* brotherhood.

In the darkness, Gordunov collided with a body rushing out of the shadows.

They both fell. The body called out in a foreign voice.

Gordunov shot him at point-blank range.

A return burst of fire from beyond the body sought him in the dark. Gordunov flattened and fired back over the body of the man he had just shot. When the body moved, Gordunov drew his assault knife and plunged it into the man's throat.

There were several foreign voices now, calling to one another. Unfamiliar-sounding weapons began to fire around him.

Gordunov peeled a grenade from his harness, primed it, then lobbed it down toward the mouth of an alley.

As the fragmentation settled Gordunov crawled into a doorway. The door was locked.

"I'm shot . . . I'm shot . . ."

Bronch. The radio.

Gordunov held still. His radioman lay sprawled in the street, his boots still up on the sidewalk. He repeated his complaint over and over, aching with the damage a foreign weapon had done to his body.

Gordunov watched the darkness. Waiting for them to come out. As if on cue, the radio crackled with unintelligible sounds. Then an electronically filtered voice called over the airwaves in Russian.

Come for it. Come on, Gordunov thought. You know you want it.

The radioman moaned, face down, his radio teasing the foreign soldiers.

Take the chance, Gordunov thought. Come on.

Movement caught his eye. And Gordunov was back in the hills of Afghanistan, brilliantly alive. He didn't let the leading figure distract him. He watched the point of origin for the covering man. When he had him fixed, he put a burst of fire into him, then shifted his weapon to catch the forward man against the side of a building.

The point man returned fire. But it sprayed wildly.

Gordunov pushed up far enough to break in the door. Then he scrambled to drag the radioman inside.

His hands slicked with blood. It reminded him of dragging a wet rolled-up tent. The boy seemed to be falling apart as he dragged him. He had clearly caught a full burst. Amazingly, he still whimpered with life.

Gordunov peeled the radio from the boy's shoulders, flicking the moisture off the mike.

"Falcon, this is Eagle."

"This is Falcon. Are you all right? We thought we saw a firefight."

"My radioman's down. I'm about a block down from you, just off on one of the side streets. Can you get somebody down here?"

"We're all ready to move out."

"No!" Gordunov screamed. He twisted his body around so that his weapon just cleared the wounded boy, and he held the trigger back until the weapon clicked empty. The approaching shadow danced backward as the rounds flashed into it, crashing against a wall. Gordunov hurriedly reloaded, then pulled out his penlight, careful to hold the point of light well away from his torso.

It was an old man. With a hunting rifle.

Stupid shit, Gordunov thought. The damned old fool.

But it had spooked him. For the first time in years, Gordunov knew he had been caught completely off guard.

The wounded boy was praying. It didn't surprise Gordunov. Religious or not, he had known many a dying soldier to pray in Afghanistan. Even political officers, professional atheists, were not above appealing to a hoped-for god in their final moments. Gordunov forced himself back to business.

"Vulture, this is Eagle."

"This is Vulture."

"What's your status?"

"We have the southern bridge. Intermittent fighting in the town on both sides of the river. The organization you requested is on the way."

"Casualties?"

"Heavy. The British ambushed us the first time we went for the bridge. But we cleared them out."

"How bad?"

"I've got about a hundred left."

"With your company?"

"Including everybody. Never found the antitank platoon. They must have gone down. We have about twenty prisoners. About the same number of wounded."

"All right. Just get in the buildings and hang on. Keep the wounded with you. I'll send a doctor down from the hospital. Get the mortars to shoot in to support Falcon. Establish a layered defense on both sides of the river."

"I'll do my best."

The radioman died. Gordunov could feel the difference in the room. When the radio went silent, it felt to Gordunov as though he were in a haunted place.

"Eagle, this is Falcon."

"Eagle."

"We can't find you. What's your location?"

"Never mind," Gordunov said. "I don't need the help anymore. Just watch for me coming in."

Gordunov sat in silence for a moment, marshaling his strength. There was no sound close in. Only the ebb and flow of firing up the street. In the bowl of almost-silence, the pain in his ankle seemed to amplify, as though someone were methodically turning up a volume dial wired to his limb.

Gordunov rose onto his knees. With a deep breath, he caught the radio on his shoulders. At the last moment, he remembered to go through the dead boy's pockets for the communications technical data pads. The papers had sponged up the boy's blood. He wiped the pads and his hands on an upholstered chair, slopping back and forth over the coarse material in the darkness. Then he climbed to his feet.

He toppled back down. His ankle would not accept the additional weight of the radio. As he fell the corner of a table jammed him in the small of his back.

Breathing deeply, trying to drown the pain in a flood of oxygen, Gordunov forced himself back onto his feet.

One step. Then another.

He stepped down into the street. No sign of Karchenko. Just as well, he thought. Up the road to the north, near what appeared to be a rail crossing, the buildings blazed, featuring the black hull of a ruptured tank in silhouette. There was firing down the first alleyway, as well.

The random bodies of the dead glistened and shone where eyes remained open or teeth caught the fluttering light. Gordunov felt no emotional response. The corpses were abstractions, possessed of no inherent meaning now. He walked upright and slowly. Each step under the weight of the radio jolted currents of pain up his leg. He pictured the pain as a green liquid fire, racing up his nerves. It was impossible to move with any tactical finesse now.

The growing fires lit the street more brightly than a full moon could have done. As Gordunov approached the network of unengaged positions by the bridgehead no one challenged him. Instead, Karchenko and another soldier rushed out to intercept him.

"Are you crazy? Get down," Karchenko demanded. Belatedly, he added, "Comrade Battalion Commander."

"Help me, Karchenko. I have a problem with my leg."

Karchenko reached out, pausing only at the last moment before touching Gordunov. Then he closed in, and Gordunov put his arm around the company commander's shoulders, easing his weight.

"It's all right," Gordunov said. "We have both the bridges."

"Let me take the radio. Here. Massenikov, take the radio from the commander."

"It's all right," Gordunov repeated. "Now we just hang on. I've been through this before."

ELEVEN

Chibisov watched the front commander eat, reckoning Malinsky's mood by his mannerisms. The old man's table manners were normally very precise. But now he absentmindedly forked up bits of cutlet and beans, simply fueling his body, as though it was just another piece of warmaking machinery. An aura of urgency had accompanied Malinsky back from his visits to the forward army commanders. Chibisov, however, remained unsure about how much of the front commander's anxiety was genuine worry and how much arose from the need to personally accomplish an overwhelming number of practical tasks, despite the support of his staff. The complexity of the contemporary battlefield was enough to break any commander who paused too long to think about it. Overall, the situation appeared extraordinarily favorable, especially in the north, in Trimenko's sector. But there were also potentially enormous difficulties, more of them each hour. Some of the difficulties had been adequately forecast, and the system had been designed with substantial tolerances. Other difficulties, such as the speed with which units on both sides essentially ceased to exist, and the tempo of movement, strained the troop control system at all levels to a dangerous point. While these difficulties had been argued theoretically in peacetime, virtually no one had internalized the practical considerations. While Chibisov himself had encountered few intellectual surprises, on a visceral level he found the reports from the formations engaged in combat almost unnerving.

As usual, Malinsky had declined to receive a full staff briefing. Although the Front Commander understood the value of ceremony and personal control, he also recognized the dangers of formalism. At the moment, continuity of effort was crucial. The staff was nearly swamped with requirements and demands, and a break in the pattern of work might have been inordinately costly. Malinsky had simply asked the chief of staff to brief him on key events and items of particular interest while he himself had a meal in his office.

"Trimenko's doing splendidly," Chibisov said, tapping the point at the deepening red arrows on the situation map. "The Dutch were too thin, and the Germans are too slow."

"Trimenko tells me that Dalyev's division is in a bad way," Malinsky interjected. "Half of the division's combat power is either gone or so disorganized it's unusable." But the tone of genuine worry wasn't there yet. Malinsky ate another trimmed-off piece of meat.

"Too much frontage," Chibisov said. "But we expected that. Dalyev had a thankless task. And the sacrifice appears to have paid off. Dalyev's attacks focused the Germans' attention. Overall, the Second Guards Tank Army is ahead of its timetable. Trimenko's got one forward detachment battering it out in Soltau, and another's running loose in the Dutch rear. He's ready to introduce an independent tank regiment to break for the Weser. Malyshev's division is up, and his lead regiments should be in contact in a few hours. The situation may not be clean enough for a demonstration exercise, but the key units are making it to their appointed places. Oh, and Korbatov has Lueneburg."

"I know," Malinsky said, dropping into his quieter personal voice. He shook his head, wearing a frankly baffled look. "Pavel Pavlovitch . . . I still think that entire affair . . ." Then he shrugged, switching his mind back to concerns within his area of decision. "Trimenko's crisis is coming tonight. He knows it. But knowing may not help. The Germans are going to hit him. I'm surprised they haven't hit him already. If they just wait a little longer, until the Sixteenth Tank Division completes its march and passes into commitment, we'll be fine. At that point, the Germans could punch all the way up to the Elbe, and they'd only be caught in a trap by follow-on forces. But the Sixteenth Tank Division must break out. Trimenko's extremely vulnerable as long as we're muddling through the commitment of a fresh division. It's a difficult function even in a peacetime exercise."

"Trimenko has already reported local counterattacks from the south against the flank of the Twenty-first Division."

"And I'll be delighted, as will Trimenko, if the Germans and Dutch continue with their local counterattacks. Let them piecemeal their combat power away. As long as they feel they're achieving little successes, it may blind them to the bigger picture." Malinsky dropped his knife and fork from the ready position, making a slight clatter as they hit the tray. He stared up at the map as though his eyes were binoculars to be focused in as sharply as possible. "If I were the German corps commander," he said, "I wouldn't strike with anything less than a reinforced division—preferably two. Local counterattacks are ultimately meaningless. It will take a powerful blow to stop Trimenko now." Malinsky scanned the known locations of the enemy forces. "If that blow doesn't arrive tonight, the Germans are fools. Or amateurs." Malinsky stared past the map for a moment. "Perhaps, Pavel Pavlovitch, we've overestimated the Germans all these years." Then his facial expression relaxed, a familiar signal to Chibisov to continue with the briefing.

"In the extreme south of the front's sector, the Twentieth Guards Army is approximately six hours behind schedule,"

Chibisov said. "The problem appears to be primarily terrain-associated. The Belgians have made very effective use of mines and obstacles along tactical directions that were already constricted. We've had to employ tactical air assaults in a leapfrog fashion to break defensive positions from behind. The situation is essentially under control, but we definitely underestimated the initial difficulties in the south. Perhaps our greatest ultimate advantage in that sector has been the experiences culled from Afghanistan in the employment of helicopter-borne infantry in mountainous terrain."

"And the Belgian forces themselves?"

"Tenacious. Very determined local resistance. I don't know what they're fighting for, really. Their greatest weakness is insufficient firepower. Further, the terrain restricts their relocation of forces to the most threatened sectors and their resupply as badly as or worse than it hampers us. We're moving forward, while they attempt to move laterally. Also, Dudorov's intelligence-collection effort indicates the Belgians have logistics problems."

"Similar to our own?" Malinsky asked.

"Some remarkable similarities, actually. Every one of our formations in contact is screaming for more tank main gun ammunition and more artillery rounds. The level of consumption seems almost impossible. It appears that we've even won several engagements by default. Nothing left for the tanks to do beyond ram each other or pull off."

"Our transport?"

Chibisov's bearing slumped almost imperceptibly, a reluctant shifting of the spine under an uncomfortable load. "We must find ways to reduce its vulnerability," he answered. "Our major lines of communication have been hit repeatedly, and to serious effect, by NATO air power. The organization of traffic is extremely difficult, and it's especially bad at the Elbe River crossing sites."

Malinsky looked troubled. "How bad?"

"Quantitatively? Acceptable thus far. But over a longer period, our hauling capability could be . . . painfully weakened."

"Painfully?" Malinsky repeated, smiling despite himself. "That's rather a theatrical expression on your lips, Pavel Pavlovitch."

Chibisov reddened. The experience of warfare on this scale, and at this level of intensity, had surpassed the careful vocabulary of the General Staff Academy in its expressive demands. Raw numbers might have aided his effort at communication, but the battlefield reporting was uneven, and Chibisov instinctively could not bring himself to trust all of it. Trained to report empirical data with unerring precision, he found himself struggling to report impressions, tonalities, and elusive feelings that insisted on their own importance now.

"NATO's air power," Chibisov resumed, "has shown more resiliency than anticipated. While *we* have achieved several impressive initial successes, the forces confronting CENTAG in the south appear to have bogged down, and the outcome of the air battle remains to be decided. If we achieve decisive superiority within forty-eight hours from now, our capability to support the ground offensive will remain at least marginally adequate. Should NATO intensify its deep strikes on our support infrastructure, however, we will experience sustainment problems within three days. It's very frustrating, really. The chief of the rear is going mad. He has the ammunition. And the fuel. As well as sufficient vehicles to move bulk supplies at this time. But attempting to link them all up and get the trucks and supplies to the right place at the right time is proving extremely difficult. Realistically, Comrade Front Commander, if the first day is like this, while we're still on the plan . . ."

"And we'll continue to adhere to the plan," Malinsky said firmly. "The tactical units and the formations can fight with what they have. The one thing that we cannot sacrifice, the one thing that is in critically short supply, is time. This is the hour when plans come into their own." Malinsky sat erectly, but his voice became intimate and direct. "If I could spare you, Pavel Pavlovitch, I'd send you forward to take a look for yourself. It's an astonishing thing. Despite all of the theory and the calculations, the endless tinkering with the tables and norms, I don't think any of us was quite ready for this. It's all . . . so *fast.*" Malinsky slowly turned his head, a tank turret sweeping the field. "I couldn't change the plan now, no matter how badly I might want to. Oh, we can adjust details. But there's no time for, no possibility of, anything greater." His eyes shone out of the darkness. "The *speed* of the thing, Pavel Pavlovitch. The speed and the power. It makes the Hitlerite blitzkrieg look like a peasant horse and cart." The front commander paused for a sip of tea, but Chibisov knew from the intensity in Malinsky's face that the old man didn't really taste it.

"I don't know," Malinsky went on. "We looked at it all in such detail . . . perhaps in too much detail. We examined the questions of mechanization and the impact of new weapons and technologies on the dialectic. We surveyed road networks and studied means of communication. We delved into automated support to decision-making and struggled with the issues raised by radio electronic combat. But somehow, we haven't done a very good job of putting them all together. What would you and your mathematician comrades say, Pavel Pavlovitch? That we haven't written the unifying algorithm? But perhaps it was unwritable. At least the enemy doesn't appear to have done any better than we have. In fact, they appear to have done considerably worse." Malinsky leaned forward, suddenly, lifting a hand, then a lone finger, as if to admonish Chibisov. But the old man was addressing an absent audience now. "Have pity on the commander without a good plan. If we have done anything correctly, it was to plan and plan and plan. Frankly, excessive planning may not work in the industrial base. But there is no alternative on the battlefield. Perhaps the difference is between problems of sequential efforts and problems of simultaneity. But I have seen the results with my own eyes. Maintain the momentum now, the momentum of the plan. Don't let up. If the enemy has a plan, don't allow him time to begin its implementation. Make him react until his efforts grow so eccentric that he loses all unity in his conceptions. Ram your plan down his throat."

Malinsky settled back into his chair, smiling with sudden gentleness. "But I'm lecturing. And to you, of all people,

Pavel Pavlovitch. Tell me about your computers. How are we doing in the new dimension of warfare?" Malinsky asked, boyish mischief in his voice.

"Frankly," Chibisov said, "there have been many disappointments. The computers in themselves are reliable enough, but the human factor is too slow. And the amount of data that must be transmitted strains even our best communications means. I believe, Comrade Front Commander, that I personally missed an important consideration. Along with allowances in the plan for such traditional measures as refueling, resupplying the units with ammunition, feeding soldiers, reorganizations, and the like, contemporary plans should also include the factor of programming and reprogramming. You recall how many officers, most of whom were simply afraid of the new technology, insisted that all of the comprehensive data accounts would be thrown out or would disappear on the first day of the war. To a limited extent, they were correct. The systems in our possession have proved to have only limited capabilities under the stress of combat, and some have failed. Yet those who denigrated automation and the volume of information to which we became accustomed were only correct in the most superficial and even tragic respects. While some of the systems and capabilities 'went away,' the requirements for the information itself are even greater than expected. We considered the symptoms, not the disease. Modern warfare is increasingly dependent upon massive amounts of highly accurate information, for targeting, for intelligence, for the rear services . . . even for the making of fundamental decisions. Those who cling to the past have made the mistake of believing that if you destroy the machinery, you destroy the need for the product. Certainly not an error a good Marxist-Leninist should make. On the other hand, too many of us fell in love with the machines themselves, confusing the relationship of means to ends. And no one from either camp fully realized the extent to which modern war would be waged on the basis of massive quantities of data." Somber at the end of his assessment, Chibisov dropped his eyes away from Malinsky's piercing gaze. "In the end, I've failed you, the army, and the Party. It all seems so clear, so obvious now, looking back."

"All of your preparation is being rewarded, my friend," Malinsky said. Chibisov winced at the unexpected choice of words. "All of the work you've done is in evidence out there." Malinsky waved his hand at the map. "I know you're having trouble with the computers. I've heard the same thing from everyone. But you're honest about it, which is a terribly hard thing for a true believer. Just use the machines within their limits now. I suspect they've already done their jobs in the preparatory phases. Perhaps the next war will be theirs. We're still in a transitional period. And now we're leaving the realm of strict military science. Now it's a matter of military art. And of strength of will."

"Comrade Front Commander," Chibisov began. There was an uneasy, stilted formality in his voice as he searched for the right tone. He had been caught totally off guard by the piercing word "friend." "I understand that your last stop was at Starukhin's forward command post. Shall I nonetheless review our perception of the Third Shock Army's situation as we see it from here?"

Malinsky's face tensed into a frown. "Starukhin! You know, he's down there shouting at his staff at the top of his lungs. I don't really understand how it works myself. One commander might shout and shout and only degrade the performance of his subordinates. Starukhin barks, and things happen. It's an amazing phenomenon. I suspect such behavior was better suited to the temperaments of past generations. But it still works for Starukhin. But I'm worried. A crisis up in Trimenko's sector could be locally contained. It is, in effect, built into the plan. But Starukhin has to come through. We must break through in the center. I've given him permission to commit his second-echelon divisions tonight. We'll pile it on, if that's what it takes. Clearly, subtlety doesn't work very well with the British. They're very stubborn boys."

"I understand his crossing was a tough one."

"One of his divisions lost an entire regiment in less than half an hour. All that remained were stray vehicles and empty-handed commanders. But he got across. And he turned the British from the south. He caught an entire British brigade from the rear, pinned them against their own minefields and barriers, and finished them. And Starukhin's moving now. But the tempo isn't all that's wanted. I don't sense a breakthrough situation. We have the British reeling back, but they've maintained a frustratingly good order. There's always another defensive position over the next hill. If Starukhin doesn't do better tonight and tomorrow morning, we may be forced to use the Forty-ninth Corps to create the breakthrough the plan calls for them to exploit. I don't like it."

"Extrapolating from our reported losses and expenditures, the correlation of forces and means is actually increasingly favorable in the Third Shock Army sector," Chibisov reported. From the staff's perspective, the British were hanging on by sheer determination and could not sustain another such day's fighting.

Malinsky reached for a cigarette. The action shocked Chibisov. Malinsky never smoked in his presence, because of the chief of staff's asthma. But, in a moment, Chibisov recognized the action for what it was: absentmindedness, a manifestation of the old man's intense concern for Starukhin's situation.

"In any case," Malinsky said, puffing a glow onto the tip of the cigarette, "Starukhin has to push through them by noon tomorrow. We must present the enemy's operational headquarters with a situation of multiple crises and apparent collapse that prevents them from implementing a truly appropriate response. We need to fragment the enemy's alliance into a conflicting set of national concerns that leads each national commander to actions or inactions based upon his own parochial perspective. And we need to drive in behind them in all sectors in order to prevent the nuclear issue from becoming an attractive option."

"Dudorov still reports no sign of a NATO transition toward a nuclear battlefield," Chibisov said.

"Keep watching it. Closely. Make sure Dudorov understands. Meanwhile, Starukhin has to keep up the pressure on the British all night. If it means committing his last tank, so be it. I've never been comfortable with night operations. I have no doubt that our enemies can see us more clearly than we can see them. But it would be fatal to stop and allow them a breathing space. We must rely on shock, on speed, and, ultimately, on simply grinding down the enemy at the point of decision, when no alternative presents itself. But we must preserve and even accelerate the tempo of combat operations. Consider it. The British have been fighting all day. Now we'll make them fight all night, against fresh forces. And we'll keep hitting them throughout the morning. If their nerve doesn't run out, their ammunition will."

But Chibisov detected an undertone of doubt in Malinsky's voice. The front commander was a powerful presence, and now it was odd, troubling, to hear even a slight wavering in his voice.

"Starukhin . . . has got to make the hole," Malinsky said. "He *must* do it." Malinsky's teeth were slightly parted, and he breathed through his mouth in the intensity of the moment. "And what about the decoy air assaults?"

"They've gone in," Chibisov said. "We had to go in with all light forces, though. The enemy air defenses limited our ability to introduce the tracked vehicles and the full range of support of the air-mechanized forces. But our troops are on the ground at Hameln and Bremen-south. Samurukov's already celebrating."

Malinsky sucked at his cigarette. "Good. I want the enemy to be looking very hard at those spots. I want him to panic, to become so obsessed by those assaults that he squanders his last local reserves on their reduction. I have never liked the notion of sacrificing soldiers, Pavel Pavlovitch. But if the Hameln and Bremen assaults do their jobs, we'll save far more, both in lives and in time, than we've lost." Malinsky chuckled, but there was neither life nor any trace of humor in the sound. His face became a bitter mask. "It's a betrayal, of course. Sending in men who believe in the sacredness of their mission, who have no inkling that they're merely part of a deception operation, and many or most of whom will die wondering why the link-up force never arrived. I console myself that, if we move swiftly enough, we may get them out of there before they're completely destroyed. But I don't even half believe it. I know I would not sacrifice momentum to save those men. But we all find devices by which we rationalize decisions with which better men could not live. Really, it's a monstrous thing to be a commander. Odd that we should so love the work."

"The air assaults on the actual crossing sites will be triggered as soon as the Third Shock Army reports a breakthrough situation."

"The timing will be critical. But you understand that."

"The enemy air defenses remain a serious threat. But their missile consumption appears to have been very high, and systems attrition favors our operations. The in-flight losses incurred by our deep assets ran just under seventeen percent. But they'll be lower tomorrow."

"Radio electronic combat?"

"Impossible to accurately gauge the extent to which the provisions of the plan have been fulfilled. Gubyshev's a busy man, though. The Operations Directorate insists he's jamming friendly nets, while Dudorov complains that he's jamming too many enemy nets of intelligence value. Then the Operations Directorate turns around and wants to know why more jamming operations aren't being conducted. The fires portion appears highly successful, but we have no tool for measuring success or failure in the electromagnetic spectrum."

"Perhaps the outcome of the war will be the only viable measure."

"Well, it's unquestionably a bit muddled. But automation has really come through for Gubyshev. He couldn't begin to manage his assets or to de-conflict frequencies with paper and pencil. And after all is said and done, Dudorov's a believer. The GRU position is that we have meaningfully impaired the enemy's ability to react on the battlefield."

"Within the contours of the plan, I trust," Malinsky said. "I'm still waiting for indications of the movement of the enemy's tactical-operational reserves to the flanks. Don't let Gubyshev queer that up. Don't let him get carried away with a sudden sense of power. What about air-battle management? Every single one of the army commanders has complained about it. Of course, I recognize that they're bound to complain. But it appears that we're having some genuine problems."

"It's certainly a bit off track. The air force is struggling with it now. The biggest problem is assessing the damages we've inflicted, then retargeting aircraft. Even the automation's overwhelmed. The air force representatives are attempting to put a good face on it, but I suspect there's a lot of guesswork going on. I do not believe that all of the available missions are being employed efficiently."

"Of course, we're speaking of relative efficiency. On the edge of chaos. Think of what it must be like for the infantryman out there in the dark, Pavel Pavlovitch. And keep pounding on our comrade aviators. But not to the degree that it becomes counterproductive. So . . . what's your overall assessment of the troop control situation? From the perspective of the chief of staff."

"Better than I feared," Chibisov said. "We can communicate, although we're often forced to rely on nonprimary means. The confusion on the ground is intense. It's a matter of continuous effort. You know our antenna farm was struck earlier? We were at minimum capability for over an hour. That didn't help the effort to maintain the automated data bases. But we're back up to ninety percent now."

"They'll hit the bunker again," Malinsky said. "And again. You'll be able to measure their desperation by how often the walls shake around you."

Chibisov nodded. He felt tired. Exhausted. Yet there was so much waiting to be done. The smoke from Malinsky's cigarette snaked into his lungs, and he unconsciously touched the pocket where he carried his pills.

"Overall," Malinsky said, "we've had better than average luck. And, while I recognize that luck is a thing best reduced to a minimum in one's calculations, I know it when it touches me." Malinsky nodded at the map, having worked his way through the mental clutter of war to a level of reasonable satisfaction. "Marshal Kribov is delighted with us—his worries are all down south. The Americans are proving tough—they're so damned unpredictable. And the Germans in the south are fighting more like Americans."

Malinsky paused for a moment, mouth slightly open at a troubling thought. "Yes, we've been lucky. But tonight will be our first big test. Tonight, and then tomorrow morning. If they piecemeal their counterattacks, and if Starukhin gives me a breakthrough by noon, they won't stop us until we're standing on the banks of the Rhine." Malinsky smiled. "And they may not even stop us then."

Leonid sat comfortably in a chair by the window, belly stuffed full, dreaming of home. His assault rifle lay balanced across his thighs. The weapon reeked with the sulfurous smell of blown powder. He had not cleaned the rifle since the battle. He had, however, taken the first opportunity to scrub the blood and filth from his tunic, and now it hung drying over the footboard of some stranger's abandoned bed.

The war seemed thankfully far away, and Leonid had convinced himself that he had done his fair share. It was up to the others now. He shifted his position, staring out into the cool darkness without focusing on any object. His slight movement ticked and clattered with the sounds of colliding plastic. He had filled his pockets with cassette tapes in an adjacent bedroom, which appeared to belong to a teenage girl. Delighted with his find, he wasn't bothered by not being able to read the labels or recognize any of the groups from the small, colorful illustrations tucked inside the cassette cases. The high quality of the printing and the lively look of the performers in the photographs promised great things.

On the far horizon, beyond a palisade of darkened evergreens, the night sky shimmered and sparkled as though a vast celebration filled the distance. Occasionally, a sputter of closer brightness disturbed the perspective, and the kettle-drum noises roamed closer, only to recede again. Leonid thought that other soldiers were undergoing experiences similar to his own of the past afternoon. On one hand, he thought it might be even more frightening at night, but he also figured that it was easier to hide.

In the aftermath of the engagement, he had found his way to the remnants of his own unit with surprising ease. The firing had diminished to a trickle, then it shut off completely, as though a tap had been closed. The barking of the officers soon replaced the noises of battle. The wounded made noises, too, but the officers seemed determined to shout them down, to bury their reality under the bullying noises of control.

Seryosha had made it through, and he told stories of machine-gunning countless numbers of the enemy. Leonid noticed that Seryosha was still laden with most of the ammunition he had carried into battle, but he accepted the tales, neither believing nor disbelieving. Their squad vehicle could not be identified, but Lieutenant Korchuk, their political officer, shepherded them to Junior Sergeant Kassabian, and they became part of a unit again. Korchuk praised their performance and asked them how they felt now that they were veterans of battle. But it was evident that Korchuk did not really listen to their responses. The *politruk* was upset because so many of the platoon group Komsomol organizers, his helpers in the political agitation effort, had been killed or wounded. It seemed apparent that the most active and enthusiastic Communists truly had led the way. When Korchuk left them, Seryosha ridiculed the fallen organizers, saying that maybe war wasn't such a bad thing if it killed off all of the boot-lickers. Then he laughed and speculated broadly about where Korchuk himself had been during the battle.

Their unit remained behind as the others lined up and pulled off in the direction of the shifting battle noises. Korchuk returned and explained to them that they were to help gather the wounded who had fallen for the cause of international peace and socialist brotherhood. The young soldiers followed the wanderings of the medical orderlies, who were clearly at a loss confronted with such devastation. An orderly would bend over a helpless figure and seem to play with it. But Leonid did not believe that the orderlies really knew what they were doing.

In one respect, Leonid surprised himself. He did not mind helping to lift and carry the wounded. He wanted to make them feel better, although their miseries made no deep impression on him. He spoke a few comforting words, repeating himself frequently, promising the unlucky boys that they would be all right. The regimen called for gathering the wounded officers first. But they, too, now were just boys and young men, no longer radiant with power, but simply shocked into silence, or weeping at their misfortunes, or groaning with their unimaginable pains. The soldiers loaded the officers into the little train of field ambulances, then they filled the few remaining spaces with badly burned other ranks. As the ambulances pulled off they began the drudgery of packing the mass of the casualties into the beds of empty transport trucks. The few wounded enemy soldiers in evidence went carefully ignored until the last, then they were loaded onto the already crowded vehicles. Most of the trucks had no medical orderlies to attend their cargoes, and two officers had an argument that Leonid did not quite understand. Lieutenant Korchuk cautiously avoided touching any of the wounded at all.

After policing their fragment of the battlefield, the soldiers in Leonid's unit loaded up onto the combat vehicles that were still operable. Leonid, Seryosha, and Sergeant Kassabian rode with a reduced vehicle crew whose members Leonid half recognized from battalion parades. The atmosphere had changed now, and the soldiers grew loose and talkative. The rain had stopped, and they drove down German country roads with the top hatches open, weapons held at a casual ready as they watched the world go by.

In the last twilight, they drove through a village whose streets seemed to have been strewn with diamonds, an effect of the light of burning buildings reflecting off broken glass. Along a street that fire had not yet touched, external blinds had been lowered over windows, sealing the houses off like private fortresses. But an artillery round exploding at the end of the street had blown all of the nearby blinds away, leaving the windows looking like dark, dead eyes. To Leonid, the last untouched houses seemed to be waiting like sheep. In the town square, bodies littered the pavement, some with a distinctly unmilitary appearance.

In the next village, the little column had to wait as towed guns with long, slender barrels moved ahead of them. Then they were delayed again, this time by a serial of military equipment the like of which Leonid had never seen. The oversized vehicles had the appearance of farm machinery, or of giant instruments of torture.

"Engineers," one of the soldiers said, eager to flaunt his knowledge.

Finally, the vehicle in which Leonid and his comrades rode was directed into position between two houses on the edge of town. Sergeant Kassabian received command of all of the dismounted soldiers. An unfamiliar officer ordered Kassabian to set up firing positions inside the house beside the road.

Even in the dark, Leonid could tell that the Germans were very well-to-do. Sergeant Kassabian made a halfhearted attempt to position the soldiers at firing points behind doors and window frames. But soon he, too, succumbed to the general desire to explore. Seryosha even tried to turn on the electric lights, but there was no power. The soldiers wandered about by the light of matches, stolen lighters, and a few candles that turned up.

The kitchen was full of food, and the soldiers ate their first real meal since their deployment from garrison. They made it into a slopping feast. There was even beer, still mildly chilled from the now-powerless refrigerator. Several of the soldiers commented on the apparent wealth of the Germans, jealous and admiring. Finally, one man said angrily that the Soviet Union could be rich, too, if it stole from starving people in Africa and Asia. Leonid did not know what to believe, but he envied any family that could possess such a house. Then one of the unfamiliar soldiers with whom they had been thrown together began to smash things.

There was no logic to it, but the mood quickly caught on. The soldiers tore through the house, upsetting furniture, hurling vases and figurines, and ripping pictures from the walls. Upstairs, the boys scattered the contents of drawers over the floor, and one soldier found a treasure of oversized women's underthings. Laughing crazily, he pulled on a drooping bra and panties the size of a big man's swimming trunks. He pranced about, throwing his shoulders forward in a parody of enticement. In an adjacent room, Leonid discovered a fine little cassette recorder and a drawer full of tapes. He doubted that he could conceal the recorder, and there were too many tapes, so he hurriedly culled the lot by matchlight, filling his pockets with the most interesting-looking items.

Out of nowhere, Lieutenant Korchuk appeared, armed with a pocket flashlight. He remained silent for a full minute, standing in the hallway, sweeping the beam of light from one room to another, inspecting the frozen revelry. Leonid expected a great fuss and heavy punishment. But Korchuk only ordered Sergeant Kassabian to reoccupy the squad's fighting positions. The political officer seemed to have taken over some level of command now, and he appeared disheartened by the responsibility. In a strained voice, he ordered the soldier who had adorned himself with women's underthings to return his uniform to its proper state.

Already weary of their fun, the soldiers acquiesced to Sergeant Kassabian's paper-thin commands. Sergeant Kassabian wielded bits of half-remembered officer talk from old field exercises, struggling to please the lieutenant. The soldiers slumped off to guard the doors and windows. Shortly afterward, Lieutenant Korchuk disappeared back into the night. But the soldiers remained in their separate rooms, as much from inertia as from duty, as quiet as exhausted children.

Leonid and Seryosha took possession of an upstairs bedroom. The furniture had been toppled, and the mattress lay on the floor, where one of the soldiers had urinated on it. The two boys put down their rifles and flipped the mattress, then lifted it back onto the bed frame. They agreed that they would take turns sleeping—Seryosha first—after Leonid cleaned his uniform top. He carefully stuffed his precious cassette tapes into his trouser pockets and bent to his labor by the light of a dying candle. Water still ran in the pipes, and Leonid soaked and scrubbed his spattered tunic in the bathtub, as much impressed by the water pressure as by the luxury of the fixtures.

Leonid sat peaceably at the window as Seryosha drowsed, then muttered a few unintelligible words before beginning to snore with martial regularity. In a state of weariness that could not measure time, Leonid watched the brilliant display of battle on the horizon, the nighttime sequel to his own experience, in a war that had moved beyond him. He thought about music, and of how painful it would be at first to re-form the calluses on the fingertips of his left hand. He closed his eyes, chording his guitar in his mind. Twice he nearly collapsed into sleep, and the second time he woke himself just in time to see a beautiful pageant of colored rockets in the distance. The colored stars trailed off in slow deaths that filled Leonid with sadness to a depth he had never before known. The thought of the most trivial detail of home gained the power to bring tears to his eyes, and when he thought of his mother, the tears fell down his cheeks in the darkness just as the distant starbursts dropped into the darkened woodlands. Pulled loose from any real sense of the hours, he concluded that the night must be nearly over, and he carefully dried his eyes and the adolescent coarseness of his cheeks. Timidly, he began the task of waking Seryosha. He felt as though he would give anything just to sleep for a little while.

When Seryosha finally forced himself awake and stamped off to the guardpost at the window, Leonid told himself that he was lucky to have such a friend. His tunic was still too wet to wear, and he lay on the ammonia-scented mattress, wrapped in a coverlet ripped by the horseplay of his comrades. In a matter of minutes, he wept himself to sleep, filled with a vast, sorrowing, and indiscriminate feeling of love for his fellow man.

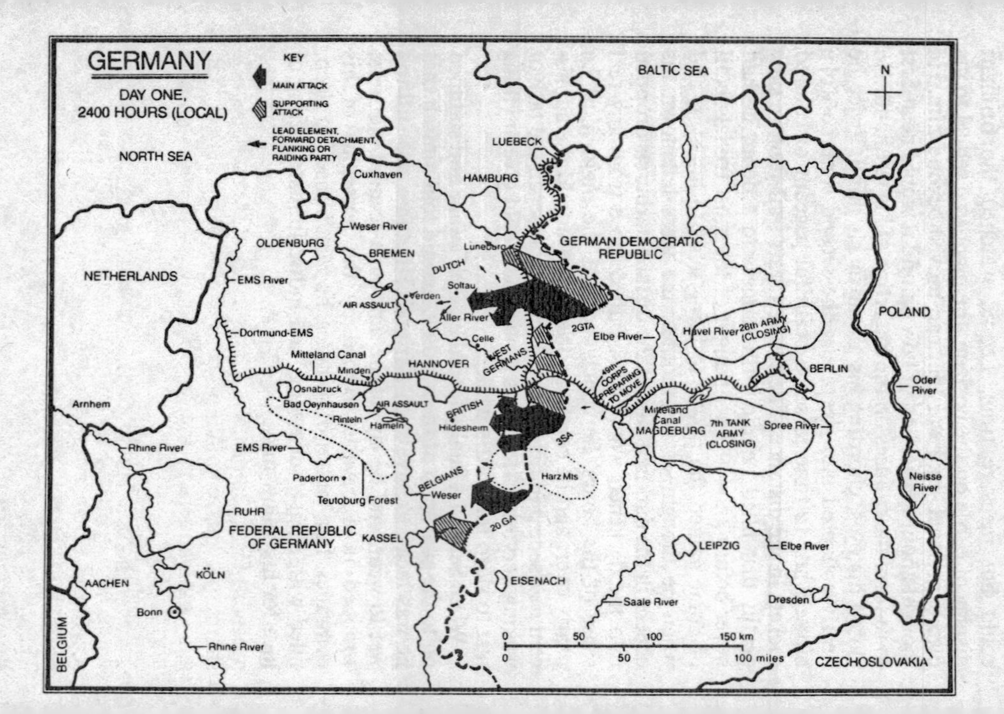
GERMANY
DAY ONE,
2400 HOURS (LOCAL)
KEY
MAIN ATTACK
SUPPORTING ATTACK
LEAD ELEMENT, FORWARD DETACHMENT, FLANKING OR RAIDING PARTY
NORTH SEA
BALTIC SEA
N
LUEBECK
HAMBURG
Cuxhaven
Weser River
OLDENBURG
BREMEN
Luneburg
GERMAN DEMOCRATIC REPUBLIC
NETHERLANDS
EMS River
DUTCH
Soltau
Verden
AIR ASSAULT
Aller River
2GTA
Elbe River
Havel River
28th ARMY (CLOSING)
POLAND
Dortmund-EMS
Celle
WEST GERMANS
Mitteland Canal
Minden
HANNOVER
49th CORPS PREPARING TO MOVE
BERLIN
Oder River
Osnabruck
Bad Oeynhausen
AIR ASSAULT
BRITISH
Mitteland Canal
Arnhem
Rinteln
Hameln
Hildesheim
MAGDEBURG
7th TANK ARMY (CLOSING)
Spree River
3SA
Rhine River
EMS River
Paderborn
Harz Mts
BELGIANS
Weser
Neisse River
Teutoburg Forest
RUHR
20 GA
FEDERAL REPUBLIC OF GERMANY
KASSEL
LEIPZIG
Elbe River
AACHEN
KÖLN
EISENACH
Bonn
Saale River
Dresden
BELGIUM
0 50 100 150 km
0 50 100 miles
Rhine River
CZECHOSLOVAKIA

TWELVE

At first, the enemy tanks were only a big, chilling noise in the darkness. Then the flares went up, and Senior Sergeant Hornik spotted the first huge vehicles working their way up along the highway beyond the meadow covered by his unit. The enemy were clinging to the treeline on the far side of the road. The steel monsters grumbled into his antitank gun's zone of fire, and he worked with the other crew members to train the gun on the vehicle in the enemy formation that had most fully exposed its flank. He ordered his crew about with sharp, nervous commands, and the voices of the other gun commanders in the antitank battery seemed to echo him.

Ranging was very difficult. The light of the parachute flares had a garish, flattening effect that simultaneously seemed to freeze everything and to create small phantom movements just off center from the observer's line of sight. The crews had been forced to hurriedly assess ranges and develop range cards with selected engagement points in the last twilight, while the engineers to their front raced to lay every last possible mine. Hornik had nonetheless felt confident as darkness draped over the guns. But now it was almost impossible to grasp the true perspective and distance to the target.

The enemy tanks sensed they were in for it. They deployed off the road, moving slowly toward the battery, hampered by the soggy terrain. Their turrets hunted targets, like animals setting their noses to the wind. Hornik felt confident that the guns were well camouflaged, and he ordered his men to remain still. But an enemy tank fired and, in an instant, the dreadful clang of a round striking metal ruptured the integrity of the treeline. Shouts and screams followed in the wake of the blast.

How could they see? Hornik wondered. How could the enemy tank have detected a camouflaged gun position in the dark?

"Fire!"

The antitank guns responded in a broken volley.

None of the rounds found their mark, and the enemy tanks returned the fire with unnerving accuracy. But their movements seemed confused by the antitank ambush. Some drew back toward folds in the ground or into the trees on the far side of the road, while others did the opposite by moving out into the open, advancing on the battery.

One of the leading enemy tanks bleached white in an explosion that seemed to ripple the metal. Hornik decided that the vehicle had struck one of the antitank mines. He could see rounds from other antitank guns striking the enemy tanks now as the gunners found the correct lay. Yet there seemed to be no pronounced damage, even when a round hit dead on. The greatest triumph of the entire battery was a shot that broke loose a track, which briefly reared like a giant snake, then flopped lifelessly, leaving the vehicle stranded in the middle of the meadow.

"Fire at the one that stopped," Hornik yelled to anyone who could hear him, and he settled himself behind the optics of his own piece. The loader hurriedly slammed another round into the breech. Hornik went as carefully as his nerves and hands would allow, realigning to seek the most vulnerable point on the enemy vehicle.

"Fire."

The round struck. But Hornik could see no difference in the state of the vehicle after the flash and sparks had cleared away. For a moment, the vehicle had seemed to be engulfed in flame. But it was all illusion.

Hornik could not understand why these monsters would not die.

"Reload," he barked. "Hurry up."

Hornik stayed with his gun. The enemy tanks came on, blasting the battery into junk. The other crew members deserted him. But Hornik struggled to get off one last shot, cursing at the top of his lungs, filled with so much hatred for the closing enemy that he felt his fury alone must stop them.

Leonid awoke to the enormous noise of Seryosha's machine gun firing through the window frame. Seryosha screamed and, for a moment, rocketing awake, Leonid thought his comrade had been wounded. But Seryosha was only shouting for help, as though Leonid might be reinforcement enough to halt the advancing enemy.

Leonid sat on the bed for a moment, unsure what to do. Outside the window, the world flashed. He felt for and pulled on his still-wet tunic, a reflex from hundreds of awakenings in the barracks. It took him several more seconds to locate his load-bearing equipment with the ammunition pouches and his assault rifle. All the while, Seryosha screamed for him and cursed at the world beyond the window.

Fitting himself in beside Seryosha and the piercing *pak-pak-pak* of the light machine gun, Leonid tried to decipher the situation. Outside, the garden and the field that led back to the treeline glimmered with speckles and broken trails of light. Fiery streaks hurtled chaotically.

"They're all around us," Seryosha shouted at him as he loaded a fresh magazine into the machine gun. *"Shoot."* And Seryosha dropped the heavy barrel back onto the windowsill.

"I can't see anything," Leonid said.

"Just shoot. Shoot at the lights."

Leonid obeyed, still trying to recover a waking balance. The noise of their two weapons firing in the small room hammered at Leonid's ears, telegraphing sharp physical pulses into his brain.

The fighting vehicle parked beside the house blew up, shaking the building and jolting the two boys against each other. Seryosha lost his balance and let go a wild burst of machine-gun fire as he fell. Leonid braced himself against the side of the window, watching in wonder as the pink glow of the burning vehicle revealed running figures. Without conscious thought, he raised his weapon and fired in the direction of a shadow scurrying along the edge of the radiance. But his effort seemed lost, devoured in the wildness of the firefight. Countless beads of light chased one another at dizzying speeds.

An unexpected blast downstairs shook the floor beneath them. Voices shouted in a stew of languages, and automatic weapons fired thunderously inside the building. The hallway flickered with light, and booted feet thumped across the floor downstairs. Leonid and Seryosha crouched behind the toppled furniture of the bedroom, weapons pointed at the doorway. Leonid watched with his mouth hanging open, breathing almost suspended.

The boots crashed from room to room. The noise sounded like at least an enemy platoon to the two boys. The enemy soldiers hunted about downstairs for what seemed an unreasonably long time. Then one pair of boots began to climb the stairs.

A voice called out in a foreign language, and another voice answered from the stairwell. Leonid expected a grenade to sail in through the open doorway. But instead, the soldier on the stairs turned about and went back down. The cassette tapes Leonid had stuffed into the pockets of his trousers cut into his flesh. It felt as though most of the plastic had splintered into shards. He wondered if the enemy would shoot him for stealing when they found him. He wondered if he should call out and volunteer to surrender. He didn't want the enemy to be angry at him. Lieutenant Korchuk had told them that the Germans and Americans always killed their prisoners. Some of the soldiers didn't believe Korchuk, but now, Leonid decided it was better not to take the chance. He lay still, doing nothing.

Incredibly, the booted feet began to leave the house, fading back into the bigger noise outside. The huge sound of tanks in rapid movement made the air tremble. The fire glow from the burning vehicle outside lit salmon-colored ripples and waves on the ceiling of the bedroom.

"We're in the shit now," Seryosha whispered.

Senior Lieutenant Zirinsky had no idea how long he had been fighting. The night seemed endless, a stubborn, miserable, unyielding thing. One by one, he had watched as his tanks were destroyed. It seemed totally unreasonable. Losing one or even a few might be expected in battle. But Zirinsky had watched six of ten explode in less than five minutes, several losing their turrets like caps popping off shaken seltzer bottles. He had almost immediately lost radio contact with the rest of his company, if any of them remained alive and capable of carrying on the fight. And he had begun the long game of cat and mouse with the enemy.

He had been ordered to hold the crossroads. The terrain ran low, with marshlands everywhere. The only practical way to pass armored vehicles through the area was to stay on the roads. And one lonely country crossroads tied the local network of roads and trails together.

Zirinsky figured that his antenna had been torn away by the artillery fire. Or that a nonlethal hit on his tank had knocked out the sets. The vehicle was so battered now it was impossible to tell exactly what cause had been responsible for each failure. He had no idea what the situation was like in the overall battalion sector, let alone from the regimental perspective. He hoped the others were in better condition than he was.

His unit had moved up from a holding area in East Germany, crossing the border in midafternoon. As they progressed deeper into the west more and more of the litter of battle had begun to punctuate the landscape. But no rounds had sought them out, and the aircraft up in the gray murk had ignored them. Except for countless unscheduled stops and starts, and the hectic confusion at the traffic control points, their march had been almost administrative in its tone, with the battle seeming to flee before them, always outside of their moving domain.

In the evening, his unit had been halted unexpectedly and ordered to deploy into hasty defensive positions oriented to face a threat from the southwest. Several of the officers were furious. They had all expected to race to the attack, to thrust deeply and dramatically into West Germany, each man in accordance with his own fantasy of himself. Then they were given the distinctly less glamorous mission of providing flank security. The battalion commander had protested that it was a poor use of his new tanks. But orders were orders. Zirinsky had occupied his defensive positions in the dark, disappointed that the battalion commander had not chosen his company to be held back behind the other two, where it could act as a mobile force in response to any threat that developed. Instead, Govolov's company had been positioned to the rear. Zirinsky wondered where in the hell Govolov was now.

The sky had cracked open with artillery fire, totally without warning, catching some of the tanks with their hatches open. Then the enemy tanks had come on swiftly, hampered only by the necessity of sticking closely to the roads. The enemy tanks were enormous Leopards, almost twice the bulk of Zirinsky's own vehicles. And the enemy's fire superiority made it clear very quickly that they had superior night-fighting equipment on board. The Leopards had initiated the engagement at what seemed an excessive range for night combat, and Zirinsky had lost a platoon before he could effectively range the enemy. Then the firefight had begun in earnest.

When you hit the enemy tanks, they died. Zirinsky had taken that one positive lesson to heart as his only consolation. He listened to the pleas of his platoon leaders for help, but he had no help to offer them. He brusquely ordered them to take control of themselves and fight back.

The engagement seemed lost. The enemy tanks surged forward behind another deluge of artillery, moving very well, unbothered by any need to maintain close formations. At first, the wet terrain seemed to cooperate, accepting the weight of the Leopards as they maneuvered off the lifeline of the road. And Zirinsky accepted that he was going to die. But he was determined to fight it out. He felt himself fill with a wordless, unreasoning hatred of the enemy, with a desire not only to destroy them, but to cause them all possible pain in the process. He let his gunner and driver know beyond any doubt that they were there to fight. He coolly began to seek fresh targets, awaiting the fatal enemy round that would finish him off and give the enemy the crossroads.

But the enemy pulled back. They had been so close. Zirinsky could not understand it. The enemy's losses had been minimal in comparison to his own.

Then they came again. Zirinsky had found a good fighting position, tucked as closely as the heat would allow behind the smoldering wreck of one of his own tanks. Again, the enemy delivered artillery in his vicinity. But this time it seemed little more than a drizzle in contrast to the earlier storm.

The enemy tanks dashed forward in bounds. Zirinsky waited, holding back his gunner until the targets were properly illuminated by the infrared searchlight. He identified three enemy tanks that could not get away if he did his work properly. They were obviously searching for him. He waited.

At the last possible moment, Zirinsky engaged the enemy tanks in quick succession, methodically destroying all three. Now it seemed as though the enemy could not even see him, as though he were a ghost. They fired in his general direction, but the rounds went wild, exploding along the treeline.

Zirinsky had already shot up half of his on-board ammunition in the series of engagements. He was especially low on high-velocity sabot now, the best tank killer. He tried his dead radio again, aching to communicate. It seemed to him that holding the crossroads was the most important thing on earth now, and he could not believe that no one had come to reinforce him.

The battlefield glowed with the light of slow-burning hulks, like random campfires. Zirinsky believed that he could count nine enemy tanks that had been put out of action.

The enemy tried a new tactic. A tank platoon raced at full speed down the road off to Zirinsky's left flank, firing smoke grenades out into the darkness. Soon, the familiar accompaniment of artillery came back to search for Zirinsky's lone tank. He ordered his driver to back up in order to reposition for a better range of shots.

The tank surged and heaved. But it could not break free of the earth. They were stuck.

Hurriedly, Zirinsky sought the lead tank of the enemy platoon before it reached the dead space behind the hulk that also served as Zirinsky's protection.

His first shot missed.

Forcing himself to execute each step methodically, Zirinsky sent off another round. This one found its mark. The enemy tank began to trail flames, veering off its course.

Zirinsky hunted down the next tank in line and killed that one, too. Two trail vehicles fired madly in his direction.

Zirinsky's universe was reduced now to the mechanics of destroying tanks. Come on, he thought. Just come on, you bastards. I'm waiting.

After the chief of staff had gone to transform the front commander's intentions into activities, Malinsky fell into an exhausted doze. The picked-over tray of food lay before him on his desk, and a last cigarette suffocated on the edge of a plate. Malinsky remained vaguely aware that countless tasks had yet to be accomplished, even as he sensed uncomfortably that events were too big for any one man to truly control. He felt as though he were struggling to manage an endless team of wild horses, their broad backs stretching into infinity, while the reins were made of frayed bits of string. Then there were only prancing cart horses, dark against snow, snorting plumes of white steam.

Malinsky recognized the scene. The Urals. So long ago. And it was all exactly as it had been. It was remarkable how little had changed. Except for the sky. He could not understand why the sky had such a golden glow. From horizon to horizon, a gilded sky stretched overhead, making a shimmering tent over the mountain peaks and ridges, shading the snow to deep copper in the crevasses and saddles. And it was very cold. His tiny son held tightly to his gloved hand. Malinsky could feel the boy trembling. They were up so very high. The valley, the houses, all of the world's familiarity and warmth, seemed lost. Paulina looked at him reproachfully. Paulina, as she had been in those early days, so neat and self-possessed. A treasure of great value, his Paulina. In her big fur coat that nearly hid her face with its collar.

He could not understand how Paulina could be so young now. And his son was only a child. That wasn't right. Malinsky felt his age pressing down upon him like tons of cold stone. Every movement was slow, difficult. He was an old man. How would he ever hold Paulina, if he was an old man? How could he explain this absurdity, this unaccountable accident, to her?

All around him, formed along the steep slope in unruly crowds, dark figures awaited an unknown event. Their faces would not hold still for him to identify them, yet they were all glancingly familiar. A performance of some sort was about to take place.

Paulina called out in fright. The boy. *The boy!*

And Malinsky saw that Anton had escaped his grasp. The boy slid away from him, sleighing helplessly down the steep slope, falling backward, skidding out of control, looking up at the old man with reproachful eyes.

Malinsky ran, tumbling, after the child.

His son. His only son.

The dark crowds watched with no evidence of emotion.

Malinsky struggled to run, losing his balance, tripping again and again. He chased madly after the boy, who always remained just out of his grasp. They were going so fast, there was no way to stop. Momentum drew Malinsky into a headlong, out-of-control downhill run.

"I'm old. Paulina, I'm too old," Malinsky called out. Yet he could not understand how it had come to be. He could make no sense of it.

He grabbed at the child, never quite reaching the boy's delicate limbs. Ahead, somehow, somewhere, he knew there was a precipice. There was a great precipice, and there were only moments before they would reach it and topple into space, and still the dark crowds watched in silence, unwilling to help him save his child.

"Help me," Malinsky shouted, half an order, half a plea. "For the love of god, help me. It's my *son.*"

But the boy slithered away in silence, skating down the icy mountainside on his back, flailing his small arms as he sought to stop himself. Malinsky could see Anton's eyes, large, dark, wounded child's eyes. He knew that he had failed the boy, that he would always fail him. Then they were sailing through dark space, beneath a gruesome, spinning golden sky.

"Comrade Front Commander," Chibisov's voice called him back, insisting that he wake. "Comrade Front Commander, wake up."

Malinsky felt Chibisov's small, firm grasp on his forearm. Just before he opened his eyes, Malinsky stirred and clapped his own larger hand over that of the chief of staff, holding it there a moment too long, reassured by its human warmth.

"The Germans are counterattacking Trimenko," Chibisov said. His voice was crisply urgent, but there was no trace of panic. Chibisov at his best, Malinsky thought. "The Dutch are trying to get at him from the north, as well. Dudorov has already identified a fresh German division and at least one Dutch brigade that had not been committed previously. They're trying to pinch off Trimenko's penetration."

Malinsky regained his faculties. "Only one German division?"

"So far."

Malinsky shook his head. "They think small. They've lost their vision, Pavel Pavlovitch. Did the Sixteenth Tank make it in?"

"The lead regiments are well beyond the counterattack sector. We're in behind the Germans. But Trimenko had to turn the trail regiments to fight."

Malinsky thought about that. "I don't like to see a division split up. Can Trimenko manage the command and control?"

"The Sixteenth Tank Division staff is controlling the lead

regiments. The trail regiments are temporarily under the control of Khrenov's division."

"Good." Malinsky wanted a cup of tea to clear his head. He pressed the buzzer to summon an aide.

"The Germans were right on time," Chibisov went on. "And exactly where expected. The roads dictated the tactical axes. Dudorov has them dead on. You need to see his map. The detail is amazing."

Following a discreet knock on the door, a young officer appeared.

"Bring us tea," Malinsky said.

The officer disappeared again.

"Well," Malinsky told Chibisov, "it's up to Trimenko now. What about Starukhin's sector?"

"He's hitting the British with everything he's got."

Malinsky surveyed the spotlit map. But all of the details were already inside his head. "All right," he said, donning the voice of command. "Trimenko's on his own. Weight the front's support to Starukhin. It sounds like the enemy has taken the bait."

THIRTEEN

Lieutenant Colonel Shilko had been waiting patiently for over an hour, but the column remained stationary. He still had two of his self-propelled batteries, his target acquisition gear, and the battalion control and fire-direction elements tucked in behind him. He had no idea where his third battery was now. All attempts at radio contact or courier linkup at former locations had resulted only in wasted breath and missing couriers. And he had been ordered to send several officers, including one battery commander, forward to fill out depleted units and to act as forward observers. It sounded as though the toll among officer cadres was very high. But Shilko accepted fate. He was pleased enough to have most of his battalion herded together and reasonably under control. He would have liked to move faster, to reach the next locations designated for his fine guns, to run them back into action. But he saw no point in joining the inevitable shouting match up ahead on the road, wherever the holdup was focused. The column would move when it was ready.

The sounds of battle were so constant that he hardly heard

them anymore. The thunder of the guns had long since worn down his already-poor hearing, and he contented himself with another cigarette. The night had grown wonderfully fresh since the rain stopped, and his peasant's sense told him there would be a fine morning in a few more hours. Pleasant weather to be out of doors.

Shilko had insured that his soldiers were fed with a bit of warm gruel from the old cooking trailers and that they had a sip or two of hot tea before pulling off of their positions. Shilko had never understood why some officers insisted on making life as miserable as possible for themselves and their men. The gaunt, baggy-pants types. Well, Shilko thought, a soldier's life was hard enough. If you had to meet your fate, why not on a full stomach? In the end, the slight delay had made no difference that Shilko could see. The march schedules and overall organization of traffic were little more than some staff officer's fantasies now.

An officer dashed down the line of vehicles. He hastened past Shilko's command car, and Shilko thought nothing more of it until the officer suddenly reappeared, slapping at the side of the vehicle to get Shilko's attention.

Shilko leaned out of the vehicle, cigarette stuck in his mouth like a stalk of straw.

"Are you the commander of this artillery?" the officer shouted. He was an agitated, ferret-faced major with all the trimmings of the commandant's service.

"These are my boys, Major," Shilko stated matter-of-factly, waiting to see what the other officer wanted. He had already made up his mind that he was not going to clear off the road and lose his place in the column, if that was what all the fuss was about.

But the major had another objective entirely. "Comrade Commander," he said, almost crying out, "we've got to do something. The enemy are up ahead. The motorized rifle troops can't hold them."

"Up ahead? Where?" Shilko demanded, quickening, reaching for his map case.

The major produced a map of his own and traced over it with a hooded flashlight.

"Here. Here, I think. In this general area. Can you fire in support?"

Shilko scrutinized the map. "There, you say?"

The major nodded urgently. But, in fact, as Shilko could see now, the target area was not exactly up ahead, but several kilometers off to the south, along a road that intersected with the one on which they were standing.

"How do you know the enemy's there?" Shilko demanded.

"Comrade Commander, I've seen them with my own eyes. I went forward to straighten out the traffic. The motorized rifle regiment's trains were backing up from the south, blocking all movement to the west—an impossible situation. I'm responsible for the movement of traffic on this route. I went to see what was happening. The motorized riflemen are hanging on by their fingernails. It must be an entire German division counterattacking."

Shilko rolled his fading cigarette in his mouth, pondering the map. It was clear to him that the local terrain would not support an enemy division in the attack. And, allowing for the commandant officer's natural exaggeration, this was probably more a matter of a reinforced battalion, perhaps leading a brigade-sized attack. But the enemy division would be spread out over multiple routes, if, indeed, there was an enemy division. In any case, there was a road running through a forested area. Any attacker would be backed up down that road. The terrain was extremely restrictive. In greater depth, there were several small towns that would also restrict any movement.

Shilko didn't trust the major's precision when it came to the current locations of the enemy. But it was clear to Shilko that the enemy, in some size, was definitely out there somewhere. Shilko took a decision.

Moving with determination now, he climbed out of his vehicle and rousted Captain Romilinsky. He ordered the fire direction center prepared for hasty action. The batteries were to come to a high state of readiness and await their missions. Romilinsky snapped to the task. Meanwhile, Shilko set to work on the hood of a vehicle, plotting fires by the light of a pocket lamp. He figured that, if he shot the long, straight stretch of road through the forest just south of where the major claimed the enemy were advancing, he would range safely beyond the forward Soviet positions, except for any that were cut off—and that couldn't be helped. The road would provide the likeliest concentration of enemy targets, and if he could strike everything behind the enemy's leading combat troops, those troops could be forced to a standstill. At the very least, if you jammed up the road, you slowed down the enemy counterattack. Shilko was rapidly becoming an expert on the criticality of roads in modern war—especially in the northern extreme of the Germanies. Now his instincts told him he had a good target.

Shilko's staff moved like a farmer's family, well-accustomed to fitting their chores together, making everything come out right. Shilko ordered the guns to elevate their barrels before pivoting into firing positions in order to avoid smashing one of the long tubes into the trees that lined the roadway. The heavy barrels elevated like elephant trunks, ready to snort fire upon command. Sleepy-eyed officers shook themselves awake and leaned over their survey equipment, doing their best in the darkness. Shilko doubted that his boys had been paying very close attention to their maps during the march, since every man was weary and willing to simply follow the leader. Paternally, Shilko hinted to them where they were presently located.

Lieutenants and sergeants shouted instructions and waved tiny signal lamps as the big guns aligned themselves in the constricted space. The tracks bit into the surface of the road, and the vehicle engines growled as if in bad temper at being disturbed in the middle of the night. Each noise, each lurching movement, attested to the power of the guns, even before a single round went skyward. The guns reminded Shilko of great, barely manageable animals.

Captain Romilinsky approached. "The first battery is prepared to accept its fire mission, Comrade Commander."

Shilko nodded. He took Romilinsky by the arm, heading for the fire-direction track.

"Comrade Commander, shouldn't we at least call the division and inform them that we're firing a hasty mission?"

Shilko chuckled. For all of his marvelous staff skills,

Romilinsky clearly did not understand how to make the system work when the situation was critical.

"You're thinking like a Prussian," Shilko said with a smile for the younger man. "Look around you. Personally, I haven't recognized a passing unit for hours. I don't know where division is located, and if I did, I wouldn't waste the time to attempt to get a mission cleared under these circumstances. You might as well try to get an apartment in Moscow on an hour's notice."

"But there could be complications."

Shilko liked Romilinsky. The captain was a terrifically serious young man, always painfully sincere and concerned. Shilko expected him to be an excellent battalion commander in his own right someday, if he didn't disappear entirely into the swift current of the General Staff officer program.

"Hesitation . . . the reluctance to take responsibility . . . is something of a Russian disease," Shilko said. "I have never suffered from it myself. Perhaps that's why I'm an over-age lieutenant colonel. But it has always been my conviction that, when things go bad and good men are in demand, there will be enough of us who are willing to say, 'To hell with it,' and do what we believe is right. Tonight I intend to harvest the maximum benefit from all the years of fine training the Soviet Army has provided me. After all, the only things a good artilleryman needs are targets and a known location." Shilko released the younger man's arm, tapping it playfully away. "Did Lenin ask permission to make a revolution? In any case, I want you to run things here while I work my way forward and get those motorized rifle boys straightened out. Listen for me on the radio. And give them hell."

Major Kolovets was unsure of which decision to take. His reinforced tank battalion, tasked to operate as a forward detachment, had simply driven into the enemy's rear after a bit of inconclusive skirmishing. All of the sounds of combat were tens of kilometers behind them now. The situation seemed absurd to Kolovets, so much so that at first he thought it must be a trap. He led his tanks over a series of good secondary roads, unchallenged. Now and again, flickers of light showed through the trees or across open fields, but no one fired a shot. Kolovets ordered his men to hold their fire unless the enemy fired first. They had driven so far that Kolovets noticed a change in the countryside, which rose slightly and had a drier feel to it. Briefly, the column became disoriented in the darkness, and Kolovets feared that his career would be ruined. But his forward security element struck the autobahn's north–south course, and it appeared the unit was in a very good situation after all.

He attempted to call in and report his location. But the airwaves were crowded with static and bizarre electronic whines. He did not know whether he was the victim of electronic attack, or if the interference was accidental. He only knew that he could not talk to his higher commander, and he felt unsure of the real object and latitude of his orders now.

He moved the main body through a narrow, unprotected autobahn underpass, working along gravel roads and trails. The path of least resistance soon drew the column toward the southwest. Several times, the flank security detachments reported enemy vehicles moving on parallel roads. Kolovets feared losing radio communications with his own security elements, as well as with higher headquarters, but local communications cut through the white noise in the air with reasonable dependability. He was terrified of being discovered, then ambushed in the forest. The situation reminded him of fairy tales told him by his mother, in which bad things always happened at night in the woods.

Kolovets repeated his instructions to all units not to engage unless they were fired upon. Then he tried once again to raise anyone in a position of greater authority than his own.

When his calls to the rear brought no response whatsoever, Kolovets halted the column along a hard-surface road in a forested area. He ordered the trail elements to close up, except for the rear security detachment, which was to guard the autobahn underpass, in case the unit had to retrace its route of march. Then he put down the microphone. He decided that the radios were junk. Why couldn't the Soviet Union at least produce decent military radios that could talk through a bit of interference? Kolovets was certain that the enemy didn't have such problems. Everything they had would be brand-new and a marvel of technology. He decided that the battalion communications officer was going to get a stinging official evaluation out of this.

Kolovets leaned out of his turret, staring into the darkness as if he might find an answer in its depths. To his amazement, a vehicle drove straight toward the column with its headlights blazing.

It was a civilian automobile, driving along as though on an outing. Suddenly, the driver hit the brakes. The automobile had been traveling at a high rate of speed, and it was comical to watch the vehicle twist and turn, attempting to weave its way to safety between the armored vehicles and the trees lining the road. The driver finally got the vehicle under control, and he hastily backed and turned. Only when the automobile had nearly escaped, shifting gears to speed off, did a burst of automatic-weapons fire send it crashing into the trees on the side of the road.

Kolovets reached for the microphone, ready to curse the man who had disobeyed his orders by firing. But he stopped himself. There had been no choice, really. The driver would have revealed their presence. Perhaps he was even a spy.

The lieutenant in command of the left flank security element reported in. Kolovets was slow to answer, filled with concern over who might have heard the firing. Belatedly, the little automobile burst into flames.

Kolovets slumped against the turret ring. Now they would have to move. He answered the lieutenant's radio call, hoping it wasn't a major problem. He just wanted everything to go smoothly.

But things were not destined to go smoothly. The left flank security element had discovered a backed-up column of enemy vehicles just to the south. There were artillery pieces, engineer vehicles, and kilometers of trucks. None of them showed any concern about an enemy presence. They were just sitting at a halt between an autobahn crossing point and a small town. Some of the drivers had even gotten out of their vehicles without their weapons. The lieutenant insisted that the column was defenseless.

Kolovets was not so sure. He had never been in combat. As an officer of tank troops, he had been able to steer clear of Afghanistan, since there were not too many tank units in the Soviet contingent, and there were always plenty of ambitious officer volunteers. Further, Kolovets had never commanded a forward detachment, even in an exercise. His receipt of the mission had resulted solely from the accidental configuration of the march serials, from his unit's immediate availability.

Kolovets weighed alternatives. He wished he had one of the fancy decision-making support computers that higher echelons used to figure things out. That way, if things went wrong, he could blame the computer. Now he felt trapped. He could attack the enemy column. Of course, that could turn out badly. What if there were enemy tanks? On the other hand, if he didn't attack, the lieutenant might report him or let something slip. Then he would be in trouble for not showing initiative. It could even be portrayed as cowardice, or dereliction of the assigned mission. Of course, Kolovets thought, he could always keep going toward the Weser River. Perhaps he would not encounter any further enemy activity. If he did make contact with the enemy near the Weser, however, he would be even farther from friendly support.

Kolovets felt as though a great injustice was being done to him. He believed that he was quite a good officer, all in all, even if he wasn't a fanatic about it like the snots who were always working on correspondence courses or reading the deadly dull stuff that came out of the military publishing houses. He was also quite conscientious and careful about the misappropriation of military goods. He never got greedy or took anything that could reasonably be missed. A bit of gasoline here and there was the commander's prerogative, just so a man could make ends meet. Kolovets did not mind all of the nonsense the system put a man through. But he did not believe that it should be his responsibility to make decisions of this sort. He was a good officer who followed orders.

The lieutenant called in an updated report, virtually begging Kolovets to attack the stalled enemy column.

In response, Kolovets tried one more time to reach his next higher commander. The attempt failed as bluntly as had all of the others.

Kolovets hated the lieutenant for putting him in such an awkward position. Probably some nasty little Komsomol twit. The kind who would run to report the slightest perceived failings in his legitimate superiors. The army wasn't what it used to be. All of the restructuring nonsense had ruined it. Nowadays everybody was a tattler, and careers ended abruptly for trivial reasons. Things had gone downhill to the point where lieutenants could criticize higher officers in the pages of *Red Star,* the military's primary newspaper. No one seemed to have any respect for the tried-and-true way of doing things.

Kolovets felt cursed. He did not have a real choice that he could see. Perhaps there really were no enemy tanks in the halted column. The enemy couldn't have tanks everywhere, could they? And even if things turned out badly, they couldn't very well punish you for fighting.

Reluctantly, feeling as though his fate had been stolen from his hands, Kolovets ordered his unit to move out of the woods and begin prebattle deployment across the high fields to the south. He had his best company commander on the guiding flank. The boy was a good map-reader, and Kolovets was not about to trust his own skills in the dark and at a time like this. He made it very plain to the boy what he wanted: no nonsense, just get everybody out on line and hit the enemy from an oblique angle. Kolovets tried to phrase the orders over the radio so that everyone listening would know that, should the attack fail, it would obviously be the company commander's fault.

As the firing calmed, moving on to other killing grounds, Seryosha suggested to Leonid that they hide in the basement. Occasional local shots, like strings of firecrackers, underscored the magnitude of any decision to move at all. Leonid felt miserable, lying in his wet tunic with splinters of plastic from the cassettes he had stuffed in his trouser pockets jabbing him in the thighs and groin.

"What if they're still downstairs?" he said. "What if they're just being quiet and waiting?"

Seryosha considered the possibility. "I can't hear anything," he answered nervously. "Can you?"

"I don't think so."

"If they come back, they're bound to find us up here. Anyway, there's more protection from the artillery and everything down in the basement."

"You know how to get there?"

"I think so."

Leonid did not much like the idea of being shut up in a dark, foreign basement. But he realized that Seryosha was right. The fighting had so shaken the floor beneath them that he had expected the house to fall apart under the strain.

Simultaneously, the two boys began to rise.

"You're clacking," Seryosha said. "What have you got in your pockets?"

Leonid pushed at his comrade. "Just go."

Seryosha led the way, stepping cautiously down the littered stairs. There was so much plaster and glass scattered about that it was impossible to be really quiet. Seryosha took one step at a time, and Leonid imitated him, pausing at each new level to await a violent response.

A scab of plaster crunched under Leonid's boot. But the rest of the house remained still. It felt distinctly empty now. As they finished with the ordeal of the stairs they could see each other's features clearly in the pinkish-orange glow of fires lowering beyond the broken-out windows.

"There was a door back in the kitchen," Seryosha said. "That had to be it."

But as they turned into the downstairs hallway, the lumpish outline of a corpse blocked their path. The dark outline of the helmet identified the body as Soviet.

Leonid and Seryosha edged past the dead soldier, careful to avoid any contact, as though the body bore a special contagion in the darkness.

They found their way to the kitchen. A fluttering glow lit

the room where they had happily stuffed themselves just a few hours earlier. Now the room lay in a jagged shambles.

"The door was over there," Seryosha said, gesturing with the long barrel of the light machine gun. He stopped, and Leonid understood that now it was his turn to go first.

All right, Leonid thought, trying to steel himself. He knew now that he was not a brave man. He felt terribly, unmistakably afraid. He forced his legs to carry him across the room. The door to the basement creaked as he opened it, and the sound seemed so loud that he was sure every enemy soldier in the area must have heard it. He stood indecisively at the top of a black chasm.

"I can't see anything. It's pitch black."

"Here. Take this." Seryosha poked a small cylinder into Leonid's hand. It took him a moment before he realized that it was a cigarette lighter, looted from somewhere.

"It's all right," Seryosha went on. "I have another one."

Leonid flicked on the little flame with his left hand, holding his assault rifle at the ready with his right.

"Get the light down out of sight," Seryosha insisted.

Leonid advanced downward into the darkness, testing the steps. He heard the reassuring noises of Seryosha close behind him. The stairs were narrow and there was no handrail. Leonid shifted his weight, tapping down to find the next level. The small ring of light from the lighter's flame failed to reach into the depths of the cellar.

Leonid felt his fingers burn, and he let the lighter go out. He halted abruptly.

"What's the matter?"

"It got too hot," Leonid whispered. "Just wait a minute."

The two boys stood in the middle of the stairs, balancing in the darkness. The sound of his own breath seemed like the winter wind to Leonid. As soon as he judged it possible, he ignited the lighter again.

Something moved.

Leonid fired his weapon in the direction of the movement, stumbling down the last few stairs, tripping, falling face down. He scrambled and rolled out of the way, firing haphazardly, until he found a wall against which he could huddle. The noise of the shots fired in the enclosed space echoed and rang in his ears. He felt as though he had been slapped hard on both sides of the head.

Seryosha brought the machine gun to bear. It sounded like a cannon firing. Leonid fired again, emptying his magazine in what he hoped was the right direction.

Someone screamed. Another voice shouted foreign words. Seryosha swept the machine gun through the darkness. But no one fired back. Streaks of light zigzagged crazily in the darkness, pinging and sparking off the walls.

"Stop it," Leonid shouted, "stop firing." He had suddenly realized that the ricochets were as likely to kill them as were any enemy actions.

Seryosha ceased firing.

"Surrender," Leonid screamed at their phantom opponents.

A female voice shrieked in response, rising over the low notes of male groans.

"Surrender," Leonid shouted, confused, his voice cracking. "Surrender."

A female voice soared hideously in a strange language, babbling.

"What the hell is going on?" Seryosha said. His voice sounded near panic.

Leonid lifted himself from the floor, all bruised knees and elbows and the burning feel of scraped skin. He lunged toward the foreign voice.

"Surrender," he ordered, his mind wild with fragments of thoughts that would not connect. He clicked on the lighter.

A heavyset girl stood with her back pressed against the wall, hands clutched to her face. She screamed in an animal fear that Leonid could not understand. It had never occurred to him that anyone might be afraid of him.

A few feet away from the girl, two bodies lay—a crumpled man and the thick form of a woman. The moans had stopped now, and the bodies lay remarkably still, with the man hunched over the woman as though he were shielding her.

It struck Leonid that the broken tapes in his pockets probably belonged to this girl, and he suddenly felt ashamed, as though he had been discovered as a thief.

The girl's screams wheezed down into sobs. Leonid let the lighter go out, shaking his singed fingers to soothe them. Seryosha clicked on his own lighter. And the girl howled again. She rubbed herself from side to side against the cinderblock wall, as though she wanted to grind herself into it.

"Oh, no," Leonid said suddenly, as the situation began to come clear to him. "No . . . I didn't mean it . . ." He wished he could make the girl understand. He looked at her, gesturing thoughtlessly with his reeking weapon. "I didn't mean it," he repeated. "It was all an accident."

The girl's voice welled up again.

Seryosha stepped forward, slapping the girl with the hand that held the lighter. When it went out, Leonid took his turn again, working the flint with his sore fingers.

"Shut up," Seryosha ordered. "You just shut up." He slapped the girl again. There was a totally unfamiliar tone in Seryosha's voice now.

The girl hushed slightly, as though she understood. But Leonid knew she didn't understand at all.

"I'm sorry," he told her again, anyway.

"You bet you're sorry," Seryosha told him angrily. Then he punched the girl. "Shut *up.*"

"Stop it," Leonid told him.

"What do you mean, stop it?" Seryosha asked. *"Who are you?* You just *killed* them. Do you realize what's going to happen to us if somebody hears her and comes down here? They'll kill *us."*

Such a possibility had not occurred to Leonid. Now it reached him in its fullness, stopping him with its power.

The girl sobbed against the wall, bleeding driblets from her lower lip. She had gone beyond words now, and she merely cried, face turned to one side. Her sounds were those of a weakening animal.

Seryosha thrust with the machine gun, jamming its muzzle hard into her chest like a spear. Then he brought the heavy stock around and smashed it into her face. Leonid watched in wonder. With clumsy speed, Seryosha beat the girl to the ground, hitting her so hard with the machine gun that she could not meaningfully resist. She waved a pudgy hand at the descending blows, then toppled to the side, crumpling in on herself. Seryosha brought the butt of the weapon down on her skull with all of his weight behind it Then he hit her again. And again.

Finally, the boy straightened, gasping for breath.

"Now she won't tell anybody," he said.

FOURTEEN

Starukhin smashed his fist down onto the map table. "Don't sing me a song, you little bastard. *Fix* it."

"Comrade Army Commander," the shattered chief of signals said, "the communications complex is a complete loss. A direct hit. It will take some time to restore—"

"I don't *have* time, you shit. I should send you down with the motorized rifle troops and let you see what war's really like. How can I run an army when I can't talk to anybody?"

"Comrade Army Commander, we can still communicate using manual Morse. And the auxiliary radios will be off the trucks and set up in no time. It's just the multiplexing that will take a little time."

"I don't *have* time. *Time* is the one thing I *don't* have," Starukhin shouted. "You should've had all of the auxiliary systems set up and ready to operate. You're a moron, a disgrace." He looked around the headquarters. "You're all a damned disgrace."

The chief of signals almost replied that, since they had just shifted locations, it was unreasonable, even impossible, to expect that all of the backup systems would be fully prepared for operations. They had still been having trouble with the microwave connections even before the enemy strike. But he realized that it was hopeless to argue. All you could do was let the army commander blow over you like a storm, then pick up whatever was left.

Starukhin suddenly turned away. He began to pace back and forth like a powerful caged cat. Without warning, he smashed a hanging chart full of figures from the wall.

"I need to *talk.*"

Colonel Shtein watched the artfully crude film of the destruction of Lueneburg on the television monitor. As he watched, the same images were being broadcast over the highest-powered emitters in the German Democratic Republic. Shtein had no doubt that the film would be monitored in the West. It would soon gather the expected attention to itself. Even if the chaotic interference in the air completely blocked a successful broadcast into the heart of West Germany, the NATO elements hanging on in Berlin would monitor it. One way or another, the message would get through. Even the satellite television broadcasts from Moscow carried the report on the regular channels.

. . . Senseless destruction . . . precipitated and carried out by the aggressive NATO forces who are bent on destroying the cities and towns of the Federal Republic of Germany . . . perhaps even turning West Germany into a proving ground for their insane theories of tactical nuclear war . . . in the opinion of experts, a nuclear war restricted to West German soil would cause . . .

And the voice-over was merely ornamentation. The powerful images of toppling medieval buildings, of women and children dashing, falling, cowering, of civilians twisted into the frozen acrobatics of death, and of the Dutch forces firing indiscriminately, were irresistible. Shtein was well aware of how far the skills of Soviet media specialists had come over the years.

Shtein was convinced that this was a war-winner. At least the overall approach. Modern war was hardly a matter of beating each other over the head with a club. Shtein saw it as a highly articulated, challengingly complex conflict of intellects and wills. *Die Welt als Wille und Vorstellung.* He laughed to himself, remembering his student days. He loved the Germans. They were so absolutely right, and so thoroughly unable to act upon the correctness of their conclusions.

We will beat them with cameras, Shtein thought. With video technology. With their own wonderful tools. He could not understand how the West could neglect so totally its vast array of technology that could potentially be used for propaganda purposes. War was, after all, a matter of perceptions. Even the most dull-witted historian could tell you that being physically beaten was not nearly as important as being convinced that you had been defeated. Shtein believed that he was one of the pioneers, one of the soldiers of the future.

He admired the wrenching conclusion of the film once again. It would be broadcast again in an hour, then every hour on the hour. It would be supplemented by other clips as the war progressed, shifting the concentration of the propaganda effort as necessary. Fighting for the invisible, for the intangible, for the ultimately vital, Shtein thought. And he smiled.

Yes. The world as will and idea.

Major General Duzov, commander of the Tenth Guards Tank Division, watched the attack from the forward observation post established by the assaulting regiment. He recognized that his presence troubled the regiment's commander. But Duzov didn't care. In an earlier assault, he had lost a regiment of tanks in two hours, in a swirling British counterattack that had ruined both the Soviet force and its antagonist. And he had not been on the scene to control the situation. Now, if his division was going to take any more catastrophic losses, he at least intended to be present.

Lieutenant General Starukhin, his superior, had been as explicit as he could be. Punch the hole, Duzov. They're worn down. Punch the hole, or don't let me see your face alive.

He had two more chances. This attack, then the commitment of the trailing regiment. Duzov would have preferred to wait until he could strike with both regiments simultaneously, as well as throwing back in the battered motorized rifle regiment that had been working the broken ground to the south and the pathetic remains of the shattered tank regiment. Duzov believed in concentrated blows. And he knew he had one of the very best divisions in the Soviet Army. He hated to see it squandered piecemeal. It went against the grain of everything he had been taught, against all his beliefs.

But Starukhin had been adamant, rising to fury. *Hit them.* Just hit them again and again. This isn't the General Staff Academy. Drive over them, Duzov. Save your maxims and elegant solutions for your memoirs.

Perhaps Starukhin was right. Keep up the pressure. Don't allow the enemy breathing space.

The earth twitched beneath his feet. The artillery preparation had begun, concentrating all available fires on the known or estimated British positions. The broad, low valley filled with light, as though a bizarre morning had arrived ahead of schedule. Shells crashed and sputtered, ripping into the horizon by the thousands. Duzov could not understand how men survived such shelling. Yet he knew that some of them always did. It was, at times, amazingly difficult to kill the human animal.

The streaking dazzle of a multiple rocket launcher barrage rose from the left of the observation post. Then the canopy of scheduled illumination began to unfold, with lines of illumination bursting in crooked ranks, four to six hundred meters apart. The British had a significant gunnery advantage in the dark, so all local units had been ordered to fire a high percentage of illumination, while the heavier rear guns concentrated their efforts on target destruction.

The attacking regiment had been well-drilled, and now, tired from the march, going into battle for the first time, struggling with the unfamiliar terrain, the subunits nonetheless appeared in good order, flooding over the near crests in company columns that soon drilled out into columns of platoons, all the while making good combat speed. Duzov admired his troops and the power of the overall spectacle.

On the valley floor, the platoons fanned out and the combat vehicles came on line. Duzov could easily pick out the positions of the company and battalion commanders, of the staggered ranks of tanks and infantry fighting vehicles, and the air-defense weaponry trailing to the rear. On the trail of the maneuver battalions, the lean-barreled self-propelled guns snooped along, ready to provide immediate fire support to the assault. Then, at the very rear, odd support vehicles and little clusters of ambulances followed. It was one of the most complete maneuvers Duzov had ever seen, and it suddenly translated into timelessness for him. It had never struck him before, but now he saw in the surging lines the perfect modern version of the old Imperial armies marching out in their ready ranks, the men of Suvorov or Kutuzov. The only difference was that today the rank and file wore layers of technology, armor, and mechanization in place of the colorful uniforms of old. In a moment of skepticism and refusal, he told himself that there was really no comparison between these squat, ugly steel bugs beetling across the valley floor and the antique brilliance of hussars and grenadiers. But it *was* the same. He could not deny it now. It was exactly the same, and the revealed truth of it burned into Duzov. What ever changed about war? he asked himself.

The British gunners and tank crews began to find targets, even with the Soviet artillery still crashing upon them. Duzov had to admire the British. He doubted that many men, especially those who had not previously known war, would even briefly attempt to stand their ground in the face of such an onslaught. Here and there, one of Duzov's vehicles convulsed into a tiny bonfire or fell, crippled, from the advancing ranks. Duzov returned to his insistent vision. It was all so much the same he could hardly believe it. The way you pictured men falling away at the first enemy musket volleys. Only now the men had been made a part of fighting systems.

Upon reaching the incline on the far side of the valley, his tanks briefly halted, not content with suppression fired from the move. Commanders' machine guns traced toward targets selected for subunit volleys. The ranks of steel rippled with muzzle blasts and recoils. Then they began to march again, picking up speed as they closed. You could almost hear the drumbeats and clipped, shouted commands issued under sweat-drenched mustaches. Close ranks, close ranks, you scum.

The artillery shifted to a deeper concentration line as the Soviet vehicles approached the military crest. Duzov watched, pained, as more and more of his vehicles fell out, some ending their journeys with volcanic explosions from which no survivors would emerge. Hundreds of garish parachute flares hung in the sky at once, and the battle took on a burnished hyperreality. The effect was as though the entire world were made of metal. The advancing lines wavered as individual tanks or platoons sought ways around local terrain impediments. But the classic, magnificent formations never broke.

As the last artillery lifted a new presence appeared over the battlefield, to the accompaniment of green flares. This element could not be fitted so neatly into Duzov's historical model. Three pairs of helicopter gunships rode in through the flare-scarred sky, coming from the right, huge flying monsters, frightening in their aspects even to Duzov. The ugly aircraft had a presence both horrid and magical, spitting rockets like flying dragons or slowing into missile-attack runs. Then they disappeared over the waves of Soviet vehicles.

The attack made the crest, and the vehicles continued down into the next valley. A radio set in the observation post squealed and coughed with requests for more illumination, even as another station reported that they had driven through the British position. A spontaneous cheer went up from the group of officers, clerks, and signalers assembled at the observation post. But Duzov surveyed the wastage in the valley and on the far slopes as the last flares sputtered into oblivion.

He turned to the regiment's commander.

"Don't stop. *Drive* them. The British will throw in everything they have now; they'll try to block you at all costs. But we have the initiative. The Three-thirty-first Tank Regiment will be up shortly after dawn. Do whatever else you must, but don't let anything stop your tanks."

Lieutenant General Trimenko closed his eyes to the false dawn that rimmed the horizon, resting as best he could in the shuddering helicopter seat. He knew he needed a few hours of real sleep. But he wanted to make just one more visit forward, to check up on the commander of the Sixteenth Guards Tank Division.

Trimenko felt a weary elation that kept him moving. He kneaded the pouch of pistachio nuts in his pocket, reflecting that he would have to fill it up as soon as he returned to the army command post. The night was going well, after all. It had been a near thing, and the situation still was not entirely under control. But the indicators were good. The German counterattack had been contained, after a few desperate hours, well south of the line of Highway 71. In the end, it appeared that the Germans had only loaded more of their forces deeper into Malinsky's trap. And the Dutch simply had not mustered enough punch to make a difference. According to the last report he had received, the lead regiments of the Sixteenth Tank were loose in the German rear, amplifying the favorable situation created by the forward detachments and inexorably closing the clamp behind the German operational grouping. Trimenko saw clearly that the only hope for the West German corps at this point was a full-scale breakout attack to the rear, followed by an attempt to stabilize the situation on the Weser River line. But there were no indications that the Germans were even considering such an alternative, and Trimenko doubted that it would come to pass. The Germans were determined to trap themselves. In any case, he was convinced that his forces would be on the Weser in sufficient strength by noon the next day to create panic. No, he corrected his weary brain. Today. Noon today. It's already today.

Trimenko slipped off his headset, sick of the pilots' blather. He settled lower behind his seat belt, thinking of Starukhin and how furious his rival would be to find that

Trimenko had beaten him to the Weser, while Starukhin himself was still struggling to achieve his own breakthrough. And why stop at the Weser? Trimenko felt confident now that he could beat Starukhin to the Rhine, as well. It was a matter of detailed calculation, of efficiency, of forcing men and events to conform to the rigorous science of war. Starukhin's reliance on ardor and native wit had brought the Third Shock Army commander up short. Starukhin had had better tank terrain, far better than the muck through which Trimenko had been forced to attack. And Starukhin had had more support from frontal assets. Really, he had enjoyed all of the advantages. But Starukhin was an anachronism.

The pilots saw the tracer rounds rising toward the windshield. The senior pilot had made the decision to fly higher than usual, afraid of snagging power lines in the morbid German darkness. He had not expected any problems with air defenses so far behind Soviet lines.

But the tracers reached insistently toward the little aircraft, pulsing up toward the pilots with a peculiar slow-motion effect. The pilot-navigator shouted from the right-hand seat, and the senior pilot tried to bank the helicopter away from the staccato flashes.

The desperate maneuver of the aircraft woke Trimenko from his reverie. Over the shoulders of the pilots, the distant battlefield turned on end until it was a vertical band of light. Trimenko's maps and papers skittered off the seat, and he grasped for anything he could use to stabilize himself. Then the aircraft jolted several times in rapid succession, and a shock of white filled Trimenko's eyes as one of his own mobile air-defense guns blasted him out of the sky.

FIFTEEN

Captain Levin stood in a deserted restaurant in Hameln, munching on bread and cold ham. Outside, small-arms fire intermittently tested the night around the air-assault battalion's perimeter, but there was a definite lull in the fighting. You could sense it as clearly as you could predict what was coming next during an uninspired political lecture or in a mediocre piece of music. Levin knew that the war would return, that the British or the Germans or somebody would come back hard at the air-assault force. They would come with well-organized firepower, with determination, perhaps in the last moments before dawn. But now, in the darkness, there were a few moments during which a man could think.

Levin tried to remember anything that he might have left undone, any small detail that might contribute to the outcome of the fighting. But his mind strayed willfully back to the experience of the air assault itself, and to the heady first minutes of combat. Levin had alternated between an awareness of his own fear and the electrifying thrill of the experience. He remembered the absolute joy of overrunning the enemy position from behind, the feeling of accomplishment disproportionate to the actual event. And the conflict with Gordunov over the importance of preserving the historical monuments in the old town. The great surprise, however, was how much he frankly had enjoyed the fighting. He had worried for years that he might be a coward, and he had expected to feel somber and troubled with cosmic guilts in the wake of battle. But the action only left him eager and confident. He felt younger than he had felt in years, almost a schoolboy at play.

At the meeting of the command and staff collective, the defense had been rationalized. To Levin's surprise, Gordunov had ordered him to take command of the approach that led from the railway station and Highway 1 to the east back to the town center and the near ends of the bridges. He had been given a platoon reinforced with an automatic grenade launcher section. Levin had not been entirely sure whether the battalion commander had given him the assignment as a reward or as an ironic joke, since the failure to hold the main road approach to the ring road that circled the medieval heart of the town could funnel the combat right into the old town itself. But it was a key position, in any case, since its penetration would split the eastern-bank defense in two.

Levin had positioned his handful of men carefully, trying to remember all of the rules learned from textbooks and training exercises. He tied in to Anureyev's company on the southern approaches and the southern bridge itself, and to the special assault platoon in the hospital grounds and on the northern bridge. A special assault squad detailed to seize the railway station had failed, but now they formed an outpost line for Levin's defense. He organized the supply of ammunition and rations for his force. Feeding the men turned out to be the easiest part of the mission, since the German shops were astonishingly full. There was even fresh bread.

Everything seemed plentiful, not just food. Despite the confusion and urgency of battle, it had been impossible not to notice the riches tumbled about in the shattered storefronts. Airborne and air-assault soldiers were highly disciplined; still, it had been difficult to keep them out of the shops. At one point, Levin had been forced to shout at and threaten several troops who were looting a jewelry store, helping themselves to watches and trophies for girlfriends back home.

Breaking up the thievery proved unusually difficult for Levin, since he could not quite bring himself to blame or disdain the boys with any heartfelt vigor. In the wreckage of the jewelry shop, the disordered contents of smashed showcases shone like mythical treasures under the beam of his officer's pocket lamp. He could not understand how the West Germans could make up their minds what to buy from so vast a selection. And, while he would never have dreamed of taking anything for himself, he had been tempted to grab up a trinket for Yelena.

In the end, he had mastered himself. He took nothing. But he had not been particularly harsh on the soldiers. He chased them away but allowed them to flee with treasures in hand.

Levin gnawed off another mouthful of ham and thought of Yelena. She had acquired a totally unexpected taste for Western things. She especially liked Western fashions now, although they did not suit her. She had grown into a woman unfathomably different from the girl with whom he had fallen in love. Yelena had always had the quickness and edge of a city girl. Yet, when they first met under the hilariously correct circumstances of a Komsomol gathering, she had spoken as a true believer, speaking her lines with conviction when the exchanges covered the triumphs of socialism and the road to inevitable communism, or the dignity of the proletariat and the need to revitalize the role of the Party through restructuring. But there had been nothing dignified or formal in her lovemaking. It was youthful, and animal, and it held Levin spellbound. It was only much later that he realized the extent to which she had led the way. He had fancied himself as serious and mature, destined to lead men. But Yelena had led him. Her father, an urban Party official of influence, had opposed their marriage at first. Levin had been at a loss to understand why, since he had a perfect

Komsomol record and he was a model student at the academy for military-political education.

Yelena had her way. They married. She was an only child, and she always had her way with her family. Levin had dutifully volunteered for the airborne forces, and, as a new junior lieutenant, he received a prized posting to the Baltic Military District.

They had a child. Mikhail. Levin, who spent his off-duty time studying and preparing his classes for the troops, was astonished when this new life appeared, as though Yelena's months of pregnancy and complaints had merely been another academic problem. Suddenly, he was a father. Now when he spoke at lectures and political-education seminars about the duty of the Soviet soldier to prepare the road to a better future for all mankind, the word "future" and the tumult of concepts and images associated with it resonated with a deeper meaning than ever before. A *better* future. A *better* world. Levin realized, to the tune of an infant's cries, how these notions really had been little more than cold abstractions for him in the past. But now it was all different. The better world would be the world in which his son would live.

Yelena changed after the child came. Perhaps she had already been changing, although he had not noticed it. But the event of childbirth seemed to unleash something unexpected in her, an uncomfortable and unwelcome new spirit. She began to joke about the Party and about Levin's beliefs. He could not comprehend the change in her. And she complained that he only had time for his books, and that he was naïve and blind to opportunity. She gained weight.

She demanded that he leave the army as soon as he could. Her father was in a position to secure him a very good Party job; perhaps he could even arrange for an early release from Levin's military commitment. He needed a job with a future, she insisted. And he knew that she meant a job with perquisites and comfort and material possibilities. He was learning fast as a father.

He, too, saw many things differently now. Yet he continued to believe. He read history, and he reviewed how far the people had come. Socialism was far from perfect. But it was continually evolving under the tension of the dialectic. And it *had* made the world a better place, Levin believed. It had rescued Russia from its fatal backwardness, and it had made the Soviet Union a great power. If the price had been high, then so had been the achievement. There was a new equity and security in the life of the average man. If there were many problems that remained unsolved, it was up to the present generation to address them, to fight inertia and complacency. Really, it was an exciting time to be alive, rich with new possibilities. He could not understand how Yelena had so fully lost her vision, how she could fail to see the dynamic at work.

And he loved the army. He found the purely military side of his duties almost more stimulating than the political, even as he enthusiastically embraced every opportunity to reach out to the young soldiers, to help mold them into better citizens of a better state. Slogans that others mocked were sacred to him, and he labored long over the most minor paperwork. He sought to perfect his abilities as a leader and his political-didactic skills.

Yelena had an affair with a moronic line officer. When Levin found out and confronted her, months after the rest of the garrison had known about the situation, Yelena stamped and screamed that he neglected her, that he did not love her, and that he did not even care enough to provide for the future of his child.

The accusations about the child hurt him most. Even though he could not accept them as true. It was Yelena who showed little concern for the infant. At times, she seemed to regard their son's care as nothing but a loathsome duty to be discharged with as little effort and conviction as possible. She was not even very clean about it all, and their cramped apartment grew slovenly.

Yet her threats about leaving him reduced him to panic. He had long loved her, and he had never wavered in that love. Now, at the revelation of her betrayal—a betrayal she had not tried very seriously to hide—he felt his love for her overripen to desperation. He hated the humiliation of it. And he loved her anyway. She let herself go. In a matter of months, she looked ten years older than her age. She painted herself with far too much makeup, becoming a cartoon of a Western harlot. And, as she took from him, he only wanted to give her more. He wondered how he could possibly make a contribution to saving the world if he could not even save the woman he loved. He begged her not to leave him, to give him a chance, leaving all of his accustomed notions of manliness in ruins.

He promised he would leave the army. He would do everything she wanted him to do. But it was too late to avoid a last posting. He had a commitment to fulfill, and even Yelena's father could not move the Soviet bureaucracy with the requisite speed. And he went to the Group of Soviet Forces in Germany. Alone.

Yelena went to live with her family until his tour ended. She wrote decent, even loving letters, and sent him snapshots of his son. He tried not to think of the men with whom she might be betraying him. Because, he told himself, they did not matter. The weakness and error of the flesh was a minor concern. It was only the future, the better future, that mattered. There would be a tomorrow of decency, fairness, and love. There would come a future without betrayals.

"Comrade Political Officer?"

It was Dunaev, a lieutenant from Third Company.

"Over here."

Dunaev searched the cavernous room with his pocket lamp, finally slapping its light across Levin's face. Then he respectfully lowered the beam.

"Comrade Political Officer, the battalion commander has sent me to relieve you. He wants you to report to him at the hospital."

"Is something wrong?"

"I don't know. He just told me to relieve you."

Levin brushed the crumbs from his hands and slung his assault rifle onto his right shoulder. "All right. Let me walk you around our positions. There's plenty of food here, by the way. The soldiers have already eaten. Just keep them away from the liquor."

"Yes, Comrade Political Officer."

Levin took the lieutenant on a tour of the platoon perimeter. The buildings, both new and old, were extremely well constructed, and the ring boulevard and the park beyond offered a perfect break where overlapping fields of fire could be established. Most of the soldiers were awake and alert, the noncommissioned officers seemed to be firmly in charge, and no one had wandered from his assigned position. Levin suddenly felt very proud of them all, proud of how much they had already achieved.

He left Dunaev back at the ad hoc command post in the restaurant and walked briskly down the main street, keeping well under the shadows of the overhanging buildings. From behind a line of gabled rooftops that paralleled the river up ahead, a vibrant glow lit the sky. The section of town on the far side of the river was burning. But the old town remained safe, even strangely peaceful, as Levin made his way through its heart.

The refugee traffic had long since stopped attempting to pass through Hameln. The next wave of traffic would undoubtedly be combat vehicles attacking to dislodge the Soviet defenders. Levin marched along, reviewing the ranks of shops. The fire's glow sent just enough light into the street to hint at inexhaustible riches. Levin had thought himself prepared for the inequitable wealth of revanchist West Germany. But now, in the bloodstained darkness, he could only wonder at the material splendor of this small city. He had studied the problem, and he knew that, somewhere, there must be horrid slums where the exploited were contained, where imported Turkish wage-slaves clung to one another in a desperate attempt to survive. Yet this casual display of riches, these shops bursting with merchandise of undeniable quality, troubled him profoundly.

Above the modern shop displays, handsomely preserved and restored medieval buildings leaned over the street, as if peering down at him. It would be criminal to destroy this, he thought. He recognized the necessity of seizing the bridges for the passage of Soviet forces, however. Now, he reasoned, it was really up to the NATO commanders as to whether or not all of this would perish. He himself had no wish to fight here, to risk the destruction of such monuments without necessity.

Past the old town hall, he turned right up another street of shops that led toward the hospital. Offhandedly, he considered the height of the old town hall, as well as its central location. This was where the battalion command post needed to be, in accordance with military logic. The hospital was too far north to allow firm control of the entire battalion. And its use was contrary to the laws of war.

He stalked by a shop whose broken window featured women's clothing. The shock of a nearby blast had toppled one mannequin into the arms of another, as though she had been wounded and caught in her fall by a friend. It would be lovely, Levin thought, to bring Yelena here, after the peace, to show her the beauty of the place, and to buy her things in these shops. How much could he afford? he wondered. Then he laughed at himself. After the peace, everything would be reordered. More would be available for all of the people. Once a great European peace had been established, military spending could be reduced significantly. The transition would take time, of course. . . .

In the meantime, there was a war to fight. Levin was proud of how well he had done in his first combat action. It was amazing how closely experience conformed to the texts over which he had labored. Envelopment was the preferred technique against a strong position . . . a well-organized defense could be remarkably strong. . . .

Why had the battalion commander called him back? Levin could think of nothing that he had done wrong militarily. And, despite their personal differences, Levin knew that Gordunov was an officer of very high technical capabilities. The Soviet military needed men such as Gordunov. It was important, however, to restrain their excesses. Levin saw no point in wanton destruction. It was not in the spirit of Socialist internationalism. The goal of the good communist was to preserve all that was good, but to surgically excise that which functioned to the detriment of the oppressed masses. Of course, you could not consider a man such as Gordunov a true communist.

Levin was familiar with the stories about Gordunov's adventures in Afghanistan. Gordunov was described as a survivor, one of the men with charmed lives who always emerged whole from the fire and smoke. But he was also renowned for his excessive violence. Reportedly, it was Gordunov's style to kill every living thing around him.

Levin had heard so many contradictory stories about the failed military assistance mission to Afghanistan that he tried to separate the tales from the main currents of his political thought. He was frankly embarrassed by his country's evident failure. But on a political level, he rationalized that the attempt to bring about a Socialist state had been premature in Afghanistan, since the inhabitants had not developed a sufficient level of political and social culture. The reports of brutality haunted his rationalizations, as well. But it had to be acknowledged that wars of that nature were always brutal. Professional officers excused the Soviet military failure in Afghanistan by pointing out that they had never been allowed an adequate level of troop strength, and that the Soviet military establishment had not been designed to fight such a war. Overall, there seemed to be two major schools of thought among the officers Levin knew personally. Airborne and special-operations officers had sought assignments to the contingent of Soviet forces in Afghanistan, eager for the combat experience and the awards. Gordunov, for instance, was one of the most highly decorated officers of his generation, and he was a very young lieutenant colonel. But officers from the other branches often had mixed feelings. Tank and most motorized rifle officers resented the difficulty of the circumstances under which mechanized forces had to operate and the lack of proportionate glamour for their branches, and support officers viewed many of their logistics tasks as verging on the impossible. The attitude of artillerymen had evolved over the years. Initially, Levin had been told, there had been so many problems with fire support that artillery officers regarded an Afghan assignment as a quick way to end a career. But the situation improved as new fire-support techniques were developed and mastered. By the final stages of the involvement, many artillery officers had regarded

Afghanistan as a marvelous place to experiment with their guns, multiple rocket launchers, and automated control mechanisms. Aviators grew to hate the place almost to a man.

Levin arrived at the broad street that fed into the northern bridge and separated the old town from the hospital complex. The burned-out hulks of automobiles in silhouette looked like obnoxious modern sculptures. On the left, the river glowed with the reflection of the burning buildings on the west bank. Great pockets of fire rose on the far side of the river, and, as Levin watched, a mortar fired a parachute flare, then another, and a distant machine gun searched out targets. Levin looked at his watch. Past four. It would soon be light. That meant the enemy would be coming soon. Otherwise, the Soviet armored columns would beat them to the crossings. Levin had great faith in the Soviet tankers. They would not let their comrades down. He pictured how it would be when the Soviet tanks inevitably arrived, rolling over the bridges with salutes for the worn-out survivors of the air-assault operation. He imagined it in tones similar to the triumphant scenes that always ended films about the Great Patriotic War. This was genuinely the stuff of heroic legends, Levin realized, and he was thrilled to be a part of it. He felt as though all of his life had pointed him toward this event. He sprinted across the street toward the hospital.

"Anureyev's badly wounded," Lieutenant Colonel Gordunov told Levin. "He's not going to make it. Shot by his own shitty little buggers in the dark."

"Anureyev's a good officer, Comrade Battalion Commander. I'm sorry."

"*Was* a good officer. He's meat for the worms now. But that's what soldiering is about, too, Levin."

"He will have died for a noble cause."

Gordunov shook his head. Levin sensed that the battalion commander had been about to say something biting, then thought better of it. "Anyway, I'm putting you in command of the entire eastern bank. You need to get down to Anureyev's positions on the southern approaches and have a quick look around. If the troops are spread too thin, pull them back. We'll make the bastards fight for every block. But no matter what happens, remember that the primary mission is to retain the northern bridge. That doesn't mean give up the southern bridge without a fight. But the priorities are clear."

"I understand, Comrade Commander."

Gordunov looked him in the eyes. The battalion commander had green eyes as noncommittal as a cat's. In the momentary silence, the smell of their still-damp uniforms mingled with the odors of the hospital.

"I hope you do understand," Gordunov said finally. "Look. As near as I can make out, you have about one hundred and fifteen men left on this side of the river. That doesn't include my headquarters section. The situation on the western bank looks worse, and I've had to reinforce it. I'm going to go over there myself and straighten things out, but I'm leaving the long-range communications here with you. We'll split the command post. I can't be encumbered over there. But I have no doubt that they'll hit you, too. They may try to coordinate an attack from both directions at once. Form a small shock assault-grouping, even if it means thinning the lines. Say about fifteen or twenty men. Enough to make a local difference. Keep them ready in a central location. Be ready to assist me, or to weight the fight at the most threatened point."

"I understand."

"I expect we have enough ammunition. But don't hesitate to make use of the captured weaponry."

A plan began to form in Levin's mind. "Where are the prisoners now?" he asked.

Gordunov stared at him, calculating. "Down in the basement. Don't get a weak stomach, Levin. If you can't control the situation, kill them."

Levin did not answer immediately. He tried to think of the best way to phrase his proposition without angering Gordunov or seeming presumptuous. In the background, hospital noises underlined the more distant noises of battle. The Western doctors were caring for all of the wounded, Soviet, British, German, military, and civilian. But that situation, too, was becoming unmanageable.

"Comrade Commander," Levin began, "if I am to control this bank, I request permission to move your remaining battalion command elements out of the hospital. If you're going across the river, let me move the communications troops and everyone else down to a central location. I can't protect them adequately up here. We'd need to extend the perimeter farther to the north."

"Have a site in mind?" Gordunov said, with no trace of his famous temper.

"The old town hall," Levin said quickly. "There's good elevation for the radio sets, it's well constructed, and it's perfectly centered. We can leave light antitank elements up here to cover the northern approaches and the bridge. And I'll outpost the choke points along the road to the north. Of course, the wounded will stay here, but I'll take our own medical personnel along with me to establish a more centrally located aid station."

"All right," Gordunov said. "That sounds logical enough. But don't go soft on me, Levin."

Levin was relieved. He had been prepared to argue his point. "And the prisoners," he said. "I'll move them into the basement of the town hall. Or somewhere nearby. I won't waste men guarding them. Two should be able to handle it."

"All right, all right. Listen, Levin. You have the makings of a decent soldier. The important thing now is to hang on, no matter how bad the situation may look. Remember, the enemy is paying a price, too. For all we can tell, he may be far worse off than we are." Gordunov paused to look Levin up and down. Levin suddenly sensed that there was something more that the battalion commander wished to communicate to him. "I know," Gordunov picked up again, "that you truly believe . . . in things with which I personally have some difficulty. Perhaps you despise me, Levin. That's ultimately of no consequence. But you must hold on. You cannot let anything interfere with the mission. There are other old buildings. Other towns. Even other men to replace the dead. But there is no other mission for us. You cannot let anything else matter to you."

Levin wanted to assure his commander that he could be

counted upon, that he would never let him down. But Gordunov wasn't finished.

"You're a different type of man from me," the battalion commander said. "Probably a better sort, who knows? But now there's this bridge. Bridges, if we're lucky. I just want you to understand . . ." Gordunov caught himself. "We've got to move. That's enough philosophy. Move the damned command post. But do it quickly. And get down and visit all your positions. Keep the men under tight control. And good luck."

Gordunov turned to go. In the muted light provided by the hospital's emergency generators, Levin caught the sparkle of an awkwardly rigged metal brace showing from beneath a slash in the bottom of Gordunov's trouser leg. Levin felt a tide of emotion sweep over him. He wanted to say something human and decent to this man after all, to recognize him as a comrade, almost to apologize. But Gordunov quickly limped away, and before Levin could sort out his feelings, the battalion commander had disappeared into the night.

SIXTEEN

Major Bezarin wanted to move. He felt his resentment swelling toward genuine anger as the hours burned away. Propped up in the commander's hatch of his tank, he focused on the tiny bead of light that marked the rear of the tank ahead of his own. It was still too dark to discriminate the shapes, but Bezarin could feel the other tanks stopped in the road ahead of him and behind him, a mighty concentration of power not only wasted at the moment, but, worse still, at risk in their compact, stationary mass. Bezarin had been allowed no choice in the positioning of his battalion. The regiment's chief of staff had halted the column without warning, telling Bezarin simply to close up and await further orders. When Bezarin asked if he could deploy off the road into dispersed tactical positions, the chief of staff had brusquely dismissed the idea with the remark that this was no time for nonsense, that the entire regiment had to be prepared to resume movement on a few minutes' notice. And with the reminder that the directive remained in effect limiting radio use to monitoring only, the chief of staff had gone to tuck in the trail battalion.

Bezarin imagined that he could feel the heavy iron breath

of his tanks, his steel stallions aching to break loose. Even with the engines cut, the pungent smell of exhaust hung on in the low-lying roadway, corrupting the cool morning air. To move, to fight, was to have a chance. But it was exasperating, a terrible thing, to be forced to wait without any information. According to the books, Bezarin knew he was supposed to be planning for his commitment and preparing his companies. But he had received no word on where or when or under what circumstances his tanks would enter the battle. He had forced his company commanders to inspect each of their vehicles for its readiness, then he had discussed abstract options with them. But finally, he had realized that he was only robbing them of sleep. Now he waited alone for the fateful radio transmission, or for a courier to ride down along the column, searching for the command tanks. But the radio remained silent, and the only sound was of the occasional tanker dismounting to relieve himself by the side of the road. Beyond the local envelope of silence, the ceaseless war sounds grumped in the distance, teasing him. It reminded him of waiting in the lobby at a film theater, listening to the muffled sound track hint at the drama behind the closed doors of the auditorium. From left to right, the horizon glowed as though the edge of the world had caught fire, flickering in slow motion, then flashing like a photographer's bulb, streaking the running clouds with gypsy colors. Bezarin wanted to enter that world of testing and decision before he could begin to doubt himself in earnest.

His feeling of helplessness was aggravated by the memory of his unit's canal crossing near Salzgitter the evening before. The flagmen had waved the vehicles onto the tactical bridging at regulation intervals, and the only signs of war were a few burned-out hulks from the day's battle. The tone of action, even the sense of urgency, was reminiscent of a demonstration exercise at which a very important observer was present, nothing more. Then, without warning, the canal exploded with fire, heaving tanks, bridging, water, and flames into an inscrutable sky. No one knew exactly what had happened, but Bezarin lost an entire tank platoon and, by sheer chance, his battalion chief of staff and operations officer. Since he had already been forced to send forward two officers to replace losses in committed units, the loss was a sharp blow, burdening him with the need to compensate personally for the cadre shortfall. At the same time, he had surprised himself by thinking frankly that he was glad he had not grown closer to any of the men who had been killed.

The unit had been quickly rerouted over an alternate bridge. But the incident felt like a warning—and a personal challenge to Bezarin. Then, in the growing darkness and confusion, they had been diverted well to the south as the attack up ahead bogged down again. The fatal crossing had been unnecessary. Now he and his tanks waited on a sunken road at the edge of a wood in Germany. Bezarin had not expected too much of Lieutenant Colonel Tarashvili, the regiment's commander. But it seemed outrageous that he had sent no word, no information on the situation whatsoever.

A compact figure vaulted up onto the deck of Bezarin's tank, almost slipping on the clutter of newly added reactive armor. The movement took Bezarin by surprise, isolated as he was in his thoughts and his padded tanker's helmet. But he quickly sensed a familiar presence. He canted his helmet back so he could hear.

The visitor was Senior Lieutenant Roshchin, commander of the Fifth Company, Second Battalion—Bezarin's youngest and least-experienced company commander. Bezarin had kept close to Roshchin's company during the deployment and march, nursing him along. Yet there was something about the boyish lieutenant that brought out Bezarin's temper. He found himself barking at Roshchin over small oversights or inconsequential misunderstandings, and his own lack of self-control only made him angrier still. Through it all, Roshchin reacted with servility and a few mumbled excuses. The boy had the feel of a spaniel addicted to his master's beatings.

Even now, Bezarin almost shouted at the lieutenant to get back to his company. But he captured the words while they were still forming on his lips. Roshchin, he realized clearly, would be nervous, frightened, unsure. Universal human emotions, as Anna would have called them.

"Comrade Commander," Roshchin said, "any word?"

The simple question seemed unforgivably inane to Bezarin, but he was determined to be decent toward the boy.

"Nothing. How's your company doing?"

"Oh, the same, thank you, Comrade Commander. Most of the men are sleeping. Always one crew member on lookout, though, just like the regulations say." He huddled closer to Bezarin, who could smell the night staleness of the boy's breath now. "The march was exhausting; you're all shaken to bits by the time you stop." Bezarin could feel the lieutenant searching through the darkness for a sign of human solidarity, but he could not find the right words to soothe the boy. "I couldn't sleep, myself," Roshchin went on. "I really want to do everything right. I've been going over my lessons in my head."

A number of sharp retorts bolted through Bezarin's mind. Roshchin was a graduate of the Kasan tank school, renowned for the poor quality of its alumni. Bezarin painted in the lieutenant's features from memory. Short, like virtually every tanker. A blond saw blade of hair across the forehead, and the small sculpted nose you saw on certain women with Polish blood. There was neither crispness nor presence to Roshchin, and Bezarin worried over how the lieutenant would perform in combat.

"The war must be going well," the lieutenant said, his voice clearly asking for confirmation.

It was as though Roshchin studied to say things that permitted no reasonable reply, as though his every utterance demanded that Bezarin make a fool of him.

"Of course it's going well," Bezarin responded, forcing the words out, sounding stilted to himself, a bad actor with a poor script.

"I wish I could have a cigarette. One smoke," Roshchin said.

"When it's light."

"Do you think we'll be able to send letters soon?"

Anna. And the letters unwritten, the words unsaid. A remembrance impossibly foreign to the moment.

"Soon, I'm sure," Bezarin said.

"I've written four already," Roshchin said. "Natalya loves to get letters. I've numbered them on the envelopes so that she'll know what order to read them in, even if they all arrive at once."

Bezarin wanted to ask the lieutenant when on earth he had had time to write love letters. But he kept to his resolve to behave decently. It suddenly occurred to him that this boy might not be alive for more than a few hours. And that he had a young wife who meant as much to him as . . . Bezarin switched mental tracks, recalling Roshchin's pride in displaying the stupid-faced bridal snapshot taken by some hung-over staff photographer in a cavernous wedding palace, where marriages were matters of scheduling and norms as surely as were military operations. The stiff, unknowing smiles in the snapshot had made Bezarin unreasonably jealous as the lieutenant insisted on showing them to his new commander.

"I suppose . . . that you miss her," Bezarin said, measuring out the words.

"How could I not miss her?" Roshchin answered. "She's a wonderful girl. The best." There was new life in the lieutenant's voice now.

"And . . . how does she like army life?"

"Oh, she'll get used to it," Roshchin said cheerfully. "It takes time, you know. Really, you should marry, Comrade Commander. It's a wonderful state of affairs."

Advice from this naïve, clumsy lieutenant was almost too much for Bezarin to bear. But he let it roll off.

"You should go and get a little sleep," Bezarin told the boy. "I don't want you to be exhausted. We'll get into the fight today."

"Do you really think so?"

If we're not caught in this stinkhole of a forest, lined up like perfect targets on a damned road, Bezarin thought.

"I'm sure of it. And I want you at your best."

"I won't let you down, Comrade Commander. I wouldn't want Natalya to be ashamed of me."

Leave me, Bezarin thought. Get out of here, you son of a bitch.

"You'll do fine," Bezarin said. "Now get back to your company."

The first morning light had crept up on the two officers during their talk. To Bezarin, the mist wrapping loosely around the trees resembled dirty bandages.

"Go on," Bezarin repeated with forced affability. "I'll wake you in plenty of time."

The lieutenant saluted. Something in the alacrity of it made Bezarin feel as though the boy were saluting a grizzled old general, or his father. Well, I'm not that old, Bezarin thought. Not quite. Thirty-one isn't old enough to be the father of a senior lieutenant.

For an instant, the terrible responsibility he had for the lives of his men glimmered in front of Bezarin. Then the vision evaporated into more conditioned and customary forms of thought. But the morning felt suddenly damp, and his head ached. He repositioned his tanker's helmet. They said that the close-fitting headgear made you go bald, if the war went on too long. What would Anna think of him with a bald pate? And what did she think of him, anyway? Did she think of him at all now? He remembered how she had liked to touch his hair. With one specific, unchanging gesture. No, a bald head would not do. My captain, she said. My fierce warrior captain. But he was a major now, and she was part of history.

Anna liked the birches when their small leaves went the color of old copper. One by one, the leaves deserted as the northern wind probed and gathered force. Then a gusting assault tore them away by the hundreds, revealing the silver-white fragility of the limbs. He remembered the feel of the buttons on a woman's dress. And if I see her again. If ever I see her again . . .

Bezarin smiled mockingly at himself. You can tell her you were supposed to be commanding a tank battalion on the edge of a battle and you thought of laying her ass down in some borrowed apartment.

But his practiced cynicism did not work to its full potential now. He attempted to turn his thoughts back to his duty. Yet he knew that she would be there now, just beyond the edge of his vision. That one time in his life he had been truly afraid. Terrified to ask a thin, laughing girl with hair the color of pouring brandy if she would marry him. Because she laughed so easily when they were alone, and he knew he loved her helplessly and that he could bear losing her more easily than he could have borne her laughter in that unarmed instant. In the subtle light he could see the broad steel shoulders of his tanks taking shape up along the road, and it struck him as absurd that he should be allowed to command such lethal machines when he could not bring himself to risk the wound of a girl's decision.

The radio spoke.

Bezarin recognized the voice of the regiment's commander, passing a brevity code. Bezarin scrambled to copy the message, then to break it out using the sheets he kept in his breast pocket.

Movement. In ten minutes.

The time was unreasonably short after so long a wait. Bezarin hoped he could wake everyone and get all of the engines started in time. It would have been better to warm the engines slowly, since they had been sitting for several hours. Bezarin thought that he would have been wiser to have been readying his force instead of indulging in reveries. But the past was unalterable, and he forced himself to concentrate on the present.

Twenty-six tanks and a bedraggled motorized rifle company. Bezarin shouted at his crew to get their gear on and start up the tank, then he hoisted himself out of the commander's hatch. It required an awkward maneuver to slip down over the jewel boxes of reactive armor that had been bolted onto the tank, and Bezarin hit the ground flat-footed, jolting himself fully awake. He ran along the column, shouting to the officers, nagged by a small, cranky worry over additional mechanical breakdowns. He found that the prospect of moving toward the battle did not bother him at all but filled him with unexpected and even unreasonable energy. He was delighted to find that he was not afraid when it mattered. Only scared of the girls, he decided.

* * *

The regiment's route, studded with traffic controllers, led them through the wreckage of earlier fighting. It was possible to reconstruct much of how the battle had gone from the position of the hulks. In one broad field, a Soviet tank company had been ambushed in battle formation. The burned-out wrecks formed an almost perfect line of battle. Bezarin felt certain that, somehow, he would never let that happen to his battalion, but he wondered simultaneously at the effect such a sight must have on his men as they rolled by with their hatches open.

The enemy appeared to be exclusively British, which both surprised and disappointed Bezarin. He had always pictured himself fighting the Americans or the West Germans. Now he wondered if his unit had not been shunted into a secondary sector, a sideshow. He felt punished by the lack of information from higher headquarters.

There were plenty of ruined British vehicles in evidence, even though visibility remained limited to a few hundred meters on either side of the road. But the obviously larger number of slaughtered vehicle carcasses from Soviet units annoyed Bezarin. The level of destruction appeared to have been terrible on both sides, but the losses were clearly not in balance. Bezarin soon stopped counting and comparing, consoling himself with the smoldering conviction that he would do better.

The British had died mostly in defensive positions, although here and there you could tell that a specific element had waited too long to pull off its position and had been caught in the open. One chaotic intermingling told the story of a local counterattack. The residue of battle left a bitter taste, as though neither side had shown the least mercy.

Bezarin blamed the superior quantitative performance of the British on technology. Of all the fears that intermittently gripped the Soviet officer corps, Bezarin knew that the greatest was of the technological edge the NATO armies possessed, all Party propaganda to the contrary notwithstanding. Often, the fear bordered on paranoia, with worries about secret weapons that NATO might have concealed for sudden employment on the first day of the war. Bezarin saw no evidence for wonder weapons now, but he cursed the mystifying superiority of the Western models of standard battlefield equipment.

One curious aspect of the battlefield was how few bodies were in evidence. Occasionally, a cluster of dead sprawled in a burned fringe around a combat vehicle or lay half-crushed along the roadway. But the greater effect was as if the battle had been a contest of machines, a tournament of systems, with only a handful of human puppeteers. That was an illusion, Bezarin knew. A troubling percentage of the stricken Soviet tanks had their turrets blown completely off. The hulls lay about like decapitated beasts. No crew member could survive such a catastrophic effect. When they died, the great steel animals devoured their human contents, as if in a last act of vengeance.

The last of the morning ground fog clung to the woodlines like decayed flesh slowly loosening from bones. The sky remained overcast, but the heaviness was gone, and the last gray would burn off as the sun climbed higher. Bezarin scanned the grayness. He could already hear the aircraft ripping by just above the visual ceiling. There was no way of telling whose aircraft these were, and Bezarin feared the impending clarity of the day. The march column moved swiftly, except for the odd accordion stop when a traffic controller faced a dilemma for which his orders had not prepared him. Yet Bezarin wanted them to go faster, to push the vehicles to the limit of their speed.

You had to close fast. That was what the books said, and Bezarin had dutifully read the books. If you closed fast, the enemy could not bring his air power or indirect fires to bear, and you cheapened your opponent's long-range antitank guided missiles. You had to close fast and get in among the enemy subunits, then you needed to keep going until you were behind him, to make it impossible for him to fight you according to his desires. It sounded very straightforward on the page. But Bezarin suspected that there was a bit more to it during the actual execution.

A loud thump-thump-thump sounded off to the right. A stand of trees bowed toward the march column, bending away from lashing, half-hidden bursts of fire.

The correct response was to button up, to seal the crews

within the armor of the tanks and infantry fighting vehicles. But the prescribed action was impossible for the vehicle commanders. As long as they remained on radio listening silence, signal flags and then flares were the order of the day. The vehicle commanders had to remain exposed until the final battle deployment began. Bezarin unconsciously worked down lower in his turret, bracing his shoulder against his opened hatch. A flight of jets shrieked by so low that the noise cut sharply through the padded headgear.

You couldn't even see the damned things.

A row of birches straggled along the road. Birches even in West Germany. Anna of the birches. Bezarin felt the grime of sleeplessness on his face, lacquered over the film of tank exhaust and sweat. Not a very romantic picture, Anna. No dashing officers here out of some ball in an old novel. We are the unwashed warriors.

Up ahead, billows of smoke and dust suddenly engulfed the march column. Bezarin saw an antiaircraft piece swing its turret snappily about, its radar frantic. But the weapon did not fire. A bright burst, clearly an explosion, flared in the lead battalion's trail company, which was separated from Bezarin's unit by only a few tens of meters instead of the regulation number of kilometers. Everything seemed crammed, condensed in both time and space, crippled by haste and necessity.

The column did not stop moving. A minute later, Bezarin's command tank turned off the road to move around a pair of burning infantry fighting vehicles. He could feel a distinct difference as the tank's tracks bit into the meadowland. The driver simply followed the vehicle to his front, and Bezarin inspected the vehicles that had been hit. The troop carriers burned in patches. There was no sign of life from within them. You could not even see what hit you, Bezarin thought. The spectacle made him want to close with the enemy immediately, to pay them back.

Bezarin's driver whipped the tank back onto the roadway. His driver had a habit of snapping the tank about, in a jaunty sort of movement that banged the occupants against the nearest inner wall. I'll break him of that crap, Bezarin thought.

The route passed a skeletal grove that had burned black. Orange veins still glowed amid the charred waste. The site appeared to have been a tactical command post. British. As soon as Bezarin realized that what he had thought to be soot-covered logs and limbs were shriveled corpses, he fixed his eyes resolutely back upon the road.

Just past a battered village, a crowd of Soviet maintenance vehicles and personnel had taken possession of the courtyard of a relatively intact farm. Lightly damaged vehicles awaited their turn in the adjacent fields, and a tactical crane held a big tank engine suspended in midair, as if torturing it. While a few of the soldiers were diligently at work, others sat about eating breakfast. They waved at the tankers hurrying to the front. It occurred to Bezarin that perhaps they were waving at the tanks themselves, convinced they would meet again shortly. Overall, the maintenance crews appeared unconcerned with the war that was perhaps a dozen kilometers away. Sitting on their recovery vehicles or on the fenders of their repair vans, they looked the way soldiers did during a lull in an exercise.

The column came to an unannounced halt in the open, just at the edge of another village. The haze continued to thin, and the exposed nature of the position immediately began to torment Bezarin.

A scout car emerged from the village and worked its way down the line. Bezarin leaned out of the turret in curiosity. The vehicle pulled up beside the command tank.

"Major Bezarin?" a sergeant shouted over the throb of idling engines.

Bezarin nodded. "Yes."

"You are to report to the regimental commander in the town square."

At last, Bezarin thought. The scout car continued on its journey, searching for the next commander in the column. Bezarin ordered his driver to work their vehicle out of the line.

Bezarin navigated the tank into the little town. There appeared to be less damage here, as though it had been surrendered without contest, or as if the battle had passed it by or forgotten it. There were no civilians to be seen, though.

Only soldiers in Soviet uniforms. A company-sized refueling point had been set up in the town square, just in front of the church. The vehicle density was such that Bezarin directed his tank into a side street and dismounted to search for the commander.

Bezarin stepped over the hoses with the skill of an accomplished soccer player. It struck him that these smells of fuel and exhaust were the real smells associated with a career in the tank troops. The reek of expended ordnance provided occasional perfume, but the requirement to nourish the machine and the stink of its digestion were constants. As he skirted the rear of one of his own leading tanks the uneven sound of its idle warned him that the engine was in poor shape. But there was no time to investigate under the engine compartment panels. He could only hope that the vehicle would make it into battle. Every fighting vehicle was valuable now.

Bezarin made a note of the vehicle number, intending to return to the matter if there was time. A nearby tank crewman offered him a cautious salute. Bezarin knew he had a reputation as a hard man with little patience. While his soldiers worked willingly enough for him in their way, he did not believe they liked him very much. Assignment to Bezarin's battalion meant higher standards and harder work than did a position in any of the regiment's other battalions. Bezarin always tried to do things correctly. He realized that there was something in the Russian spirit that sought the path of least resistance, and he revolted against the shoddy work and low standards that too often resulted from the desire to simply get by from one crisis to another. When his soldiers were scheduled for training, he made certain that they trained. When it came time to perform maintenance tasks, no matter how simple and seemingly trivial, Bezarin stayed with his men to make sure that they did not simply doze off inside their tanks.

The penalty for all of this was that Bezarin had no close friends in the regiment. The other officers regarded him with a mix of jealousy and suspicion, and it was clear that he made them nervous. He knew that the regimental commander did not like him personally. But Bezarin performed so well on training exercises, and he so raised the unit's statistical performance, that Lieutenant Colonel Tarashvili tolerated him and allowed him to run his own battalion. Rumor had it that the regimental commander was involved in black-market activities. Whether such accusations were true or not, Bezarin had little respect for the man. He did not believe that Tarashvili really understood military matters, except for those garrison duties that kept everyone out of trouble. Bezarin did not even believe that his regimental commander cared for his profession at all.

Now they were at war, and Bezarin had waited all through the night for the least scrap of information on the situation. His respect for his commander had deteriorated still further.

Bezarin spotted a group of officers working over a map spread on the hood of a range car. As Bezarin closed on the group Tarashvili looked up and smiled.

Lieutenant Colonel Tarashvili was a dark, handsome Georgian with a rich mustache and a beautiful southern wife. He was also an excellent military politician, capable of talking circles around political officers and Party officials. Now he touched his mustache with his thumb and index finger, a habit Bezarin recognized from the tensest moments in peacetime exercises.

"Well," Tarashvili said, still smiling, "Comrade Major Bezarin has arrived. That makes all but one."

A few of the gathered officers muttered or gestured greetings to Bezarin. He recognized the key members of the regimental staff and the commander of the lead battalion. The regimental chief of staff was missing, however. Bezarin figured he had been sent to the rear to sort out one problem or another. Additionally, there was an air force officer present whom Bezarin did not know.

Bezarin drew out his own map and worked his way into the group. He could already see that the colored lines and arrows of axes and control measures were completely new. Bezarin hurried to copy down as much of the information as possible. Before he could finish, the last battalion commander appeared.

"Good," Tarashvili said. "Good. Now everyone's here.

Pay attention. There's very little time. In fact," he said, looking uncertain, "we're late. Not our fault, of course. The routes were not clear. The damned artillery had them tied up half the night. We should have gone in at dawn. But it doesn't matter . . ."

Tarashvili continued in a rambling, confused manner, prompted now and again by his staff. Bezarin's anger and frustration grew until he was not certain how much longer he could control himself. The situation slowly became clear. The British defense had been ruptured during the night. Some Soviet units were already fighting on the outskirts of Hannover. But in the division's sector, the confusion within the Soviet movement control system had allowed the British to patch together one last defense on the approaches to Hildesheim. The regiment had been intended to exploit, but now, due to a late arrival, they would have to fight through the reorganized British position. Tarashvili assured everyone that the British were fought-out and that they had been thrown into hopeless confusion. But Bezarin remembered the litter of destroyed vehicles along the approach route. Tarashvili went on about a divisional feint to the north while the regiment struck the weakened British right. Bezarin quietly gave most of his attention to the map. The traces showed British defensive positions in the vicinity of a ridge between the towns of Wallersheim and Mackendorf. Most of the terrain between his current location and the enemy was open and rolling.

"Will we have a smokescreen going in?" Bezarin asked, hardly caring now if his question seemed to interrupt.

"Absolutely," the commander of the regiment's artillery battalion said. "In any case, the fire strikes on the British positions will be of such intensity that little will remain for the maneuver forces to engage."

"Really, it's very simple," Tarashvili resumed. "A matter of drill. We'll have the opportunity to bring the entire regiment to bear. The effect will be overwhelming."

The plan called for the battalions to move into the attack unencumbered by unnecessary attachments. The artillery would remain under regimental control, and the air-defense subunit would also be centrally managed. Tarashvili talked the assembled officers through the attack, from prebattle deployments to the exploitation phase. Suddenly, Bezarin had the unexpected revelation that Tarashvili was doing his sincere best. But the lieutenant colonel's best was appalling. The plan, the coordination measures, the assumptions had the sterility and thinness of the scheme for an unimportant bit of field training. There was no imagination or even routine polish to the plan. In essence, it was nothing more than a regimental drill, with the subunits deploying at distances measured back from the estimated British positions. Bezarin realized as he listened to the staff respond to questions that no one had bothered to go forward to conduct a personal reconnaissance.

"Division stresses that no one is to stop. Just keep going, no matter what," Tarashvili said, repeating himself as he sought a firm way to close the briefing. "The intention, remember, is to reach the line of Highway 1, then to wheel left, and to advance along it to the west. Whoever first achieves the breakthrough becomes the regiment's forward detachment. The initial mission of the forward detachment is to open Highway 1 between Hildesheim, northwest of our present location, and the Weser hill country to the west. Upon reaching this area"—Tarashvili pointed to the map—"the forward detachment then turns northwest for Bad Oeynhausen and the Weser River crossing site, which is the objective of the day."

Bezarin evaluated the mission. It was a long way to Bad Oeynhausen. "The crossing site due west at Hameln is considerably closer," he observed. "Are there any provisions for seizing it, should the situation appear favorable?"

Tarashvili looked at him in annoyance, eyes nervous. "Division has specifically identified Bad Oeynhausen as being of primary importance. We are obviously prohibited from moving on the Hameln site. Look here. You can see the control measures on the map. They're self-explanatory."

Bezarin, in a black mood, felt obliged to press the issue. Hameln was the obvious objective on their tactical direction. "Do you have any idea why we're not interested in Hameln, Comrade Commander?"

Tarashvili looked at Bezarin with a semblance of fear in

his eyes. Bezarin figured that the regimental commander had no answer and was embarrassed by the fact. But Tarashvili mastered himself. "Perhaps someone else has the Hameln mission. In any case, division has its reasons. Bad Oeynhausen is the objective of the forward detachment. Our air assault forces are undoubtedly already on the ground there. But we're wasting time."

"How much time are we allowed to inform our subunits of the mission?" Bezarin asked.

"Until the vehicles are refueled."

That was a matter of minutes. Bezarin felt as though he needed hours to prepare his companies.

"That's barely enough time to locate all of the company commanders."

"There's no time. We're late now. We will proceed according to drill."

"Shouldn't we at least conduct a commander's reconnaissance?" Bezarin asked.

"No time. We're wasting time now. The order has been issued."

Bezarin stared at Tarashvili.

"Go on, everyone," Tarashvili said, forcing a smile. "Comrade Major Bezarin, you may remain and address any other questions to me."

Bezarin felt the clock working against him. He turned to leave with the others. But Tarashvili surprised him by catching his sleeve.

The regimental commander waited until the others were out of earshot. Then he turned his dark brown eyes on Bezarin. In their depths, Bezarin thought he glimpsed the soul of a man who wanted to be anywhere else but here, perhaps at home with his splendid-looking wife.

"What do you expect?" Tarashvili asked. "What do you really expect, my friend?" The lieutenant colonel seemed painfully sincere, as if he valued Bezarin's approval after all.

Bezarin did not know how to respond. He wanted it all to be by the book, to match his personal visions. He wanted time to issue battle instructions to his companies in a concealed jump-off position, to prepare each last detail.

"We all want to do our best," Tarashvili continued. "I don't know what more you can reasonably expect."

Bezarin found himself at a loss. The words that came to mind seemed laughably formal and pompous now. Behind his back, he heard his tanks readying to move.

Tarashvili reached into the officer's pouch he wore slung over his shoulder. Smiling, he produced two chocolate bars.

"Here," he said. "Spoils of war. The West Germans make wonderful chocolate, you know."

The oddity of the gift and its timing startled Bezarin. He sensed that Tarashvili, for whatever reason, was trying to give everything he had. Perhaps it was guilt over the wasted years and opportunities. But now it was evident that the regimental commander was lost and knew it.

"Take them," Tarashvili begged. "It's all right. You'll be glad for them later." The lieutenant colonel seemed almost pathetic. It struck Bezarin that he himself rarely considered other men as real human beings with complex problems of their own.

Bezarin reached out and took the chocolate bars. Trying to bribe me with chocolate. It's the only way he knows how to do business, Bezarin thought. But he found unexpected compassion in this image of the other man now. It was pitiful that Tarashvili had come to this.

Bezarin forced out a word of thanks. So this, he thought, is what war is really like.

In the winter, Lvov seemed to be the grayest city in the world. Dirty snow piled up along the streets, making trenches of the sidewalks. When fresh snow failed to come, the snowbanks slowly blackened along the shabby rows of old imperial buildings, architectural remnants of the years when Lvov had been Lemberg, the heart of Austro-Hungarian Galicia. The once-stately offices and departments resembled women aged beyond any possible dignity as they crumbled away between the cinder-block-and-concrete structures from the Stalinist twilight. In the winter, in the crowded silence of the streetcars, it seemed as though the last feeble capacity for joy had been crushed out of the people. The men and women of Lvov trudged through the short winter days like weary soldiers, marching past closed peeling doors and frayed posters announcing events already past. He had met Anna in the winter, in Lvov, and she had stood out from her background like a match struck at midnight.

Bezarin remembered his route through the purple-gray of the faltering afternoons. He recalled the streetcars with their worn seats and their smell of urine, winter clothes, and chemicals. From the headquarters barracks, you took 23 to Konev Square, then 35 to the office block where the classrooms were located. In the old Austrian barracks, well-built and ill-heated, there was never quite enough space for all of the officers and men and activities. The streetcars, too, were overcrowded, but sometimes you got lucky coming in from the barracks and you found a seat before the benches had all filled up. Then you could read over your notes. There was insufficient room at the university, as well, and the special classes for officers were held in makeshift classrooms at an agricultural cooperative administration center. Everyone was happy with that because there was a tearoom for the cadres that still had cakes and other snacks in the late afternoon, when more public establishments had long been emptied. It became a joke among the officers that the agricultural officials, whom the officers nicknamed "our kulaks," would never run out of food. Anna was a joke among the officers, too, but laughing about her in her absence was the only way they could cope with her.

She was an unexpected girl, this young candidate of literature. With hair that swirled around the collar of her winter coat like cognac in a proper glass. When she took charge of the class, her style had the sharpness of brandy, as well. No nonsense, Comrade Officers. Attention. The tiny Polish girl is in charge here.

The officers had come to the class for assorted reasons. The military district commander maintained very close relations with the regional and city Party officials. And he had fully committed himself to the military's current mania for improving the educational achievements of officer cadres, as well as seeking improved contacts between the military and the community. The result was a variety of special university-sponsored courses offered in the late afternoon and evening. The older officers generally considered the courses a waste. But the younger ones, the hungry junior officers who had not had the career advantage of a tour of duty in Afghanistan, were all for the courses. The classes also meant a bit more time away from the drudgery of duties. The most popular courses were in fashionable subjects such as automation techniques. Bezarin had been one of the few to sign up for a series of writing classes. He sincerely wanted to improve his level of staff culture, but he also envisioned himself as a future contributor to the military journals, offering suggestions that would be respected and that would result in tangible changes. Most of his classmates had taken the course because it sounded like the easiest of the lot. Then the little Polish girl with the bothersomely elegant features had swept in and taken charge, and there was plenty of work for all. The officers nicknamed her "Jaruzelski's Revenge." And Bezarin, who had little experience with female instructors, thanks to his long years as a Suvorovets cadet, then the years at the academy and higher tank school, fell in love with his teacher.

Bezarin had always thought of himself as a firm, decisive man. But he found that he dreaded poor marks from this girl as though she were a savage commanding officer. Conscious of his short stature, he hurried to be in his seat before she arrived. At work, his mind wandered from training plans and range allocations to the way Candidate Saduska looked when she came in fresh from the street, cheeks stung red above her high collar and scarf. He did not know what to say to her. Then he discovered that she, too, had found out about the tearoom and had begun to arrive early so that she could eat her fill. Marshaling all of the courage the bloodlines of three generations of tankers and cavalrymen had given him, he waited for her one day. As she peeled back the winter layers he approached her, carrying a tray with two cups of tea and a mound of sweet rolls.

She looked at him with fierce green eyes, a revolutionary judge deciding a profiteer's fate.

Finally, she said, "Sit down, Captain Bezarin, please. I have been meaning to talk to you."

And the spring came early to Galicia. The muddy end-of-cycle maneuvers brought with them the first small flowers, and warm winds rolled up over the Carpathians from the golden south. None of the few girls Bezarin had known had been like this one. She gave him Chekhov to read, and he dutifully reported. The officers in the play did not seem concerned about their duties, and that was why the Imperial Russian Army had performed so poorly against the Japanese. And the three sisters never did anything but complain. They were not content with anything. Overall, he declared the play irrelevant to contemporary conditions.

"But this one," she insisted, with the park a fresh, windy green all around her, "*this* story is one of the great masterpieces of Russian literature. Doesn't it move you at all?"

He wanted to share her enthusiasm. But in these stories and plays of a bygone era, all of the men appeared indecisive, and the women were petty adulteresses.

"It's all too artificial," he answered at last, exasperated. "You. The two of us sitting in this park, now that's real. Your 'Lady with the Pet Dog' is dead and gone."

She laughed and told him the army had ruined him for life. He laughed, too, filled with unaccustomed fears that she might be right and that she would not go with him. Yet their love seemed to work: the hours in borrowed apartments and the dutyless Sundays in a countryside that had never seemed so rich before. Low hills that had until recently inspired him only to analyze terrain and ranging considerations gained a golden-green existence all their own, called to life by Anna's words and gestures, and by the faint gorgeous smell of her when the wind blew down from the mountains and swept through her hair and over her shoulders. He gained confidence, only to have it desert him again. He knew that she liked his body, which was athletic, if short. She was a very small girl, with a frame that seemed far too light and frail for the spirit that enlivened it. And she liked his sobriety, and his earnestness, even when it made her laugh. But he could think of so little else that he had to offer. Officer's quarters in some remote post in Kazakhstan, perhaps, where there was still no running water and where even a captain's family had to share crude communal latrines.

In the end, he could not even ask. He had been the lucky one from the entire garrison, selected for attendance at the Vystrel command course, to be followed by early battalion command.

But Anna? Would she be waiting? Could she even consider waiting for him? And if he was posted to the Trans-Baikal? Or to Mongolia? Afghanistan, too, had been a possibility. Notions that once had filled him with visions of glorious achievement began to echo with time and distance, and he was quietly ashamed of himself. In the end, he left without asking her, without perhaps really knowing her at all. The new computers at the training school worked more often than had the earlier models, the tactical problems were simple for him, and there was much about which an ambitious officer could be optimistic. But his cowardice haunted him. During their last awkward hour, in a park that raced with fallen leaves, he had found he could not ask her. He resolved to write his feelings down. But later, he could not do that, either. All he could do was to think of her, wondering if she was teaching yet another group of young officers now, and if she ever thought of him, and whether any of her new students liked Chekhov.

Bezarin led his column through the cluttered rear of the combat area. The road network was superb, allowing his vehicles to move with what felt like irresistible speed and compactness. He had hastily restructured the battalion's internal order of march so that he could personally guide the deployment of the three tank companies by visual means. The combat task of the motorized rifle company was to follow and be prepared to clear overrun positions, if necessary. The battalion's rear services trailed, with instructions to break off the road when the battalion deployed into company columns but to remain mounted and ready to follow.

His small staff and his company commanders had worn

solemn faces as Bezarin attempted to give them adequate verbal instructions. Nothing in their training had prepared them for this sudden acceleration of events. Fear showed openly on Roshchin's face. The boyish company commander listened to Bezarin's coaching with his mouth opened partway, revealing slightly buck teeth that made him appear hopelessly naïve and immature. Dagliev, Bezarin's most reliable company commander and a good improviser, looked ten years older from lack of sleep. The last tank company commander, Voronich, stood slouched, grumpy, as though his shoulders and spine were declaring, "This is pig shit, and we all know it." Voronich was cynical to the point of being theatrical, but he was competent at his job. Lasky, who commanded the motorized rifle troops, looked like an orphan boy. Bezarin knew that the motorized rifle officer expected to receive the dirtiest tasks and the least thanks. But there was no time for coddling now. Bezarin did his best to answer their worried questions, even as his officers tried to phrase their queries in words that sounded as tough and masculine as possible. It occurred to Bezarin that they were a distinctly unheroic-looking group, huddling around the spread map in their filthy coveralls. The faces had a slightly lunatic appearance, broken skin smeared black and framed by hair skewed wildly in pulling their headgear on and off. Bezarin did not give them all of the details that would come into play should they become the designated forward detachment. He felt his officers had enough to work through in the little time available. But he was determined to be the commander who punched through.

Now, speeding along the road from village to village, Bezarin felt as though nothing could stop him. Intellectually, he realized that there was great danger, especially from enemy aircraft, since the heavy air-defense weaponry remained under centralized control. The battalion had to rely on a few shoulder-fired missiles, which, in turn, required soldiers—boys—to calmly expose their bodies under combat conditions. The army gave them a few weeks training and, sometimes, an armored vest to shield their torsos. Some of the newer soldiers had never even fired a live missile. But there was nothing to be done. And emotionally, he was already in the attack.

The column passed battery after battery of guns and howitzers, their tubes raised as if in salute from the midst of broken orchards or under hurriedly erected camouflage nets in open fields. Closer to the direct-fire battle, readily identifiable artillery reconnaissance groups marked off and surveyed still more firing positions. The road passed a medical clearing station where wounded soldiers lay in rows upon the ground. Communications vans filled a sports field at the edge of a shot-up village, and uncollected corpses littered the village streets. A lost-looking young soldier stood beside a broken-down truck, watching Bezarin's tanks race by.

Suddenly, the artillery preparation began. The volume of fire from the massed artillery created a disturbance in the air that was so palpable Bezarin could feel it in his stomach. The effort felt solidly reassuring. It was difficult to believe that anything could survive such a barrage. The country had opened out into dry, rolling terrain, and the impact of the artillery was partially visible along a sweeping ridge running north and south several kilometers in the distance, astride Bezarin's line of advance. Smoke began to rise, as though storm clouds had settled on the earth.

Bezarin knew that the lead battalion was already in its start position, waiting for him to come up on the left. The roadway traced over a small bridge. Bezarin checked his map, then looked off to the right. A shattered motorized rifle company appeared to be regrouping, and Bezarin went cold. But a moment later, he saw the company columns of his sister battalion drawn up in a grassy valley beyond the tattered subunit. Everything appeared intact and ready. The lone motorized rifle company was probably getting ready to displace after being relieved of local responsibility.

Bezarin hurriedly unrolled his signal flags and stood erect in the turret. He stretched out his arms, directing prebattle formation, company columns abreast. Then he ordered his driver to slow down so that the trail companies could come up after crossing the bridge. In the middle distance, the wall of smoke looked dense enough to gather in your arms. Bezarin led the center company off the road, watching

Dagliev hurry to catch up on the left. Dagliev's company briefly disappeared in a depression, then reappeared exactly where it was meant to be. Bezarin looked right.

Roshchin was on the right, on his own now. But Bezarin felt it was the best position for the boy. He would have an entire battalion on his right flank, and the bulk of his own battalion on his left. All that Roshchin had to do was execute his company drill and keep up. At least for now, Roshchin appeared to be in control. Minor obstructions staggered the progress of his company slightly, but the frontage would be approximately correct. And beyond Roshchin's line of armor, Bezarin could see First Battalion breaking out of a line of trees and hedges from a parallel route.

Bezarin tried to gauge the distance to the wall of smoke, then he rose again and signaled platoon columns. He ordered his driver to slow, allowing the tanks of Voronich's company to overtake them. On the right flank, First Battalion surged visibly ahead, almost ready to assault the line of smoke. Bezarin signaled an increase in speed, hoping the company commanders were paying attention.

The local roughness of the terrain tossed Bezarin against the rim of the hatch, and he steadied himself as best he could. The smoke and artillery fire were still a kilometer out but already felt too close. Bezarin dropped the signal flags into the belly of the tank. The next command would be given over the radio.

As his tank crested the low ridge Bezarin saw that First Battalion had begun to pull hard to the right. He started cursing at the developing split in the assault formation, but then he saw the cause of the problem. A wind gap was opening in the smokescreen, exposing the center of the line of attack. The artillery had stopped firing smoke rounds too early. Bezarin looked to the rear, struggling for elevation, searching for any sign of an artillery observation post. The attrition within the division's artillery establishment had been so great that Bezarin had not even received an artillery officer to direct fires in support of the battalion, but Tarashvili had promised that regiment would handle the requirement. Now the only vehicles Bezarin could see to his rear were the meandering trucks of the battalion's rear services, hunting for a place to tuck in for the duration of the attack. Visibility to the rear was splendid. But there was nothing to see.

The textbook response called for Bezarin to guide his battalion to the right, to maintain contact with First Battalion at all costs. He nuzzled the microphone closer to his lips. But he could not order Roshchin into the gap. Whoever drove up between the parting curtains of smoke would be sacrificed. And, as his company commanders began to bring their tanks on line, Bezarin could not see the ultimate sense of throwing away a company, perhaps more, to briefly maintain contact that would inevitably be lost in the smokescreen. He felt his battalion surging with a life of its own, a long wave of steel moving at combat speed toward the towering gray wall of smoke. He waited for the first report of the guns.

Bezarin glanced left to check on Dagliev. And he noticed an aspect of the terrain that his hasty map reconnaissance had not fully brought home to him. The ridgelines on which the smoke had settled threw a long spur out to the southeast. It was obvious now, on the scene, that the finger of high ground would shield any attempted British counterattack until it reached the rear of the attacking Soviet units. All the British would need to do would be to allow the Soviets to move past the spur into the trap. On the other hand, it offered Bezarin an opportunity to take the British in the rear, if they had failed to cover their extreme flank.

Bezarin decided to take a chance.

As he spoke his first words into the microphone British artillery fire began to crash down just behind his formation.

The British knew.

"Volga One, Two, Three, this is Lodoga Five. Amendment to combat instructions. Three, move left six hundred meters. Get on the reverse slope of that spur. Use the smoke. Follow it in behind the British positions." Bezarin paused. The artillery had not yet adjusted to hit them, and Bezarin realized that the smoke was of some value after all. The British were guessing, executing preplanned fires. Then he found he could not remember the call sign for the motorized rifle troops. Exasperated, he called, "Lasky . . . Lasky, you follow Three. Stay close to him. Three, you get on their damned flank and roll them up. Call me if you have trouble. Acknowledge."

"Ladoga, this is Three. We're losing contact with First Battalion."

"Damn it, I know that. Just get up on that ridge and kill everything you see. Meet me on the far slope. *Do you understand?*"

"This is Three. Executing now."

"Volga One, Two . . . let's get them. Into the smoke. Independent fires on contact."

"One, acknowledged."

"Two, acknowledged." That was Roshchin. Bezarin could hear the nervousness in the boy's voice.

"Ladoga, your hatch is flapping."

Bezarin reached out, trying to snag his hatch cover. The jouncing of the vehicle as it moved cross-country made it difficult. A hatch could crush your hand or break an arm. Finally, he caught the big steel disk and smashed it down, fastening it.

Bezarin felt as though he had suddenly gone underwater in the sealed belly of the tank. He always felt cut off from the real world when the vehicle was fully sealed. He leaned his forehead against the cowl of his optics. But the smoke began to shroud his vision.

The tank jolted hard. It seemed to lift to the side. Then it stopped. The shock smashed Bezarin's brow hard against his periscope. He began to curse his driver, just as the tank resumed movement.

The smoke grew patchier. Bezarin's ears rang, and he did not know why.

More speed, Bezarin thought. Every nerve in his body seemed to want to move faster. Yet he knew that he could not afford to pull the line apart any worse than the movement to contact in the smoke would do by itself. He resisted the temptation to order an all-out charge. He feared that, in the smoke, they would soon begin killing one another if they became disordered.

"Target, right, one thousand," the gunner called.

Bezarin looked right. A tank in profile, firing toward First Battalion, clearly visible in a corridor between waves of smoke. Bezarin had missed it.

"Load sabot."

The automatic loader whirled into action.

"Sabot up."

"Fire," Bezarin ordered.

The tank rocked back. The breech jettisoned its casing, and the reek of high explosives filled the crew compartment.

The round missed.

"Load sabot," Bezarin shouted, forcing himself to go through the precise verbal and physical motions.

The regimental net scratched like an old phonograph record. "This is Ural Five. I'm in trouble. *Ambush. Ambush. They're all around me."*

First Battalion was in trouble. Bezarin half listened for a response from regiment. But none came. Bezarin realized there was nothing he could do for his sister battalion now except to fight his own fight as well as he possibly could. But it troubled him that there was no reply whatsoever from Tarashvili or one of his staff officers.

"Range, seven-fifty." Bezarin focused with all of his strength. The British tank sat perfectly on the aiming point. As he watched it began to swing its turret around.

"Fire."

A splash of flame lit the British tank. The turret stopped turning.

"This is Two. Ladoga, this is Two. I've lost two tanks."

Roshchin. He sounded near panic.

"Keep moving, Two. Just keep moving. Fight back. You're all right." But Bezarin suspected that the boy was not all right.

"This is Ural Five, calling any station. *I need help."*

"Ural, this is Ladoga. I hear you. But I'm in a fight myself."

"Ladoga, can you reach regiment? They're ripping me apart."

"I'll try. But I haven't heard a thing." Bezarin cleared his throat, rasping at the fumes inside the tank. He attempted to raise a regimental station. But there was no response.

"Target, six hundred," Bezarin shouted to the gunner as another enemy tank appeared. It was nerve-wracking to play this deadly game of hide-and-seek between the billows and eddies of smoke. "On the right."

"God, oh, God. *They're killing us all.*" It was Roshchin. Bezarin knew beyond any doubt that the boy had lost control now.

"Roshchin," he called. "Get a grip on yourself. Fight, you son of a whore, or they *will* kill you." Bezarin remembered the loneliness and self-doubt of the boy in the early morning hours. But he could not pity him now; he felt only anger. Roshchin had a job to do, and all of their lives depended on it.

"Five hundred . . . *fire* . . . selecting . . . sabot up . . . adjust to four-fifty . . . *fire* . . ."

Bezarin's tank suddenly emerged from the smoke into the painful clarity of daylight. In his optics, he could see three British tanks and four of his own in a murderous shoot-out at minimal ranges. As he watched, the tanks destroyed each other in suicidal combat.

"Smoke grenades away," Bezarin screamed, fumbling at his controls. *"Target . . ."*

"Got the bastard."

"Three, can you hear me?" Bezarin called, his desperation rising.

Nothing.

"Where are you, Three?"

Instead of Dagliev, Roshchin came back on, pleading for help. Bezarin coldly ordered him off the net. An enemy tank appeared in Bezarin's optics, so close it seemed as though they were bound to collide with it.

"Target left. Get on him," Bezarin yelled to his gunner.

"Too close."

"Fire." Bezarin's field of vision filled up with blast effects. But they had gotten the British tank first. Bezarin felt weak, almost nauseous, yet his pulse throbbed as though his heart would explode.

"Volga One, this is Ladoga . . . is that your element mixed up with the British on the crest?"

"This is One. I'm still in the smoke. It must be Two up there."

At the mention of his call sign, Roshchin came back up on the net. He was weeping. "They're all gone," he said, "everybody's gone."

Bezarin's gunner screamed. A British tank had its gun tube aimed directly at them.

"Point blank," Bezarin yelled. "Fire." He did not even know what kind of round, if any, was in the breech.

A burst of sparks dazzled off the mantlet of the British tank's gun. A moment later, the enemy vehicle began to pull off of its position without firing. Bezarin sensed a kill and methodically directed his gunner. The next round stopped the British tank, and smoke began to climb from its deck. Roshchin cried into the battalion net as though he had lost his sanity. Bezarin found himself cursing the boy, even wishing that the British would kill him, just to stop him from blabbering. He feared that Roshchin's panic would become contagious.

"Roshchin," Bezarin said, disregarding the last radio discipline. "Roshchin, take command of yourself. You're still alive. You can fight back. You're all right."

Bezarin could not even be certain that his transmission had reached the boy, who had begun to broadcast incessantly.

Suddenly, Bezarin lost his temper. "Roshchin, if you don't get off that radio, I'll shoot you myself. Do you understand me, you cowardly piece of shit?"

For the moment, Roshchin dropped from the net. Bezarin's driver barely avoided colliding with another Soviet tank in a last pocket of smoke. The driver halted the tank to let the other vehicle pass. Bezarin used the pause to help the gunner replenish the automatic loader's ready rack.

Roshchin called again. This time his voice was marginally more rational. "They're behind us," he cried. "I have enemy tanks to my rear."

"We're behind them, you stupid fuck," Bezarin called back. "Just shoot."

Kikerin, the driver, set the tank back in motion, throwing

Bezarin off balance. As soon as he recovered, he tried to piece his unit back together over the radio.

"One, where the hell are you?"

"Can't talk," Voronich answered. He sounded out of breath. "We're fighting it out with an entire company. I think they lost their way in the smoke."

All right. At least Voronich was fighting. "Volga Three, this is Ladoga Five." No answer. Bezarin wondered if he had squandered an entire company, and his best company, at that, by sending them around the spur. He ordered his driver to head for a copse of trees that sat slightly higher than the tank's present location. As the vehicle moved Bezarin watched the treeline warily.

A British armored personnel carrier bolted from the grove like a flushed rabbit. Kikerin knew enough to stop the tank, and the gunner already had the target in his sights.

"Fire."

The British troop carrier exploded in a spectacular bloom of flame.

"Get in against the trees and halt," Bezarin ordered. He had lost control of his battalion in the smoke and the fighting. But he did not see how he could have done otherwise. Now he could only hope and gather what remained of his battalion to him. He did not even know for certain who was winning. If the radio net was to be believed, the fight had been a disaster. Yet here he was, on the high ground atop the broad ridge, with a trail of destroyed British vehicles to his rear. It was hard to make sense of it. At any rate, there was a perceptible change in the level of combat in the immediate area. A pocket of quiet seemed to have grown up around his tank.

He tried again to contact Dagliev, hoping that his position on the high ground would make a difference.

"Volga Three, this is Ladoga Five. What is your situation?"

Dagliev replied as promptly and as clearly as if he had never been away. "This is Three. I'm behind them. Clean. Killing them one after another as they pull off. It's just like firing on the range."

"Your losses?"

"None. They never saw us coming. They must've been totally fixed on the smoke and what was going on in front of them. We ran right through their artillery batteries."

"Good. *Won*derful. When you're done at your current location, I want you to sweep back to the east toward me. Close the trap completely. I'm up on the high ground. Just watch what you're shooting at as you close."

So perhaps things were not so bad after all. Bezarin felt a tremendous satisfaction in having sent Dagliev around the enemy's flank.

"Volga One, this is Ladoga Five. Situation?"

"Wait. *Load sabot.* I'm still in the shit, but it looks about even."

"Are you all right?" Bezarin was surprised at his good luck, after all.

"Yes. All right. But Roshchin's gone. *Now. Fire.* I saw his tank go up. Catastrophic kill. I watched the last of his company go. In seconds. They came out of the smoke at an angle, driving right up between my tanks and the British. It was a matter of seconds."

So. Perhaps, Bezarin thought, wishes had a dark, unforgiving power. But he could not let himself think about that now.

"All right," Bezarin called. "Just stay off the crest of the ridge. Three's coming in behind them now."

"I heard the transmission."

"Good luck." Bezarin switched over to the regimental net.

"Ural Five, this is Ladoga Five."

Silence. Then a bit of faint, eerie music.

"Kuban Five, this is Ladoga Five."

"Target, left," Bezarin's gunner screamed.

"Hold it, that's one of ours," Bezarin said. He tried the microphone again.

"Kuban Five, this is Ladoga Five."

No response. Where was everybody?

Bezarin angrily unlatched his hatch cover and shoved it up hard. Unreasonably, he felt that if he were out in the open air, he would have a better chance of reaching someone.

"Comrade Commander," the gunner called, trying to stop him.

Bezarin ignored the tug on his overalls. The air, laden with the acrid residue of the artillery barrage, of the smoke and the tank fight, was nonetheless marvelously fresh after the poisonous fumes in the interior of the tank. The noise of battle was still there, but at a reduced volume. Then Bezarin noticed the huge black scar on the side of the turret. There was a break in the reactive armor plating that gave the appearance of a section of mouth where teeth had been knocked out. Bezarin suddenly remembered the tremendous jolt that had shaken the tank early in the fight. It made him feel weak in the bottom of his belly to realize how close he had come to dying.

Bezarin was startled a second time by the appearance of Voronich's tank leading five others up the hillside behind him. Several of these tanks also bore visible scars where the reactive armor had saved them.

Shaking his head, Bezarin pressed the microphone closer to his lips. "Volga One, this is Ladoga Five. Put your tanks in the woodline just below my position. Cover the saddle you just worked up and the crest to the north." Six tanks, Bezarin thought, plus his own. Seven. And Dagliev had reported no losses at the time of his last transmission.

Roshchin was gone. And it sounded like the greater part of his company had gone with him. But Bezarin hoped that a few of them, at least, would show up alive and well as the last smoke dissipated.

Bezarin called Dagliev. "Three, what's your current position?"

At first, there was no response. Bezarin was just about to try a second call when Dagliev responded.

"This is Three. I can't talk now. I'm in it hot."

Bezarin's newfound confidence began to dissolve.

"Three, where are you? I've got seven tanks up here. I'll come to you."

"It's all right," Dagliev answered. He sounded annoyed at the suggestion that he needed help. "We're just shooting as fast as we can. We caught their reserve right in its ass end."

"One, this is Ladoga. Prepare to move."

"Acknowledged."

Bezarin knew that they had the British now. He wanted to finish the job. But he was worried at the complete silence on the regimental net.

"Ural, Kuban, this is Ladoga. Can you hear me?"

"Ladoga, this is Beechtree. I hear you clearly."

Bezarin had no idea who Beechtree was. He tried again.

"Ural, Kuban, this is Ladoga. What is your situation?"

"This is Beechtree," the unidentified station insisted. "Regimental artillery. The attack has failed; it's all over. Air and fire strikes hit Kuban as he was moving up. Ural never reached the British positions. All of the battalions are destroyed. It's all over."

"Like hell," Bezarin said. "We're in behind them. They've pulled off the southern portion of the ridge. We have their positions. Now we're going to roll them up from south to north. Can you support us?"

The net was silent. Then:

"Ladoga, this is Nevsky Ten. Do you hear my transmission?"

The transmitter was clearly very powerful. Whoever Nevsky Ten was, his voice dominated the static and distant stations on the net.

"I hear your transmission," Bezarin said.

"Execute your decision," the godlike voice commanded. "We will support you. Antitank helicopters are closing from the north at this time. You roll up the British from the south. Be prepared to mark your positions with flares. I will stay on this net. If you have any problems, call me immediately. Stop. Beechtree, answer your vertical net. But priority of fires is to Ladoga, is that clear?"

Bezarin no longer had any doubt about the identity of Nevsky Ten. It was Major General Duzov, the division commander.

The British were in a trap. Bezarin turned his tanks northward behind the last line of enemy positions as smoothly as in a demonstration for visiting dignitaries, working up along a broken plateau atop the high ground. He felt as though he was absolutely in control. Most of the targets were infantry fighting vehicles and transporters now, with few tanks in evidence. Bezarin concluded that the British had run out of antitank ammunition, since they so often failed to return fire effectively. Their surprised vehicles scurried about like mice surrounded by cats. As Bezarin's armor overran one of the positions a British soldier emptied his rifle at the command tank, then charged the forty-ton vehicle, swinging his empty weapon as a club. Bezarin cut the man in half with machine-gun fire.

The last of the smoke disappeared, and Bezarin's tankers fought under blue skies. The Soviet tanks halted along the cleared ridge, pursuing the fleeing enemy with their fires. The long slope up which Bezarin's sister battalion had attacked presented a chilling testament as to what could happen when a hasty attack became so rushed that it degenerated into recklessness. Most of the battalion's vehicles sat inertly or burned, sending pillars of dark smoke heavenward. The encounter had been devastating for both sides, overall. The British had killed, and then they had been killed. The combination of Bezarin's sweep and the converging attack helicopters had turned the tide. Bezarin switched his attention to rallying what remained of his battalion and the survivors of First Battalion's debacle.

Stray vehicles gathered around Bezarin's position. Leaderless, the disoriented crews' general confusion was evident in their tendency to draw too close to one another, as if for protection by virtue of proximity, and in the slackness of their behavior. Vehicles simply halted in the open in the middle of the seized positions, their crews convinced that the work had been done and that they could relax. The tautness of battle ebbed dangerously now.

Bezarin acted quickly. He had not forgotten the forward detachment mission, and he did not want to be deprived of the opportunity to lead his tanks into the enemy's rear ahead of everyone else. He ordered Dagliev to take one platoon of motorized riflemen along with his tanks and push on northwest toward Hildesheim, clearing the road. Then he organized every stray tank he could locate that remained in running order into a heavy company under Voronich, his remaining company commander. His rear-services officer provided a pleasant surprise by appearing on the scene before the last tanks had stopped firing. The rear-services captain, an especially preachy communist who was laughably naïve about much of the corruption in the regiment's rear services, had come through, living up to all of the hollow-sounding phrases about the need for good communists to take the initiative. A representative from Beechtree, the regimental artillery commander, came up as well, maneuvering warily in his artillery command and reconnaissance vehicle. It was a captain, a battery commander. His guns were ready to move out and follow Bezarin. Evidently, the division commander's directives to Beechtree had shocked him into action.

Bezarin delayed calling Nevsky Ten until he felt he had assembled a sufficient, if lean, grouping that could act as a forward detachment. He personally dashed among the congregating vehicles, insuring that they moved to the correct radio frequencies and ordering them into local positions that provided at least partial protection from ground and aerial observation. The clear sky showed webs of jet trails, and Bezarin felt it was only a matter of time before the enemy would attempt to strike back. The best of his tankers had quickly learned new priorities now, and they hurried to restock their on-board units of fire from the limited quantities brought forward on the battalion's trucks. Bezarin urged them to hurry, convinced that time was pressing, that the afternoon was waning. When he finally glanced at his watch, he was amazed to find that it was not yet ten in the morning.

As Bezarin remounted his own tank the gunner told him that Nevsky Ten had been calling.

Bezarin was horrified. "Why didn't you come and get me?"

The gunner shrugged. He was a gunner. Command communications were not part of his responsibilities.

Bezarin hastily pulled on his headpiece. "Nevsky Ten, this is Ladoga Five."

Major General Duzov responded quickly. "This is Nevsky Ten. What's your situation?"

"We've cleared the ridge. I've formed a grouping by

combining my battalion with the remnants of First Battalion. Overall strength, battalion-minus of tanks, with one motorized rifle company attached and a battery of guns moving to join us. We are prepared to act as a forward detachment. I've already dispatched a reinforced tank company to clear the approach route in the Hildesheim tactical direction."

Bezarin's body tensed in anticipation. He wanted this mission. He wanted to lead. He had tasted blood, and he liked it. He felt as though he could take on anything the British had to offer. His battalion had earned the right to be the first to reach the Weser River.

"This is Nevsky Ten. Do you have a clear understanding of the mission? Do not respond with details in the clear. Just yes or no."

"Yes. I understand. We're ready." Bezarin knew this was a slight exaggeration. It would be at least ten to fifteen minutes before he could get everyone back aboard their vehicles and organized into march order.

"All right. Do you have any long-range means of communications with you?"

Bezarin thought hard. What he needed was a regimental command tank or vehicle.

"This is Ladoga Five. I have a special artillery vehicle with me. I can use the artillery long-range set, if necessary."

"Good. Get your vehicles on the road. And whatever you do, keep moving. We will all be behind you."

The gravity in the commander's voice, and his simple choice of words, moved Bezarin. He switched over to his battalion radio net, anxious to send out the words that would set them all in motion. He knew that his tanks needed more time to resupply, that the stray vehicles had not been sufficiently integrated into the grouping to do much beyond merely following the vehicle to their immediate front. But he knew that now, with a great hole punched through the last line of the enemy's defense, time was the dominant factor. He felt simultaneously elated and half-wild with small, cloying frustrations. He worked his radio in a fierce, uncompromising voice that had matured in the space of a morning. Major Bezarin wanted to move.

SEVENTEEN

The morning mist floated off the Weser, blending with the slow-moving darker smoke from the burning buildings. Gordunov sat concealed on the bank, alone, allowing himself a brief rest, fighting against his body to maintain the strength to lead. He had expected an assault at first light, but the dirty air had been growing paler for an hour, and still the only sign of hostility was the occasional rattle of a spooked rifleman or machine gunner in an outlying position. Communications checks with the network of observation posts returned only reports of vehicle noises back in the hills. Gordunov could not understand the delay. The reduced visibility provided by the mist and smoke offered perfect cover for an attacker. Later, after the mist burned off, an assault would have a much tougher time of it. Gordunov could feel the change in the weather. The last of the rain had sputtered out during the night, and the day would be warm and clear.

He was certain of one other thing, too. There would be little mercy shown on either side. As he'd made his tour of the perimeter in the first light he had been startled by the number of dead civilians in the Hameln streets. House fires had obviously driven them from their hiding places right into the midst of the fighting. In the night, they would have been impossible to distinguish from combatants. Dark running forms. A foreign language. Both sides would have shot them down. But Gordunov understood the psychology of the situation. The blame would fall solely on his men. When the enemy returned, they would see only the victims. They would not pause to consider that their own fires might have been as much at fault as Soviet weapons. And they would not be inclined to take prisoners. His men would get the message quickly enough.

So be it.

In many ways, so many ways, this was a totally different war from the lost war in Afghanistan. You rarely had such a heavy morning damp, or such thick mist off slow rivers. In high Asia, the air was thin, and the mountain torrents plunged through impassable gorges down into ruined valleys. You did not have so sturdy an urban area as this outside of Kabul itself. But haunting similarities remained. As a brand-new, unblooded officer, just off the troop rotation plane with the first windblown grit in his eyes and teeth, he had been garrisoned at Bagram, where the new airborne leaders learned the ropes. A priority then had been reopening the road to Kandahar. The Afghan forces failed, as always, and Soviet forces received the order to do the job. Gordunov commanded a company in a battalion equipped with airborne-variant infantry fighting vehicles. They road-marched south, a small part of a much larger operation, nervously awaiting an ambush that failed to materialize. Gordunov had not tasted combat directly that time. But he got his first look at war up close.

The column halted in a ruined village, whose dirt streets were littered with fly-covered carcasses. At first, he had only recognized the dead animals, large and obvious. Then he realized that the clumps of rags lying about were human bodies. Scavengers circled overhead, like gunships awaiting targets. The column idled in the stench and the heat, anxious for orders that would call them to support a combat operation ongoing in the next valley. But vehicles began to cook over, and still no word came. Gordunov dismounted to relieve himself, and he walked a few meters away from the column, hunting a place where the flies would not hurry off a nearby corpse and attack him before he could finish his business. He turned into an alley between two ruptured mud buildings. And he faced a carpet of human bodies, butchered until they were stacked three corpses high. The alley was at least fifteen meters long and perhaps a meter and a half wide. It ended bluntly against a masonry wall. The natives had been driven into the enclosure, then methodically murdered. Now they lay turning to leather in the sun. A few pillaging birds lazily lifted away at the sight of Gordunov, unsure of what he portended but too bloated to hasten. A fly pinched Gordunov's cheek. He batted wildly at his face, gagging at the thought of some strange and hopeless infection. He struggled to master his insides just as a hand seized his slung weapon from behind.

It was a special-operations major, grinning. "Interesting, don't you think, Captain?"

Proud, Gordunov struggled to mask his emotions. But it was useless. He still had many things to master.

"We . . . *we* certainly . . . didn't do this," Gordunov said.

The special-ops major laughed, releasing Gordunov's weapon. The major's skin had cooked a dark brown, almost as brown as the exposed, dehydrated corpses. He looked as though he lived in these mountains.

"Of course not," the major said. "This village was loyal to the government." And he paused, smirking, allowing Gordunov time to settle himself a bit. Then he continued, "We only do this sort of thing in villages that support the dushman. But get yourself an eyeful. And buy yourself a nice little camera in the bazaar. You'll see plenty more, if you don't go home in a tin box first. And you'll want pictures to help you describe the glorious successes of our efforts at international solidarity." And he walked away. Gordunov hurried back to the stalled column, seeking shelter in its vigor and familiarity. He pissed against the road wheels of his track, thinking about the special-operations officer, trying to understand him. He had failed in his efforts that day. But later on, he came to understand the man very well, indeed. Death became more trivial than a spilled drink.

Gordunov remembered standing there in the stink of death and shit and diesel fumes, wondering how the veterans could sit in their turrets spreading tinned meat on bread and eating it. In six months, he, too, had learned the art of not seeing.

Now he waited, exhausted, in a damp uniform, with the remnants of his battalion. He was a lieutenant colonel, fighting a civilized enemy half a world away from the land where he had first gotten to know himself. But as he walked through the litter of charred, or ripped, or fractured bodies in the streets of Hameln he knew it was going to be the same.

He placed his hand on the fender of a burned and blasted tank. A faint warmth lingered under the slick of the morning dew. He stared up calmly at the tank commander whose body had been caught halfway out of his hatch. In the fire, the body had shriveled so that it resembled a blackened monkey.

There was no point in trying to understand it all. The point was simply to win, to outlive the other bastard.

Gordunov limped back to the building near the northern bridge where a communications detachment had rigged an antenna. He sat down on the edge of a table, taking the weight off his hurt leg, and slowly worked out a coded message to send back to headquarters. "Bridges secured. Forty-five percent strength. Holding."

He checked the code groups, then passed the message to a communications specialist he didn't recognize, but who had taken charge of the long-range set. If they couldn't communicate from this station, Gordunov was prepared to try again from Levin's east side of the river, where the remainder of the staff and communications platoon had set up headquarters.

"Make sure you do it right. Get an acknowledgment."

"Yes, Comrade Battalion Commander."

Gordunov stepped back out into the chilly dampness,

restless. He felt exhausted, but unable to calm down. He worried that he had almost reached the point where men made bad decisions. Bad luck about the leg, he thought. The pain had taken a lot out of him. Then he heard the first ripple of organized fire.

The initial assault was coming against Levin's side of the river. Gordunov had not expected that. The deep reserves should have been on the western bank. Perhaps the enemy was having difficulty organizing his assault in the west. Perhaps only ill-trained reservists remained, grandfathers and pot-bellied family men. Perhaps they had even lost their will to fight. Gordunov wondered how the rest of the war was going. Where was the Soviet armor? How long would it take to arrive?

He ducked back inside the communications station. Picking up a field telephone, he rang the circuit. As the answers came he told everyone but Levin to drop off.

"Can you assess your situation yet?"

"The enemy is at the outpost line," Levin said. His voice, too, sounded weary, its present excitement nothing but raw nerves. "No sign of them on the ring boulevard yet, but they'll be down here as soon as they realize how little we have out front. The damned problem is all the little alleys. I'm afraid they'll infiltrate the defense. I have a few men up on the rooftops, spotting, but nobody in the sewers. If they come that way, we'll just have to fight them where they turn up."

"Just get one or two men down in the sewers. Establish listening posts, so you at least have a bit of warning. Otherwise, you've made the correct decision. You can't waste any firepower. The rooftops are more important."

Another station cut into the line.

"Command, this is Outpost Four. There are vehicles moving in the treeline at the base of the hill."

Outpost Four lay on Gordunov's side of the river. The enemy would be coming from both sides.

Before Gordunov could respond, artillery rounds began to strike close by. Gordunov hit the floor, just before a blast smashed open the door.

The shocks continued, shaking the building and shattering the last surviving bits of glass. Between impacts, Gordunov could hear shouting. The rounds were falling too close to the command post to be a random volley.

"Everybody out of here. Out the back."

The bastards had an observer in the town. It was the only possible explanation. Still, Gordunov was surprised at the intensity of the shelling. This was their town, these were their people.

The bridges, Gordunov thought. They must need them very badly.

He helped his men gather up the electronics while shock waves made the walls quiver and sifted plaster and dust from the ceiling.

"Come *on.* Move."

Gordunov grabbed the field phone and rang the net one last time. He tried to speak between blasts, waiting for the wires to go out at any second.

"This is the commander. I'm changing locations. The enemy has this site fixed. Each sector must be aware that there are enemy observers inside our perimeter. Men from the rearward positions are to sweep all buildings with good fields of observation. End."

Gordunov disconnected the phone and threw it to the last of the communications specialists to leave the building. Outside, the troops huddled together in the alley, cowering at each blast, waiting for instructions.

"Follow me," Gordunov commanded, although he was not completely certain where he was going. He did not want to move too far from the northern bridge, but there was a dangerous slice of open ground between the first buildings and the river. He led the men southward, attempting to work out from under the shell fire, rushing from one building to another.

The shelling lifted. Gordunov could hear the heavy throb of armored vehicles beyond the perimeter.

Armored vehicles—the noise of their engines—had become the modern equivalent of war drums, Gordunov decided. The rumbling chilled your guts.

He pointed across the boulevard that connected the two bridges on the western bank, indicating the German post-office building. "Set up your equipment in there. Report to Captain Karchenko, if you can locate his company command post. Try to get wired in again." He looked at their faces. Children. Not the sun-scarred faces of the men with whom he had survived Afghanistan. He had not seen the communications officer for hours. Another worthless bastard, he decided. He selected the least frightened-looking soldier. "You're in charge of the communications collective now. I'm appointing you to the rank of junior sergeant. Do your duty for the Soviet Union."

Gordunov left them. He limped across the boulevard to the west toward the sound of the enemy armor. The brace on his leg helped, but each step still jarred him with pain. He had selected the brace himself at the hospital, and he had worked it onto his foot and calf, unwilling to surrender himself to any other man's care.

The sound of small arms exchanges intensified behind his back, on Levin's side of the river. On his side, the sound of the armored vehicles changed.

They were moving.

Gordunov came up behind Lieutenant Svirkin's platoon. The lieutenant had a field phone that was still operational, and Gordunov called Levin.

A soldier answered. The comrade captain was up forward, in the fighting. But he had sent back the message that the attackers on the eastern bank were British regulars.

Levin would have his hands full, Gordunov thought.

Lieutenant Svirkin appeared confident, almost eager. He was new to the battalion, and Gordunov had not yet had a chance to take his measure.

"You understand? You *must hold.* There is no alternative. Our tanks are on the way."

"Yes, Comrade Commander."

Gordunov stumped off to check the next line platoon's defenses.

Firing erupted ahead of him. The sound of the enemy vehicles suddenly seemed impossibly close.

As Gordunov watched, a direct-fire round smashed into a corner building. A moment later, two soldiers stumbled out with their hands over their heads.

His men. Giving up. Gordunov shot them down with his assault rifle.

The lead enemy tank had already reached the Soviet positions. Everything happened too swiftly to be managed. Gordunov watched in horror as the enormous vehicle, twice the size of a Soviet tank, rolled toward the bridge, spraying machine-gun fire to its flanks, apparently unstoppable. He rushed back toward the platoon he had just visited, going in short dashes on his hobbled leg. The enemy tank either did not see him or didn't care about the lone man's actions. Another tank appeared just behind the first, also heading for the key northern bridge.

Gordunov raged at the thought of the bridge falling back into enemy hands so easily. It seemed as though the air assault force defenses had simply melted away. No one returned the fire of the tanks.

Gordunov cut around the corner of a building, screaming orders at his men not to fire at him. Lieutenant Svirkin rose to meet him, his face blank.

"Where's the nearest antitank grenadier?" Gordunov demanded. "Have you got anybody close by?"

Svirkin thought for a moment, infuriating Gordunov with his slowness. "I think . . . there's a launcher back down the street."

Gordunov seized the lieutenant's arm. "Where? Show me."

The lieutenant obediently led the way. Rushing across intersections, the two officers fired blindly in the direction of the tanks. Beyond a pair of dead civilians, they found two soldiers lying flat behind a wave of rubble. One of them had an antitank grenade launcher.

Gordunov could hear the tanks firing. It sounded as though they were very close to the bridge.

"Get up," he ordered the soldiers. "Come with me. You, too, Lieutenant."

He led them in a rush down behind the post-office building. Whatever Karchenko was doing in his company command post, it wasn't stopping tanks. Gordunov felt a sickening sense of collapse. His instincts told him that this section of the defense had gone wrong, that Karchenko simply had not had it in him as a company commander to handle the mission. Gordunov regretted that he had not relieved him the night before when he had failed to bring back the body of the battalion chief of staff.

Gordunov waved them all down. The soldiers fell flat in the street, weapons ready. But no targets were visible.

"They're up around the next corner," Gordunov told them. The whirring and grinding of the tanks as they worked through the wreckage in the streets was unmistakable. Then a quick pair of explosions, followed by bursts of Soviet fire, signaled that somebody was fighting back.

"You." Gordunov singled out the grenadier. "Come with me. Svirkin, you stay here and make damned sure we don't get cut off."

The lieutenant nodded. But Gordunov had no confidence in him now. He was familiar with the pattern from Afghanistan. Men who had performed reasonably well suddenly reached their limit, triggered into a near-stasis either by an unexpected, demoralizing event or simply by nervous exhaustion. No one was completely predictable. And few were consistently brave.

Gordunov expected to get shots into the rear of the tanks. But as soon as he and the grenadier reached the target intersection, a third tank appeared, bringing up the rear. The two men were caught in between the lead tanks and the trail vehicle.

"Shoot that one, get the bastard," Gordunov screamed.

The grenadier knelt, shaking. He balanced the weapon on his shoulder and fired. The round struck just below the mantlet of the gun, near the turret ring. But the huge trail tank kept coming, firing its machine guns.

The grenadier jerked up from his knees, then collapsed. The machine-gun fire kicked his body backward, rolling it over.

Gordunov pressed himself as flat as he could against a covering wall. As the tank passed him, impossibly loud, it concentrated its fire down the side street up which

Gordunov and the grenadier had come. But the vehicle had its hatches sealed, and its field of vision did not include the spot in which Gordunov lay. As the tank rumbled past he dashed for the grenade launcher, scrambling the last few meters on knees and elbows. He ripped at the dead boy's pack, from which the trails of two more antitank rounds jutted. Each moment, he expected gunfire to strike him. But he managed to work the pack off the heavy, bloody body. He slung it over one shoulder and rolled back toward the slight cover available. It was foolish to commit tanks into a built-up area without infantry support, and Gordunov was determined to make the enemy pay for it.

He thought he remembered how to work the device, how to sight it. He loaded a round, snapping it into the launcher with a reassuring click. He remembered that the logical order of the hands had to be reversed for a proper hold and balance. He slung his rifle around crossways on his back so that he could pull it quickly into a firing stance. Then he rose and ran for the intersection again, moving as swiftly as his crippled leg would carry him.

The rear of the tank that had killed the grenadier was completely exposed. Beyond it in the distance, Gordunov could see that the lead tank was smoking. The scene elated him. His men were still fighting. Someone had killed the lead tank. Gordunov shouldered the launcher, aimed for the back of the trail tank's engine compartment, and fired.

The target was so close that he could feel the shock of the impact through his body. As a minimum, he figured that he had gotten a mobility kill. And the tank did, indeed, lurch to a halt, smoke rising from its rear deck. Gordunov scuttled to a nearby doorway, laying down the launcher and tugging his assault rifle around into his arms. He took aim, waiting for the crew members to emerge.

The crew appeared reluctant to abandon the tank. They attempted to traverse the gun to the rear. But the narrowness of the street would not permit it, even with the gun at maximum elevation. Gordunov grew so involved with the spectacle of the turret's attempts to turn on him that he almost missed the movement beneath the tank as the crew slipped out of an escape door in the bottom of the hull.

Gordunov waited for a second man to drop to the street. When no other crew members appeared, he swept the area between the tank's tracks with his assault rifle. He could see the reaction of the trapped, stricken men, like nervous puppets. He emptied an entire magazine into them, then reloaded. When the bodies remained still, he reloaded the antitank grenade launcher.

The middle tank in the column continued to fire wildly, aware that it had been trapped. Gordunov approached in bounds, closing to where he could get a clear shot. They had tried to take his bridge. But it was not going to be that easy. He felt wonderfully capable again, unbeatable.

He positioned himself behind the cover of the flank of the vehicle he had just killed, angling the grenade launcher for another shot. In the moment of aiming, his location in time and space blurred. He was back on the road to Kandahar, and fighting his way out of mountain ambushes, and soldiering in a thousand places he could not recognize. There was only the enemy, a timeless thing, waiting. Gordunov tightened his finger on the trigger.

A surviving crewman from the wrecked tank shot him in the back with a pistol.

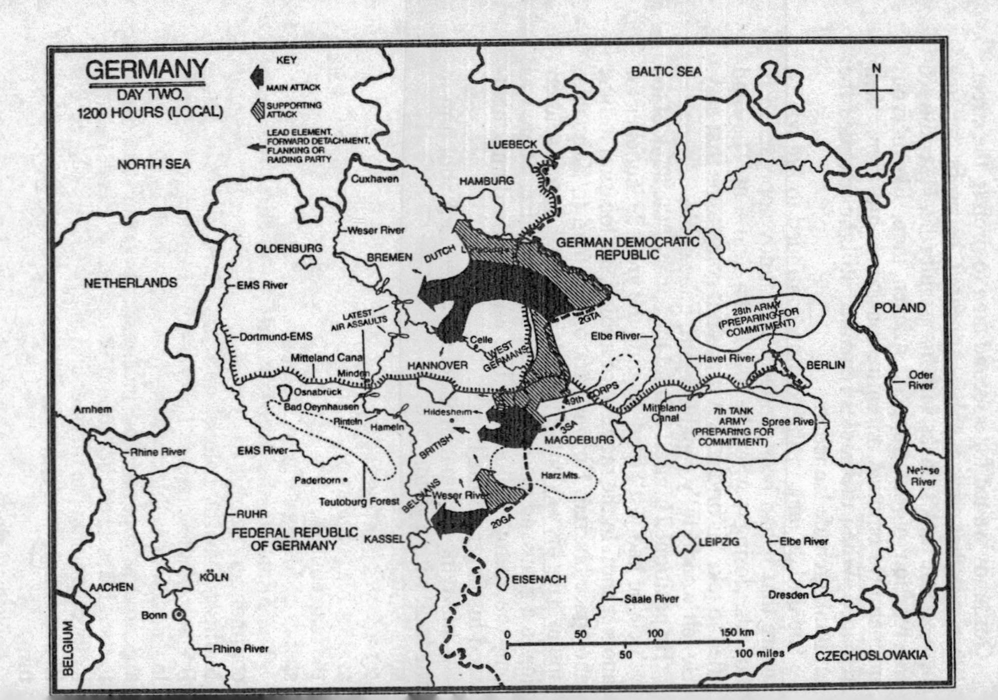
GERMANY
DAY TWO,
1200 HOURS (LOCAL)
KEY
MAIN ATTACK
SUPPORTING ATTACK
LEAD ELEMENT, FORWARD DETACHMENT, FLANKING OR RAIDING PARTY
NORTH SEA
BALTIC SEA
N
LUEBECK
HAMBURG
Cuxhaven
Weser River
OLDENBURG
BREMEN
DUTCH
GERMAN DEMOCRATIC REPUBLIC
NETHERLANDS
EMS River
LATEST AIR ASSAULTS
2GTA
POLAND
28th ARMY (PREPARING FOR COMMITMENT)
Dortmund-EMS
Celle
WEST GERMANS
Elbe River
Mitteland Cana
Minden
HANNOVER
Havel River
BERLIN
Oder River
Osnabrück
49th CORPS
Arnhem
Bad Oeynhausen
Hildesheim
Mitteland Canal
7th TANK ARMY (PREPARING FOR COMMITMENT)
Spree Rive
Rinteln
Hameln
3SA
MAGDEBURG
BRITISH
Rhine River
EMS River
Paderborn
Harz Mts.
Teutoburg Forest
BELGIANS
Weser Riv
RUHR
20GA
FEDERAL REPUBLIC OF GERMANY
KASSEL
LEIPZIG
Elbe River
KÖLN
EISENACH
AACHEN
Dresden
Saale River
Bonn
0 50 100 150 km
0 50 100 miles
Rhine River
CZECHOSLOVAKIA
BELGIUM

EIGHTEEN

A blackened man with no forearms walked straight toward the front commander's son, fanning the air with his stumps like a medieval beggar giving a performance, possessed eyes hunting the beyond. Anton instinctively backed against his command car. It seemed impossible to him that the man could be alive and walking at speed, trailing burned strings of his uniform in the bonfire heat.

The casualty half strutted, half staggered past his brigade commander, admitted to a different reality. Anton Malinsky, guards colonel and commander of the Third Brigade of the premier Forty-ninth Unified Army Corps, looked about helplessly. The few whole men on the scene appeared as separate and incapable as Anton felt himself to be. He sensed he should be giving orders, dramatically organizing the disaster and alleviating its effects. But it was simply too big, and there was no one to whom to turn.

Fools had done it, Anton told himself. Unpardonable fools. Behind a row of gutted hulks, a fresh fuel explosion stirred the metallic air. Anton hunched behind the flank of his vehicle, but the blast was too far away to reach him. He understood intellectually that he had just lost an entire combined arms battalion that had yet to see the combat for which it had been so finely organized and equipped and for which it so long had trained. Gone, in moments. Yet he could not quite get at the totality of the event.

He felt the pulpy wastes building up pressure in his intestines again. Since the previous evening, he had come down with diarrhea so severe that he had not been able to ride in his command track but had had to remain in his range car during the road march so that he could pull off suddenly without interrupting the entire flow of traffic. During a helicopter liaison visit to Major General Anseev's corps mobile headquarters, he had almost soiled himself. He felt increasingly weak. The brigade surgeon had given him pills but had sufficiently doubted their potency that he'd recommended that Anton chew a bit of charcoal as well. Anton had taken the man's advice, forcing down the grit in his desperation to overcome the terribly timed illness. But now, at the sight of the burning alive of perhaps a thousand human beings, he doubted he could manage any more of the charcoal.

He fought the need to go off into the smoldering woods, struggling to hold out until one of his staff officers or a subordinate commander made his way forward. It was forbidden, even for a brigade commander, to employ radio communications during the march. The commitment of the corps was to have been a sudden shock, its stealthy momentum propelling it deep into the enemy's rear area. There was an intricate system of heliborne and road couriers, of predesignated rest, provisioning, and information points, structured to move the entire corps without resort to the electromagnetic spectrum. Yet how, Anton asked himself, could anyone have expected to hide such an enormous organization during a hasty daylight march on the exposed road network between the Letzlinger Heide and Hannover? There were too many obvious bottlenecks and water obstacles, and the border crossing sites were huge naked gashes on the countryside. It was well known that the enemy had sophisticated technical means of reconnaissance. The dialectic had shifted, perhaps decisively, and men refused to face up to the consequences. How could his own father have permitted such a thing to happen?

Even as he tentatively oriented the blame for his loss toward the enormous image he carried of his father, Anton realized that the old man had reached so grand a position of authority over his fellow man that the loss of this battalion was levels removed from his concern. No, this was not his father's doing. This was the work of a chain of lackadaisical staff officers and of commanders intoxicated by the confusion and pace of the operation. It was, finally, his own work.

Still, it infuriated him that all of the rules had been so readily discarded. Of course, even darkness was no longer much of a shield against modern intelligence systems. Yet there was a margin of advantage. Or was it nothing more than the psychological security the darkness brought to the man with something to hide? Anton could not think the problem through now. He began to feel slightly faint. His bowels pressed outward, swelling in him, a body in mutiny.

He stopped attempting to analyze and relaxed back into his initial anger. The foolishness, the collective idiocy, that had created so perfect a target seemed beyond belief. On an open and obvious high-speed route, the last common sense and measure of security had been sacrificed for speed. Company-sized refueling stations had been clustered about an intersection with a network of feeder roads in such a manner as to allow an entire reinforced battalion to refuel simultaneously. Then the site had taken on a life of its own, obeying the secret law that a nucleus of military hardware inevitably attracts more hardware. It did not require sophisticated detective work to recognize the types of tactical sites in the burned-over wasteland. The burst sausages of the reserve fuel trucks had been parked in the disorder endemic to rear-services troops. And the stricken companies, his companies, unlucky in their timing, lay slaughtered where they had been calmly sucking at their fuel tits. Quite near the intersection itself, the commandant's service had marked off its own little fief. And some technical-services officer, spotting an opportunity, had put in tracked- and wheeled-vehicle repair sites, running the two functions close together at a location where they could troubleshoot vehicles pulled over to refuel. Clever peacetime efficiency had turned deadly in war. Amid the blasted repair vans, stranded assemblies and major components lay strewn about in the chaos that Soviet soldiers achieved at the least opportunity. But perhaps worst of all, field hospital tentage had been set up against the treeline. The tents had blown down during the attack, burning their smothering occupants alive. All of the rules of dispersal had been ignored in the natural human tendency to crowd. And death had come in an instant, from a source that remained unknown.

Anton recalled reading articles that warned of Western assault breaker systems and reconnaissance strike complexes, the new bogeymen of the technological battlefield. And he had intellectually understood the implications. But words on a page could not prepare any man for this. Anton had been well over a kilometer away from the target area, working his way along the endless columns of his brigade, when, without warning, gigantic blossoms of flame had sprouted above leaves of midnight smoke, filling the horizon and dazzling his eyes so hard they ached. The blast waves seemed to lift his light vehicle off the roadway.

He had automatically ordered his driver to push forward, aware that this was his duty. But the continuing secondary explosions and the impenetrable heat had erected a barrier in the atmosphere, holding them back for long minutes. The inferno seemed to guarantee an end to all life within its radius.

Yet, as the densest smoke opened out into the blue sky, heading off in a trail that had to be dozens of kilometers long, a few living men had become evident, despite the impossibility of survival. And the man whose forearms had been torn away and whose face had been burned to an African grimness had wandered out of the dead landscape. His face reminded Anton of the pathetic look of the students from Patrice Lamumba University or the Third World military students at the Frunze Academy experiencing their first Russian winter.

Anton felt absolutely powerless. He knew he had to take actions to protect his remaining units and to reestablish the required march tempo. The plan demanded the corps' commitment beyond the Weser in the Third Shock Army's breakthrough sector during the coming hours of darkness. And they were already slipping behind schedule. The trained officer in him knew it was critical to maintain momentum. But his soul expected that somehow, after this, sensible men would agree to call it all off. How could such things be allowed to continue? It was madness.

A tracked command vehicle skirted noisily up along the blocked column, pluming exhaust. It was the brigade's operations officer. As he dismounted to report to Anton he got his first good look at the devastation, and the routine formula of the military greeting broke apart in his throat.

Anton felt his lower belly quaking; the pressure of his sickness threatened to overpower him. He wanted to grasp his abdomen and bend over the pain. An unbearable cramp struck him, and he no longer had the control to await his subordinate's report.

"Get them moving," Anton shouted, his voice driven off balance. "Get them all moving. Move around this . . . this . . . *Get the bastards moving."*

The operations officer did not reply, except to salute haltingly and quickly turn to his mission. Already moving, Anton looked about him for anything that might shield his impending nakedness from passing vehicles. He rushed dizzily toward the blackened no-man's-land, clutching his map case, thrusting his hand inside to seek notepaper, anything with which he might cleanse himself. He felt as though he were exploding with filth.

Shilko found it unreasonably difficult to accept the lieutenant's death. Intellectually, he understood that men died in war, and that the calamities of the battlefield did not discriminate between good men and bad, or between young and old. But he could not reconcile himself to the senselessness of this particular death. The thought of his lost gunners troubled him, as well. They were all his children. But the pathos, the stupidity, of the lieutenant's end haunted him.

Following the delivery of hasty fires during the chaotic night battle, Shilko had rounded up his battalion to resume the march. Traffic controllers diverted all of the local movement down the same stretch of highway upon which Shilko's guns had worked until they exhausted their on-board loads of ammunition. In the light of a clearing day, Shilko had gotten to see the results of his craftsmanship.

The forest road had been a well-chosen target, and, after some initial adjustment, his gunners had hit it dead on. Even after enough of the wreckage had been bullied aside to allow the great snake of Soviet vehicles to pass, the human and material devastation in evidence was such that Shilko could barely muster the hollowest feelings of professional pride. He felt no joy or moral satisfaction as the victor in this engagement. The Germans had been slaughtered; there was no other word in Shilko's vocabulary that fit the scene. The enemy vehicles had been backed up in close order along the highway, unable to turn off into the thick stands of trees. Virtually every arm of the enemy's service was represented in death. Artillery pieces sat enshrouded in soot, and the buckled skeletons of high-bedded trucks had the feel of dead draft animals. Burn scars and lacings of junk marked the locations where fuelers or ammunition haulers had been stricken. Even medical carriers had been caught by the blind artillery rounds, and a series of red crosses on white fields had been discolored by waves of flame. The clearing party had piled the dead from the center of the roadway into disorderly mounds against the treelines, where the bodies looked like plague victims already partially burned.

If there were such a thing as a God . . . such a being, Shilko told himself . . . He might not be able to forgive this. But at the same time, Shilko knew that he would do it again, instantly. Perhaps that made him hopelessly damned. But he would do his duty.

They reached their next designated firing locations just behind the artillery reconnaissance group that was responsible for preparing the site. The quartering party had been delayed and all movements seemed to be out of sequence. The assigned unit location had also been allotted to a signals unit, and a muddled engineer bridging company blocked the ingress of Shilko's guns, then became entangled in their deployment. When an oversized pontoon section backed into the side of a gun carriage, Shilko lost his temper. He screamed at the engineer company commander, calling him an asshole with arms. Then Shilko took over the engineer company himself, straightening them out by sheer force of personality and tucking them into a nearby treeline that would not do for his batteries. Shilko's staff officers were more startled by the outburst than was the engineer officer, and as Shilko calmed himself down and settled back into his usual demeanor, his subordinates moved with unusual caution in his proximity. Even Romilinsky had been jarred by the evidence that there was an alligator inside of Shilko after all.

Miraculously, resupply trucks appeared, most of which carried rounds of the needed caliber for Shilko's guns. The breakdown of the ammunition and the trans-loading had to be done largely by hand, but everyone had been shocked back into wakefulness, and the men worked as swiftly as their growing exhaustion permitted. Soon, the battalion began to receive fire missions. The data link would not be reestablished for some time, if ever, and the missions came in clear text over the radio. Shilko pushed his communications officer to lay land lines as swiftly as possible, but the first missions could not wait.

The program of fires alternated between artillery duels and shelling of enemy concentrations cut off in and around the town of Walsrode. Shilko was ordered to fire white phosphorus into the town to flush the enemy out into the open. The enemy counterfire appeared less organized than Shilko had expected. The day before, there had been extremely heavy attrition of lower-echelon Soviet artillery and multiple rocket launcher units. But the enemy did not seem interested in responding to Shilko's powerful volleys. He wondered if they were short on ammunition, and he began to feel at ease as his pieces threw their huge rounds toward their distant targets.

Shilko was drinking a cup of tea when disaster struck. Enemy rounds landed on top of one of his gun platoons with artistic precision. Shilko hurried down to the battery position even before the secondary explosions had subsided, outraged that anyone could have hurt his boys and his guns.

As he left the fire direction center he screamed at Romilinsky to prepare to displace.

The gun platoon was finished. One gun lay on its side like a fallen horse, nuzzling its long tube into the dirt. The last of the resupply trucks had been caught just as they were about to depart. The support soldiers had lingered to watch the big guns at work. Now a soldier's corpse, still physically intact, waved limp paws down at Shilko from the branches of a tree, while other corpses smoldered with tiny patches of fire. There were many wounded men; not one soldier in the immediate area had escaped untouched.

The platoon commander, who was doubling as senior battery officer, lay open-eyed on his back, gasping as though he were trying to swallow the entire sky. The lieutenant was the sort of officer who excelled at everything, yet who had a guilelessness and natural generosity about him that prevented his peers from growing jealous. He was, above all, a wonderfully likable young man, seemingly immune to life's inevitable indecencies and indiscretions. He appeared relatively unharmed, only scratched here and there, and sooty-faced. But the boy's eyes were lucid and quick with the intelligence of mortality.

"Damn it," Shilko shouted at the medical orderly leaning dumbly over the lieutenant, "he can't breathe. Open the airway, man."

But the orderly appeared desperate to pretend that he did not hear or did not understand. He only called to a companion who knelt, wiping cotton over another sufferer. The second medic came over and stared down at the lieutenant, mimicking the first orderly.

The lieutenant's chest shook with his efforts to breathe. Up close, Shilko could see that his jaw was strangely out of line with the rest of his skull, and there was, indeed, blood sliming out over the grimy skin.

"The trachea," Shilko told the orderlies, "you've got to open his trachea." He could not understand their inaction. He would have knelt and done the operation himself, but he did not know how.

The second orderly obediently drew a medical knife from his kit. His hand shivered, and he had to steady it by grasping himself under the wrist. He punched the blade into the lieutenant's neck, but the windpipe seemed to jerk out of the way. Blood poured out. The orderly gripped the lieutenant's neck, trying to hold it still as he stabbed him a second time. The lieutenant rasped at the sky, eyes huge. The boy was trying to scream.

Shilko smashed the orderly aside with an oversized fist. He knelt in the mud and placed his left hand firmly on the boy's scalp, feeling the matted hair flatten under his callused fingers. He desperately wanted to repair the incompetent damage to the boy's neck, to rescue him for other, better days, to see him promoted and married and moved to a better assignment than this. But he had no idea where to touch, or how.

A fountain of blood played into the air, then fell back. Another crimson plume followed, then another, matching the dying boy's pulse.

The lieutenant was crying, tears sparkling in the soot-rubbed corners of his eyes and streaming down his temples to catch at his ears. Shilko realized that the boy knew with certainty that he was about to die.

The first battery sent another volley toward the enemy. The kick of the big guns shook the earth under Shilko's knees. Then a second volley followed the first, firing one last mission before moving.

"It's all right," Shilko said. "It's all right, son." And he kept on repeating himself until the last life settled out of the boy and his eyes fixed upon the fresh blue sky.

Levin stared at his own death. Apart from the helpless revulsion he felt at the sight of the murdered men, he also recognized with sickening clarity that, if relief forces did not break through soon, he would die. In the excitement of battle, the thought of surrendering had never occurred to him. Yet now, with that option suddenly and irrevocably closed to him, he felt his resolve weakening, his confidence slipping through his fingers. He tried to convince himself that he was only feeling the effects of exhaustion and stress. But he realized that if he was captured, they would hold him personally responsible for this butchery, and they would kill him. He knew how the Germans had treated captured commissars in the Great Patriotic War—a single shot in the base of the skull. And the political officer, on a humbler level, was heir to the mantle of the commissar. Even if the enemy today was not as crudely barbaric as the Hitlerite Germans, they would nonetheless associate him, the battalion's deputy commander for political affairs and the senior officer remaining in Hameln, with the massacre.

The soldiers attempted to explain what had happened. The event even had its own sordid logic. A few of the prisoners of war tried to rush the two tired guards. But the prisoners were too slow. The guards cut them down. But the two frightened boys had not stopped at that. They continued to fire into the basement room full of prisoners, their fear blooming into a momentary madness. They emptied all of their magazines before the communications detachment from the upper level reached them. The signalmen found the guards stalking through the room, firing single shots to guarantee that each of the prisoners was dead.

Summoned by a panic-stricken young sergeant, Levin had, for the first time in his life, experienced the feeling of willful disbelief of what the eyes took in. He could not believe that such a thing had happened under his command. Stunned, he could not even lose his temper. He simply walked through the dungeonlike room in a wordless daze, surveying the gore with his pocket lamp. His boot soles smacked and sucked at the wet floor. The dead men in the British uniforms at least looked like soldiers, hard-faced boy-men, and NCOs with broken teeth. But the German reservists, for the most part, looked like fathers and uncles, hapless men caught up in events for which they were utterly unprepared. The smell had been of a slaughterhouse, with the reek of burst entrails catching at the top of the throat.

Levin knew that the British or Germans would kill him for this. It even occurred to him that there might be a peculiar justice in the act.

He sent the two guilty soldiers out to fight on the line. He could not judge them. Somehow, it was all too easy to understand. He should not have left them alone, unsupervised. Yet there had been no realistic alternative. The only officer who remained fit for combat, other than Levin himself, was Lieutenant Dunaev, to whom Levin had assigned the defense of the northern bridge. The sergeants were of little use. Gordunov, the battalion commander, had been missing since early morning. Captain Karchenko was dead. The defense of the west bank had collapsed, and the isolated firing from that side of the river sounded as though the enemy were methodically rooting out the last resistance.

The situation at the northern bridge had broken down into a standoff. The enemy held the western approach now, but they could not get across. Dunaev's handful of defenders killed every vehicle that approached, and the automatic mortars husbanded their last rounds to support Dunaev whenever things got too hot. The southern bridge had been lost back to the enemy in its entirety, and British regulars had pushed the defending air-assault troops north behind the ring boulevard. The only thing holding the British back now was their apparent reluctance to take the casualties one big rush would cost. The air-assault troops had run low on everything, including combat-capable soldiers. To Levin, it began to seem miraculous that they had held on for so long.

One quarter of the old town had caught fire, and flames separated the defenders from the enemy at the southern bridgehead. The beautiful old houses burned enthusiastically, as though they had grown weary of their existence. The destruction no longer struck Levin as tragic. He was too worn down for grand feelings. The spreading conflagration merely saddened him, sapping a bit more of his psychological juice. Perhaps, he thought, Gordunov had been right. It did not matter when you looked at it from the grand perspective. There were other old cities, even other men to replace those dying here.

Levin left the old town hall without trying the radios again. He had not been able to reach any distant stations since dawn. The location in the river valley was poor to begin with, on top of which the enemy jamming made communications impossible. Perhaps the burst transmissions had gotten through. But no responses had arrived. He wondered how the war was going overall. He had fully expected to greet Soviet tanks by now, to enjoy a scene like those in the old patriotic films. He had even imagined that he might be a hero, and that Yelena might take a renewed interest in him, and that they might be happy again. Now, weary beyond much emotion, he reflected that he might never see his son again, and that Yelena would not really mind losing him. He had been a mistake for her; her father had been right. Yelena would not be content with the things that contented him, not ever. She would not miss him.

Levin dashed across the little square, followed by the skip of a distant machine gun. In a well formed by a protrusion of buildings, a mortar section hurried lobbed rounds to help Dunaev push the enemy back one more time. Levin felt the enemy noose tightening. He strained to hear greater battle noises in the distance, the sound of Soviet tanks. But there was only the close-in chopping sound of automatic weapons and the dull thuds of grenades and mortar rounds. The enemy had concentrated an inordinate amount of force to reduce the bridgehead. Obviously, it was a critical objective. Why, then, hadn't his forces made a greater effort to break through? It made no sense to him.

Keeping the burning area to his right, Levin worked his way down a series of passages and alleys, past garbage bins and a pair of civilian corpses. At a loss for decisive actions now, he automatically began to inspect the perimeter positions one more time. He worked in through the back of a barroom where a machine-gun post anchored the corner of the defense.

The entire front of the building had been gutted. He had to look hard to distinguish the bodies of his soldiers.

The enemy had gotten through. He could not understand how he had avoided running into them. He tried the battered field phone in the outpost's wreckage. But the device was dead.

Levin retraced his steps, assault rifle at the ready. Soaking with sweat, he experienced real fear now, concentrated in a pain behind his eyes. The situation was out of control.

Foreign voices startled him. He drew back into a blown

doorway. Footsteps slapped down on the cobblestones, the sound of men running.

Two British soldiers dashed down the alley and across Levin's line of sight. He tensed to rush out behind them, prepared to kill. But he held back at the last moment, grown newly cautious. His easy courage of the night before seemed to have sputtered out of him like air out of a balloon.

When the footsteps faded, he hustled across the alley to the covered passageway down which he had come. Off to the side, he heard firing. He realized that he had behaved badly. The British soldiers he had allowed through were engaging his men.

Levin ran. But when he reached the end of the tunnellike passage, he discovered that the broad shopping street before him was the scene of a wild firefight. The headquarters elements in the town hall fired out of the window frames. The mortar section he had so recently passed had been overrun, and the crew members lay dead around the tipped-over weaponry.

He did not know what to do. His men were still fighting, cut off here and there. He knew that he, too, should fight. But the very knowledge of combat behavior had gone out of him. He felt that the situation was hopeless, in any case, and that he was uselessly small and ineffectual. He thought of the bodies in the vaulted basement room. None of the men in the headquarters element would survive five minutes after the town hall fell.

He knew that he did not want to die. Not here, and certainly not like this. He had once pictured himself falling, heroically and painlessly, in dramatic combat, a hero of the Soviet Union. Now the notion, with its childish images, seemed like a revoltingly childish game. He felt as though all of his actions of the past night and day had been taken without any realization of their consequences, as though it had all been play.

Foreign weapons bit into the walls and street. Levin backed up a pair of steps, pressing himself against the cool masonry. Then he turned away from the fighting and worked his way along the back alleys until he found a door that had been broken open. A cluttered passage smelling of mildew led into a department store. He found himself stumbling through a shadowy maze of baby clothes, still perfectly displayed on their racks.

Clothes the like of which his son would never have. At least not purchased by a natural father's hand. The accompanying set of images, in which Levin would not have indulged at any other time, struck him hard now. He could not resist the strangely warming melodrama of his vision. He began to cry.

Stray bullets smashed glass and punched into the wall ahead of him. At first, he thought his presence had been detected. He wanted to shout apologies, to beg, to swear that he had not meant any of it. But no other bullets followed the initial burst.

He climbed a motionless escalator with no clear aim. He absently considered seeking out a place to hide, even though he knew they would find him. He wished he could find the strength to die a hero's death, to at least avoid shaming himself. He knew he had fought well. But his actions of the evening and night before seemed to have been the work of a different person. He could neither understand nor master his sudden inability. He kept thinking back to the tangled bodies in the town-hall basement, picturing his own corpse among them. He could not steel himself to return to the fighting.

He wandered through displays of women's clothing. They were so rich. It did not seem fair to him. He had worked so hard all of his short life, and he had been an honest man to the extent of his capability. He had believed in the ultimate goodness of his fellow man. Now he would die in a burning town in Germany, and he would not see his son again.

As he meandered through the men's clothing department it occurred to him that he could dress as a German, and that he might just be able to conceal his identity until Soviet forces finally arrived on the scene. He set down his assault rifle and stripped off his combat harness. Pulling at his paratrooper's tunic, he began to hurry himself into clumsiness, almost into panic, tearing at the unwilling garment. He tried to identify a shirt in the correct size, but it was all too confusing. He tore open packages until he had freed a shirt that looked right. He grabbed a tie. Without bothering to find a mirror, he hurried into the shirt and pulled the tie into a knot. Then, in shirt and tie and undershorts, he rooted through the racks of men's suits, settling for a gray jacket and trousers that had a lovely, expensive feel. The trousers were too loose, but he cinched them in snugly with a belt. He drew on the jacket.

Somewhere, there had to be shoes. He could not see any shoes, and he began to shake with nerves. He tore down the aisles in disbelief. There must be shoes, fine Western shoes.

In his rampage, he caught an unexpected glimpse of himself in a mirror. He stopped. And he began to laugh uncontrollably. He stared at himself through wet eyes.

His face was filthy, blackened by the residue of battle, and a clotted cut stood out above one eye. The fine jacket hung limply, ridiculously, and the trouser cuffs dragged along the floor. He looked like a child masquerading in his father's suit. His dirty hands had fatally soiled the shirt.

He collapsed onto the floor in his laughter, sitting down hard. The noise he made broke into sobs. He cried into the fine gray cloth of the jacket sleeves. He was a fool. He even looked like a fool. He could never pass himself off as a German. He was ridiculous, and a coward, as well. Levin the fool. He doubted that he could even pass himself off as a human being anymore.

He crawled back toward his abandoned uniform, watched by the dead eyes of the massacred prisoners. He slapped his assault rifle out of the way and buried his face in the damp, stinking material of his tunic. He rocked onto his side and drew his knees up to his chest. Then he got a last desperate, fragile hold on himself.

Levin sat up. He pulled the camouflage uniform back on, fighting childishly against the unwillingness of the legs and sleeves. Then he reached for his holster. He thought of the men murdered in the basement room. He sensed them back in the shadows, behind the piles of sweaters and the absurd variety of socks. A sound like ocean waves drowned the noise of battle. He thought helplessly of his son and his faithless wife. Then he became angry at it all, hating for the first time in his life, hating indiscriminately.

He dropped his shoulders back against a wooden display rack and cocked his pistol. He closed his eyes. The taste of the metal was foul on his tongue. It was a relief to pull the trigger.

NINETEEN

The radio reports from his forward element had not begun to prepare Bezarin for the scene in the valley below him. He had painfully worked what was left of his battalion—now designated as a forward detachment—through the confusing network of roads southwest of Hildesheim. There had been fighting down in the small city, where another forward element on a converging axis had been engaged, and funnels of black smoke rose high into the blue sky. Bezarin labored to keep clear of the action in Hildesheim, following the path blazed by Dagliev and his reconnaissance and security element. The mission was to reach the Weser at Bad Oeynhausen—not to get bogged down in local actions unless it proved absolutely unavoidable.

Dagliev had reported back to Bezarin about the backed-up traffic along the east–west artery of Highway 1, which was the main line of communication Bezarin hoped to exploit. The company commander became emotional over the radio, searching for adjectives, describing the scene up ahead in apocalyptic terms. But Bezarin had only his mission in mind. He ordered Dagliev to stop acting like a nervous little virgin and get moving.

As Bezarin's tank broke over the ridge the view forced him to halt his march column. Dagliev had not been succumbing to emotionalism. Stretching across the landscape, civilian vehicles packed the vital highway, all struggling to move west. There was so little vehicular motion in the jammed-up lanes that, at first glance, the column appeared to be at a complete standstill. But once the eye began to seek out details, slow nudging movements became apparent, really more nervousness than actual progress. Along what had once been an eastbound lane, a column of military supply vehicles smoldered where they had been caught in the open by Soviet air power. Here and there, clusters of wrecked or burned civilian automobiles and small trucks further thickened the consistency of the traffic flow. Some vehicles had evidently been abandoned by panic-stricken occupants, and on both sides of the road, a straggling line of civilians with suitcases, packs, and bundles trudged along. Bezarin judged that this was the last wave fleeing southwest from the major urban center of Hannover and its satellite towns, trying to get across the Weser to an imagined safety less than fifty kilometers away. It was a pathetic scene, but Bezarin forcibly reined in his sympathies. The enemy would have put the Russian people in the same condition, if not in a worse one, had they been allowed to strike first. He doubted that a West German or an American tank battalion commander would have wasted as much thought on the situation as he had already squandered. He pictured his NATO counterparts as fascist-leaning mercenaries, fighting for money, unbothered by human cares.

Bezarin gave the order to move out, deploying cautiously into combat formation to facilitate a safe crossing of the high fields that tapered down to the highway. He still had no heavy air-defense protection, and he worried about getting caught in the open. He ordered the self-propelled howitzer battery to remain on the ridge, covering the movement of the tanks and infantry combat vehicles. His spirits had fallen off sharply. He had imagined that, once in the enemy's rear, the roads would be clear. Now he had to work around this exodus. He could not see how he would be able to make adequate time.

But remaining static would not solve anything. Bezarin figured that, at a minimum, he could stay close to the refugee column, exploiting them as passive air defense. The enemy would have to strike his own people to hit Bezarin's tanks. Bezarin was far from certain that the NATO officers would show any compunction about such an action, but it offered a better chance than driving openly through fields all day long. Bezarin wondered if the West Germans had perhaps even planned this, using their own people as a shield to block the progress of the Soviet Army on the roads. Well, he would make the most of this situation, too.

He found himself thinking of Anna. She did not fit in here, but her image was insistent. She scolded him, flashing her high Polish temper, demanding that he see the mass of frightened humanity down on the road as a crowd of terrified individuals, seeking nothing more than safety.

All the same, the refugees were an annoyance. Bezarin felt like a cavalryman with new spurs since the engagement along the ridgeline with the British, and he wanted to drive his steel horse faster and faster, to water it on the banks of the Weser.

His tattered battalion unfolded from the high road and the crown of trees, opening into a quick, if somewhat ragged, battle formation. The self-propelled guns sidled off to firing positions as the wave of tanks, followed by infantry fighting vehicles, plowed toward the valley floor. The warriors who had survived the morning's engagement had a changed feel to them now. Bezarin could sense it even through the steel walls of the tanks. It was, he suspected, the feel of men who had tasted the blood of their enemies.

Tanks sprayed dirt and mud in their trails as they maneuvered across the declining slope. Turrets wheeled to challenge the flanks. Bezarin saw only the readiness, the will to combat, ignoring the unevenness of the line. He knew that his demanding approach to training, despite the resentment it caused, had paid off. He felt that he could match his tankers against any in the world.

Along the highway, still nearly a kilometer distant, the refugees on foot began to run at the sight of the skirmish line of tanks. First a few of them ran, then other runners gathered around the first clusters like swarming insects. Some fell. Others discarded their last possessions.

At first, this response surprised Bezarin. It had never occurred to him that this slow river of humanity should be afraid at the sight of his tanks. The idea of causing them any intentional injury had never crossed his mind. In a moment's revelation, he saw the world through the fear-widened eyes of the refugees. Despite the seal of his headset over his ears, he imagined that he could plainly hear their screams.

Bezarin was about to redirect his formation toward a secondary road heading off to the west, refusing his right flank, when the first muzzle blast flashed from across the valley.

Beyond the stream of fleeing civilians, an enemy force of undetermined size either had been waiting in ambush or had just reached the wooded ridge on the opposite side of the valley. Other muzzle blasts flared in quick succession, and Bezarin's tanks maneuvered to take advantage of the sparse local cover. They had been caught fully exposed on the slope.

On his right, Bezarin saw one of his tanks erupt, its turret lifting like the top of a mountain raised by the force of a volcano. Some of his platoons had begun to fire back, but the enemy was at extreme range, and the tanks had to fire from the halt to have any hope of hitting their targets.

Another of his tanks began to burn.

Good gunners, Bezarin thought. The bastards.

His first instinct was to pull everyone back up into the treeline. His ridge was considerably more commanding than the one occupied by the enemy.

"Attention," Bezarin called into the radio mouthpiece. "Do *not* return fire unless you have positively identified a target. Voronich," he called, dispensing with call signs, "your task is to identify targets for volley fire. The artillery is to suppress the enemy position along the treeline. Neshutin, you—"

Bezarin froze. The enemy were coming out. It was senseless. They had good concealed firing positions. They were willingly putting themselves at the same disadvantage Bezarin's vehicles were in.

Then he got it. They were trying to rescue, to cover, the refugee column. Again, Bezarin was startled by the enemy's apparent perception of the threat his tanks posed. But he did not waste time on moral philosophy. The enemy had just told him, frankly, where their values lay.

"Everybody," Bezarin called over the radio net. "All tanks and fighting vehicles. Move forward *now.* Full combat speed. Get in among the refugee traffic. Use the automobiles for cover. Fire smoke grenades and move *now.* All tanks back on line. *Now."*

His vehicle lurched forward at his command. Bezarin triggered the reloaded smoke grenade canisters and drove headlong into the rising puffs. His vehicle jounced wildly over the uneven field.

The smoke made him cough. But he did not want to seal himself in the belly of the tank. He was afraid he would lose control of this engagement, as he had lost control in the morning's fighting.

Beyond the thin screen of smoke, the column of automobiles soon blocked the enemy's fields of fire. Bezarin looked quickly to the right and left, unsure how many tanks should be there now, but satisfied with the grouping he saw. Quick armored infantry fighting vehicles nosed their sharp prows in among the tanks, losing drill formation in the headlong dash for the highway.

Bezarin's tank roared through an area of low ground from which the column of automobiles on the built-up road actually stood higher than his turret. Then the tank slanted back upward, heading for the multicolored column of civilian vehicles.

The last drivers deserted their automobiles, leaving doors wide open in their haste. Bezarin's tank shot up over the berm of the road and slammed down on the pavement of the highway. His driver only halted the tank after its glacis had crunched into the side of a big white sedan.

The meadow beyond the road had filled with running figures, their bright clothing like confetti thrown over the green fields. The refugees scrambled toward their own forces. But now the tables had turned. The enemy tanks had lost the race to the road, and they stood embarrassed in the open fields, uncertain sentinels attempting to cover the human flood. Bezarin could see that the enemy unit was weaker than his own after all, its vehicles scarred by combat and spread thinly across the long slope.

"Get them," Bezarin screamed into the mike, "get them while they're in the open. Don't let them get away. Platoon commanders, direct fire." He felt himself bursting with adrenaline; his determination to destroy his enemies was so powerful he felt it could propel him into the sky. He had not paused to consider his choice of words as he issued his command.

"Target," Bezarin said, dropping into position behind his optics. "Range, six hundred meters."

"Six hundred meters."

"Correct to six-fifty. Selecting sabot."

"Six-fifty. Sabot loaded."

"Fire."

Bezarin's tank rocked back, and an instant later an enemy tank jerked to a stop, lifting slightly, like a man punched hard in the lower belly. The enemy tank failed to explode, but smoke began to fluster from its vents.

Bezarin was in a killing mood.

"Repeat target," he said. "Six-fifty."

"Target fixed."

"Sabot."

"Ready."

"Fire."

Bezarin's tank rocked again and, before it settled, the enemy tank dazzled with sparks. A moment later its deck blew skyward. Magazine strike, Bezarin thought. And he scanned the fields for another target.

His optics found a changed scene. Most of the civilians had dropped into the high grass, caught in the middle of the battle. Then Bezarin saw one running group jerk into contorted positions and fall. Someone had intentionally gunned them down.

"Comrade Commander, *target.*"

Bezarin saw the tank. Lumbering down, as if to rescue the survivors, its long gun fired above the bodies prostrate in the grass. It looked like a defiant, protective lioness. Bezarin understood, even sympathized with the commander of the enemy vehicle. The maneuver was brave, and suicidal. Bezarin fixed the target in his rangefinder.

The headset had grown chaotic with a litany of calls. Bezarin tuned them out until he had fired on the lone, brave enemy tank. Two other tanks also fired on it in quick succession, and they managed a catastrophic kill. The enemy vehicle burned its wounded crew alive.

The surviving enemy vehicles had pulled back into the distant treeline, and Bezarin's supporting battery pounded their positions, forcing them back yet again. The firing of tank guns subsided very quickly. It had been a swift engagement, determined by the single factor of Bezarin's tanks beating the enemy to the highway by less than a minute. Bezarin searched the horizon for any last targets. But all of the visible enemy vehicles remained stationary, either blazing or smoking heavenward. Bezarin watched as a lone civilian rose and ran up the hillside, only to be tossed about by a burst of automatic-weapons fire. Bezarin watched as though the action were occurring on a movie screen. Then he snapped back to his senses.

"Cease fire, cease fire," he shouted into the mike. "I will personally shoot the next man who fires on a civilian."

He opened his turret, climbing up into open air only to be greeted by choking black smoke. At first, he thought his tank was on fire, that it had been hit and that they had not even realized it. Then he located the true source of the smoke. A burning automobile stood just to one side of the tank. The heat seared Bezarin's cheeks. His vehicle, already battered, wore a cloak of black soot down the side.

The continuing volume of small-arms fire alarmed Bezarin. There was nothing left to shoot at. And there were too many shouts, screams.

He dropped back into the turret, ordering his driver to back up out of the grasp of the fire and smoke. Then he called his subordinates and ordered them to get their men under control, to halt all firing immediately. In a rage, he stripped off his headset and drew his personal weapon. He climbed out of the turret and jumped down from the tank, trotting through the smoke in the direction of the greatest density of noise.

Countless automobiles had taken fire, or had been wrecked in their last desperate attempts at flight. Between the drifting curtains of smoke, islands of clarity revealed dead and badly wounded drivers and passengers, slumped over steering wheels or spilling from opened doors. Dead civilians lay scattered about the roadway, some of them crushed. A heavily built middle-aged woman's flowered skirt lofted on the wind, dropping high up on the back of her sprawled legs.

Beyond the next drape of smoke, Bezarin surprised a group of motorized rifle troops with a girl. They had stripped off her skirt and underpants, leaving her clad only in a sweater, and they were teasing her, driving her screaming from one man to another. The girl wailed in mortal terror, and his men laughed. Whether or not she could ever be pretty, her fear had wrought her young face into a mask of revolting ugliness. Her eyes were those of an animal beaten almost to death, but with just enough spark of life remaining to want desperately to live.

The girl shrieked in a foreign language, and one of the soldiers grabbed her sweater, tearing it as she tried to break out of the circle.

Bezarin fired at the ground, putting the round very close to the girl's tormentor.

All of the men turned to face him, one even lifting his assault rifle. As soon as they recognized an officer, they all straightened, backing away from the girl as if it was only an accident that she and they were discovered in the same place. The soldier who had raised his weapon quickly lowered it.

"Pigs," Bezarin shouted at them. "You shit-eating pigs. What do you think you're doing?"

None of the soldiers responded. Bezarin cursed himself empty, then could find no sensible words to express himself, and a difficult silence enveloped them. He almost launched into an angry series of platitudes about their duty and mission and the trust of the Soviet soldier. But this was all much too immediately human and terrible for classroom phrases.

Bezarin shook his head in disgust. "All of you. Get back to your vehicles. *Now.*"

The soldiers obeyed immediately. Bezarin watched them go, weapon at the ready. He did not fully trust these strangers now.

And yet . . . they were his soldiers. They had fought together, and they would undoubtedly be forced to fight together again before the war ended for them.

Bezarin turned to the girl, embarrassed more by what his soldiers had done than by her charmless nakedness. He took care to look only at her face, which was red and beyond the range of normal expression. Still, she backed nervously against a smashed automobile, as though she expected Bezarin to become her next tormentor.

"Go," Bezarin said. "Get out of here. Your people are up there." He pointed, wishing he could tell her in her language.

"Go," he barked. He did not know what else to do. There were still shots and cries, and he had no doubt that his experience of what his soldiers were really like had not yet come to an end. He wanted to get away from here, away from this lost girl. But he was afraid to leave her alone.

The girl covered herself with her hands, tugging down the torn sweater in a hopelessly inadequate gesture. Bezarin closed on her, watching her fear grow. But he had no time to waste. He grabbed her by the upper arm and dragged her along so swiftly that she could not resist. He drew her to the edge of the highway, facing the now-silent ridgeline from where her would-be guardians had come. Another small horror awaited him as he discovered a tumbled clutter of bodies in the drainage ditch by the roadside and trailing away from the raised berm.

"Go," Bezarin ordered, pointing the way with his weapon. Visibility was far too good, despite the residue of battle smoke, and he worried that enemy aircraft would descend upon them. He knew he had to get his troops back under control, to get moving again.

He pushed the girl toward the enemy's hill. She looked at him in fear and confusion. He pointed again.

Either the girl finally understood him or she simply obeyed what she perceived to be his desire. She began to pick her way down between the corpses. As her foot touched one of them the body moved with a life of its own, and Bezarin realized that, surely, there were many wounded along the column and out in the fields. But he could not cope with that issue now; he had no assets, and he had a mission to fulfill. He struggled to shut his mind to the welling visions.

He stepped back behind the cover of an abandoned vehicle and watched the girl go. She was a scrawny thing, little more than a child, and her naked behind looked like two stingy pouches of skin tucked onto a skeleton. Bezarin could not imagine anyone having sexual feelings for her. As she worked her way up through the field her half nakedness called up nothing in him but a sense of human weakness, of the miserable level to which human life was reduced in the end.

At the sound of a single shot, the girl flung an arm into the air, as if waving to someone in the distance, and dark blood splashed from the hollow under her shoulder. An instant later she collapsed, disappearing into the shimmering grass.

Bezarin's other officers had been more successful than their commander, and he was pleased to learn that none of his tankmen had abandoned their tanks to participate in the free-for-all violence with the motorized riflemen. He took some comfort in the thought that the men he had trained himself remained disciplined soldiers.

Bezarin threatened Lasky, the commander of the attached motorized rifle troops, with a court-martial under wartime conditions in accordance with the provisions of Article 24 if he lost control again. Failure to act, under battlefield circumstances, could be punishable by death. Bezarin made the threat just as his anger peaked, and as he began to realize how deeply the episode had shaken Lasky, he regretted having made it. None of the motorized rifle officer's school training or unit experience had prepared him for this. Lasky stuttered, half-pleading, insisting that such a thing would never—could never—happen again. Bezarin had read and been told many times how war made boys into men. Yet the very opposite seemed true. Men who swaggered across the parade ground and bullied their way through the administrative rigors of peacetime soldiering became as helpless as children in the face of battle. Bezarin thought again of Tarashvili, his regimental commander, and of Lieutenant Roshchin, the boy who had broken down on the battlefield and perished with his company. Lasky appeared to be so unnerved that Bezarin wondered if he would go into shock. Where in the program of instruction did they teach you how to handle officers who went to pieces in combat? Or who were frightened into stasis by the unexpected behavior of their men? Having begun by raging at Lasky, Bezarin found himself spending precious time in an attempt to rebuild the officer's confidence, to put him back in control of himself and his men. He assured Lasky that there would be a chance to even things up at the river, if not before, although he knew that there would be a price to pay for this massacre—Bezarin could find no other word for it—and that he and Lasky were the two officers most likely to face a military tribunal.

"It's all right," Bezarin said. "The men are back in their squad groups with their vehicles. All you have to do is go through the motions. They'll listen to you. They've got it out of their systems. Just show them you're in control."

But the motorized rifleman could not control his hands well enough to light his cigarette. Bezarin lit one for him, then guided it into the other man's hand. Lasky's fingers felt like electric wires, frantic with too much current. He gripped the cigarette so hard that the small paper tube bent as he jammed it between his lips. Bezarin turned his back, unable to spare another moment. He felt as though he had squandered his efforts reinforcing failure. Lasky would have to make it on his own, as would every one of them, in the end. The thing now was to move.

Bezarin had lost two more tanks and three infantry fighting vehicles, along with most of the crew members. He loaded his wounded into the largest, sturdiest civilian vehicles that remained in running order, then he put a medical orderly in charge of two riflemen who claimed they could drive. Bezarin directed the orderly to retrace the detachment's route as best he could, stressing that it was essential to put enough distance between his charges and the scene of the engagement to disassociate the wounded men from the massacre. He worried that any enemy forces or even civilians in the area would take vengeance upon his wounded. Bezarin wished the orderly luck, unhopeful.

Nothing more could be done. The Germans or the English would have to tend their own casualties. Bezarin forcefully shut his mind to the suffering around him. But a part of him felt as though he were the lone occupant of a fragile boat in the middle of a storm at sea. All a man could do was hang on.

He moved along his disordered line of vehicles, shouting at officers and men to mount up, to regroup their platoons. He screamed and cursed at them all until his voice began to fail, and even then he forced the mingled commands and obscenities out of his raw throat. He sensed that the only way to hold his dwindling unit together was by sheer force of will.

The unit pulled together. The vehicles had a battered, overloaded look, a caravan of military gypsies. Camouflage nets trailed over decks, and stowage boxes had been torn open. Vehicle fenders had twisted into chaotic shapes, and cartridge casings littered every flat surface on the infantry fighting vehicles. The self-propelled guns worked their way down from the ridge, and, at Bezarin's wave, the little column began to move again. He had heard nothing from Dagliev's advance element, but he contented himself with the thought that he had told the company commander to use the radio only to warn of trouble ahead. He took the quiet as a positive sign.

Bezarin had directed that the vehicles maintain twenty-meter intervals, but the difficulty of moving along the refugee column soon squeezed that distance down to an average of less than ten meters. He allowed the crowding as long as they marched immediately beside the panic-stricken traffic, sensing that his enemy would not stage an air attack against his column as long as it hugged living refugees. Besides, he did not want to lose control of a single vehicle.

He had issued strict orders to cause no wanton damage. But the panic that flowed like a bow wave in front of the armor caused the refugees to harm themselves in their desperation, and collisions proved unavoidable. Bezarin clenched himself as tightly as possible, forcing his mind not to accept the implications of the string of small tragedies that marked the path of his tanks. He peered forward, unseeing, as his war machines rumbled to the west. He scanned the sky and the rising line of mountains that hid the Weser, shutting out everything but the mission of reaching and crossing the river. His tanks rode the berm of the highway or took short detours along parallel routes and across the fields wherever the debris and confusion of the human flood threatened to become overwhelming. Here and there, bombed-out enemy march columns blocked the way, blackened trucks steering into eternity, their drivers crude, shrunken figures carved from charcoal. Several times, enemy aircraft boomed overhead. But their rockets and bombs never sought Bezarin. He did not know whether or not they were even aware of his column, whether their ordnance was predestined for other, greater threats than the one his presence posed. He only knew the sudden intervals of terror, almost impossible to master, as the jets came screaming down along the highway, seemingly aimed straight for his tanks, only to blast on by to the east.

Intermittently, Bezarin's forward detachment surprised enemy soldiers in stray transport vehicles or perched along the side of the road, tasked to administer the rear area. Some attempted to fight it out. Bezarin's vehicles cut them down. Others, astonished, simply raised their hands in surrender and went ignored. Bezarin refused to permit his tiny force to be diverted. He wondered what had become of Dagliev's advance element. When he tried to raise him on the radio, there was no answer. Neither was there any sign of his passage. Bezarin relegated the Dagliev problem to his list of lesser concerns so long as things were going well.

The column seemed to be touring the guts of the enemy formations now, the individually unimportant targets that joined in a great combination to make a modern army function. The Soviet tanks and infantry fighting vehicles merely raked the sites with machine-gun fire from the move. The only sharply focused efforts at destruction were directed against enemy vehicles with antennae in evidence. Bezarin did not intend to give the enemy any free intelligence on his location. When the path to the west led his tanks around a congested village and right through the middle of a British vehicle-repair site, Bezarin almost lost control of his force again. The target seemed too rich to be passed by, crowded with equipment and technicians, and officers and men took it upon themselves to destroy as much as possible. Bezarin screamed into his microphone, whipping his officers back into column formation with more curses and threats. Even as he shouted, he wondered how much longer he would be able to keep it up, how long his willpower would endure. Then he barked another command and forced his self-doubt down into a private dungeon. The unit pulled away from the support site, spraying suppressive light-weapons fire in its wake to prevent the British from employing any man-packed antitank weapons.

Bezarin felt certain that the enemy must know his location by now, and he pounded at the rim of his turret hatch when another clot of vehicles at a valley crossroads brought his tanks to a halt. Threats and warning shots failed to undo the great knot of vehicles, and Bezarin finally directed his driver to batter the civilian vehicles out of their path. The destruction seemed vicious and senseless and unavoidable to Bezarin. As if in punishment, one of Lasky's infantry fighting vehicles threw a track as it attempted to work its way up out of a field and across a lateral road. There was no time to repair the vehicle, simple though the operation would have been, and Bezarin ordered that it be further disabled. Then the crew mounted up with their more fortunate comrades. Bezarin felt as though fate were chipping away at him, defying him to reach the river. Yet there was good fortune, too. His tanks were obviously moving faster than the enemy could react, and none of the bridges over the tertiary streams had been blown. The passage of local water gaps, which might have held up the column, merely involved clearing off the refugee traffic. And as Bezarin's vehicles raced past still more British support sites, it was apparent that none of them had been forewarned. The British were in a process of dissolution without even knowing it.

Twilight began to wander down out of the side valley and treelines. The darkening shapes of low mountains rose, threatening to bar the way to the river like black fortress walls. As his column worked its way along the valley bottoms Bezarin recognized the possibility of an ambush from which there would be no way out. But the anticipated enemy fires failed to materialize, and each minute brought the Soviet tanks closer to the river.

Dagliev finally reported in. The advance element, intended to provide security and reconnaissance for the main column, had long since branched off on another route to the northwest, weaving into the mountains. That at least partially explained to Bezarin why the British had so consistently been unprepared for his arrival. Dagliev swore he had been trying to call in for hours but had been unable to raise Bezarin on the net, probably because the intervening mountains had blocked him from radio line of sight. Bezarin lost his temper. He could not understand how Dagliev could have diverged so widely from the anticipated route. Dagliev made a series of excuses, but the most telling point was that, despite his error, the company commander was within a half-hour's march of the Bad Oeynhausen bridgehead. He had found an open road into the Weser hills. Accepting the situation, despite the residue of his anger, Bezarin ordered Dagliev to push on for the bridgehead without delay and link up with the air-assault forces.

Bezarin could not sort out his feelings with any clarity. Part of him tensed with jealousy that Dagliev had pushed so far ahead of the main body. By sticking to the most obvious route, Bezarin had lost time in the exodus of refugees. Dagliev had almost reached the objective, while he was struggling up the valleys, skirting to the north around the pink glow over the ridges that marked Hameln, and accomplishing little more than frightening a few British mess sergeants. Additionally, Bezarin felt newly vulnerable now that he knew for certain he had no security force in front of his column, and his mind filled with the varieties of possible dangers. Still, he decided that it would not do to stop and push forward another reconnaissance and security element. His force had shrunken to too small a size to permit any further detachments, and he was not even sure he had an officer left that he could trust to find his way efficiently in the dark. Bezarin decided to alter his course to reach the river valley as directly as possible. He calculated that he could strike the river at Rinteln, then work up the river valley. He reasoned that the refugee flow would have little reason to move northwest along the route he anticipated taking. In any case, he wanted to get clear of the mountain valleys.

The twilight deepened into a pale darkness, with night descending over the landscape like layers of silk. He would keep his force together and move as fast as he could. They were so close now. All the consequences could be sorted out later. The repercussions from the massacre along the highway were likely to be so severe that Bezarin reasoned he could do little to worsen the situation. It was time to take risks. Even if they were to court-martial him and have him shot, Bezarin had made up his mind on one thing. They would not do it before he reached the river.

Bezarin's force seized the Weser River bridge at Rinteln almost by accident. It had not been part of the plan. The objective remained the crossing site at Bad Oeynhausen. But just as the remains of Bezarin's unit straggled down out of the hills toward the river road junction at Rinteln, Dagliev radioed in with news both good and bad. He had managed to link up with the air-assault forces on the near bank at Bad Oeynhausen. But hard fighting continued at the crossing site, and he could not get his armored vehicles across the bridge because it lay in a direct line of fire from enemy positions on high ground just to the south. The enemy had not managed to blow the bridge before the air-assault forces seized bridgeheads on both banks, but now they were shelling it with everything they had, trying to drop it into the water or at least prevent anyone from crossing it. Still, the artillery could be managed. It was the direct fire threat that had brought any further progress to a halt. The twin Soviet bridgeheads could not move to support each other, and Dagliev suspected that the enemy would attempt to counterattack, reasoning that it would be foolish to waste any more time. The tension in Dagliev's voice reassured Bezarin's battered ego, and he felt a fresh surge of energy. There were problems to be solved, and he was the man to solve them.

The map showed a bridge at Rinteln. If it had not been blown, its seizure would allow Bezarin to move up behind the enemy on the west bank of the river. If the bridge was blown, or if he failed, he risked losing precious time in a fight in the town, perhaps even losing his force. But he could not see how his vehicles would make much difference if they simply marched up to the same near-bank bridgehead that Dagliev had reached. Bezarin took one last hard look at the map, inspecting the road net on the west bank of the river. There appeared to be a direct road along the Weser that would bring him out in the enemy's rear. If he could get across at Rinteln. Bezarin took his decision.

He led his shrunken column directly for the bridge. He hoped to achieve surprise, to seize the crossing before the enemy could prepare or implement the destruction of the bridge. Immediately, everything seemed to go wrong.

On the outskirts of Rinteln, Bezarin's tanks hit another traffic jam. More refugee traffic had been held up in an effort to evacuate a British column of artillery to the west bank of the Weser. Bezarin ordered his tankmen to open fire on the guns, and to sweep the support vehicles with machine-gun fire. But his objective was not the destruction of enemy forces. They were distinctly secondary to the prize of the bridge and the importance of reaching the bridgehead at Bad Oeynhausen. But nothing could be done about the situation. To reach the bridge, they would have to fight through the British column; yet, as they destroyed the British vehicles, the hulks blocked further progress.

The firefight threw brilliant lines of color across the night, while the explosions of on-board magazines and soft-skinned support vehicles soon decorated the edge of the town with a garden of fire.

"Lasky," Bezarin called into his microphone, "get those little bastards of yours out of their vehicles and go for the bridge. Just follow the main road. I'll try to work the tanks around. But get to the damned bridge before they blow it."

Lasky acknowledged the order. His voice sounded excited, but not as shaken as it had come across back on the highway, amid the shot-down refugees. Bezarin hoped Lasky would be able to do his job this time.

Bezarin led the tanks in a detour around the back of the town, looking for another way in. He feared getting bogged down in street fighting, where a few soldiers with antitank weapons could put an end to his mission on the spot. But he saw no alternative to running for the bridge.

The firefight had nearly blinded him, and he ordered his driver to turn on the running lights, aware that he was setting himself up as a perfect target. But he found a side street that opened into the fields. He led his tanks into the town.

They moved through a residential section, chewing curbs into dust and grinding down fences and hedges. From a distance of several hundred meters, Bezarin could feel the secondary explosions from the stricken British column. He ordered his self-propelled battery to assume hasty positions on the edge of town. There was no point in simply dragging them into town behind the tanks.

The streets wound in arcs and twists. Bezarin had a sense of simply wandering about in circles as he struggled to find a main artery that would put him on a course for the bridge. At each small intersection, he rose in his turret, scanning the alternatives, waiting for a light antitank weapon to seek him out.

In his urgency to reach the bridge, Bezarin turned his tank into a street that soon began to narrow dangerously. The buildings converged so tightly that he feared his tank might get caught in a vise between them. The bent fender of his vehicle scraped noisily against concrete. When Bezarin looked behind him, he saw the looming black shapes of his remaining tanks tucked in so closely on his tail that it would take an hour to back them up and turn them around.

"Can you make it?" Bezarin asked his driver.

"I don't know, Comrade Commander."

So. The decision was his alone.

"Go," Bezarin said. "Let's try it."

The tank's exhaust coughed, like a giant clearing his throat. The tank's metal screamed along the walls in the narrow alley.

In a moment, they were through. Released, the tank shot ahead.

"Stop," Bezarin shouted. *"Halt. Back up."* He had caught a glimpse of something as they rolled across an intersection.

He guided his driver backward just as the next tank in line came up in their rear. The vehicles almost collided. But off to the left, down another, blessedly wider alley, Bezarin could see the dark span of an intact bridge rising against the sky.

Bezarin helped his driver turn the vehicle in the cramped space, sweating, shifting his eyes back to the bridge again and again. He expected it to erupt in flames at any moment.

"Lasky," Bezarin called, "can you hear me? Where are you?"

The motorized rifle officer did not respond. Bezarin wondered if he had even taken a dismount radio with him.

As his tank nosed out into the open near the deck of the bridge Bezarin could see the vivid traces of action back in the center of the town. The guardians of the bridge were giving Lasky a tough time of it. But they had left the bridge itself virtually undefended. A few British military policemen fired their small arms at the tank, forcing Bezarin down behind the shield of his hatch cover. But his machine gun soon drove them to ground. He hoped there would not be too many more of them. He was nearly out of machine-gun ammunition, and he had no main-gun rounds to waste. As the next tanks in column came up behind him Bezarin ordered his driver forward. They had approached the bridge at an awkward angle, and it proved difficult to maneuver up onto the deck of the bridge. To his rear, the next tank worked its pivots.

It was possible, he realized, that the British were set to blow the bridge, that they were only holding off until Soviet vehicles filled its span before they dropped everything into the river. But he could not wait for Lasky's dismounted troops to work their way up to check for demolitions. Success could be a matter of a few minutes, of seconds. At the same time, Bezarin's overwhelming emotion was not fear, but a peculiar sort of joy, of fervor. He had reached the river. If he had to go, this was as fine a moment as he could imagine. But he did not really believe that he was going to die. He felt as confident as he had ever felt in his life. His tank snorted and began to accelerate.

The bridge had cleared of traffic during the assault. Bezarin rolled across a span that lay empty save for a single broken-down British personnel carrier. He rode high in the turret again, ready with the last few rounds in his machine gun. He sensed that he had just become a part of history, and it filled him with a thrilling bigness. He felt as though he could accomplish anything in the world. Below him, the dark, murky waters seemed almost alive, and resentful. The river caught fractured patterns of light from the fires back in the town. But there was no beauty to it. It reminded Bezarin of a sewer.

He looked to the rear. His second tank followed him, and a third was steering around the obstructions to come up on the bridge. Suddenly, small-arms fire broke out from the shadowy clutter of buildings on the far shore, and random shots pinged off the glacis of Bezarin's tank. He dropped back inside the turret. The tank's infrared searchlight revealed a few probable vehicles well up on the far bank, arranged to exploit the intermittent fields of fire allowed by the antique cram of the village. But they didn't look like—didn't feel like—tanks. And no main guns fired at him. Bezarin ordered his gunner to hold his fire. They were too low on main-gun rounds to waste a single shot, and they would need to fight their way into Bad Oeynhausen. Bezarin decided to take the risk of simply racing through the funnel of the built-up area. He got on the radio and ordered his other tanks to follow him, but to hold their fire unless it proved necessary to suppress local targets.

He tried again to call Lasky. But there was nothing on the airwaves except intense static and faint ghosts of other men's voices. He wanted to direct Lasky to remain and hold the bridge at all costs. But, unable to contact him, he could only hope that Lasky would grasp the dictates of the situation. Bezarin did not intend to accept any further delay. He would take his remaining tanks on to Bad Oeynhausen. The motorized riflemen, the artillery, everyone else could remain at Rinteln. Nothing, not even unit integrity, was more important than time.

Bezarin's tank rolled off the bridge. Roaring up the canyon of shops and houses, he paid out a few more rounds of machine-gun fire, hoping to discourage any hidden antitank grenadiers. A signature in the path of the infrared searchlight baffled him for a moment. Then he realized that the crossing site was well-protected, indeed, but against the wrong threat. The path of Bezarin's tanks led through the middle of a NATO air-defense missile unit. The enemy had anticipated air assaults or air attacks on the Rinteln crossing. But they had not expected Soviet armor to penetrate so deeply so fast.

Bezarin managed to contact his self-propelled battery, which lay on the other side of the river now, deployed against an orchard. He ordered the battery commander to wait five minutes for the tanks to transit the area, then to open fire on the far side of the river. He also directed the artilleryman to use his long-range radio set to contact any higher station he could raise, reporting the situation at Rinteln and that Bezarin was leading his remaining tanks directly on Bad Oeynhausen. Finally, the battery commander was to track down Lasky and order him to remain and hold the bridge, literally to the last man.

Bezarin's last tank in column reported that it had thrown a track making the pivot up onto the bridge.

Bezarin sensed that he could not wait. And he wanted the artillery to destroy the enemy air-defense unit before it could move. He ordered the crippled vehicle to remain where it was to support the motorized rifle troops. Bezarin's tank had already reached an open expanse of highway, where the thoroughfare was bothered only by intermittent wreckage and the occasional lost or straggling refugees. First he would go west, then, picking up the river road, he would wind around until he turned northward for Bad

Oeynhausen. There were still tens of kilometers to cover. But the way was clear. He tried to call Dagliev, to assure him that help was on the way. The geography of the river valley prevented his attempt at communicating. But Bezarin remained marvelously calm. Another few kilometers and he would try the radio again. And he would keep on trying until he raised Dagliev. And then he would reach the objective with his tanks. In the meantime, Bezarin allowed himself to relax, ever so slightly, and to enjoy the feeling of driving unopposed through the heart of West Germany.

Bezarin's handful of tanks shot their way onto the high ground south of Bad Oeynhausen with their last rounds. One last, vital time they managed to surprise the enemy, and they caught a series of tank and infantry fighting vehicle positions in the rear. The enemy vehicles had been positioned so that they could kill anything that tried to cross the main highway bridge to the north. But they had become so preoccupied with that task that they had totally neglected the possibility of a threat from behind their positions. Bezarin's tanks destroyed every enemy vehicle on the hill.

Hurriedly, he radioed Dagliev to tell everyone in the bridgeheads to hold their fire. Then he split his tiny force in two, leaving half of it to hold the high ground and taking what amounted to a platoon of tanks down the hill toward the big bridge, firing colored flares to indicate to the air-assault troops that his was a Soviet force. Some small-arms fire came his way, despite his precautions, but it only managed to force Bezarin back inside the turret.

Dagliev had moved his tanks over the bridge as soon as he saw the firefight on the high ground, and he awaited Bezarin just off the western approach to the bridge. The air-assault unit commander came out to meet Bezarin as well. The officers hugged each other, oblivious to the nearby impact of artillery rounds that a single day before would have sent them scrambling for cover. Dagliev looked filthy, even in the darkness, covered with oil and the residue of gunnery. The air-assault lieutenant colonel looked even worse, grimed with blood, soot, and mud. It was all very much unlike the movies about the Great Patriotic War in terms of glamorous appearance, Bezarin thought. But the emotional power seemed incomparably greater.

The air-assault commander was disappointed to learn how few tanks Bezarin had with him, and he was alarmed to hear that they were virtually out of ammunition. But Bezarin felt confident. Surely, the enemy had received reports that Soviet tanks had entered Bad Oeynhausen. That would slow down any planned countermeasures until the enemy assessed the impact of the change in the situation.

Bezarin ordered Dagliev to recross to the east bank and block any enemy counterattacks from that direction, then he returned to properly position his remaining tanks against a threat from the south or west. Small-arms engagements continued to flare in the center of the town, but the noise did not seem to worry the air-assault commander. The bridge, after all, was everything.

Now it was a matter of waiting to see who would arrive first, an enemy counterattack or formations of Soviet armor. Bezarin expected more high drama, perhaps even a sort of siege. But reality disappointed him. More small Soviet elements began to filter in, while some reconnaissance elements pushed on to the west. Another forward detachment found its way through, and its commander was disappointed that Bezarin had beaten him to the linkup. Regimental forward security detachments and advance guards arrived, often with vehicles from different units jumbled together. Lead elements from an army corps appeared, demanding that their vehicles receive unconditional right-of-way. The orders of march often made little sense, judged by the prescriptions of the manuals. But within an hour, enough combat power had crossed the Bad Oeynhausen bridge to hold the area against any counterattack the enemy was likely to launch. When Bezarin reestablished radio contact with his elements left behind at Rinteln, he learned that other Soviet units were crossing there, as well.

Mission accomplished, Bezarin attempted to make out his after-action report, huddled in the stinking interior of his tank. He felt a desperate need to explain the day's events from the perspective of his battalion. He was unsure whether he was a hero or a war criminal. He intended to be as honest as possible about the situation that had gotten out of hand during the engagement amid the refugee column. He wanted to get it out in the open. He did not intend to live with it as a secret, like one of the tormented characters in Anna's beloved novels. In any case, he doubted that it would be possible to hide it. It was too big, too terrible. He remembered the girl in the torn sweater, how her arm had flown high over a spray of blood in the moment before she fell. In his imagination, he could see each of her bony fingers, reaching higher and higher, even though she had been too far away for him actually to have made out the fine details he now traced in his mind. Then the fleeing girl was Anna, reaching to touch the coppery leaves of a birch tree in the Galician autumn, and it all made perfect sense to him as he fell into an iron sleep.

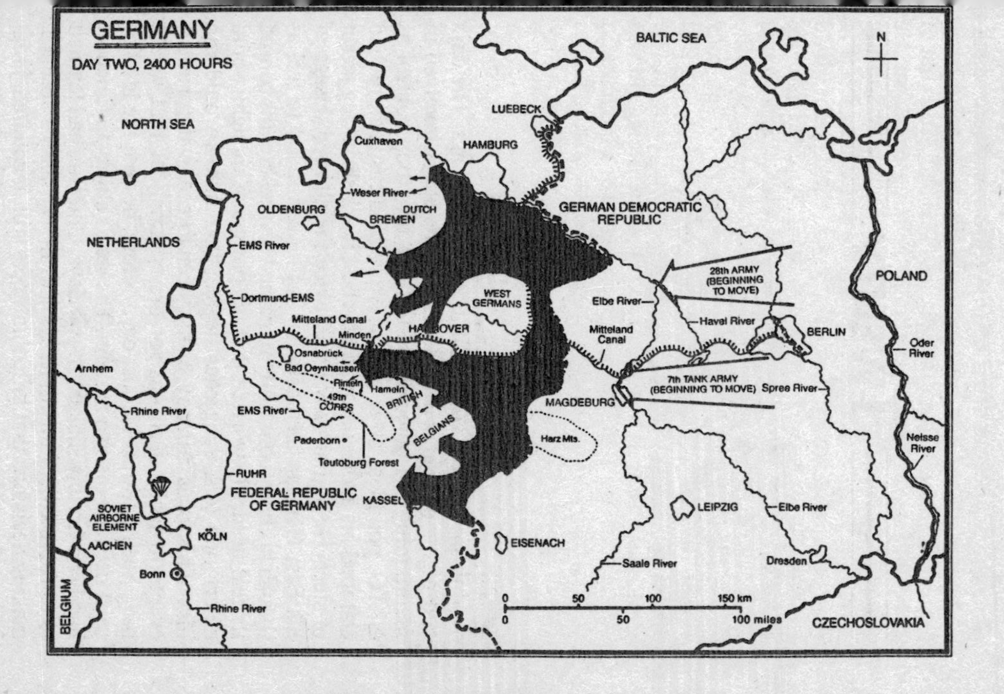

GERMANY
DAY TWO, 2400 HOURS
NORTH SEA
BALTIC SEA
N
NETHERLANDS
Arnhem
Cuxhaven
Weser River
OLDENBURG
DUTCH
BREMEN
HAMBURG
LUEBECK
GERMAN DEMOCRATIC
REPUBLIC
POLAND
EMS River
Dortmund-EMS
Mitteland Canal
Minden
WEST
GERMANS
Osnabrück
Bad Oeynhausen
Rinteln
Hameln
49th
CORPS
BRITISH
BELGIANS
EMS River
Rhine River
Paderborn
Teutoburg Forest
RUHR
FEDERAL REPUBLIC
OF GERMANY
KASSEL
SOVIET
AIRBORNE
ELEMENT
AACHEN
KÖLN
Bonn
Rhine River
BELGIUM
28th ARMY
(BEGINNING
TO MOVE)
Elbe River
Havel River
Mitteland
Canal
BERLIN
Oder
River
7th TANK ARMY
(BEGINNING TO MOVE)
Spree River
MAGDEBURG
Harz Mts.
Neisse
River
LEIPZIG
Elbe River
EISENACH
Saale River
Dresden
0
50
100
150 km
0
50
100 miles
CZECHOSLOVAKIA

TWENTY

Chibisov felt the strain of the war in his lungs. The days and nights of near-sleeplessness and the stress involved in maintaining the objective conditions for troop control as NATO pounded away at the front's infrastructure had clamped his asthma around his chest like a shrinking jacket of steel. He had already taken twice the allowed dosage of his East German medications, but he continued to feel as though his body constantly remained several breaths behind its real need. He worried that his powers of thought would deteriorate to a dangerous degree, that illness would rob him of his focus. Already, he had been forced by the crush of events to make decisions for the commander that would have been unthinkable just days before, despite the level of trust between the two of them. The staff's ability to function had been terribly shaken. In two days, Chibisov had learned to make drastic, immediate choices in Malinsky's absence, making decisions that killed numbers still uncounted, judging only by the powerful law of the plan and his insights into Malinsky's approach to military operations. Sequential and even concurrent methods of support for decision-making and planning had largely broken down. The truly crucial decisions had to be made upon the immediately available information in the executive manner. Under the circumstances, Chibisov did his best to be a perfect chief of staff and deputy commander for the old man, struggling not to insert his personal views, always seeking to act as a pure extension of the commander's will. But now Chibisov worried that he might make a false move out of the sort of temperamental spitefulness that sickness brought out in the human animal.

He had not been outside the bunker since the beginning of combat operations. Malinsky flew around the battlefield, applying his personal skills and attention at the points of decision, while Chibisov remained at the main command post, working the routine levers and gears. Chibisov had no doubt that Malinsky's presence forward made a difference. The old man had the knack, the touch of the born general, able to see through the fog of war to the essence. Perhaps, Chibisov thought, there was something to bloodlines. Perhaps all of the centuries of family soldiering had made this difference in Malinsky, breeding a special, ultimately undefinable perfection in the man.

Chibisov smiled bitterly at the shortness in his lungs. Yes, and if bloodlines determined fate, then what did that imply for him? A little Jew from the ghetto of Kiev or Odessa, sputtering the arcane formulas of a new metal religion. Worshiping the correlation of forces and means, the norms of consumption and the mathematical coefficients of combat results. He sensed that he was, after all, an impostor. How could he be otherwise? How could any of them have been otherwise? His father had fought for the Soviet Union and the international cause of socialism in Spain, and had nearly died in Stalin's camps for his suspicious voluntarism within a viciously capricious system. Only the German invasion had saved the man from death in the snows of Magadan. As with Malinsky's father, Chibisov well knew. And he laughed. What would the Hitlerite Germans have thought had they known that their invasion actually freed

Jews? To fight them from Maikop to Potsdam. Jews who would have sons to fight their sons.

Chibisov was never fully aware of the extent to which he accepted his Jewishness in the end. He mocked it to himself, working to hate it. Yet he inevitably cast himself in the term against which he so rebelled, insinuating it into the speech and thoughts of his comrades.

Yes, he thought, the great socialist experiment has been a failure for some of us. May we never annihilate the past? My father came out of the camps without reproach or even a question, to join the struggle as though he had only been on sick leave. And his father's father had played cat and mouse with the Okhrana, the czarist secret police, plotting the future by smoky lamps in back rooms in the near-medieval Ukraine. His grandfather had manned the barricades, fighting fanatically to bring a new world to birth. In the years of the troubles, he had withheld food from the starving, from his own people by any definition, to shorten the long and agonizing labor. Every weapon had been justified. The final result was to absolve all guilt.

But there never was a final result. The golden age receded again and again. Next year in Jerusalem, Chibisov thought sarcastically.

Why did we believe? Why us, out of all of them? The Russians and Ukrainians, wretched in their superstition and drunkenness . . . it was easy to understand their blindness, their madness. But how were *we* so deceived?

We deceived ourselves, of course. Because we, of all the peoples of this earth, wanted most passionately to believe. Religious natures, with a weakness for mysticism. And the new religion of the revolution, of shining, benevolent socialism, the ideology of an unprecedented dispensation, of a new holiness . . . that was the new Jerusalem. New heavens and, above all, a new earth. It was, Chibisov thought, as though history had painstakingly set us up to be the fools.

And yet, we had to believe. What else was there except belief? Belief in any religion. Even the religion of war. Am I of the blood of David, of Joshua and Gideon? Or the crouched asthmatic son of willing fools?

Chibisov knocked lightly at the door to Malinsky's private office. The old man had returned exhausted from visiting the front and army forward command posts, and despite the compounding successes of the day, he had ripped through the staff, unusually biting in his comments as he demanded key pieces of information. Chibisov had been relieved when he finally managed to steer the old man off for a bit of sleep.

Now, all too soon, he had to disturb Malinsky. This was not a matter he felt he could address by himself. It was, potentially at least, far too big. The one great variable.

Chibisov wondered to what extent Trimenko's death had upset Malinsky. Of course, any flying would be hopelessly nerve-wracking after that. No. The old man would not have worried about the personal danger. But the unanticipated loss of Trimenko had been a blow to them all. If Starukhin was a wild bull who could break down the stoutest fences, Trimenko had been the front's cat, always able to find a quick and clever way around the most formidable obstacles. Chibisov sensed that, with Trimenko's loss, some intangible yet important balance had been upset within the front. Oh, his deputy commander would do well enough. This was a powerful new generation of leaders, and the situation in the north met all of the objective conditions for success, with the Germans encircled and Soviet forward detachments on the west bank of the Weser at Verden and Nienburg. The Dutch forces who had not been pushed out of the way and trapped against the North Sea on the Cuxhaven peninsula were dying piecemeal. But the loss of Trimenko was somehow greater than its purely operational significance.

Perhaps that's only my view, Chibisov thought. My unjustifiable emotional prejudice. Because Trimenko was like me in his methods and in his fondness for numbers and machines that emulate the more dependable aspects of human thought. Perhaps I merely feel a bit more alone.

Chibisov knocked again. But there was still no response from within Malinsky's office. He wished he could let the old man sleep. But there was important intelligence from the Western High Command of Forces, laden with rumors of political movement. And, internal to the front, the situation was growing troublesome in new respects. As

NATO's deep attacks destroyed more and more intelligence-collection systems Dudorov's splendid picture of the battlefield was rapidly deteriorating. The loss of intelligence platforms and the resultant clouding of the battlefield left Chibisov with the sensation of a man going helplessly, relentlessly blind.

Chibisov let himself in. Much to his surprise, he found that Malinsky was not asleep. The old man sat before the map, staring at its intense intermingling of friendly and enemy symbols. Despite the labor of clever staff officers, the situation map now appeared almost as though the different colors of the opposing forces had been thrown on randomly between the East–West German border and the Weser River. Here and there, a cluster of enemy symbols showed some integrity. The Germans, for example, had been pocketed in a vast area between Hannover and the southern forests of the Lueneburg Heath. But in other areas, expanding red arrows had overwhelmed the diminishing enemy markers. In between, it appeared as though the colors had been swirled together. Enemy forces remained behind the Soviet advance, while the Soviet elements that had penetrated most deeply appeared stranded in the blue rear. Chibisov made a mental note to order one of the operations officers to come in and clean up the map. So many units had been depicted that the graphics no longer telegraphed their meaning with directness and clarity—indispensable requirements for a commander's map.

Malinsky turned his head in slow motion. Chibisov felt that they were both captives of the same wearying spell in the darkness. He moved closer to the lighted magic show of the map.

"Oh, it's you, Pavel Pavlovitch," Malinsky said, as though he had bumped into an acquaintance on a city street.

"Comrade Front Commander," Chibisov began, armored in his formality, "we have a bulletin from the High Command of Forces Intelligence Directorate."

Malinsky looked up at him. The old man's face appeared ashen, almost lifeless, in the harsh pool of light near the map. There was no lack of the accustomed intelligence or dignity. But there seemed to be a profound change in

Malinsky's age. The quality of the eyes and skin, of simple health, had altered radically in a matter of days.

Chibisov experienced a rush of emotion, which he refused to allow into his outward expression. He wished he could do still more for this man, to lighten the burden weighing so heavily upon him. But he could think of nothing acceptable to do or say, always terrified of revealing any emotional weakness, conditioned by a solitary lifetime to withhold the most trivial symptoms of human vulnerability.

"Comrade Front Commander, the Intelligence Directorate of the General Staff has informed the High Command of Forces that the American and British militaries have requested nuclear release. Apparently, there is a great deal of turmoil within the NATO alliance about granting the request, as well as about the terms of nuclear weapons employment, should release be granted. The West Germans are reportedly reluctant—perhaps the propaganda broadcasts and the business with Lueneburg have had some effect, although it's natural enough not to want your homeland turned into a nuclear battlefield, in any case."

Chibisov had expected a shot of energy to enliven Malinsky at the mention of nuclear weapons. But the old man merely raised his eyebrows slightly, as at the poor taste of a cup of field tea.

"There are no indications that nuclear release has been granted at this time," Chibisov went on, "and Dudorov's convinced the Germans will disrupt the process. But measures must be taken—"

"Sit down, Pavel Pavlovitch," Malinsky said, interrupting him. "Sit down for a moment." Chibisov stiffened at first, spinsterish, unused to being interrupted even by Malinsky. Then he calmly took a seat. The smoke of burned-down cigarettes hovered in the lamplight, as though the smoke of battle were drifting up from the situation map. Chibisov labored to control his breathing, to conceal the weakness he felt diminishing him.

"Look at the map," Malinsky said. "Just *look* at it. And if they do get their nuclear release? What will they do with it, Pavel Pavlovitch? How could they strike us now without slaughtering their own?"

"Comrade Front Commander, they could still strike deep targets. Inside the German Democratic Republic or Poland. Our assessment shows that an unacceptably high level of strike aircraft remain operative within the NATO air forces."

Malinsky brushed at the air with his fingers, dismissing the idea. "The best measures we can take are to proceed with the plan. Push deeper into their rear. And load everything onto West German soil that we can." Malinsky turned his eyes on Chibisov, narrowing them until he looked almost Asiatic. "And hostages. Give me hostages, Pavel Pavlovitch."

For a moment, Chibisov could not follow the old man's train of thought. The notion of hostages seemed so out of character. To Chibisov, hostages meant frightened illiterates herded out of lice-ridden kishlaks in the valleys of Afghanistan.

"We must refocus our efforts slightly," Malinsky went on. "You told me earlier about the problems with prisoner transport. But you sounded proud of the problems, Pavel Pavlovitch, you truly did, because you solved them with your usual efficiency." The old man smiled slightly. "What good are prisoners to us? We need to watch them, feed them, move them, even protect them. And we haven't time. Much better to have hostages." Malinsky pointed at the map with a nicotine-stained finger. "*There.* Hannover. And the entire area still held by the German operational grouping. That . . . is a collection of hostages on a nuclear battlefield. Let them dare toss nuclear bombs at us. No, Pavel Pavlovitch, we must insure that our commanders do not tighten the more critical nooses too snugly. We must leave the bypassed or surrounded enemy forces just enough spatial integrity to make them prime targets. And drive them into the cities. NATO military units and formations backed up into German cities, that's what I want. Then let them rattle their nuclear toys."

Chibisov had never heard quite this tone in Malinsky's voice. Even in Afghanistan, where the demands of military operations and the pervasiveness of small brutalities had not brought out the best in men, Malinsky had seemed above the rest of them—a soldier, but with no special lust for killing, no trivializing callousness. Chibisov realized that he had, in fact, considered Malinsky essentially a warmhearted man, one who loved his profession and his soldiers, and who adored his wife and son. To Chibisov, Malinsky had come to personify the goodness of Russia, the possibilities latent within the frustrating Russian character. Now, to hear him speak so coolly of replying to any future NATO nuclear strikes by methodically destroying German cities and military forces that had ceased to pose an operational threat, Chibisov again felt his own baffling difference from all of them. He realized that he had, indeed, underestimated what it meant to be born a blood Russian.

"I do not want to precipitate a nuclear exchange, if one can be avoided," Malinsky went on. "We all have enough blood on our hands. But should it become apparent that our enemy will resort to such a course, he must be preempted. He cannot be allowed to strike first. It's no longer a matter of political bantering and competing for the international limelight. I want you to begin preparations—with an appropriate level of discretion. Have the nuclear support units move to the highest readiness level. Wake up our friends from the KGB and have them visit me. We will begin to put our formal mechanisms into motion. I will tell you, though, Pavel Pavlovitch, that I expect the devolution of nuclear targeting authority as soon as it becomes apparent that NATO is seriously preparing for a nuclearization of the battlefield." Malinsky picked up his shoulders, regaining his usual erectness in his chair. "Meanwhile, see that the reconnaissance strike apparatus is reorganized to exploit nuclear targets. I do not want an atmosphere of rumor and panic. Employ the strictest security measures. But release the commander's reserve of missile troops. Let Voltov position them as he sees fit, but make sure he understands the psychological-political dimensions of the problem, as well as the purely military considerations. We'll see what our chief of missile troops and artillery is made of."

"Comrade Front Commander, I'm afraid we may all see what we're made of."

Malinsky smiled. His voice returned to the normal, vastly

more personable tone to which Chibisov had become accustomed in their private exchanges. "Personally, I do not believe the battlefield will turn nuclear. It's too late. They waited too long. They would have had to reply immediately with nuclear weapons in order to stop us. They were fools. And we may be thankful for it." Malinsky sat back in his chair. He turned his face from Chibisov to gaze at the map again. "You know, I suspect that I have always undervalued the essential brilliance of the Soviet system. I became preoccupied with the endless problems, with the imperfections. It's easy, of course, to discount the system because of its obvious inefficiencies—perhaps the only thing of which I have never found a shortage." Malinsky laughed. It was a special, heartfelt laugh that he employed only when he was laughing at himself, at his own folly, and it was not shared with many other human beings. "Yes, inefficiency may be the only item that has never been in short supply within our Soviet state. But in the end, we are too easily taken in by superficialities. We condition ourselves to be cynical, to see only the inefficiencies, while our opponents are masters of the superficial accomplishment. We even came to question the system's central focus, one might say its preoccupation, with planning. Well, the system was right after all. The plan remains the thing." The front commander shifted in his chair, leaning closer toward Chibisov. "Consider how differently we and our enemies approached the long preparation for war. Nearly half a century's preparation, although its directness is only evident in retrospect. We followed the correct policy, whether we all liked it or not. *We* fit the military plan to the overall political framework, all the while resenting even that much compromise. But our enemies in NATO tried to force a political plan into a military framework. The beauty in our system is that it restrains the military, often uncomfortably for us, but does not interfere in the internal details of military operations. *We* are the warriors who enjoy the essential freedoms. Our enemies allowed political considerations to dictate not just the decision to use force, but even the practical details of military planning. Their forward defense policy, for example, proved disastrous—but it placated the West Germans in peacetime. When it mattered, they could not even implement it effectively. They avoided squabbles and discomforts in peacetime at the price of crippling their abilities to wage war. Look at the wastage evident on that map. All of their splendid equipment. And their expensively trained soldiers. Squandered for a political convenience that failed them in a time of crisis. Our opponents forgot what armies are for. And we are very fortunate. I have always been jealous of their marvelous equipment, and even, I must admit, of their soldiers. Pavel Pavlovitch, whenever I reviewed the special wartime tables for correlation calculations, I always told myself that, were I in command of NATO, the Warsaw Pact forces would not stand a chance. And who knows? Even now the tide of battle could turn in a moment. I do not believe it will. But perhaps I underestimate the nuclear bogeyman at this point. I do not believe the West Germans will consent to nuclear usage on their soil. I believe we have already won—for now. The outstanding question is, how much have we won, and for how long? But we've won. Or perhaps it would be more honest to say that our enemies have defeated themselves."

Chibisov rose and moved close to the map, recalling through the layers of weariness that his report was incomplete. He circled a large area in the mountainous region south of the Ruhr. "Comrade Front Commander, Dudorov has drawn a blank here. From the Ruhr right down to the Taunus, almost to Frankfurt, we have insufficient current data, only the sketchiest notion of what's happening in there. The attrition of our technical means of reconnaissance is hampering our collection effort, and our human intelligence and special-operations effort has been disappointing in its results. Only the systems can provide the volume and detail we require on the contemporary battlefield. And we're losing those systems at an intolerable rate. The attack on our intelligence infrastructure may be the most painful aspect of the NATO defense at this stage in the war. In any case, Dudorov is convinced that our sister front to the south does not have an accurate accounting of the current dispositions of all of the NATO-CENTAG forces."

Malinsky leaned slightly toward the map, but he either

remained magnificently imperturbable or was nearing the point of true exhaustion. "The Americans?" he asked the map. "Does Dudorov believe the Americans will move north?"

"He believes our sister front has overcounted the U.S. Army formations that are currently committed. It's psychologically natural for them to do so, based upon their failure to sustain a substantial penetration in the south. Dudorov is convinced that the Americans have been attacking our intelligence structure unilaterally, trying to blind us. He feels they're up to something big."

"It's a different war down south," Malinsky said. He paused for a moment, shifting his eyes, scanning thoughts that remained hidden from Chibisov. "Of course, I received the privileged position. Our comrades down in the Second Western Front have a thankless task. How well would we have done attacking the best-equipped, heaviest enemy formations on terrain that almost defends itself? No one really expected great gains in the south, of course. The object is simply to fix them while we break through and conduct the operational-strategic envelopment down the west bank of the Rhine. But it must be a heartbreaking mission for our comrades to the south. And now Dudorov thinks they may have botched the job? Does he really believe the Americans can move north fast enough to intercept us? Does he really think they're coming?"

"He doesn't believe the Americans will ever allow the British to be destroyed. And the Americans aren't the fools we'd like them to be. They must see the threat to their lines of communication if we reach the west bank of the Rhine. They have to move at some point."

"But are they moving already? How quickly can they move? Will the routes support an operational movement? How long will it take? And *where* will they try to strike us?"

"Dudorov's working the problem. But we just can't *see* back into those mountains down south." Chibisov paused, playing through a mental war game. "The Twentieth Guards Army is moving slowly, and a gap is beginning to open up. The Americans could theoretically move north almost anywhere between the Weser and the Rhine."

Malinsky pushed himself back into a more comfortable position. "Well, we can fight the Americans, too. Dudorov needs to get moving. Concentrate all of the available intelligence assets. Find their formations, if they're really out there. And you and I can sit down and choose our ground. Now, how's the passage of the Forty-ninth Corps progressing?"

Chibisov almost began his reply with "Your son's corps," but he caught himself. He answered crisply. "The lead brigades of the Forty-ninth Corps are crossing the Weser at Bad Oeynhausen and Rinteln at this time. We had a splendid stroke of luck. A forward detachment grabbed the Rinteln bridge while working its way up to Bad Oeynhausen."

Malinsky nodded, but his face appeared troubled. "Our luck has been almost too good for my tastes, Pavel Pavlovitch. Dudorov really needs to pay attention now."

"The trail brigades of the corps are following the same routes. Their lead elements should cross within the next hour. The biggest problems remain the refugee flow and clutter on the highways, but we've managed to clean up the priority routes. The transit of the Forty-ninth Corps has, however, meant a cessation of other reinforcement and resupply throughout the night, except for what we can push up on secondary routes. Maintaining the broad integrity of the Forty-ninth does, of course, give us the option of turning the entire corps or the trail brigades to meet a threat from the south. But we would need to send them combat instructions within the next few hours. Otherwise, they'll be too deeply committed to the push for the Rhine."

Malinsky peered at the map. Chibisov could sense the old man war-gaming various options, doing his own vital staff work now in a matter of seconds. "We'll see," Malinsky said. "I don't want to change their mission just yet. Stick to the plan. We'll take the risk. But Dudorov has to work the problem with the Americans. I do not want to send the Forty-ninth Corps chasing ghosts on the wrong side of the Rhine. But I don't want to be unpleasantly surprised by the Americans. Really, an operational-scale American attack is a more likely threat than a nuclearization of the battlefield.

Stick to the plan. For now. Get the lead brigades of the Forty-ninth to the Rhine and across it. We will only turn the lead brigades if we have no choice. But warn the corps of the possible danger to their left flank. Direct that the trail elements be weighted to the south, ready to conduct a spoiling attack, fight meeting engagements, or, if necessary, assume a hasty defense. Speed them up. Get them all through the Teutoburg Forest tonight."

"We can expect to fight for some of the passes in the Teutoburg. It's the last practical line of defense."

Malinsky waved the problem away. "That's a purely tactical problem. The enemy is beaten. They have too little left to stop us. Our commanders must not be timid."

Chibisov thought again of Malinsky's son. Guards Colonel Malinsky. The son had a reputation as a painstaking officer, but a loner, even more so than his father. Not at all the gregarious sort of Russian to which one became accustomed in the officer corps. Chibisov also knew that the son was supposed to be a very talented musician, and that he had a wife said to be eccentric and overly given to Western tastes. He knew that the old man loved his son more than he loved anything else in the world. There were endless stories about how Malinsky so relentlessly stressed that his son should have no special treatment that everyone assumed that he was actually hinting that he wanted to insure that the son received very special treatment, indeed. Chibisov suspected that he might be the only officer in the entire army who never doubted Malinsky's sincerity. Malinsky just did not make sense to others. A high-ranking officer who did not press ruthlessly for his son's advantage made no sense within the Soviet system. Malinsky was a genius in some respects; in others he seemed as naïve as a child. He never seemed to fully grasp the selfish motivations of other men.

Now the son would have a chance to perform on his own. Perhaps against the Americans, with their magnificent weapons. Chibisov wished the son luck across the dark distances. For the father's sake.

"Shall I call for tea or some refreshments, Comrade Front Commander?" Chibisov asked.

Malinsky nodded. Yes. But it was really an unconcerned

gesture. The old man was engrossed in the map again, seeking out advantageous ground and constructing hypothetical situations for a possible clash with the Americans. He had come back from the depths of weariness one more time, rejuvenated by the prospect of another combat challenge, of a new enemy.

Suddenly, Malinsky turned from the map, smiling. He stood up with the sprightliness of a boy. "We'll beat them, Pavel Pavlovitch. They've waited too long. I don't believe they can reach us in time to make a difference." Malinsky set his face into a resolute expression, and Chibisov felt as though he were staring at the personification of the long history of Russian military struggles. "Damn them, let them come, the Americans. We can beat the Americans, too."

Malinsky surprised his chief of staff by taking hold of his upper arm. Chibisov automatically recoiled from the human touch, then mastered his reflexes and forced himself to endure the grasp. He felt as though his armor had been penetrated, as though even this friendly grasp might fatally weaken his tenuous control over his lungs, over his fate.

"You realize that we had to fight," Malinsky said passionately, vividly Russian in his tone of confidence. "Do you see that, Pavel Pavlovitch? It wasn't only the political situation. We've been through worse crises. But we had to fight them now. It was the last chance. They were beating us without ever firing a shot. They forced us to fight so long with their weapons—technology, economics, their entire arsenal for destroying us in peacetime. And we could not compete. We were losing, and it became so apparent that even a fool could see it. They were laughing at us, Pavel Pavlovitch. But they aren't laughing now. There is one thing we can still beat them at. Look at that map. We'll beat the Americans, if they come. We have no choice."

Major General Borchak, special KGB representative to the front's military council, labored over his daily report. Writing official correspondence was an art, and Borchak prided himself on his mastery of it. You had to write in such a way that it provided indisputable facts for future use by your superiors, but you had to arrange those facts in such a manner that they did not directly affix blame, so that they could be given an innocent, sober interpretation, should the individual about whom you were reporting ever attain access to his file or gain unexpected power over you. Borchak struggled to communicate his grave doubts about Malinsky and his clique, but to do so without the sort of crude directness that might one day become a liability.

He did not like Malinsky. Overall, he found army generals a bit too puffed up, too convinced of their indispensability. Certainly, the regular military forces had a role to play. But the ultimate guarantor of Soviet power was and always would be the state security apparatus. Military commanders were narrow-minded, greedy, and naïve. For the most part, they could be managed. But Malinsky made Borchak uneasy.

Borchak would have much preferred the front commander to have a few obvious vices. The most desirable traits in a high-ranking military officer, from Borchak's point of view, were occasional weaknesses toward alcohol or women—or even a reasonable appetite for material corruption. Officers who had such traits inevitably left a trail that could be exploited should the need arise. A man like Starukhin, for instance, could never be a threat in the long term. He would always say something in his drunken belligerence that was potentially fatal. But Malinsky was too clean. Of course, you could always make a case of sorts out of his bloodlines. Such a stale approach was not much to Borchak's taste, however. As a matter of professional pride. He would have much preferred something immediate and powerful, with an unmistakable taint of filth, to hold over the man.

He considered how Malinsky could be painted before a tribunal or special committee. For one thing, Malinsky had a tendency to underutilize the military council. He certainly did not adequately consult with the representatives of the state security apparatus at every opportunity. He was willfully independent. In fact, Malinsky possessed several distinctly unsocialist habits. He even seemed to foster a small-scale personality cult with his staff and subordinate commanders. Nor was morale in the front everything that could be desired. The reports of Article 27 cases, unauthorized leaving of the field of battle, and of Article 25, 30, and 31 cases, were sufficiently numerous to undercut the man's reputation as a dedicated communist. Abandonment of equipment, plundering, and violence against the civilian population were among the most serious military crimes. It was obvious that Malinsky had not placed adequate stress on the inculcation of communist values and discipline within the formations under his command.

The trouble was, of course, that Malinsky's forces were doing too well. Thus far, their successes had dramatically exceeded Borchak's expectations. Had progress been a bit slower, had the fighting been more difficult, had there been more local reverses, the situation would have been more to Borchak's liking. He wanted the armed forces of the Soviet Union to win. But it would not do for them to perform *too* gloriously. The KGB had learned its lesson from Beria's fall, decades before. There would be no Zhukovs, no kingmakers, this time. Afghanistan had had several of the ingredients of a model war, in Borchak's eyes. Failure had put the military in its proper place.

If NATO granted nuclear release to its forces . . . it might be possible to manage the situation so that the ground forces took a bloody nose, and Malinsky and those like him could be brought back under firm control. Now Malinsky wanted authorization for preemptive strikes at his discretion. Borchak was firmly committed to fighting that request through KGB channels. As always, the military were taking a very short view of things. They could not see beyond the battle to the peace. Of course, the whole timing of the nuclear business would have to be precise. The mission was to defeat NATO. But the balance of power between the Party, the military, and state security had to be maintained.

If Malinsky made a mistake, if a substantial part of his operation failed . . . then, even though ultimate success was achieved, he could be charged with making unjustified decisions, with failing to employ the full range of decision-making support tools and the proper methodology available to him as a front commander. He could be portrayed as subjectivist, too prone to making executive-style decisions, while ignoring the objective conditions for success postulated by Soviet military science. The military's own toys could be turned against them in the end.

An alternative would be to work on the son. Malinsky's boy was not the strong figure his father was. He was ridiculously infatuated with his wife. And wives could always be managed. Nonetheless, such an approach was a bit too Byzantine. And the father might just cut his ties and sacrifice the son. You never could tell. Borchak much preferred the thought of something directly implicating Malinsky in corruption or disloyalty, no matter how slight the evidence. The point was not to destroy the man, after all, but simply to harness him, to chop him down to size if he ever became a threat of any kind.

Borchak disliked Malinsky the way a man might dislike a particular food. But he hated the front commander's chief of staff. Borchak could not even stomach looking at Chibisov. His purpose was to manage Malinsky. But he would have enjoyed destroying his smug little Jew of a deputy.

The Jews had always been and always would be a problem. Until they were finally expunged from Russia. Oh, the Jews could make revolutions. But they never knew when to stop. Borchak found it impossible to believe that Chibisov was truly loyal to the Soviet Union. But the chief of staff was clever. And Malinsky protected him.

Of course, that might open up new possibilities. If Chibisov could be implicated in something unsavory, and if Malinsky could be induced to defend his subordinate a bit too publicly, a bit too vehemently . . .

There was always a way. Every man had his weakness, his flaw, his instant of poor judgment, and it would be vital to keep the military firmly under control after the fighting ceased and the real work began. The military men thought they were so grand. But the difficult part of it all would be the occupation, the painstaking rebuilding of an acceptable government on the Rhine, the deals, the seeming compromises, the appearance of civilized, even generous behavior as the undesirable elements in reformed Germany were quietly eliminated. Entirely new formulas had to be developed to keep the Germanies divided, to maintain a sufficient degree of hatred and rivalry between them. The Soviet Union had not paid so great a price in blood to see the Germanies unified. Such a thought was anathema to all sensible men. . . . Borchak was aware of the intense debates in Moscow over what sort of restrictive federalism might be safely permitted, and over what contours the occupation would take on. So far, as his own boss had told him with a bitter laugh, the only thing anyone agreed on was that the new capital would be Weimar.

Borchak finished his report. He was not completely satisfied with it, but he felt that he was beginning to build up his arsenal of weapons to bring Malinsky low. Should the need arise. When you could not strike a man directly, you needed to weave a web of incidentals around him. Borchak was confident that he could do the latter.

He slipped the completed report into his courier briefcase. But before he went to the special communications center to send it, he drew out another message form and addressed it privately to his office-mate in Moscow.

"Dear Rodion Mikhailovitch," he began, "please look in on Yevdokia and the children, if you can find the time. Greet them from me; tell them I love them and that my thoughts are with them. Tell Yevdokia I said to go ahead with the plans to add the additional room onto the dacha before winter, but also that she need not be overly extravagant. I look forward to seeing all of you again. Greetings to Irina. Arkady."

TWENTY-ONE

The brigade's operations maps decorated the wall of the German living room. Battery-powered lamps shone their harsh, flattening light about the crowded room, striking Anton's eyes as he moved from officer to officer, checking, correcting, struggling to remain lucid despite his building fever.

At midnight, he had led his wounded brigade across the big bridge at Bad Oeynhausen. He had dismounted to empty his bowels yet again and to watch the progression of bristling war machines on the march, their spiky outlines silhouetted by fires burning out of control in the town. The bridgehead had been in a chaotic state, guarded by a crust of air-defense batteries, hastily dug-in antitank positions, grubby air-assault troops, and a battered assortment of scarred-up tanks and infantry fighting vehicles. Major General Anseev, the corps commander, had flown down in a light liaison helicopter, a brave act given the density of nervous gunners packed into the bridgehead. He hastened to brief Anton on a possible change in the situation. Indicators were building of a possible counterattack by U.S.

Army forces coming up from the south. The information only consisted of bits and pieces, and the corps commander even acknowledged that there might be nothing to it, just the imaginings of overwrought staff officers. But Anton had to rush his force through one designated pass across the Teutoburg forest ridge, a distance of more than fifty kilometers on a network of secondary roads, then to prepare for a possible wheel to the south. If an American grouping did appear, it was imperative to hold them west of the Teutoburg and south of the Paderborn–Soest–Dortmund line. Anton was to prepare contingency measures for a meeting engagement opened from the march, as well as for a hasty defense, as dictated by the developing situation. The corps' attack helicopters would forward base west of the Weser by first light. Since he was marching on the southern flank of the corps, Anton would have first call on the aircraft. Further, he would receive heavy multiple rocket launchers and additional tube artillery from the corps artillery brigade.

Images fuzzed in Anton's head. He understood what the corps commander said, but it only sounded hopelessly difficult, an unreasonable burden. He would have to pull in his commanders and hastily reorganize, without sufficient time for even the most rudimentary staff procedures. The additional assets made available by the corps commander only sounded like additional headaches. It all seemed so nightmarishly hard to manage, impossible to keep under control.

"The front is making every effort to locate the American grouping, if such a force is actually out there," the corps commander said. "If anything critical comes up, I'll personally open the long-range net. You may, of course, open up the net upon initial contact. But I don't think there will be a problem before daylight, at the earliest. The Americans couldn't move that fast." The corps commander stroked his mustache. "In the meantime, go like the wind. Speed is the best security."

Anton nodded. A part of him hoped with the hope of a child that the corps commander would see how ill he was and relieve him of his responsibilities on the spot. But the corps commander seemed totally immersed in the military problem.

Anton braced himself. He told himself that his diarrhea was slackening, although he knew he was running a high fever. How would it do, he asked himself, for the son of General Malinsky, the *privileged* son of the *great* General Malinsky, to miss the war because he had a case of the shits? But the sarcasm did not work. And Anton knew that he would keep on going until his body physically quit on him, paying the price of his father's terrible love.

Anton cared less and less for his personal pride now. But he could not imagine letting the old man down. Not without absolute physical failure. Or death, Anton thought, before dismissing the notion as the morbidity of illness.

He wished he were home, in bed, with Zena caring for him. He could lie propped up in his bed, drinking tea, and Zena could read to him. Perhaps a lesser tale by one of the giants whose pens had swept across the Russian earth before the Revolution. And he could draw Zena close to him, until her straight thick red hair blazed on the white of the bedclothing.

I'll do this for my father, Anton thought, growing undisciplined in his mental processes. I'll do this for him. Then that's the end. Then it will be *my* life, the days will belong to me . . . and to Zena. But he refused to trace his fantasy through its practical dilemmas.

The corps commander flew off into the clear night. Anton dispatched his couriers, then he remounted to leap along the column with the core of his staff. They erected a temporary command post in an abandoned German house that stood by yet another crossroads. Anton felt magnetized by the inevitability, the irony of that. It was as though the war were all about roads, and no matter the obvious vulnerability, crossroads determined all events of significance.

His officers, as they filtered in, appeared both tired and anxious. Yet there was a reassuring readiness in them, a clumsy energy that was largely nerves, and the determination to get into the fight. Anton wondered if any of the rest of them were ill. He had had his share of experiences in training areas and on maneuvers with diarrhea, even dysentery and hepatitis. But somehow, he had assumed that those were peacetime problems, and that the seriousness of war would make them go away. Now he wondered if he alone was suffering, or if other men were similarly weakened by sickness.

Anton had always been fastidiously clean, with scrubbed nails and well-fitted uniforms. Now he sensed that he must stink of his own waste as he moved about the room full of officers, and he felt as though this, too, made him smaller and less capable.

His officers wanted to get back to their units, to prepare for combat. They had felt cheated in their waiting impotence, remaining in the rear as their comrades died and the war raced on without them. These were largely picked men, the best the Soviet army could offer. There was a bit of nervousness about the Americans, since they were, after all, the great, almost mythical enemy behind all of the other enemies. But there was a willingness, too, even a desire, to get right to the heart of the issue with the ultimate opponent. The thing that most bothered them was the restriction on employing radio communications prior to contact with the enemy. They felt, as a body, that here in the enemy's heartland, west of the Weser River, speed alone could provide sufficient security. They complained of columns breaking up and units lost on the wrong routes.

Anton disagreed. He reiterated his position, backed as it was by the corps commander, that radio transmissions were not allowed prior to contact with fresh enemy forces of at least battalion strength. Anton knew that some of his subordinates had already broken the rules in the confusion of minor skirmishes, but he ignored the violations. He, too, missed the ease of coordinating through the airwaves. But he still wanted to take every possible measure to conceal the brigade. To hide, he told himself frankly, no matter how hopeless the attempt might be. To hide against the terrible magic deaths of a new age.

As the hasty briefing session came to a close and the officers prepared to chase down their units in the dark

Anton slipped away to the toilet, lighting his way through the dark house with a pocket lamp. Behind him, his staff officers were already stripping the maps from the walls, preparing to jump forward to maintain control of the brigade on the move. Anton went slowly, careful in his weakness. Even in the narrow beam of light, it was evident that the house was gorgeously furnished. Very rich, even by the standards to which he, a high-ranking general's son, had become accustomed. It was the sort of house he wished he could provide for Zena. Fine, dark polished wood and brass. Oriental carpets of silken feel even through the heels of combat boots. There was a baby grand piano in one of the rooms through which he journeyed, and at any other time, he would have paused to touch the keys to life. But the oppression of the situation and his cramping bowels hurried him on.

As he crouched alone in the dark Anton thought of his father once again. The old man was pulling it off. He was beating them all. Anton felt gladness for the old man, but no pride. He could not summon up any pride in the achievement because it was all so thoroughly his father's triumph, echoing in the night with the son's lifelong inadequacy. He remembered how, when he was a child, his father had proudly, delightedly, taken him to military parades, reveling in the pageantry that his army and his nation staged so well that it temporarily redeemed a host of other failures. Anton remembered how he thrilled to the brilliant clanging of the music, enraptured more by the tonal spurs to the imagination than by the big metal reality of the parade. His father held him up to see the tanks and the big guns and the sleek new missiles, affirmations of might and capability, of the nation's greatness. But Anton had only been frightened by the stinking, growling monsters of steel. He watched them warily, anxious for them to be gone and for the wonderful music to come again.

General Malinsky's personal helicopter pilot had been with him since the hard days in Afghanistan. A major and a pilot-first-class, he had developed the habit of calling Malinsky's attention to interesting features along the flight route. His younger eyes were far sharper than Malinsky's, and he had shown a knack for spotting details that other men would have flown by in ignorance in the stony mountain deserts of Afghanistan.

Now, however, the details were evident even to Malinsky's tired eyes. The night flight took them through corridors of fire, where towns and cities burned like enormous lamps to mark their course.

"Hannover coming up on the right," the pilot declared. "That's the big group of fires at one o'clock."

Malinsky saw a demonic blur of light.

"You can see Hildesheim cooking if you look out the left side, Comrade General."

The pilot was terribly excited about it all. There seemed to be no human reality, no implied misery in it for him.

Well, Malinsky thought, perhaps that was to be preferred. If all soldiers, or even just the officers, fully perceived the human consequences of their actions, it would be impossible to make war with them. No, it was probably better to have this stupid gleefulness, this naïve awe, in the face of the destruction of an enemy's land.

As the city of Hannover drifted by on the right side of the aircraft Malinsky examined his handiwork. The blur began to be defined. He could see now that the conflagration actually consisted of a series of smaller fires. Not all of the city burned, and he sincerely regretted that any of it was ablaze. But you could not make war neatly. The Germans and some of the British had backed into the city, drawing the Soviets after them like steel filings to a magnet. He had ordered Starukhin not to close the encirclement too tightly. The front had neither the time nor the troops to get bogged down in a significant level of urban combat, and the city's primary value was as a hostage. But one of Starukhin's division commanders had let himself be drawn into a fight for an outlying district. And the battle of Hannover had begun, taking on a life of its own against the will of either side. Soviet aircraft had gone in to pound the enemy positions. And the heavy guns had come up. Malinsky shifted in his seat, restrained by his safety belt. It was hard to destroy a city, especially a modern one. No doubt, when the smoke cleared, the damage would not be all that bad. But Malinsky knew that the city had not been officially evacuated, and he wondered what it was like for the remaining residents and the soldiers trapped in the inferno.

In the end, his vision did not move the soldier in him. He realized that it would be naïve to imagine that war, given the modern technology of destruction and the timeless characteristics of the human animal, might have grown any nicer. And in the end, it was better for German citizens to die than to lose Russians. After all, hadn't the Germans begun this themselves almost a century before? Malinsky had long believed that future historians would stand back and look at the twentieth century only to marvel that its inhabitants could not see its fatal continuities. It was, in a sense, the century of the German problem, and its wars, so neatly packaged as distinct world wars in prologue to this encounter, really constituted one long struggle, a new hundred years' war, with Germany at the center of it all.

Below the helicopter windows, strings and stars of miniature fires marked the residue of smaller actions. Vehicles in catastrophe marked the highway lines like poorly spaced flares. Malinsky had received reports of engagements fought amid refugee columns getting out of hand, and of isolated units committing atrocities. But even as the thought of needlessly killing civilians revolted Malinsky as unsoldierly, he nonetheless realized that such tragedies were unavoidable. He had issued strict orders stating that unit and formation commanders would be held personally responsible for instances of indiscipline committed by their subordinates, and they would be charged under the provisions of the Law on Criminal Responsibility for Military Crimes. But he recognized that restraint could only be a matter of degree. He was, in fact, relieved that the situation had not degenerated further and on a broader scale. The conditions of warfare that brought some men to sacrifice and great heroism turned others into beasts. War was the great catalyst for the terrible chemistries dormant inside humanity.

Malinsky shut his mind to the collateral destruction issue. In a tired blankness, he listened to the throb of the helicopter, feeling its heartbeat through his seat. He had refused to modify his methods of leadership, his habit of going forward to visit critical sectors, despite Trimenko's death. He even wondered now why the army commander's death had come as such a shock to them all. It was inevitable that helicopters would be lost, some to friendly fire. Malinsky pictured a nervous boy with a powerful weapon on his shoulder, dizzily searching the sky, or another young man blind to all realities except that portrayed on his radar screen. Missiles and shells did not discriminate between ranks or search out the less essential beings. Generals could die as easily as privates. The thought brought Malinsky an odd, unexpected comfort.

He had talked with Starukhin over secure means prior to lifting off, bringing the Third Shock Army commander up to date on the developing situation. Dudorov had been right. The Americans were coming, although difficulties remained in fixing their exact location and targeting them. Too many intelligence-gathering systems had been lost, and those that remained were straining at the limits of their serviceability and survivability. The situation had proven too dynamic for human intelligence, agents and special operations teams, to have the expected effectiveness. Dudorov estimated, working against a curtain of darkness, that the Americans could have diverted combat power equivalent to one heavy corps, which would have the approximate combat coefficients of a Soviet army-level formation. Malinsky felt it in his belly now that the Americans were indeed coming, and that they would come hard. The question was how fast they could move. By daylight, he would be favorably deployed to meet them.

The situation remained extremely favorable along the front's operational-strategic direction. Powerful thrusts had been successfully developed in each of the subsidiary operational directions. The Weser River line had been breached across a broad front now, with multiple crossings in the sectors of the Second Guards Tank Army, the Third Shock Army, and the Twentieth Guards Army. Remnants of the enemy's Northern Army Group clung desperately to a last few bridgeheads, but those pockets would soon become traps.

Malinsky thought briefly of the Hameln operation. There

had been no contact with the Soviet air-assault force for several hours, and he had to assume that the enemy had retaken the town. The deception plan and the diversionary attack had worked almost perfectly, and the British Army and the German Territorial Forces had squandered combat power in their efforts to dislodge a few air-assault forces, losing all perspective on the greater situation. Still, Malinsky could not help thinking of his men who had been sacrificed at Hameln. They certainly had not known that they were part of a deception operation. And they had bravely played out their roles. *In sacrifice.* The idea of sacrificing his soldiers, of ordering them quite literally to their deaths, repelled Malinsky. It was not a course of action to be taken lightly. Yet he had done it. Twice in Afghanistan, on a much smaller scale. And now here. *Sacrifice.* The word held no splendor for him. It was only another word for death.

But the river line was open now. The Forty-ninth Corps, functioning as an operational maneuver group directly under the front's control, had passed three of its four maneuver brigades to the west. The hastily reorganizing divisions of Starukhin's army were readying themselves to follow in force. The first follow-on army was approaching the border, hurrying along the cluttered, broken roads, despite the desperation of NATO's air attacks.

Trimenko's army had reported . . . Malinsky stopped himself. It was no longer Trimenko's army. Trimenko was dead, replaced by his deputy commander. Nonetheless, the Second Guards Tank Army had reported a lone forward detachment approaching the Dutch border with no opposition, while a reconnaissance patrol mounted in wheeled carriers claimed it had reached the banks of the Rhine across from Xanten on the western side. The advance party of an airborne division that had been subordinated to the front had struck the Dusseldorf civilian airport, although the outcome of that operation had yet to be decided. Due to the heavy transport losses going in, Malinsky had decided to hold back the heavy lifts. He counted on the Forty-ninth Corps moving quickly. One of the leading brigades was in position to reach Dusseldorf within twelve hours, unless the Americans put in an early appearance.

The business with the Americans gnawed at Malinsky. He realized that he was behaving in a less-than-scientific manner, counting on his luck to hold just a little longer. The battlefield, for all of the front's fine successes, had become quite a fragile thing. The first-echelon armies were out of breath, and even a beast like Starukhin could only whip a horse back up onto its legs so many times before the animal gave out. The Forty-ninth Corps would have to carry the initiative for the front until the initial follow-on army came up. The front had moved so far, so fast, and had suffered such losses, that the units and even formations were disorganized. There was a lack of control out there that Malinsky could sense through the darkness, a battlefield on the edge of anarchy. If it materialized, the American attack would need to be dealt with swiftly and violently, before it could discover and exploit the front's weakness.

He expected the Americans to attempt to sweep north across the Paderborn plain. Theoretically, an attack into the base of the operational penetration would be more desirable, but it was impractical at this point. The Americans would be desperate to blunt the penetration before substantial Soviet forces reached and crossed the Rhine. And if the Americans did attack in the Paderborn direction, the trail brigades of the Forty-ninth would have the mission of stopping them. His son's brigade would be directly in the line of attack. Malinsky recognized the danger but refused to think about it in any more depth. Such were the fortunes of war, and his son would fight well, he had no doubt.

If the corps alone could not break the American attack, Starukhin would have to do it. His divisions were badly disorganized and intermingled, but there was still substantial combat power available, and Starukhin would just have to sort it all out. If they couldn't hold the Americans west of the high ridge of the Teutoburg, they could always shape them into a pocket between the ridge and the Weser. And the Second Guards Tank Army could close the trap behind them, from the north.

The material logic was correct. And the follow-on forces were closing as fast as they could. But Malinsky worried about the psychological aspects of the coming fight. He might, at least temporarily, be forced onto the defensive, until the next echelon came up. And Malinsky did not trust the defensive at all, after what he had seen his forces do to the Northern Army Group over the past two days. He made a mental note to call the Second Guards Tank Army main command post and stress that they must further increase the tempo of the drive to the Rhine. Sheer movement carried the initiative now. He considered bringing the mechanized regiments of the airborne division into holding areas close behind the Third Shock Army's spearheads and giving them to Starukhin to employ as a light armored reserve. The Twentieth Guards Army to the south would be of little help now, since they were spread thin with the task of blocking any Central Army Group counterattacks against the base of the penetration, closer to the East–West German border.

Malinsky tried to keep it all in precise order in his head. But he could feel the effects of stress and sleeplessness beginning to tell on him. Small details had begun to elude him for long moments, and he wondered how much longer he could go on without becoming a menace to his men.

The helicopter started losing altitude. Malinsky saw discreet guide lights directing them onto the landing area. He was anxious to get out and hear the latest on the situation from Starukhin. And, he admitted to himself in a moment of weakness, he desperately wanted to know what was happening to his son's brigade.

Major Barak enjoyed the clean feel of the night air on his face as his tank cruised down from the mountain. His battalion constituted the advance guard of the Third Brigade, and he had worried as his column approached the Teutoburg Forest, then began the climb along the tree-lined mountain road. It was inconceivable to him that such a perfect choke point would go undefended. But no one had fired a shot. Now it was an enormous relief to emerge from the narrow pass, running down through the tight corridor of a village and out onto an open highway. His tanks were headed west for the Ruhr, and for the Rhine beyond.

The rumble of the armored column penetrated the roar of his own vehicle, piercing the padded headset and filling Barak with a sense of irresistible power. If the Americans showed up, they would have the devil beaten out of them. And if they failed to appear, Barak intended to see the Rhine before sunset.

Barak enjoyed leading the way this time, despite the obvious risk. He worried about the brigade commander. Colonel Malinsky had been visibly ill at the hurried meeting a few hours before, and, when questioned, the brigade staff admitted that the colonel had a bad case of the shits. The situation made Barak uncomfortable. He did not care much for Malinsky, in any case. The colonel was far too remote, too self-involved for Barak, who liked noisier, more sociable commanders who did not mind sharing a drink with their subordinates. Drinking with his superiors had long been a successful practice for Barak, and he resented Malinsky's aloofness, telling himself that the elegant young colonel had simply ridden on his father's coattails.

Malinsky was too much of an intellectual, as well. Barak distrusted the bookish sort of officers, the ones who could always tell you what Gareyev or Reznichenko or some other theorist had to say about an issue. Barak was convinced that all of the restructuring nonsense was ruining the army. How could anybody who was afraid to knock back a few drinks be any good in a fight? Barak suspected that the deep thinkers were the ones who had almost ruined the army in Afghanistan. He doubted the brigade commander would be much of a fighter, even without the runs.

Distant points of light on the southern horizon caught Barak's eye. It was an odd little display, and he could not determine what caused it. Then he saw more points of light. Some of them seemed to be moving. But the night beyond the roar of the column felt silent, dead.

Without further warning, Barak's vehicles began to erupt. Instantaneous clangs and blasts underscored spurts and billows of fire. Dark shapes careened through the air as burning tanks spun off the highway into ditches and fields, fuel tanks blazing.

Barak dropped into his turret. He could not decide what to do. He ordered his driver to find a building, anything, to hide behind.

He could not remember the call sign for the air-defense troops. He had never spoken to them in the past, regarding them as second-class soldiers. He broke open the radio net.

"Air-defense commander, air-defense commander, this is the battalion commander. Do you hear me?"

No response.

A lurching motion smacked Barak against the inside of the turret. Attempting to steer the vehicle off the road, the driver had misjudged the angle of an embankment. The tank began to slide to its left.

Now that Barak had opened the net, everyone tried to speak at once.

"Everybody clear the net," he shouted, as though raising his voice would empower the transmission. "Clear the net. Air-defense commander, where are you?"

"This is the air-defense commander."

"Enemy helicopters. Why aren't you firing? What good are you?"

"We *are* firing. The targets are out of range. We can't even pick them up on radar."

Barak clung to the inside of the turret. The driver fought the slide of the tank and seemed to have arrested it. Barak tried to understand how he could be attacked by something at which he could not strike back. How could the enemy be out of range, or invisible? What were the air-defense troops for, after all?

"They *can't* be out of range," Barak insisted. "Fire at them."

Abruptly, the tank resumed its slide. The sickening motion felt tentative at first, then it gained in velocity. Barak stared wildly down into the hull. The tank stopped with a jerk that banged Barak down against the gunner. The big vehicle had come to rest at a forty-five-degree angle.

"We're in the mud," the driver said matter-of-factly, as though it were something to be routinely expected.

"Get it out," Barak ordered. "I don't care what you do, but get us out of here." He switched from the intercom back onto the radio net. "All vehicles clear the road. Get in among buildings or trees. All vehicles take cover."

Barak's tank growled and shook, then powered back down. The driver tried again, filling the compartment with fumes. The efforts only seemed to grind them deeper into the mud. Barak knew from experience that they would need to be towed out.

He switched over to the long-range radio, calling brigade headquarters. Again, he received no response. The airwaves buzzed with static and surrealistic tones. The enemy were jamming everything. He sent his message anyway, hoping that someone would copy it, reporting that he was under heavy attack by enemy antitank helicopters. Finished with the transmission, he began to climb out of the tank, intending to take over a vehicle that remained mobile.

The sight of his battalion stopped him. Dozens of vehicles stood ablaze, marking the long trail of the battalion in the darkness. There were more fires than he could count, stretching down the road as far as he could see. It seemed impossible, a joke. It had been minutes, seconds. Here and there, an untouched vehicle moved against the fiery backdrop like a stray dog scavenging. One of the roaming vehicles exploded just as Barak turned his eyes to it. Then another went up. It was as if some godlike enemy were out there, patiently exterminating them all. Barak almost jumped to the ground and fled. But he took command of himself, unwilling to be a coward, no matter how hopeless the situation. He slipped back into the hold to order his crew to evacuate the helpless vehicle with him.

A noise enormous beyond imagination stopped him.

The brigade's senior officer of transportation troops watched helplessly as his supply column began to explode. He had pulled off the road on a hilltop, positioning his vehicle so that he could count the trucks of the matériel support battalion as they passed, wondering how many had fallen out. And without warning, the faint dawn blew up. Enemy tanks, sleek, with flat, angular turrets, emerged from the murk across the valley, bristling into small-unit formations as they rolled north. They used their main armaments sparingly, raking the column of trucks with machine-gun fire. The steel phantoms seemed to float over the terrain, enhancing the ghostly effect of their unexpected appearance east of the Teutoburg forest. The transportation officer's concern with lone lost vehicles quickly disappeared.

A motorized rifle subunit assigned to protect the convoy tried to deploy and return fire. The transport officer watched with a surge of hope as sparks flew off an enemy turret. But the tank kept coming, impervious to the weapons of the infantry fighting vehicles.

The tanks opened up with their main guns to engage the guardian combat vehicles, destroying each with the first shot.

The transportation officer ordered his assistant and driver to take cover in the trees, where he joined them after securing his classified materials. The trio hunkered in the brush, watching the panorama of destruction. There had been no warning, except a casual mention of stray pockets of enemy resistance. But there was nothing feeble about this attack. It was determined, and big. The ammunition carriers and fuelers threw such spectacular fireworks into the air as they were hit that the enemy slowed, then briefly halted. At an unheard signal, the tanks opened volley fire on the precious transports, then backed off slightly, shying away from the secondary blasts, reorienting the angle of their attack before resuming movement.

The transport officer's abandoned vehicle lifted off the ground on a cushion of flames. The driver, lying nearby in the brush, screamed in pain, caught by a random fragment of steel.

The enemy tanks swept up over the hill, passing within a hundred meters of the transport officer's hiding place. Large, boxy infantry fighting vehicles trailed the tanks. The transport officer tried to get a count, but too many of the vehicles were hidden by folds in the terrain or blurred in the bad light. Phantomlike, the war machines disappeared back into the darkness, headed north. They seemed marvelously, almost supernaturally, controlled in their strange open formations. The transport officer knew they were not supposed to be this far north, that this was critical information. But his vehicle, carrying his radio, was a smoldering pile of junk.

After the whine of the engines subsided, he ordered his assistant to see to the driver. Then he started down into the burning valley on foot, cautious about the continuing blasts as ammunition cooked off and streaked across the lightening sky. Even though the enemy had passed, it sounded as though a great battle was still raging.

A radio, he thought. If they only left me a radio.

TWENTY-TWO

Anton felt the situation collapsing around him with irresistible speed. The Americans had hit him broadside, hours before they were expected to appear, catching the brigade at its most vulnerable, with units strung out on both sides of the Teutoburg ridge. The first fragmentary reports had driven him to hastily establish his command post in a nearby grove so that he could get his communications gear fully set up. Reports from elements in contact came in broken and chaotic, and the number of enemy forces reported seemed impossibly high, multiplied by panic. A few things were clear, however. The Americans had found a gap between the forward elements of the Twentieth Guards Army, which had bogged down in the southeast, and the bulk of the Forty-ninth Corps' combat power, which had been pushing southwest and west as rapidly as possible. Anton's brigade had been a perfectly positioned target for the American onslaught from the southern flank. Helicopters or some special weaponry had catastrophically destroyed his advance guard, and other units reported contact at various points along the line of march. Feverish, Anton could not discern the pattern of the American attacks. His head would not come clear. He stared at the urgently plotted locations on the map, trying to make sense of the situation. His brigade was dissolving.

"Comrade Brigade Commander," his chief of staff called, "can you please listen to me?"

Anton turned slightly. He had not even been aware of the man a moment before. He felt disgracefully weak. The surgeon had given him shots for the fever, but Anton could detect no improvement in his condition. Sleep, he thought. You can't get better unless you sleep.

He drew himself up erect before the map and the eyes of his staff, unsure of how much longer he would be able to remain on his feet.

"Look," the chief of staff said, "the brigade transport officer reports enemy tanks here, working their way north beyond Lemgo."

Anton tried again to focus on the map. To take in the reality of the scrawled colored markings. He wanted to sit back down and close his eyes.

"That's impossible," he said. "That would put them behind us."

"Yes, Comrade Commander. Behind us. I've verified the coordinates. The transport officer swears he saw them with his own eyes. They overran the brigade resupply column."

Anton turned his head to look into the face of this bearer of bad news.

"Damage?"

"Severe."

This cannot be happening, Anton thought. I have no control over any of this. He laid his hand on the map, bracing himself, but attempting to disguise the action as a gesture of decisiveness.

"Order all units to halt where they are and assume a hasty defense. *All* units this time." He looked at the map. The colored arrows seemed to be teasing him, refusing to hold still. If the Americans had already slipped some elements behind them, his brigade could still block any forces that tried to follow in the wake of the lead elements. Yet no one seemed to know exactly where the enemy was located. It was all such a mess. There were too many possibilities.

Anton swept his hand along the trace of the brigade's march routes. "Defend the intersections. Block them. Commandeer any civilian vehicles in the area and build antivehicle barricades. Use our support vehicles, if necessary. But I want every major intersection blocked and covered with fire."

"Artillery?" the chief of staff asked.

Anton tried to think. He wanted to be firm, to offer a worthy example to his staff. But it all seemed a bit distant and dreamlike.

"The guns will be positioned near the roads, where they can bring direct fires to bear in an emergency." Anton thought. There was a dull physical pain associated with each new thought now. "Protect the rocket launchers. Position them at a central location where they can support as much of the brigade as possible."

He felt nauseated. Dizzy. He had to sit down. Hold on, Anton told himself. Just hold on. It can't last forever.

General Malinsky carefully avoided contradicting Starukhin in front of the Third Shock Army staff, but he watched and listened closely, ready to intervene if the situation became critical. He had complete faith in Starukhin in the attack, but he worried that the passionate aggressiveness that served an advancing force so well might prove unsuited to the very different demands of a hasty defense and the give-and-take exchanges required to stabilize a major enemy counterattack. Malinsky found himself wishing that Trimenko were still alive and in command of this sector. Trimenko had possessed balance, a cool mind behind a steel fist. Malinsky looked at Starukhin's broad back. He realized that the army commander was behaving with unusual restraint in his presence, aware that Malinsky did not like incessant displays of temper. It was like a game between them.

Would nuclear weapons soon be a part of a greater game? Since the alarm in the night, the High Command of Forces had been silent on the subject, and the KGB boys were pulling their own twisted strings. Malinsky dreaded the thought of a battlefield turned nuclear. But he did not want to be caught unprepared. He did not want to give the enemy the first blow. It was bad enough now with the damned Americans.

The Americans had moved more quickly and powerfully than anyone had expected. The bits and pieces of intelligence information that had been trickling in now seemed like obvious clues in retrospect. But they had all committed the age-old sin of underestimating the enemy.

Malinsky shrugged to himself. He was not interested in history lessons. But he made a mental note. For the next war. The technical means of reconnaissance were sufficiently powerful. But the men behind them, who had to analyze the data and make judgments, needed further development. One good man like Dudorov could not do it all by himself.

Starukhin's quartering party had selected a fine site for the command post, tucked into a row of West German warehouses spacious enough to hold all of the command and support vehicles. The lessons of the first two days had been assimilated very quickly. Command posts set up in the countryside could be located and targeted almost effortlessly. The cover and concealment of built-up areas at least offered a chance at survival. Increasingly, this was a war of cities and towns, and of roads.

The din of generators wrapped the command post in a cocoon of noise within the outer shell of the warehouses, and fumes clotted the atmosphere. But the opportunity to work with all of the lights turned on around the clock more than compensated for the bad air.

Starukhin suddenly raised his voice, drawing Malinsky's eyes. The army commander quickly got his temper back under control, but it was clear that things were not going well. In the rear, the encircled German corps was attempting a breakout from the Hannover area. Malinsky believed that the inner ring of the encirclement was sufficiently powerful to hold the Germans, or, at a minimum, to channel them onto routes where they would become hopelessly vulnerable and impotent to affect the main thrusts of the front. Still, the added pressure of yet another subbattle was hardly welcome at the moment.

Starukhin dispatched a nervous staff colonel on a mission, waving his big paws in the air. Then the army commander turned toward Malinsky, wearing the look of a dog who suspects he might have a beating coming.

Starukhin came up so close that Malinsky could smell the big man's stale sweat. The army commander looked down at his superior, clearly ill at ease.

"What is it?" Malinsky asked.

"Comrade Front Commander . . . the situation along your son's route of march has become critical."

"You mean the situation along the route of march of the Third Brigade of the Forty-ninth Corps," Malinsky corrected, struggling to control his facial muscles.

"Yes, the Third Brigade," Starukhin agreed. "It's very bad, Comrade Front Commander."

"What does the corps commander have to say? Does Anseev believe he can master the situation?"

Anton. Malinsky knew that it was not right to think of the boy now. He risked losing all perspective. Thinking of the boy who had grown into a man, yet who would always remain a boy to him. Malinsky ached to see his son. And, he realized helplessly, he wanted to protect him. To shield him from the harms of the grown-up world.

But Anton was a soldier. A guards colonel in the Malinsky tradition. In the *Russian* tradition. He would have to do his duty.

Anton. Malinsky could see his son's fine, clear features before him. Surely, he would look disheveled now. Black circles. The boy would be tired. He had been on the march for a long time. Malinsky imagined the scene at the brigade command post. Anton weary, but firmly in control, a pillar of strength for his subordinates. Or perhaps he had already gone forward, to direct the combat action in person. It was, of course, a difficult question, given the temporal and spatial issues of modern war. To what extent could a commander permit himself to be drawn into the fight? How much distance did he have to maintain to retain an adequate, objective overview? Malinsky felt confident that his son would evaluate the situation and do the right thing.

"Comrade Front Commander," Starukhin continued, "we have temporarily lost communications with the corps-level command posts. We can talk to your son's—I mean the Third Brigade—however."

"You can't have lost all means of communications."

The buildings trembled as distant explosions walloped the earth, dusting the already bad air.

"The Americans are conducting extensive radio electronic combat operations to support their attack."

Or they've hit Anseev's command posts, Malinsky thought. Anseev was a good man. Why couldn't he get his corps under control?

"Have you tried the corps' rear control post?" Malinsky asked.

Starukhin nodded. "Oh, yes. We can talk to them. But they can't reach Anseev, either. The rear is in the dark worse than anybody."

Malinsky pondered the situation for a moment, then reached for a cigarette. Calmly, he told himself, do it calmly. Do not let him see a trace of emotion.

"And your situation? Tell me about the Third Shock Army."

"We'll manage. We'll hold them. They'll never cross the Weser River line."

"What about the Hameln crossing site? They could be heading straight for it."

Starukhin wiped a paw across his unshaven chin. "They'd have to break in. I have a tank regiment on the west bank. And if they broke in, they'd never get back out. The British force in Hameln is sealed off. They're fighting like savages to keep us out, but they'll just provide that many more prisoners in the end."

"Any further communications from our air-assault force in Hameln?"

"Nothing further," Starukhin said. "Not since yesterday."

Malinsky carefully lit his cigarette. "Go on."

"I'm moving covering troops and forward detachments

across the river at multiple points. The first line of defense will be in front of the hills beyond the river. The Tenth Guards Tank Division holds the Bad Oeynhausen sector, with a grouping from the Seventh at Rinteln. The Forty-seventh Tank Division and the Twelfth are committed to the encirclement of the German operational grouping and the Hannover fight, in conjunction with elements of the Second Guards Tank Army. I'm reorganizing my East German division as a counterattack force."

Malinsky was surprised. "They've done well, then, our little German comrades?"

"Good tools," Starukhin said. "They make very good tools, the Germans." He smiled.

"All right. But don't commit the counterattack force without my approval. I want to know exactly where the Americans are headed. We must not commit prematurely. Also, I'm going to order the release of a mechanized airborne force to you. You'll have two reinforced regiments. I want you to employ them as light armor, working around urbanized terrain."

Starukhin bobbed his head in agreement, obviously pleased with the gift of additional forces, minor though they were. Malinsky knew that Starukhin would fight hard with every weapon put into his hand. It was only his impulsiveness that worried the front commander.

"Yes," Malinsky said. "The most desirable thing is certainly to hold them west of the Weser and south of the Rinteln–Herford–Borgholzhausen line. I don't want them interfering with the progress of the Second Guards Tank Army. And we need to hold open as many bridgeheads as possible for follow-on forces."

"How long do you think we'll need to hold on," Starukhin asked, "before fresh divisions come up?" It was unprecedented for Starukhin to ask such a question, so totally devoid of swagger. It brought home the seriousness of the situation to Malinsky.

The front commander put down his cigarette and pushed back his sleeve. He checked his watch. To his surprise, he found that it was full morning. It would be broad daylight outside.

"Twelve hours," he guessed, wishing Chibisov was on hand, ready with his clear-cut, confident answers.

A staff officer approached the two generals. From the movement of his eyes, Malinsky could see that the officer was far more worried about Starukhin's possible reaction to his presence than about Malinsky.

Malinsky's stare caused Starukhin to turn.

"Well?" Starukhin said, in a voice of measured restraint.

"Comrade Commanders," the staffer said, looking back and forth between them. "The Third Brigade of the Forty-ninth Corps is being overrun."

The sounds of combat action reverberated in the middle distance. When large-caliber shells struck, the roughly erected tentage sheltering the area between the vehicles of Anton's command post shivered, jouncing the maps lining the canvas walls. The radios sputtered with grim updates. The manning of the command post had been reduced so that a defensive perimeter could be established at the edge of the grove. There was still no enemy contact in the immediate vicinity, but American forces had passed by on both flanks.

"Try to raise corps again," Anton said to the staff at large. "There are helicopters. We've been promised helicopters." He half remembered a meeting in the night with the corps commander. They had spoken of helicopters that would come to the rescue.

Anton had a budding suspicion that his staff had begun to work around him, struggling to carry out his orders to block every key intersection and to establish a hasty defense. They had been caught, and caught badly. The brigade, the entire corps, was a splendid offensive weapon, well-structured to fight meeting engagements. But they had moved too swiftly, brigades out of contact with one another, and with gaps between elements of the individual brigades. It had all been too fast, and the intelligence had been too slow, and now they were paying the price.

Yet even if all of that was true, the failure remained his, Anton realized. He tried to blame the acid sickness in his guts and the fever and his flesh rubbed so raw it hurt to sit.

And the dizziness that made it difficult to stand. He should have turned over the brigade to someone more capable.

But to whom? Where did duty end? What would his father have thought? Perhaps even that he was a coward. A Malinsky brought low by a bad digestion. In any event, it would have shamed the old man. And Anton would not do it. No matter what it cost.

He thought of Zena, of all the things he had to tell her. They often talked together. They shared everything. Yet it seemed to him now that an incredible amount had been left unspoken.

"Where are the helicopters?" Anton asked suddenly.

"Comrade Commander, we can't reach the corps."

"Try manual Morse."

"Comrade Commander, we've tried everything."

"Don't tell me that you can't do this and can't do that," Anton shouted. *"Get the helicopters.* Do you understand me?"

"I'll try to relay through the Fourth Brigade."

"Why didn't you tell me we have communications with the Fourth Brigade?"

There was no response. Anton looked around him. Work had almost stopped. Several officers stared at him.

"What is the situation of the Fourth Brigade?" Anton demanded.

"They are . . . in contact. To the north of us. Comrade Commander, you listened to the report as it came in."

Anton tried to make sense of this. The north was the wrong side. He remembered that much. And the Americans were to the north of them now.

"Report on subordinate units," Anton demanded. "We must form a counterattack force." He tried desperately to remember the formulas, the rules, how the schools and manuals insisted it must be done. But he only remembered faces without names.

Then Zena returned. Zena enjoyed nakedness. She said she wanted to live where there was always sun and no one needed to wear any clothing at all, and Anton always pictured that place as Cuba, but empty of everyone but the two of them. Beaches. Sun. The sun was enormous now, blinding him.

"Report," Anton insisted. He felt his belly beginning to cramp again. He would need to go outside soon. But he struggled to wait until the last possible moment, punishing himself. He would not abandon his post.

"Comrade Commander"—the chief of staff placed his hand on Anton's shoulder—"Comrade Commander . . . " He shook Anton slightly. Anton realized what was happening, but he found it difficult to respond.

"Colonel Malinsky," the chief shouted at him.

Anton looked up at the man. He was unshaven. Officers needed to shave, to set the example.

"Your father is on the secure radio. He wants to speak to you. Can you talk to him?"

His father. Anton rose quickly, a bit too quickly. As though he had been caught committing an indiscretion. Letting his father down.

The chief of staff helped him across the command post to the vehicle containing the secure radio sets. An operator pulled up a stool for Anton. But Anton would not sit. Not in the presence of his father.

"Your call sign is 'Firebird,'" the operator said. "The front commander is 'Blizzard.'"

Firebird. Blizzard. Anton took the microphone, steeling himself.

"Blizzard, this is Firebird."

His father's voice came to him, instantly recognizable even through the disturbed airways. "This is Blizzard. Report your situation."

Anton sought to order his thoughts. "This is Firebird . . ." he began. "We are in heavy combat. Enemy units have penetrated . . ." He forced his speech to behave, to conform to military standards. It required an enormous effort, the greatest of his life. "We have been penetrated by American armored forces attacking on a minimum of two axes. We have suffered heavy casualties, especially to enemy attack helicopters. Our current course of action involves the establishment of a series of local defenses, oriented on retaining control of vital intersections. We are attempting to channel and slow the enemy's attack."

The voice at the other end was slow in responding. Did I make a mistake? Anton wondered. Did I get something wrong? He stared out through the open rear of the vehicle, straining to read the situation map's details from an impossible distance, desperate to offer his father whatever he wanted.

"Firebird, this is Blizzard. Your decision is approved. Continue local defensive actions. Do all that you can to break the enemy's tempo of attack and to disrupt his plan." The voice paused, and Anton thought for a moment that the transmission had come to an end. He nearly panicked. He wanted to tell his father . . . he wasn't certain . . . but he knew there were important things to say. Yet how was he to say them now, using this means? The officers and technical specialists around him stared. The hull of the vehicle had grown very still, as had the entire command post. They were all listening. Only the irregular sputterings of fire off in the distance offered any covering noise at all.

"You must hold out," the voice came back, and Anton imagined that he could detect a note of human warmth in it now. He realized with perfect lucidity what such a breach in his rigorous personal discipline must have cost the old man. "You must hold out. We will support you. We will support you with every available sortie of attack aircraft. You may expect relief by our ground forces in twelve to eighteen hours . . ." Again, the voice paused. "Can you hold on?"

Anton straightened his back. "Blizzard, this is Firebird. We will do our duty."

"I know you will do your duty," the distant voice said. "I know that all of your soldiers will do their duty. And you will have all the support the Motherland has to give you. Good luck." And his father formally ended the transmission.

Anton stood still. He felt as though a critical link had been severed, not just in a military context, but in his life. He wanted to hear his father's voice a little longer. Anything not to let go of the old man.

Voices picked up around him, calling in nervous haste.

The chief of staff yelled for the ranking forward air controller. Yes, sorties. Aircraft. We'll hang on, Anton thought.

His stomach rebelled. The pang hit him so violently that it bent him over the radio set, and he feared he would lose all control on the spot. He hurried for the entrance flap in the canvas.

The chief of staff touched him. "Comrade Commander, can I help you?"

"I'm all right," Anton said, pushing by. "I'm all right. I'll be back in a moment."

He blundered at the tentage, extricating himself with difficulty. Outside, he had to step carefully across deep ruts cut by the vehicles as they positioned themselves between the trees. He looked around, trying to spot the perimeter guards. He did not want anyone to see him.

His intestines bit him again, struggling to empty themselves. Anton staggered. He decided that he could not worry who saw him. He touched a tree trunk for stability and caught himself around an antenna line. He broke free in an angry fit, charging past the tethers. Bushes caught his trousers.

He forced himself to march a little longer, to put a few low shrubs between his act and the field command post. Then he tore at his clothing, stripping down. He lowered himself against the trunk of a tree in his agony, straining to crouch on burning calves.

He knew he had failed. He had failed at everything for which he had spent his lifetime preparing. Now his father was trying to rescue him. He had even corrupted his father.

Anton stared, sweating, up through the trees. The sky shone a hot, magnificent blue. He wheezed, waiting for his body to finish punishing him. He felt that all of his strength was at an end.

The roar of the jets came up fast. They flew very low. It was a big, rushing noise, commanding in its power. The jets, he thought. Already. His father had sent him these gifts.

But the forest began to burn around him. He was on his side, lying in dampness. Another blast picked him up and slapped him against a tree. He sagged, crying. The noise engulfed him. He wasn't certain whether the ground was shaking or if he was shaking on top of it. He felt as though he were tumbling. He was tumbling in the waves, playing with Zena. It was Cuba, and the sea was salty and warm, and the sky was a splendid cloudless blue. And the sun. The sun came closer and closer. And he rolled in the sea. It was too rough for Zena. He called to warn her. And the enormous sun came closer still, colliding with the earth.

Anton opened his eyes. Everything around him was on fire. Then he realized that he was burning, too. His hands were burning. The rags around his ankles were burning.

He scrambled to his feet, stumbling, waving the torches of his hands.

Zena, he cried out, or thought he cried out. *Father. Not like this, god, not like this.*

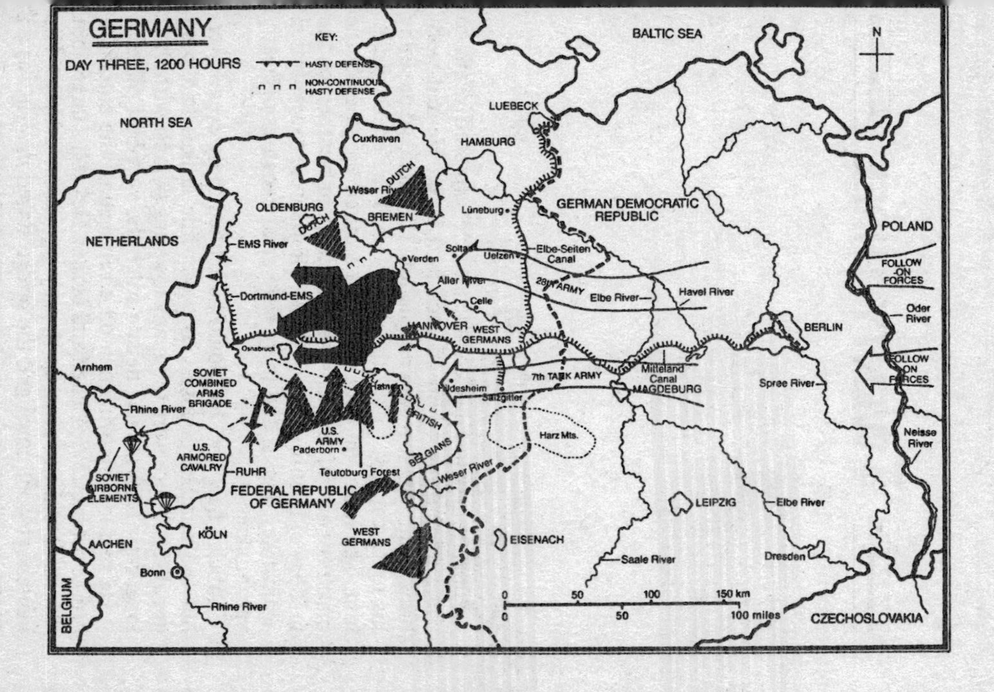
GERMANY
DAY THREE, 1200 HOURS
KEY:
HASTY DEFENSE
NON-CONTINUOUS HASTY DEFENSE
N
NORTH SEA
BALTIC SEA
NETHERLANDS
BELGIUM
POLAND
CZECHOSLOVAKIA
GERMAN DEMOCRATIC REPUBLIC
FEDERAL REPUBLIC OF GERMANY
Cuxhaven
LUEBECK
HAMBURG
OLDENBURG
BREMEN
DUTCH
Weser River
EMS River
Dortmund-EMS
Verden
Soltau
Uelzen
Lüneburg
Elbe-Seiten Canal
Aller River
Celle
28th ARMY
Elbe River
Havel River
HANNOVER
WEST GERMANS
Osnabruck
Arnhem
SOVIET COMBINED ARMS BRIGADE
Rhine River
U.S. ARMY
Paderborn
Hameln
Hildesheim
Salzgitter
7th TANK ARMY
Mittelland Canal
MAGDEBURG
BERLIN
Spree River
FOLLOW ON FORCES
Oder River
Neisse River
BRITISH
BELGIANS
Harz Mts.
U.S. ARMORED CAVALRY
RUHR
Teutoburg Forest
SOVIET AIRBORNE ELEMENTS
KÖLN
AACHEN
Bonn
WEST GERMANS
EISENACH
LEIPZIG
Saale River
Dresden
0 50 100 150 km
0 50 100 miles

TWENTY-THREE

Sobelev had lost his confidence. He expected death to come up and meet him on each next flight. He had worn himself through fear into resignation. He would go on doing his technical best to kill the enemy until the enemy killed him. The losses on both sides had scoured the skies of the masses of aircraft evident, despite the poor weather, on the first day of hostilities. Now the air efforts were concentrated against key points, and there were great expanses of nearly vacant skies.

Sobelev flew low. He would have liked to fly even lower, but the number of losses to power-line strikes had been appalling. There were too many towering pylons, with their long, ropy lines set like nets to catch the very best pilots.

He had lost his wingman on a run against the autobahn bridge between Wiesbaden and Mainz. He hit his target, but the strike did not seem to do any significant damage. His lieutenant went down and the bridge stayed up—it was an enormous structure—and the enemy retained its use.

It took all of Sobelev's experience and talent to fly the aircraft now. Exhausted, he continued to worry that his own error would get him before the enemy did. He had a terribly difficult mission this time. Close support of ground forces in a battle with no clear front line. He had never believed that pilot training for close air support was really adequate, but he prided himself on his professional skills, and he did his best to improve himself. He had spent endless hours in the flight simulator, although he never really felt that the simulations were of sufficient quality. The voice commands never had the panic encountered on a real battlefield. Still, whatever the deficiencies of the system, the ground troops continued to scream for air support.

"Zero-Five-Eight, Zero-Five-Eight, I think I've got you on my radar." It was the target control and identification post. "Is your wingman hugging you tight? I can't discriminate."

"This is Zero-Five-Eight. No wingman. Solo sortie."

"Roger, Five-Eight. I am vectoring you on an azimuth of two-four-five from your known point. You are about to become army property."

The ground rushed by under the belly of the aircraft, and the treetops seemed to surround the fuselage. Sobelev's tired mind fought to maintain control, to make everything hold together.

"Roger, I have the known point."

"You're in the box, Five-Eight. Passing you directly to your tactical controller."

A new voice came up. "North Star, this is Orion. Passing this one directly to the forward."

"Roger, Orion. Did you copy that, Five-Eight?"

"Heading, two-four-five," Sobelev confirmed. "Waiting for voice from your forward."

Sobelev did not like this kind of mission. He preferred to know in advance exactly what kind of target he was going in after and exactly where it was located. But the Third Shock Army sector was apparently in trouble, and every available aircraft had been scrambled with only the vaguest of mission briefings. Now Sobelev had no idea if he would be directed against tanks or infantry, artillery positions or an enemy command post. And any one of those targets would be very, very difficult to identify from a hurtling aircraft flying low. The controller on the ground had to do his job correctly, or the mission was wasted.

Sobelev flew right through an artillery barrage. The aircraft shook and nearly bolted from him. We're down in the shit now, he thought.

"Unidentified forward, this is Five-Eight. I'm climbing. Tell me when you have me visual." Sobelev mastered the aircraft up into the sky, hoping that none of the air-defense troops, either Soviet or enemy, would decide to knock him down.

Everything went incredibly fast. Below him, lines of military vehicles crowded the roads, and clusters of equipment blurred by in the fields where units had deployed. In most cases, it was impossible to identify the vehicle types. Columns of smoke marked a nearby engagement, and islands of fire soon developed into an archipelago along the trace of the main road.

"Five-Eight. I have you visual," the forward air controller called. *"Decrease speed."*

Like hell, Sobelev thought.

"Marking own troops with green flares," the controller said, rushing the words. "Hit the far treeline, *hit the treeline."*

Just in front of his aircraft, Sobelev caught sight of the flares arching into the sky above billows of black smoke.

"Visual on your markers. Here we go."

Sobelev corrected slightly on the flares and searched beyond the smoke for the designated treeline in the last quick seconds. He thought he had it, hoping it was the correct one. Terrain features rushed up so fast he could not see any enemy vehicles at all. He saw nothing but a fringe of trees.

He half heard the controller verifying that he was on the correct heading as he cast off his ordnance. Ground-attack aircraft had stopped doing initial orientation passes after the first day of the war.

Behind his tail section, the entire planet seemed to shake. The aircraft shimmied, and Sobelev prayed that it would just hold together and do what his fingers ordered it to do. He came out in a hard turn, heading back toward home.

Kill them, until they kill me, he told himself, sweating and shaking so badly that he could hardly guide the aircraft. Kill them, until they kill me . . . kill them . . .

The new mission startled Bezarin. He had expected to be withdrawn into a reconstitution area where his scattered unit could be reassembled and his tanks could be repaired and rearmed. But the orders, delivered by a staff officer in a hurry, were to dig in and prepare to defend the western bank bridgehead against an armored assault.

It made no sense to Bezarin. Certainly, the smothered thudding of a great battle had arisen in the distance. But it was inconceivable to him that the torrent of Soviet armor that had been pouring across the river since midnight could possibly be driven back to depend on his handful of battered tanks.

An engineer vehicle appeared to prepare defilade positions for his unit. Bezarin almost laughed. He was very much in favor of protected fighting positions, but he did not think they would be of much use unless he received some ammunition. In the light of day, his remaining tanks looked like wrecks that would hardly be accepted by a vehicle cannibalization point. Reactive armor had blown or torn away, and the thinner plates of metal twisted up to scratch the air. Little remained of the equipment racks and stowage boxes, and the snorkels, useless in the best of times, were hopelessly perforated by shell fragments. Bezarin roused his men and forced them to perform basic maintenance chores. He believed that, with ammunition and a bit more fuel, his unit could give a good account of itself in an emergency. But it seemed absurd to expect his tiny force to hold back any threat that could devour the unscathed new-model tanks that had passed in such great numbers to the west.

The bridgehead had taken on the character of a small military city. Air-defense systems crowned the surrounding hills. Supplementary bridges lay in the Weser at intervals of several hundred meters, emplaced to augment the highway bridge or replace it, should enemy aircraft finally succeed in their efforts to drop the prize span in the water. The canvas of administrative entities had already begun to appear, although many organizations preferred to exploit buildings on the edge of the smoldering town. Bad Oeynhausen was quickly turning into a forward command and control center. On the eastern bank, artillery batteries poked deadly fingers into the sky. And in the midst of it all, the traffic controllers from the commandant's service waved their arms and shouted and argued, straining to sort out competing priorities on the roads.

Probably, Bezarin figured, his orders simply reflected caution. A systematic response to an enemy counterattack, aimed at preventing any Soviet forces from suffering the sort of surprise his tanks had inflicted on the enemy the day before. He set his face into his "I'm in command here" expression and marched down among his vehicles, guiding the efforts of the big engineer tractor and refining individual zones of fire. He felt a profound surge of pride in his dirty, knocked-about tanks and in the new brotherhood of men who crewed them. Come what may, they would do their duty.

Still, Bezarin thought, it would have been nice to have a bit of ammunition.

Shilko felt as though he had stumbled into a cache of hidden treasures, like the hero in a folk tale. Splendid farm instruments crowded the barn, a harrow and a shining plow, a seeder and a hay mower of a new type with which Shilko was not familiar. And this wonderful assortment of devices for bringing life out of the earth apparently belonged to one private farmer here in West Germany. It did not seem fair. Shilko thought about how such tools would ease the tasks of his little agricultural collective back in garrison, and how much more they could produce. He reveled in the mingled smells of hay and dust, breathing lustily until it made him sneeze. In his heart, he grudgingly suspected that the Germans did, indeed, have superior talents or values in some respects. He sat on a bale of hay, leaning over his belly to rest his elbows on his knees. He envied the absent

German farmer. He envied all of the farmers of the world, and it came to him that he had wasted his life.

Shilko rarely wandered off by himself, always preferring the crowding and company of his battalion officers, his second family, unless he needed to rest or faced a particularly unpleasant writing task. He loved to be surrounded by other men. Refusing to be suspicious—sensible, his wife called it—he warmed to every man who gave him the opportunity. There would be plenty of time to spend alone in the grave. Life was meant to be enjoyed in the company of other human beings.

But now, west of the Weser River, perhaps a day's journey from the fabled Rhine, riding the currents of victory, Shilko's unruly thoughts had led him off for a few moments of solitude. He was not a man given to serious reflection, yet it seemed there were so many things that needed to be mulled over. Sitting in the rich twilight of the barn, with brilliant rays of light slicing through the amber gloom, he tried to sort things out. But he could not quite get a grip on any single train of thought. He wondered if he had ever understood anything about the world at all, or if he had merely gone through his life in a waking sleep. Whenever he thought of the face of the suffocating lieutenant, it seemed to him that that single moment of helplessness had revealed to him the failure of his entire life. Men were dying by the thousands, by the tens of thousands. But only the pathetic death of his lieutenant had made it real for him.

His guns had done well, and he credited Romilinsky with much of that. His staff had been a wonderful support to him, a team. And his soldiers fought well. Shilko was determined to do his best by them, to fully shoulder his responsibility. But sitting in this German barn, surrounded by these life-giving tools made of the same steel as his precious guns, Shilko felt that all he really wanted to do was to grow things, to be a farmer, on whatever terms were offered. Surely, the peasant generations from which he had come had learned to hate war the hard way, just as they naturally loved the green shoots bursting up through the holy soil.

Perhaps, he thought, Pasha, his son, could help him. Perhaps the Party needed someone to help in the renewed agricultural effort. Surely the Party could make use of his talents, especially since he expected so little in return. A chance to muddy his boots in peace.

Shilko rose to return to his place of duty, accepting the inevitable. The control post had been erected in the farm courtyard, with Shilko barking like a friendly old dog to insure that his men did no unnecessary damage to the place. No sooner had the post gone operational than the airwaves crowded with reports of a German attempt at a breakout to their rear, and a linkup operation on the southern flank, with rumors of a massive American counterattack down in the Third Shock Army sector. In the haste of the moment, no one had bothered to send Shilko missions for his guns. But he knew that the missions would come when the time was right. He had turned over control to Romilinsky and strolled off. His men were enraptured by the war, intoxicated by victory. Even with the reports of trouble across the front, his men remained full of confidence. Shilko wondered why, after all of his years of preparation for this, he could not share their enthusiasm any longer. He laid his hand on the snout of a compact green tractor, petting it as though it were a draft animal. Reluctantly, he took his leave of the quiet stable of machines.

He wandered across the farmyard, past a low barn where imprisoned pigs snorted and stirred. The control post boiled with activity. Radios crackled, and grimy hands scrawled on clean sheets of paper. The chief of communications whined that every time he laid in wire to the guns, some bastards knocked it down or drove over it. Romilinsky worked at the situation map with the care of a surgeon. Here and there, men ate as they worked, making the most of the stores of food discovered in the farmhouse. The senior duty sergeant brought Shilko his tea.

"Any change?" Shilko asked Romilinsky.

The captain shook his head. "The situation is extremely confused. The number of missions assigned to the divisional guns remains low, but the regimental guns are firing up everything they have. It's hot up front. There's a great deal of intermingling of forces. I'm afraid the target acquisition program isn't working very well."

The sounds of battle were clearly audible from behind a low range of hills. But the valley in which the battalion had been ordered to halt and deploy remained at peace. Shilko hoped that the war would not come here to destroy the fine machines in the barn or the animals, or any of the other manifestations of the absent farmer's good husbandry.

"Forward progress of the Americans?"

"The reporting from the flanking units is intermittent. I've been monitoring the division net," Romilinsky said, eyebrows lowering in concern. "It sounds like a mess down south. But right now I'm more worried about the Germans up here. We even seem to have Dutch units counterattacking. Everybody thought they were knocked out of the war."

"Desperation," Shilko said matter-of-factly. "They're fighting for their homes. It must be a terrible thing to be on the other side just now."

Romilinsky looked at him in surprise. Then the crisp staff officer recovered, ignoring his commander's musings. "All of our elements are in position. A total of eight operational guns, and we're working to get Davidov's number-three gun back up. Seems to be a hydraulic problem. And still no resupply of ammunition. But we have enough rounds left to make it hot for somebody, Comrade Commander."

"And everyone is positioned so that they can engage in direct fire? If it should come to that?" The muddled reports on the artillery command net made it clear that it was time to expect the unexpected. Still, the idea of attempting to employ his heavy guns in a direct-fire competition with enemy tanks or infantry fighting vehicles seemed absurd and wasteful to him. Poor husbandry. But Shilko was, at bottom, a very stubborn man, and no matter what his personal feelings, he would fight to the last gun against any attacker.

"We're positioned to sweep the main arteries with direct fire," Romilinsky said. "Hopefully, we'll have a bit of warning."

"Just be ready. I don't want to lose a single man because we were unprepared."

The big dull thumps in the distance sounded like a clan of giants beating the earth with clubs. The volume had increased noticeably, reaching Shilko's ruined ears. Perhaps, he thought, the war would come to them after all. He tried to cheer himself by telling himself that his ears were so bad they played tricks, and that he was a very tired man, incapable of judging the situation with perfect objectivity.

"I want everyone in a fighting position," Shilko said. "Every last cook. We've come too far to throw away success."

Romilinsky moved sharply to act on the order. Shilko had decided that, whenever the war ended, he would recommend Romilinsky for honors and early promotion. And he intended to quietly do everything he could to secure the captain a better assignment where he would have more scope for advancement. Romilinsky deserved that.

Shilko listened intently to the hammering in the distance. Discontented, he put down his heavily sweetened cup of tea and stepped back outside, trying to hear more clearly. The traffic noise had diminished significantly, since all units had been ordered off the roads and into hasty defensive positions. The roads had been cleared for tank reserves.

But no tanks passed at the moment, and the area around the farmyard seemed deceptively peaceful, a rustic paradise. The signs of war were most obvious in the sky, where laces of jet exhaust adorned the blueness. Shilko tried to judge the distance to the nearest fighting by the reverberation of far-off guns, coaxing his ears to respond to his desires. He realized that his ancestors must have felt the same way, listening for hoofbeats or shots, or for the terrifying shouts that signaled the approach of a raid or an invading army, too late for any response but submission and hope that the massacre would not be complete, that enough food could be saved to feed the survivors through the winter and enough seed preserved to plant again in the spring.

As Shilko listened it seemed as though the sounds of battle diminished, responding to the wishes in his heart. The distance to the discharges and impacts did not recede, but the volume of fires slackened. After a few minutes, the difference was unmistakable even to Shilko's career-damaged ears.

His pulse quickened. Perhaps the counterattack had been

defeated. He had remained perfectly calm under the threat of an enemy breakthrough. But the possibility of some end to the fighting, however temporary and for whatever reason, made his heart race.

The sound of the guns stopped completely.

Romilinsky hurried out from under the canvas wall of the control post, visibly excited.

"Comrade Commander," he shouted, absolutely exuberant, almost dancing out of his controlled staff-officer persona, "Comrade Commander, the West Germans have requested a cease-fire."

Epilogue

Chibisov emerged from the bunker into the light of day. The sight of the splintered forest, with its ashen wounds, shocked him. Throughout the period of hostilities, he had heard and felt the impacts of the enemy's weaponry hunting over the surface. Yet unseen was somehow unimagined. Beyond the pockmarked outer door, large bomb craters and black scars marked the landscape, and the acridity of explosives lingered in the air. Yet a blue sky blessed the living and the dead, and even this pungent air tasted gorgeously fresh after the staleness of the bunker.

Soon, he would need to visit a good doctor, perhaps even take a cure at the sanatorium. His breathing never came normally to him anymore, and despite his determination, Chibisov had begun to doubt that he could continue to shoulder serious responsibilities much longer.

Aircraft still cut the heavens, and vehicular traffic continued on the roads. But the volume, the noise of it all, was far less than it had been. The sounds of combat had stopped.

Shtein, the revolting creature from the General Staff with his little movies, had been right in the end, as had Dudorov.

The Germans caved in. Chibisov remained unpersuaded that Shtein's unpleasant films and broadcasts had played as grand a role as Shtein himself readily declared. Even the best propaganda had its limits. But there would be adequate time for the chroniclers to argue about whose contributions had been the most important. For Chibisov, it was all part of an indivisible whole in the end. Examined in detail, one saw appalling failures and incompetence. Yet the sum of the Soviet way of war had proved greater than its individual parts. Finally, the result was what mattered.

Assailed militarily, politically, emotionally . . . the West German government had broken down over the issue of nuclear release. The Americans and British had demanded it, and the French made their own unilateral preparations. But the West Germans had experienced a failure of the will, of nerve. Paralyzed by the speed of their apparent collapse and the unanticipated level of destruction, they had refused to turn their country into a nuclear battlefield. The Germans had decreed NATO's military policy in peacetime, and they reaped their harvest in war.

Chibisov realized, as did only a few of the privileged, how close the battlefield outcome had been. The American counterattack, really the centerpiece of a counteroffensive, had nearly broken them. Perhaps the follow-on forces would have contained them, but the Americans and the surprisingly resilient forces of the Northern Army Group had hit hard. Not even Dudorov had correctly estimated how much fight the battered NATO corps had left in them. The counterblow had stormed to within a dozen kilometers of the Weser crossing site at Bad Oeynhausen when the German plea for a cease-fire halted them.

The West German government had declared a unilateral cease-fire and had demanded that all NATO forces halt offensive actions on German soil in a bid to conciliate the Soviets. All NATO combat forces were to withdraw west of the Rhine within ninety-six hours, and to leave German soil entirely within fifteen days. Intact Bundeswehr units would also withdraw west of the Rhine. Numerous Bundeswehr commanders had resisted the cease-fire, but their rank and file had proved unwilling to follow them. And as the NATO armies withdrew, Soviet tanks closed the rest of the distance to the Rhine without firing a shot.

And that was it, Chibisov believed. There was no point in going any further. The Rhine was the natural Soviet western frontier, and the control of Germany meant the control of the rest of Europe. The French would ultimately accommodate themselves to the new order. An occupation of France would have been far more trouble than it was worth. And the British could remain an American outpost, for all the effect that would have on the new Europe.

Some high-ranking officers within the Soviet military wanted to drive on. Most of them had not experienced the war firsthand, and they spoke more blithely of resuming the offensive than did those who had gotten a good taste of the battlefield. The most worrisome estimate making the rounds prophesied that the Americans did not regard the war as finished but were preparing to strike elsewhere. And there were clouds on the eastern horizon. Would the war enter an Asian or Pacific phase? Personally, Chibisov hoped it was over. He hoped the Americans would have the good sense to turn their backs on a Europe that took their lives and money and gave them nothing in return. He could not quite believe the Americans would find any of this worth fighting over any more. But he wondered. The Americans remained an enigma.

Intellectually, Chibisov appreciated that the Soviet way of war was scientifically correct, integrating the military and political elements into one overwhelming program. Unity of effort at the highest levels. But in the end, it was not so much the Soviet tanks that had defeated NATO, but NATO's own foolishness. Watching the progress of the war from his unique perspective convinced Chibisov that the issue could very easily have gone the other way. For instance, the surrounded German operational grouping northeast of Hannover was currently being disarmed, with its soldiers and limited support equipment allowed to move west of the Rhine. But the Germans might easily have been the captors. NATO had the combat power but lacked unity of purpose and strength of will. On a practical level, their lack of a cogent and unified military doctrine had destroyed them. The tools and the workers had been available, but everyone had insisted on using his own blueprint. Chibisov was grateful.

A black bird settled into a splintered tree, and Chibisov thought of Malinsky's son. The remnants of his brigade reported that Guards Colonel Malinsky had been killed by an air strike. But no body had been recovered, and the old man refused to accept his son's death. The general went forward in person to conduct the search.

Chibisov felt deeply sorry for his protector and comrade. It seemed stupidly ironic that he, of all men, should lose so much at such an hour. Chibisov did not know the young colonel well enough to feel much sorrow for the fallen officer. The elder Malinsky drew all of his emotion. In a way, he knew, the loss of his son would be harder for Malinsky to bear than defeat on the battlefield would have been.

Of course, plenty of sons had died. Chibisov tried to rationalize the old man's misfortune away. But the image of Malinsky would not leave him. He pictured the old man stepping over the blackened waste that had once been a forest, peering into the gutted shells of command vehicles. Blinking his eyes to control any sign of the intensity of his feelings, Chibisov realized, helplessly, how much he loved the old man. How much better if an asthmatic renegade Jew, who could not find a home in any camp, had died in place of the cherished son.

Chibisov remembered his mother. His father, a determined communist, had tolerated no mention of religion in their home. But his mother had wrapped her child in the wonder of fairy tales and remembrances. Chibisov had not realized until much later that some of the fairy tales had been stories from the Old Testament. He smiled the smile of middle age at this bit of maternal deviousness, recalling how he had been terrified by the story of Abraham and Isaac. As a boy, Chibisov had had no doubt that his father would have sacrificed him, had the modern gods demanded it.

His thoughts returned to Malinsky and his son. A perverse twist on an old tale, in which God does not relent, or forgive, or show mercy. A god for the world as it is, rather than as it was supposed to be.

Of course, it did no good to romanticize death. Chibisov looked up at the crow on the broken limb. The bird immediately spread its wings and rose skyward, as though Chibisov's gaze made it uncomfortable. Chibisov took a deep breath, filling his withered lungs. And he turned back to the bunker to sort out the combat statistics.

"They cut us off," Seryosha told the little crowd of soldiers gathered around his bunk. "We were entirely cut off. Enemy tanks everywhere. You can't imagine it. But we held out. We held our assigned position for two days, and we killed every German soldier who came near us."

Leonid accepted the tale. Seryosha had told it so many times now that it had acquired a truth of its own. He and Seryosha never exchanged a word about the incident in the basement in the little German town. When they left the house, it was as if they had signed a compact never to speak of it. And really, there was nothing to say that would change anything. They had simply hidden in a barn until Soviet forces returned. The unit had been a fresh organization from the Soviet Union and had not arrived in time to see any combat. The unit sent the two veterans to the rear, to a holding facility for soldiers who had become separated from their units. They were quartered in a large barracks near the town of Bergen. The barracks had been hit by shells a few times during the fighting, but the quality of everything, from bunks to plumbing, remained amazingly good. Leonid did not mind the arrangement at all.

Two separate groups of soldiers existed within the holding area. The larger group, containing Leonid and Seryosha, was assigned to crowded barracks where they underwent nearly constant roll calls whenever they were not out in the countryside on work details to recover military equipment or to load or unload trucks. Every day, shipments of soldiers left to rejoin their units, while fresh herds of lost privates arrived. The food was not bad, and the officers stayed so busy doing whatever officers had to do that there was even a little bit of free time to sit around the barracks and swap war stories.

The smaller group of soldiers lived in barracks behind barbed wire. Armed guards patrolled the perimeter. These soldiers, the political officer warned the more fortunate, were deserters, men who had thrown down their arms or fled from battle, who had betrayed the sacred trust of the Soviet soldier. They were all to be charged under Article this or Article that. Every time the topic came up, Leonid went cold inside. He suspected that the difference between deserters and soldiers such as he and Seryosha was perilously slight. One rumor held that the difference was whether or not you still had your weapon when you were picked up, but Leonid trusted there was a little more to it than that.

"Anyway," Seryosha went on, "we finally ran out of bullets. There was nothing to do but go to ground and be prepared to fight with our fists, if it came to that. We thought it was all over. Then our troops came back up, late as usual. They told us we held the farthest point inside the enemy lines. No one else had been able to hold out."

Most of the war stories received challenges from the more cynical listeners. But Seryosha retained his gift for convincing others. It was remarkable to Leonid. Seryosha had already ingratiated himself with the facility's political officer, and he had begun to draw away from Leonid once again.

Leonid didn't mind. He wanted to put the events of the war behind him. He wanted to go home, and he listened avidly to rumors that all combat veterans would receive home leave, while those who had not fought would remain behind with the occupation forces. Yet Leonid suspected that, if anyone received a leave, it would be Seryosha. Well, that was all right, too. Sooner or later, they would all be discharged. The army couldn't keep you forever. And he would go home and play his guitar. He had managed to rescue two looted cassette tapes from destruction, half-surprised when they were not confiscated upon his arrival at the holding facility. It turned out that nearly everyone had a souvenir or two to show for his battle experience.

A voice loudly called the barracks to attention. It was almost time for the political officer's daily world-events class, and Leonid assumed that either the lecture would be a bit early today or this was yet another of the endless roll calls.

He was wrong. Instead of the political officer, the warrant officer in charge of work details appeared beside a new captain. The warrant officer announced that a very sensitive mission, one of great honor, required a platoon of soldiers for its immediate execution. They were all familiar with this particular litany. It meant that more bodies had been located. It was the worst detail imaginable.

Leonid knew he would be selected. It was just his luck.

Bezarin sat on a concrete slab at the water's edge, watching the withdrawal of the last American forces across the Rhine. His new medal dangled from the blouse of the fresh uniform he had been issued for the presentation ceremony. General Malinsky, the front commander, had flown in to present several dozen awards at a gathering hosted by General Starukhin, commander of the Third Shock Army and of all occupation forces in the Ruhr. The banquet undoubtedly continued, with passionate drinking of cognac, back at the Japanese luxury hotel that served as the provisional Soviet headquarters in Dusseldorf. But Bezarin had no thirst for alcohol at the moment, and he had slipped away to think about Anna and the rest of his life.

Between daydreams, he watched the Americans passing in the distance. Ugly, venomous-looking attack helicopters covered the crossing from midriver and from the urban industrial tangle of the far bank. Tanks crossed the big bridge with their main guns at the ready, swiveling around to cover the eastern bank behind them. The Americans moved very well, with superb march discipline. They did not look like a beaten army to Bezarin.

But they had been beaten. If not on the field of battle, then at the greater level of political decision. Bezarin remembered waiting on the heights at Bad Oeynhausen, surrounded by his surviving tanks, out of ammunition, as the American spearheads slashed up through the forwardmost Soviet formations. Their advance had been halted by a miracle, a few kilometers from his position.

Bezarin inspected his opponents. He figured he could beat them all right. But he had not particularly wanted to face them without any main-gun ammunition. The big, solid-looking tanks rolled smoothly over the roadway of the bridge, partially obscured by its sidewalls. The Americans, the great enemy. Now they were leaving, and it seemed as if a lifelong nightmare had finally come to an end.

He had attempted to report honestly on the tragedy that had occurred along the highway behind Hildesheim. But no one wanted to hear it. As far as his chain of command was concerned, it was all history—regrettable but, viewed from the grand perspective, unavoidable. The Soviet Union needed war heroes, not war criminals.

And Bezarin became a hero. One of the brilliant heroes of the Weser crossing operation. And in his own mind, the horror of the massacre along the highway had already begun to undergo a subtle change, receding in importance in comparison to the already codified achievements of his battalion. He tried to write to Anna about the tragedy, expecting that she would somehow understand and help him. But he could not put the words on paper. The incident seemed to demand forgetting. To be buried, like the dead themselves. Bezarin knew that certain images would remain with him, below the surface, occasionally rising to remind him of what he and his soldiers had done. But now he spent more time thinking of Anna, remembering the fragrance of the sparse Galician spring, and the smell of the woman he had held in his arms. Instead of writing his confession to her, he had found the strength, at last, to write and say he loved her.

He had no idea how long a response would be in arriving, if one were to come at all. He feared that his letter or her reply would go astray in the disruption of events, and he had decided that, if no response came within a month, he would write again. And again. He would not be defeated now by his fears of a little Polish girl.

At the same time, he felt haunted. His mind filled with terrible images of Anna in another's bed, of her special admissions spoken to another man. He worried that he had already become no more than a bit of finished personal history to her. But he was determined not to surrender without a fight.

A vehicle pulled up on the quay. Bezarin stood. He was not supposed to be off on his own; there were reports of violent assaults against Soviet officers and men throughout the occupation zone. At a minimum, two officers were always to go together, and it was much preferred that officers remain near their place of work or assigned quarters unless official matters called them elsewhere. The soldiers and sergeants were closely restricted.

Bezarin touched his holster.

The sight of the major surprised Malinsky. He had neither wanted nor expected company. He simply wanted to see the Rhine up close, to savor his moment in history as best he could. To confirm the value of his sacrifice. And this nervous major appeared, reaching for his pistol. Malinsky decided to make the best of it.

"I would be grateful, Comrade Major, if you didn't shoot me."

The major reddened, embarrassed. He stammered out a barely intelligible apology.

"Don't worry," Malinsky told him. "It's always a good thing to be on your guard." He recognized the major as one of the men on whom he had pinned a medal not an hour before, and he offered him a cigarette, which the major clumsily declined. It struck Malinsky as odd that this fresh-baked hero would be alone, when Starukhin was holding court for all of his heroes at what promised to be one of the great parties of the century. Malinsky had excused himself so that Starukhin and his boys could relax and drink themselves sick. Starukhin seemed to Malinsky to embody much that was eternally Russian—big, loud, vainglorious, generous, abusive of his personal power, desperate for comradeship, alternately slothful and passionate, and capable of great cruelty.

Well, who knew what devils chewed at this lone major?

The war had very different effects on different men. Malinsky examined the younger man. The major's face looked bright enough. Not as intelligent, and certainly not as sensitive, as Anton's face had been. But it was the type of clean, earnest face that would go far under the new regime. Certainly, this Hero of the Soviet Union would not be a major much longer.

"Married, Comrade Major? Thinking of your wife and family, perhaps?"

The major had begun to recover from his embarrassment. But he remained ill at ease.

"No, Comrade Front Commander. I'm not married."

Malinsky flicked his cigarette ashes toward the river. The storied Rhine was a bit of a disappointment to him, running grayish-brown, with eddies of garbage against the shore. "A girl, then?"

The young officer nodded, stupidly eager. "Yes, Comrade Front Commander. A wonderful girl. Very well-educated."

Malinsky sensed that the major wanted to gush details and descriptions of his beloved. But the younger man had the discipline to restrain himself.

"Well," Malinsky said, "you must marry her. Marriage is a wonderful institution. I highly recommend it. And you must have children. The Motherland needs to preserve the bloodlines of her heroes."

Malinsky suddenly wanted to turn the discussion off, to drive the major away so that he might be alone. He thought of his wife. He would not see her for some time yet, and she would have to bear the news of Anton's fate alone. It seemed terribly unfair that his wife should be alone at such a time. A soldier's wife never had the comforts or conveniences of a normal life.

Anton's wife, too, was alone. More alone than his own wife. No one would ever come back to the girl. Malinsky thought of Zena, a silly, irresponsible red-haired girl, impossible to dislike. Swollen with the energy of life, bursting with it. She had possessed none of the makings of a soldier's wife except the ability to love his son. And that love had made his son so happy that Malinsky found it easy to indulge the girl's artistic pretensions and ridiculous behavior. Yes, he thought, she made my son happy. I must take care of her.

Malinsky felt tears rising in his eyes, and such a display would never do. He fought for and regained control of himself, flicking the butt of his cigarette carelessly toward the river. But he could not reconcile himself to Anton's death. He could not bear it. He would have been glad to die, to die miserably, in his son's place.

He looked at the major, who had averted his eyes. Why should this man live instead of his son? There was nothing special about this major, nothing without which the world could not keep turning. His face bore none of the high traces of honor and breeding that Anton's fine features had carried. Why, of all the sons, did Anton have to die?

Malinsky understood the mundane logic of it. He understood war. He even comprehended the minuscule importance of his son's fate in the shadow of events that changed the world. But he could not, he would not, reconcile himself to it. He raged at the death, refused it, holding Anton alive in his heart.

The last of the Malinskys, he thought bitterly. Now we will be nothing more than a footnote in unread historical treatises.

Anton.

Malinsky followed the major's stare out over the polluted water to the commanding span of the bridge. The Americans were going. Malinsky knew how close they had come to embarrassing his plan. They had almost beaten him. But "almost" was a word that carried no reward.

He felt no special hatred for the Americans. He admired the good order of their formations, their unbroken feel. He thought of how bitter this march must be for them, when they had fought so well. He believed he could have stopped them at the Weser until follow-on forces arrived. But he was glad he had not had to try.

Malinsky cut short his ruminations. It was time to go. He had other ceremonies to attend, other medals to award, and a host of tedious issues to resolve between toasts. He felt an urge to salute the Americans before he left, the tribute of an old soldier. But he doubted that the major would understand the gesture. The old traditions were dying, and you could not keep them alive artificially, no matter how hard you tried. A new and thoughtless age had overtaken them all. In the end, Malinsky simply wished the major luck with his girl.

Author's Note

The land power elements of the Armed Forces of the Soviet Union have not been known officially as the Red Army for many years. Yet in our informal conversations, in the bold colors of our war games, and in many of our bleakest mental images, the Soviet military remains indelibly Red. Certainly, that shorthand term "Red Army" was the accepted terminology of my childhood in the nineteen-fifties, when my classmates and I practiced huddling under our school desks as a defensive measure against nuclear attack. And we have accepted that "Red Army" as a cliché both verbal and mental, conjuring a "faceless mass," with only the rarest attempts at differentiating between its individual members as human beings.

Red Army suggested itself as a title because it speaks so directly to that deeply ingrained mental image. It is *not* a book about lethal gadgets. While seeking the highest possible level of technical accuracy for its backdrop, this book is about behavior. How would that other system *behave* at war—and how might its individual members prove like us or distinctly unlike us in their responses to the stress of combat? This book is not about the hardware or even the mission, but about the men. This is the area where I have personally found intelligence products grossly deficient, yet understanding the human dimension is an essential element of battlefield success or failure. It is not enough to memorize the technical parameters of missiles, MIGs, and battlefield lasers. We must, somehow, get at the consciousness behind the controls. My fundamental goal in writing this book was to attempt to bring those men to life in their rich human variety, to see them as a bit less faceless and enigmatic, in the context of modern battle.

For more than a dozen years, I have been frustrated by my inability in formal briefings, lectures, and documents, either in the mud of gunnery ranges or in the comfort of theaters, to adequately transmit anything sufficiently meaningful about the men behind the Soviet guns. When asked what the Soviet military is "really like," I have often joked that it's a lot like sex: Much that you've heard about it isn't true; when it's good, it can be amazing; but when it's bad, it's inexpressibly embarrassing. Yet such a pat answer only deflects an important question. What *are* they really like? While it would be impossible ever to fully answer such a query even were I Russian-born, the format of fiction, with painstaking fidelity in detail, seemed my only hope for bringing "the other guys" to life for my comrades and countrymen. This novel does not pretend to answer all of the questions. Instead, it is aimed at provoking thought and a new consideration of those men so tragically made our opponents by the events of this grim century.

Could *they* pull it off? Could they achieve the success the book allows them? If we examined only the achievements of Soviet military theory, the answer would be an emphatic *"Yes!"* The body of contemporary Soviet military theory is tremendously impressive—far more sophisticated and comprehensive than the often-dilettantish concepts cobbled together in the West. But wars are not won by theory alone, and the area in which the Soviet military is perhaps the least impressive is in the lack of suppleness and honing of their tactical units and subunits. The gap between soaring aspirations and limping reality has long been manifest in many fields of Russian, then Soviet endeavor, such as philosophy, politics, economics, science—and the military. A Russian is rarely short of fabulous ideas—and Soviet "military science and art" dazzle us with their intensity and incisiveness. But between those brilliant theoretical constructs and the muddy boots lies a range of operational question marks that only combat could satisfactorily answer. Were a war to occur in Europe "tomorrow," the Soviet military *could* conceivably pull off the victory related in the book—but the luck of the battlefield would have to be running almost entirely on their side. The Soviet military system seeks methodically to reduce the impact of "luck," of chance, of friction, and even of what they term "native wit"—the individual human talents of which *we* are inclined to make so much, rightly or wrongly. Yet the overall military balance in the European theater is such that luck in its broadest sense would have a great deal to do with the outcome on the battlefield: who would be "lucky" enough to have the right men in the right positions; whose analysts would properly assess the disparate bits of intelligence information appearing amid impressionistic conditions of confusion and evident disaster; who will have figured out the most acute employments for modern battlefield technologies; who might take the proper risks at the decisive times; who would get to the good ground first . . .

This book is hard on NATO, because everyone else is so anxious to handle it with exaggerated delicacy. I am personally firmly committed to this most successful of all alliances, but I also believe that we have allowed NATO to evolve into something of a spoiled child at an unacceptable relative cost to the security and economy of the United States. NATO has tremendous latent combat power that may fail to show to full effect on the battlefield simply because we have all been so anxious to avoid sober self-criticism in peacetime. As a citizen of the United States, I place a value beyond words on the preservation of western civilization (with all its discontents), yet I cannot rationalize the sacrifice of a single American soldier's life because we acquiesced to folly in fear of an ally's tantrum.

This book does not presuppose that a war is either imminent or inevitable—indeed, the declarations of Mikhael Gorbachev offer grounds for careful optimism—and it should be clear from the events described in these pages that war is not becoming any more attractive an option for the solution of our problems as military technology improves. Authors are marvelously privileged in that they can kill tens of thousands without shedding any real blood, but the paper war in which the reader engages is only a comfortable shadow of the potential horror of modern land warfare. This is ultimately a work of fiction; a cautionary tale on one level, an effort at creative investigation on another, it frankly means to entertain. If there is a conscious message between its covers, it is not that there *will* be a war with that differently uniformed collection of human beings east of the Great Wall of Europe, but that, should such a war occur, we will be opposed by other men of flesh and blood, with their own talents, ambitions, and dreams. Thankfully, I believe that the great majority of them resemble the great majority of us in their desire simply to get on with the business of living.

About the Author

Ralph Peters is a veteran U.S. Army intelligence officer, with extensive tactical experience in Europe. A Soviet analyst and linguist, he has published widely on military affairs, and his work has been translated into various foreign languages. An earlier novel, *Bravo Romeo,* appeared in 1981.

"RED ARMY is about the men behind the Soviet guns," he writes. "My fundamental goal was to bring those men to life, in their rich human variety . . . to see how they might respond in the context of modern battle."